"Fail gloriously and have the experience. Do what you must and let the outcome be what it will. Be a human for a change and not part of a machine!'"

Coming Soon from Jeri Shepherd Books:

Faulted Reasoning
Faulty Methods
Double Fault
Faults Exposed

In addition to compiled story collections:

The At Fault Canon
The Faulted Reasoning Canon
The Faulty Methods Canon
The Double Fault Canon
The Faults Exposed Canon

If you are interested in helping to create the canon stories for the *Fault Lines Series*, please email JeriShepherdBooks@gmail.com with the subject line Canon Contests for full contest rules. Lucy's Lantern Literature, Jeri Shepherd Books, and the *Fault Lines Series* creators look forward to discovering new authors, paying them for their work, promoting them in the world of science fiction, and allowing them to contribute to the intricate world and complex characters already developed and still to come in the Earth-After-the-Melt world of the *Fault Lines Series*.

AT FAULT

BOOK 1 OF THE FAULT LINES SERIES

JERI SHEPHERD

Lucy's Lantern Literature

Cover Design by: Michael Nicloy, Nico 11 Publishing & Design
Cover Art by: Sara Risley, Sara Risley Art
Series Symbol, Linda's World Map, Miriam's World Map, and Series Dinkus by: Cas Mayhall
Contributing Editor: Stacy Lewerenz
Contributing Editor: Amy Oaks

ISBN 13: 979-8985696004

From Jeri Shepherd Books – A Lucy's Lantern Literature Imprint

www.AtFaultBook.com

Printed in the U.S.A.

Linda's World

EARTH AFTER THE MELT — YEAR 2552

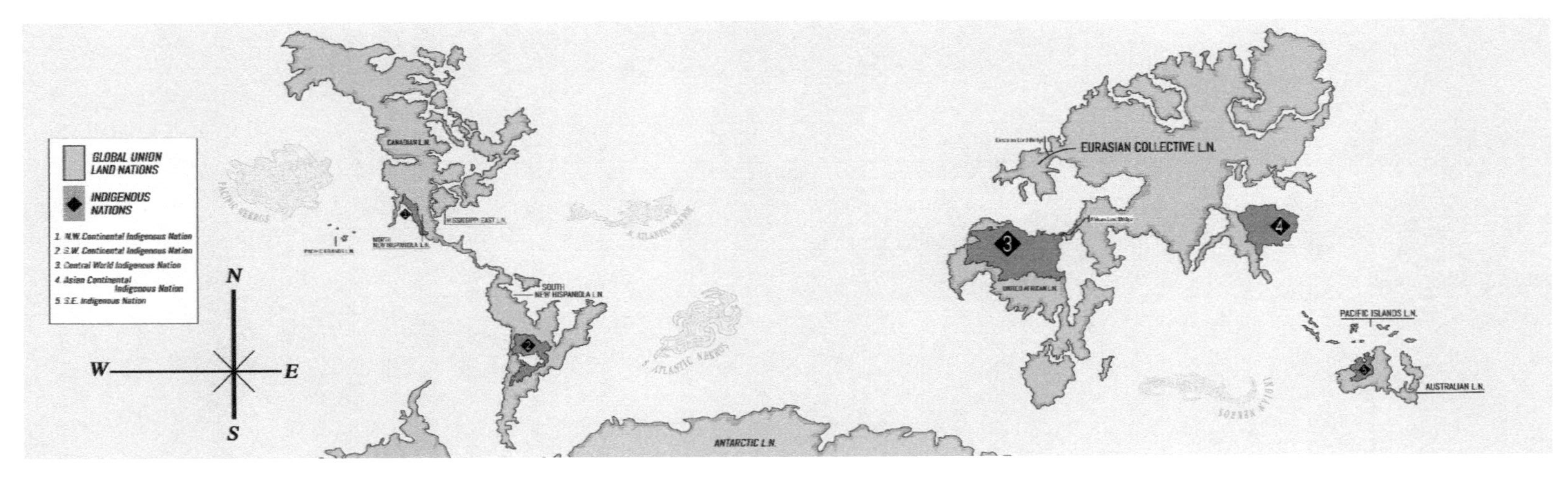

GLOBAL UNION LAND NATIONS
INDIGENOUS NATIONS
1. N.W. Continental Indigenous Nation
2. S.W. Continental Indigenous Nation
3. Central World Indigenous Nation
4. Asian Continental Indigenous Nation
5. S.E. Indigenous Nation
N
E
S
W
CANADIAN L.N.
MISSISSIPPI EAST L.N.
NORTH NEW HISPANIOLA L.N.
SOUTH NEW HISPANIOLA L.N.
PACIFIC ISLANDS L.N.
EURASIAN COLLECTIVE L.N.
UNITED AFRICAN L.N.
AUSTRALIAN L.N.
ANTARCTIC L.N.
Excavator Lord Bridge
Yukon Lion Bridge

CHAPTER 1
YEAR 2552

Baja Province
Northern Territory of New Hispaniola Land Nation
Global Union

This time, she hoped he'd kill her.

It's not that Linda welcomed death, but neither did she fear it. She was just so damned tired, and that tiredness overwhelmed any justified fear. There wasn't a cell in her being that didn't feel exhausted. Spent. Heart, mind, body, and soul were devoid of all vitality. The empty numbness of fatigue was her robe. She drowned in it like a small child donning her mother's gown. The idea of lying down forever seemed appealing to her and that was at least a feeling. So little could elicit an emotion anymore.

Existence in the Global Union, the GU, met every physical need, but emotions and spirits were neglected. The presumably perfect system's mundane monotony had turned humans into data processors and factory parts. Would the machine even miss her after she was gone, or would she just be another cog to replace? Human loss was negligible.

Linda's temple throbbed from the most recent strike, and it made her head feel too heavy for her neck. She reached up to touch the spot where she'd been hit and discovered warm moisture. What had she done this time? Mismanaged their allotted funds? Allowed them to run out of food leaving them to insipid nutrient bars until the ministry's next deposits? Used their unassigned energy rations without clearing it with him? The wondering furrowed her aching brow.

Lukas threw her to the ground like a rag doll, but time moved slowly for her as she fell. Her perception was distorted. Linda's feet went sideways, and her form turned in the air. With no control over her body, she fell onto her side with her full weight pushing her into the floor against her forearm. Her arm crunched before going pain-fully limp. She could picture the bruises spreading straight to her bones. In the time it took her to land, Linda felt herself ironically cov-ered by a blanket of gratitude. She was grateful for the fact that the two of them were never able to have children. Even once their permit was selected, no matter how many times he bedded her against her will, they couldn't conceive. It was as though her body rebelled biologically where she was unable to do so physically.

That Linda could leave this existence guiltlessly was emotion-ally purgative. Guilt and shame drained out of her with each exha-lation. Absorbing this final drubbing without a daughter looking on meant there could be no impressionable still human thing seeing a man dominate her. No little girl could view her the way she had once looked onto her own mother – full of pity, sadness, and fear, as well as grief for the soul that had left the body long ago.

Linda never blamed her mother. Getting beaten was just a fact of life for the women in her family. Her grandmother said she'd had it good. She used to brag that her partner only beat her when she'd done something to deserve it. The man she knew as her uncle, though he wasn't blood, unleashed only when he drank while at the bong bar of the local vice lounge. Her uncle's son thought he'd bro-ken the cycle until his administrator, a mere woman in his words, had to demote him to a lower-level employ. She caught him making illegal trades for more credits. He beat her into a coma and then went home and hanged himself.

It would end with her. She would be the last woman of her line to submit to the fists of a man. As if inextricably bound to a torturous inheritance, Linda managed to find in Lukas a family outsider who still held the ugly traits of men from the damaged generations before them – misogyny and violence. Domestic abuse never really waned but it usually at least manifested behind closed doors. Lukas and men like him wore machismo with pride. She wondered, if she'd been able to carry a baby when their birth permit was approved and then extended, maybe Lukas wouldn't be beating her. It would have allowed them more energy rations, more food, more work, more of the things of existence.

No!

She pushed the thought out of her mind. Linda refused to feel at fault in her last moments. He could take her will to live. Hell, he could even take her life. But with her final heartbeats, she was going to reclaim that heart as her own along with her own mind and her own reality. She was stealing it back from the virile and radical indoctrination he had imparted upon her for too long.

Lukas kicked her in the stomach. She didn't tense up as she usually tried to do. Linda let her belly go soft so that it could swallow the full force of his work boot. Squishing deep into her tender flesh, her abdomen consumed his foot and the reinforced toe of his shoe seemed to tap her spine like a reflex hammer.

She fought the urge to cry out. He couldn't hurt her anymore. She wouldn't let him watch her writhe. She had enough defiance left for at least that illusion. The lack of agony she showed only angered him more. Lukas's fair skin grew red hot with rage beneath the thinning, short-cropped hair she'd stopped finding attractive years ago. Linda's life partner had light hair, blue eyes, and a pale complexion. All three together was a rarity in the Northern Territory of the GU's New Hispaniola Land Nation. Yet he had a poisonous belief that his genetic makeup made him better than others.

There weren't many men left who openly thought like Lukas in the Baja Province – pure, he called himself. He wasn't afraid to share such an antiquated ideology in public, either. He saw no need to hide it. Linda's Global Union home in Earth-Before-the-Melt, the EBM era, had become a multicultural potpourri of the world's people – islanders and Latinx populations blended with those of European,

Asian, and African descent all sharing countless different languages together instead of a singular unifying one.

Earth-After-the-Melt was something even more homogenous as the physical features of humankind had grown to be less reflective of one's ancestral nationalities. In the midst of a sea of mixing immensely deep and intricate, few but a handful of pockets around her EAM homeland identified themselves by their national origins or religions anymore. Most were just human, fellow GU citizens with their brothers and sisters around the world, regardless of beliefs or DNA. At least, that's what the Global Union education system would have one believe. It had taken them centuries to learn to stop labeling themselves and more centuries to stop self-segregating based on those arbitrary and archaic ideologies.

But Lukas? He coveted the days of separation. He was pure, after all. Pure what, she wondered? Pure in the way of boiled white chicken. Nothing was added. She hated boiled chicken. No development. No layers. No complexity.

Lukas and Linda had always kept a chicken in the twelve years they had been together. They only had room for one in the small, GU-provided coop beneath their garden box. She preferred them to the goats that were allowed for those who lived in the ground-level quarters of their building – the residents who had access to the courtyard. She sometimes traded eggs for goat's milk, but she felt the creatures weren't as personal. A chicken was much like a pet. Pets hadn't been kept by people for a century and the practice of inviting an animal to be part of your family was something that always fascinated Linda.

Linda had hoped her aptitude test would have landed her in an animal sanctuary or agricultural assignment. She often speculated on how her life could have differed in the Australian Land Nation caring for primates or raising GU chickens. The idea of bonding with an animal was precious to Linda. Those who had goats shared them with two or even three other families. Each of her chickens by contrast knew her as their one and only caretaker.

Linda and Lukas usually afforded only an aged hen, five or six years old. They would get a year or two of egg-laying out of it, and then—when the egg supply dwindled—the chicken was traded to the poultry merchant for a chicken packaged as a meal. Her pet would live its days out in one of the animal sanctuaries until it died and became some other citizen's meal chicken. This is the way it had been ever since the ethical protein farming standards were put in place.

It always made Linda melancholy to take the meal chicken in place of her own, knowing that this animal, too, had likely once been a pet. Nonetheless, she knew it was a delicacy to get real meat protein. Some primordial part of Linda's psyche was enveloped in a longing to honor the animal. She knew it was ridiculous to think it mattered that the sacrifice comprised a special meal after it was gone, but it didn't stop the hope that somebody else would do the same for the chickens for which she once cared.

'Shie shie,' she imagined some recipient saying to one of her favorite chickens. *'Thank you,'* in the global tongue of Post Babel. *'We know you served your citizen so well, Henrietta. We'll be seasoning you with ginger and sage, and you'll be accompanied by some browned wild rice mixed with fresh celery and sweet potato cubes. You had a long life and we're grateful.'*

It was part of the cycle. And she would love the next chicken as much as the one given up for the health and well-being of a Global Union family.

Again, Lukas kicked.

Deep inside of her, something cracked. Linda wasn't sure if she was hearing the muffled sound of it vibrate through her bones or if the blow was echoing outside in the air around her. It was all happening both too slowly and all at once. She swam drunkenly through the dizzying in-between of time, incoherent to how much of it was actually passing. It was enough for her to believe the end would come soon. Her sweet release. Her time would pass from this life much like it had for her chickens. She meditated on what value she would leave behind . . . if any at all.

Throughout her life, Linda had let Lukas erase her again and again and again. He erased her imagination, the dreams she once had of contributing to the world, telling her how irrational that thinking was for a low-aptitude citizen like herself. He erased her womanhood, taking her as his own whenever he wanted her, while also demeaning her for not being able to fulfill their child-bearing permit. He erased her community, forcing her to take the most mind-numbing and lonely of employs offered to her skill level in order to limit human interactions. When she had nothing left but their quarters, he even erased her pride in that, belittling her attempts to make it a home with virtual art or entertainment upgrades. He eventually erased her from the smallest of tasks that still brought an inkling of joy, like bringing her chickens to play in the courtyard or cooking in their quarters.

Lukas always felt the cooking of their meal chickens was his to control, even while Linda could have stretched the meat so much further, done so much more with the creature that had once sustained another citizen and that would now sustain them. She felt he always ruined it, and—usually along with it, almost as painful punctuation—the last bit of their cooking water. The water would foam with the fat of some citizen's former pet all the while the chicken turned into a lump that was both dry and slimy at the same time.

Linda languished that her last thought might be of bland chicken, but now the image was trapped in her head. She saw Lukas ruining some citizen's pet much like he'd ruined his own pet – her.

Linda couldn't shake the image of a chicken just like Henrietta, naked and blanched in a pot of way too much water, boiling away on their one burner. She worked to change the vision the way one tries to manipulate a dream from the inside while it's happening. Lucidly, she reversed the process. She turned off the burner, pulled the chicken out of the water – painlessly burning her own skin in the process, puzzled the raw flesh back together, replaced the head, feet, and feathers, and closed the sleeping creature's beak. It was plush again with down of brown, black, red, and even some deep bluish-purple feathers. She made it look just like her Henrietta. It was lovely but still dead. Beautiful . . . but lifeless.

Just like me, she thought.

Her mouth began to fill with blood. It pooled in the loose cheek of her face that lay against the floor. The metallic flavor was nauseating. The lining of her throat grew thick with mucus obstructing her airway. She was consciously aware of breathing with a gurgle through the tiny straw-like opening that remained unobscured at the back of her throat. She pushed the blood out of her mouth with her tongue to make room for air. She wasn't sure why she did it. She had fought to live so many times that doing so had become involuntary despite feeling ready to die.

Lukas took a break, fatigued from his fury. He was crashing like a student coming down off the high of his mandated focus drugs prescribed during aptitude week. He grabbed the full bottle of fermented cannabis spirit out of their small cold storage and sat down to drink it while watching the digital headlines scroll across their screen wall. He knew she couldn't move from where he'd left her.

Time must have clicked on as Linda, in and out of consciousness, had glimpses of various programs that she couldn't conceive her mind of having created on its own. Severe flooding was overtaking lands near the Mediterranean Sea. The African Land Nation was experiencing drought and fires on its east coast. Revolts were continuing on the Caribbean Islands Province of the Mississippi East Land Nation. The GU could not safely reach them with rations while extreme weather continued. It was the standard headlines – single lives lost were ruefully memorialized while entire societies dying were turned into statistics.

At one point, Lukas approached Linda with a knife. He scraped it across her left palm in the place where her identity tattoo had been lasered. When scanned, the Global Union code on her hand gave her access to everything she could need in this world and also gave information about her to anybody who might need it – an employer who tracked her hours, a physician who needed her medical records, or an administrator who would assign quarters or rations. At first, as Lukas ran the blade over her skin, it only felt hot, then it became raw, and finally it was exposed and bloodied. He pushed his thumb into the wound. It was excruciating. Linda's tears fell to the floor in place of the screams she yearned to release but for which she did not have strength.

"You're a nobody now," he said more to aggrandize himself than to diminish her. He watched what remained of her palm scan weep blood onto the floor. Her identity physically drained from her being.

Lukas walked out of Linda's field of vision and she went back to her dream to lie with Henrietta, face to face, sorrow to sorrow, death to death. In her mind, she opened the beak of the bird and exhaled, blowing what might have been the last of her own air into the body of the still fowl, giving it new life. It blinked, ruffled itself up, stood, cocked its head curiously to one side, and then sat back down, folding its little claws beneath itself and taking up a quiet vigil with its keeper. She smiled at it sleepily. It looked at her in return and it transformed into something different. It was majestic and regal, an animal with overlooked beauty finally puffed up in the strength and pride it deserved.

Then, Henrietta began to shake.

Linda began to convulse.

Their whole world trembled.

This is it, she thought.

Linda and her feathered friend would be done with this place in a final stand that only existed in her imagination. Her eyes unwillingly tore open, away from the dream and into the nightmare. Lukas was returning. She couldn't focus through the slitted vision of her eyes. Her pupils watered and burned. Lukas held something in his hand to once and for all finish the job. His power hammer? A kitchen tool? It was hard to make out through her deliria.

Lukas shook from head to toe. The world appeared to be crumbling in her final moments, raining down on the two of them. The very wall behind him shimmied. The sterile, bluish LED light above him began to swing from side to side like Newton's Cradle. She was sure she must be losing her mind when the single window that opened out over their standard garden box shattered.

Linda remembered now.

She'd forgotten to save one of the many-eyed potatoes to plant in their ravaged soil. That's why she was about to die. She was as tired of white potatoes as she was of blanched chicken. Tired of assigned jobs and assigned homes and assigned food. Tired of allotted energy and directed travel. Tired of the inhumanity of human existence.

Nothing to miss here.

Linda imagined Lukas's death in her place. He fell beside her full of fear that she refused to reflect. The obscure object in his hand flew into the air and came down in the center of his head, right in the middle of his pale pure face which bloodily cracked open in an immediate body-paralyzing deathblow.

The floor of their top-level quarters opened up and swallowed him whole, dropping him deep, deep down to the earth below, the very ground that Linda assumed was her own awaiting grave. The walls around her were shorn off to the dust-filled sunshine rays outside before the solid floor below her own body compacted, taking her down like an elevator to the underground levels of their quarter building.

In Linda's mind, Henrietta's wings opened over her form as the chicken landed on her with a weight greater than she should have had. The hen spread her beautifully colored feathers wider than all of Linda's body, protecting her from the crumbling sky. Water rushed in around her and washed Lukas and the rest of the world away.

Sirens and flashing lights and echoing robotic voices filled the air but—below Henrietta's wingspan—Linda was safe. Death was safe. It could be as easy as going to sleep. Sleep sounded so inviting.

As her world continued to shudder, she closed her eyes and shut the sound away. She curled her body up beneath the large, protective Henrietta of her imagination as the bird let out a single cluck of comfort. Finally, she could release herself into the darkness. Linda could spend her last moment with the hen to whom she had given life.

CHAPTER 2
YEAR 2908

Governor's Residence
Zoe Baja
Zoelands Concord

"**D**aylight," Miriam sighed out loud.

The governor's first word of the day projected hoarsely. The room-darkening shades rose above the window, retracted into the ceiling, and revealed the blinding pool of orange and yellow light that made up the sunrise on the east side of Zoe Baja. The northeast coast of Miriam's homeland is where the governor's residence stood since the mid-2700s and she was sure that this early morning view was the primary reason the architects chose the location.

Miriam's eyes had been open for half an hour. She stared into the darkness and dreaded the crucial conversations that would take place over the next week. Confrontation was right up there with claustrophobia on her list of least favorite things. She far preferred playing the role of peacemaker over that of boat-shaker.

She tried to recall what hour she'd finally fallen asleep the night before. The last time she checked the clock, it was 1030 coordinated universal time, or UTC. The racing thoughts in her mind ricocheted off one another all night as they vied for her prioritization.

Would Prefects Enele Chen and Lilibeth Phillips think her proposal was too risky? Could Zoe Baja really manage if it lost its cooperation with one of the Global Union's largest land nations? Her heart felt suspended in her throat as she pondered the ideas she could not bear to say out loud. How much longer could her home sustain plant life and if the answer was not long—or worse, not at all—what would happen to them? And what next – always, what next?

Everything in her being told Miriam she was taking the right step, but she couldn't see the steps after the first one. She had no way of knowing whether she could lead the Zoeans through those next unseen steps. She never wanted the job of governor, but—now in it—she couldn't bear the thought of letting down Zoe Baja.

Between the low morning fog and the early dawn light, the overflowing metropolises of New Hispaniola, twenty-three kilometers east across the Sea of California, were not visible. Maybe that was a good thing. This could be the last days of their uneasy cooperation together. At least she wouldn't be forced to start this inevitable journey with a woeful glance on her ancient sisters across the water.

"Window open," Miriam said, and the pane of glass shifted outward with a mechanical hum. Sweet salty air slipped into her room through the bamboo fibers of her screen that had been tightly spun to near transparency.

She closed her eyes once more, inhaled slowly, and counted one, two, three, four, five in her head as she allowed the air to infuse her with fortitude. Then she sat up and placed both feet, with deliberate intention, flatly on the cool, hard floor. She took another couple of breaths and meditated on the idea that her toes were immersed in the dirt, bare and wiggling in the rich soil of the gardens. The moment was enough to remind her of the world for which she was fighting. She opened her eyes, this time for good.

Miriam let the sheet fall off her naked dark-skinned body as she stepped away from the bed. She felt invigorated by the breeze as it swept through her sleeping quarters and across her curves and muscles.

Miriam considered herself average in appearance, not because she was an unattractive woman but more because she did not put in much effort to enhance her features. Hair dying, semi-temporary tatua, facial inlays of precious metals and stones, bejeweled fingernail dips, and the intricately knotted and colorful fabrics that were commonplace amongst Zoeans of influence and affluence never looked right on her. When she dressed in such trends out of necessity for important events or celebrations, she felt like she was in a costume.

Miriam manually started her shower and straightened the relatively common travel clothes she'd chosen while the water warmed. The collection of black and gray pants ensembles with scarves would be fitting attire for meetings with land nation diplomats. The outfits were added to by a formal gown for the Cityship Tatsu's Unity Dinner, pajamas because she was always cold at sea, and an orange sweater given to her by Inoke when they were just friends and not the professional cohorts they had since become.

She glimpsed herself in the mirror as she made her way toward the water closet and a refreshing shower. She had lost some weight with the stress of leadership, but that was nothing to complain about. The bags beneath her eyes were a different story. They seemed to stretch all the way to her freckled cheekbones, and they had grown as gray as her eyes from lack of sleep. A couple of strain-induced white hairs appeared at her temples. Her mother had worn silver hair so beautifully before she died and, while Miriam didn't love the idea of them framing her own face, she did like the way she was able to see her mom looking back at her.

Miriam missed the simple days of working the gardens outside the Heirlinda Museum before she became governor. The sun and fresh air never let her reflection down. They kept her young and vibrant, at least in her own mind, even as her forties were closing in. She sighed deeply with the feeling that she'd aged ten years in the last two. Another six years of leadership were ahead before she could return to the gardens.

Stepping into the water, Miriam's shower-streams were inconsistent, spitting at her from some pipes while others seemed to rush and gush. The water had begun to have a gamey scent to it. The salt was going to make her red and brown curls completely unruly. She decided to embrace it. After the four days it would take her to reach the Pacific Islands Land Nation via Cityship Tatsu, the result would probably be the same even if she'd have chosen to tame the mane from the start. Nonetheless, she made a note to herself to have the residential water filters replaced while she was out on negotiations . . . one more thing for the growing list in her head.

"Top headlines," she said to no one in particular from between the sputtering shower heads around her.

"CHANNEL?" responded a voice that was likely meant to be comforting and friendly when initially created, but time and routine had turned it into an annoyance.

"New Hispaniola," Miriam decided reluctantly. News from the Global Union always came with its share of propaganda, but she could wash the stink away just as easily as the dirt on her body. The voice began to read out the world's constants and concerns:

> ROLLING BROWNOUTS CONTINUE TO PLAGUE SEVERAL NATIONS OF THE GLOBAL UNION, DESPITE EFFICIENCY EFFORTS. PREFECT MARSHALL RELEASED A STATEMENT SAYING THAT THE GLOBAL UNION WILL BENEFIT GREATLY FROM CREATING ITS OWN RELIABLE SOURCES OF ENERGY CAPTURE.

> AFTERSHOCKS CONTINUE TO ROCK CITIES ALONG THE COCOS AND PACIFIC PLATES. SOME GEOLOGISTS ARE RAISING ALARM THAT THE TWO ACTIVE TREMOR ZONES SO CLOSE TO ONE ANOTHER MAY BE SIGNS OF A MORE SEVERE EARTHQUAKE CAUSAL SEQUENCE COMING IN THE NEAR FUTURE.

GOVERNOR MIRIAM HEIRLINDA OF ZOE BAJA WILL BE WELCOMED BY THE PACIFIC ISLANDS LAND NATION THIS WEEK AS THE ALLIES CONTINUE IN THEIR ENERGY NEGOTIATIONS AND THE GLOBAL UNION CONTINUES TO CARE FOR ITS ZOE NEIGHBOR IN THE MIDST OF THAT REGION'S RECESSION AND FOOD SHORTAGES.

Miriam huffed out a laugh to herself. Never a note about the Zoelands without a plug of self-gratitude for the Global Union.

THE ANTARCTIC LAND NATION HAD A SUCCESSFUL LAUNCH OF TWO LUNAR MINING DOMES VIA RAIL GUN.

MODERATE WEATHER CONDITIONS CONTINUE IN THE SOUTHERN PROVINCES OF NEW HISPANIOLA WITH SUNSHINE, WIND FROM THE EAST, AND A COMFORTABLE THIRTY-SIX DEGREES CELSIUS. GET OUT THOSE JACKETS AS THE NORTHERN PROVINCES DROP TO JUST TWENTY-FOUR DEGREES CELSIUS.

RESIDENTIAL EVENING LIGHTS WILL GO UP AT OH FIVE THIRTY.

"GOOD DAY AND GOOD LIVING, CITIZENS," Miriam mocked in unison with the voice as she manually turned off her shower.

She lingered in the stall a bit longer. She allowed the water to drip off her skin and away down the drain while she quietly considered the greater implications of the headlines. Even the weather report spoke of a world that was dying – cooking, really. The literature of Earth-Before-the-Melt spoke of beach trips and outdoor activities in the same temperatures that felt almost cool to her generation. Humanity itself had evolved to the world they had so drastically changed. And then there were the tremors that continued to spike on the moment scale. Each of those aftershocks surely had lives lost but death as a result of quakes and storms were so common that they were rarely even reported anymore. Mining on Mars and Luna were commonplace, and Miriam contemplated if there may be a time when the Lunar and Martian off world colonies would support as many citizens as they did operational teams.

The mechanical voice began again meaning Miriam had been standing still for five minutes.

ROLLING BROWNOUTS CONTINUE TO PLAGUE SEVERAL NATIONS OF THE GLOBAL UNION—

"Music, please," she cut off the report. "Contemporary mix. Five decibels."

The voice was replaced by an upbeat blend of hide hoop drums and digitized scatting voices backed by a counter melody shared between ukuleles and suona horns. There were times that music gave Miriam a jolt for her work, but not today. She finished getting ready while barely aware of the songs as they played. She didn't have much need for makeup, but after she dried her body, she liberally applied lotion to her salt-ashen skin before she got dressed in one of the simple outfits and then packed the others, along with her toiletries, into her travel tube. Miriam secured the luggage with a code and set it aside for pickup by the staff. It would await her in her assigned travel quarters when she boarded the Cityship Tatsu the next morning.

"Music off. Window closed," she said as she left her quarters. She followed this with, "Good morning," to Chief of Staff Inoke Kalua. He waited two steps from her room, a cup of coffee for her in one outstretched hand and his handheld digifile in the other. Miriam ravenously wrapped both hands around the old-fashioned, ceramic mug filled with the hot morning liquid she craved.

"Shie, shie," she gratefully uttered to Kalua.

She drank the beverage in completely with her nose before it ever touched her lips. Immediately Miriam was nudged just a bit more to life. A small, close-mouthed smile crossed her lips. The governor had her first couple of swallows through which her chief of staff patiently waited, before she finally said, "Jambo," the casual hello from an EBM African language. It was as if she were greeting him for the first time and her chief was sure he was merely an afterthought to the coffee.

"I can't believe you drink that stuff, Miriam. Energy patches work faster and are far more convenient."

"It's not about the effect, Inoke. It's about the ritual."

The two turned and walked at a moderate pace toward the offices.

"To business, we shall," Kalua said formally. He bowed his head slightly and it caused his deep purple coif to bob. The image made Miriam's lips finally part in a full smile.

She raised one eyebrow suspiciously. "So proper this morning."

"Yes, ma'am." Then, almost apologetically, "Deputy Governor Francisco is waiting in your office."

An expletive slipped out over the surface of her coffee causing ripples across it as she drank the rich, dark java.

"And what do you have for me of import?" she drawled in an affected tone as they moved through the corridors from the private to the public side of the structure.

Unlike Miriam, Inoke was known to be cotisuelto, fashionable, always on top of the latest working-men's trends. Today, he wore green bottoms that moved as a skirt over one leg and fit as a tight pant on the other. His fiberoptic eyelash extensions had been programmed to match. His tailored asymmetrical suit coat crossed his body and buckled tightly on his hip. The fitted top accentuated the V-shaped physique one would assume belonged to the satellite program stars who were draped in admirers. The loose skirt side of his bottoms rippled like wind through a field of grass during their brisk walk. He would have fit in at a fashion function far better than he did here.

With rebellious opinion, Miriam was appreciative he chose the latter. She genuinely liked him and that was better than she could say for most in government. She also trusted him, which was even rarer. To top it all off, he knew the job. Likability, trust, and competence in one person? Miriam wasn't sure how the hell she could manage her role without him and was grateful she didn't need an answer to that conundrum.

"The basin moderators are ready to give their reports on the kelp farms and fish nurseries first thing this morning. The zip chopper will take you to the central coast for that review, followed by the shoreline erosion reports from Mr. Ramos," Chief of Staff Kalua continued down his list, making sure to get at least a curt nod of approval from Miriam after each bullet point before moving on. "You have a visit to the southern solar farm, as well as to Weston. That's where you'll tour the desalination plants and pick up Dr. Bradley. Cityship Tatsu is scheduled to dock this afternoon at the northeast port gate. Trading and battery loading will take place today and then dinner with the captain."

"Did I schedule that?"

"Your dad did. He's the host home for Captain Ridgelin, remember?"

"He's what?" Miriam exclaimed, stopping dead for a moment.

"I assumed it was your request. I didn't even ask. Nina and I are joining you. We don't have to. I could talk to her," he offered.

Shaking her head and continuing their morning march, Miriam noted, "It's my father that needs the talking to, not you!"

Sheepishly, "So, we'll be there at oh two hundred UTC?"

"Apparently you should check with Jomo Heirlinda on that one. I don't suppose you know what he's cooking, as well?"

"Your dad? I think he said seaweed salad and some sort of root stew."

"I'm sure it will be a nice enough night," Miriam shot, but her chief saw the dimple appear on her left cheek as she held back a smile. Despite her vocal protestations, Inoke knew Miriam appreciated the excuse to spend time with her dad. After her mom drowned three years earlier, the two of them treasured the rare moments they were able to spend together.

"First thing in the morning," Inoke went on, "a whistler will pick you up and security is in place for your stroll through the northern wind farms."

Miriam stopped once more in the middle of the corridor and turned to her chief-of-staff with an exasperated expression. "Inoke, Please tell me you realize how ridiculous that sounds. Security for my stroll?"

"Disculpas, Governor," he apologized. "Deputy Francisco said he wants to make sure you are safe up until the second you are en route to your negotiations."

"That man just can't wait to put my pants on for a few days, can he?"

Inoke chuckled uncomfortably but stopped himself short of a full laugh.

"It's okay, Inoke. It is funny," Miriam said flatly as she grabbed the digifile from him and began to read through it herself, sipping her coffee all the while with her other hand. "And besides, you know it's true."

"Yes ma'am, he definitely wants to get in your pants."

Miriam pursed her lips and winced away the words as she handed the digifile back to Inoke.

Inoke nervously stuttered, "Governor Heirlinda, I didn't mean—"

"Relax. Nobody wants to move on from that image more than I," she said as the leaders began walking once more.

The chief was shaking his head. "I still don't know why you work with him."

"He was second in the gubernatorial election, so it's not as if I chose him."

"That's tradition, Miriam, not law."

"You know as well as I do that not honoring that tradition with Roberto Francisco would have been terrible optics. The human equality groups would have been all over me for passing him up."

"That's ridiculous. You've always been an ally to their causes. You don't dislike Francisco because of his deformities. You dislike him because he's a crumb!"

"Which is all the more reason I selected my own chief of staff. It's your job to keep him at arm's length for a measly six more years," she couldn't hold back a familial laugh for her friend.

"Are you sure you don't need me to come along to the negotiations?"

"Nice try," Miriam said. "I need you here."

"Just offering. You have until the morning to think about it. That's when you embark on the Tatsu and head to the talks," he continued walking through the agenda. "Executive Officer Kate Murphy will review your schedule for the extended travel to the Pacific Islands Land Nations once you're on board."

"Oh, I always liked Kate," she said. "Even before she started dating your sister."

"We like her, too."

Miriam stopped one last time. Inoke paused with the governor like a partner in perfect step. They were in the middle of the hall directly before the double doors that would take them to the public side of the residence. On this side of the doors, they were pals who had known one another for twenty years. On the other side, they were politicians – Governor Miriam Heirlinda and Chief of Staff Inoke Kalua.

Miriam held back a sigh and surrendered to the tension that she knew would set in the moment the entrance opened. She turned to face Inoke with her side to the door and she took a long indulgent swallow of her coffee.

Stalling, she asked "How are your chicks doing?"

"Mish mushkela!" he said excitedly, while mirroring her. Any remaining air of servanthood dropped. "No problems! For a while there, we thought we might lose the littlest one. It was always last to the food. But it's been standing up for itself a bit more and Nina and I believe all six will make it!"

"That's great news. I love that you enjoy caring for your animals. That's supposed to be the point," Miriam said, now drinking her coffee more intently to enjoy every last ounce.

"It doesn't hurt that my partner is Zoe Baja's Head Poulterer."

"I miss Nina," Miriam said sincerely. "It will be nice to see her tonight. The two of us used to catch up at least once a week and, other than in passing, I don't think she and I have sat down in," the governor shook her head sadly. "Oh. It must be months."

"She understands."

"And your sister, Sefina? I didn't even get to see her off after her last break. She's managing well at the university? I've heard that final year is brutal."

Nodding, "She's working hard, but Sefi finds ways to get out into the community, too."

"Does she fit in okay in the Canadian Land Nation?"

"Yes. They treat her very well."

"I hope so," Miriam exclaimed. "If they didn't, they might have a diplomatic crisis on their hands! I had to pull in a lot of favors to get her student travel papers."

"She truly does love it there. She's taken to oceanography. Wants to intern on one of the cityships. Maybe the Zhu."

Miriam shivered on hearing the word and she wrapped her hands a bit more tightly around her mug. "No kidding. Cold up there. She likes the Hudson waters?"

"Ideally. She's somewhat familiar with the work they do since it's the ship closest to her. They have a lot of university partnerships. She wouldn't mind working on the Greater Lake, either."

"The freshwater seastead? Interesting." Miriam chimed in.

"Maybe the seastead or maybe the Cityship Yahng. That's the cityship with a route that passes the seastead. Both are part of the Cityship Regatta," Inoke confirmed. "Sefina isn't picky, though. Two seasteads and twelve ships across the whole world doesn't leave room for many entry-level opportunities. I'm sure she would be satisfied with any chance to come her way."

The many floating cities around the globe dotted a handful of passageways on the open seas. Miriam was always fascinated by the gargantuan vessels but didn't much enjoy being on them. She was made for the land. Still, there was something romantic about the great historic race to the sea—the Cityship Regatta, as it became known—that took place centuries earlier. As a child, she always enjoyed the nostalgic tales of the original cityship captains as they found and transformed old ships into homes, communities, and—eventually—vital world partners. Even though it wasn't the path for her, Miriam was glad that Sefina, somebody she loved as family, would be able to enjoy a life at sea one day.

"She always took to the water industries. I'm sure it's why she and Kate work so well together," the governor responded as she downed her last drop of energy.

Her procrastination was officially drained from the mug. Miriam looked at her empty cup with sad dissatisfaction, as though she could will it to refill itself. She and the chief of staff stood silently for a moment. They knew that they could not delay the workday any longer.

After finally releasing the resigned sigh, Miriam looked up at Inoke. "Alright, then, let's get this day started, Chief!"

The two passed through the double doors to the public side of the governance building while Miriam simultaneously handed her empty coffee mug to Inoke. He in turn passed it off to the first worker by whom they walked. With their morning chat and first coffee behind them, the buzz of business was now in the air.

"And what should I do about Deputy Governor Francisco?" Inoke asked, submission back in his voice as show for the rest of the personnel.

"Let him wait in the office. He probably wants to consider redecorating for the short time I'll be gone."

"Yes, ma'am," he laughed openly this time, proud to show the camaraderie he had with the governor in front of the other workers.

Inoke desired the staff to see him as reverent toward the office of Governor Miriam Heirlinda at the same time that they saw her reflect a mutual respect for her chief of staff. She was so impressed with how well he played the game. He had true charm and it showed. The colorfully attired parade of professional government Zoeans snapped to attention when the two of them passed by. It was unnecessary. Miriam hated pageantry.

"Your security awaits," Inoke jested.

CHAPTER 3
YEAR 2552

Baja Province
Northern Territory of New Hispaniola Land Nation
Global Union

The first thing she noticed was the unorganized barrage of sound.

With her eyes still closed, Linda listened to her surroundings: footsteps running back and forth, calls for supplies and other orders shouted between people across what must have been a massive room based on the echoes, beeping, buzzing, and alarms of digital machines, the muffled sounds of Global Union zip choppers overhead outdoors, something wheeled by – squeaking as it passed on a hard floor. And then there were the voices of countless people, too many to distinguish, as a chorus under the GU soloists who pretended to be in control. The choir was crying, moaning, whispering, and begging. The noise was all blended together into a single symphonic soundtrack. It was the soundtrack to confusion. To chaos. To pain. To loss.

Linda didn't plan to open her eyes again after the beating she withstood but the sounds around her indicated a world that expected otherwise. Slowly, she forced the slits of her eyes to widen. It was painfully jarring to awaken on an all-white bed in an all-white room. She squinted against the crisp brightness of the foreign place where she found herself.

She was surrounded by other beds squeezed so tightly together that, had she wanted to, she could have reached out and touched the man next to her. He was perfectly still. She turned her head to look at him, a tiny act that unexpectedly brought dizzying pain. She could not see his chest rising and falling. She stared harder but nothing changed. Her eyes slowly traveled up to his face. His skin was yellow and gray, and his mouth was unmoving and slack with a tube hanging out of one foamy drool-covered corner of his parted and cracked bluish lips. A muted hissing was the only sound coming from the bed, the tube in his mouth blowing air that was no longer being breathed. No. She did not want to touch the man.

Linda wasn't sure if it was her imagination or her reality that caused the smell to hit her at that moment. It was rot, but so much stronger than she'd ever experienced. It was an assault on her nose comprised of vomit, feces, compost, and something somehow even worse. Death, she thought. No. It wasn't her imagination. She knew in her soul that it was the scent of death. There was disinfectant, too, but its failed attempts at covering the other odors of decay made it just another complex layer to the air she didn't wish to inhale or invite into her lungs. She gagged and looked away from the empty body beside her.

It was the gagging that made Linda aware of her next unpleasant sensation. Her throat closed on something foreign. It felt hard and tight and scratchy. Her mouth and throat were dry. She looked down at herself as much as she could with her eyes, not wanting to repeat the pain of lifting or moving her head. She became keenly aware of her present condition. Panic settled in her chest as she realized the number of tubes connected to her. A digital core monitor claustrophobically closed over her torso. The machine took scans every minute or so, giving readouts of her heartrate, blood pressure, circulatory blockage, vitals, and general healing process. Or, maybe dying process, she pondered as she tried not to think about the man beside her.

The monitor scanned from right to left and back again, humming as it moved across her body and sending readouts to a screen at the foot of her bed. Linda realized much of the beeping, buzzing, and alarms she'd heard had come from right here – above, and around, and attached to her body.

She hurt.

Everywhere.

She was groggy and sensed that she might hurt a whole lot more if whatever was making her feel groggy wasn't being pumped into her system. Maybe it was the sensation of pain and not the sounds in the room that had awaken her. Throbbing began to return, at first to her head, but soon to her back, abdomen, and eventually everywhere that she could feel. Her whole body was pulsing with a dull ache that was growing more intense. As if on cue, a mechanical arm moved over her face. Padded braces came up out of her bed and held her head in place while the mechanism angled in toward her jugular and, with a metal-tipped tube, pushed a painkiller into her neck.

After the muffled puff and as the needle drew away from her, everything went black once more.

The next time Linda remembered waking, her bed was shaking violently, a cacophony of rattling tubes, wires, and mechanisms. A medical technician was unclasping the core monitor from one side of the bed.

"Dr. Richards, help me out!" he screamed to a passing woman who was juggling her own handful of equipment.

"Olive, I can't. We're leaving this floor." the doctor said to the young man, "I'll drop these if I stop," she added, as if completing that one task had become her unfailable mission.

"Those are supplies. This is a citizen. Go ahead and drop them and get over here! If the monitor falls while it's over her, she'll get crushed!"

The doctor attempted to put the equipment in her hands down onto a counter, but they crashed to the floor just a moment later, adding to the deafening clatter around them.

The two worked while tremors rocked the facility. Lights flickered on and off. A pipe burst in the ceiling, dropping a flood of water down onto an occupied bed – the patient in it had the ability to move and was joined by a nurse leading him away. Digital tones filled the air joined by panicked human voices.

All the while, a booming announcement echoed outside:

"...NEAREST GROUND-LEVEL SHELTER. CITIZENS OF NEW HISPANIOLA, THIS IS YOUR GLOBAL UNION EMERGENCY ADMINISTRATOR. WE ARE EXPERIENCING EARTHQUAKE ACTIVITY. PLEASE MOVE TO THE NEAREST GROUND-LEVEL SHELTER. CITIZENS OF NEW HISPASNIOLA, THIS IS YOUR GLOBAL UNION EMERGENCY ADMINISTRATOR..."

"This is the fourth largescale aftershock in half as many days," the doctor said in a haze. "And dozens more that they don't even report on anymore."

"Days?" Olive said shaking his head. "Aftershocks? You can't buy that," Olive returned. "We have been in this season of earthquakes for longer than any time in human history. Each tremor is stronger than the last. Does that sound like aftershocks to you? We're in the fifth year of this – FIFTH YEAR! It used to be months between quakes, then weeks, and now, we're lucky if we get a day between the ground shaking us to our knees. When the hell will the GU acknowledge that something bigger is happening?"

Helplessly, Linda watched as they struggled to detach complicated clamps that remained in constant motion. She wanted to assist but wouldn't have known how even if she had been physically able to do so. She absorbed their conversation but had neither the strength nor the ability to form enough a thought to allow her to contribute. She felt like an invalid. She was.

"Did you hear that they lost more of Philippine Islands Province? More than two hundred and this time, some of the inhabited ones, too." Dr. Richards shared, not responsive to anything outside of her own thoughts. "Just gone. That's seven million Pacific Islands Land Nation people dead or evacuated."

"I hadn't heard. That's on top of those we've lost in our own provinces and I've been too busy trying to keep us from losing any more. The announcements are background noise to me these days. It's the only way to stay focused."

"And the latest tsunami took out Lanai." The doctor continued in a cloud of shock. "Another of the islands gone. That leaves just three," she was spiraling.

"Doctor," the tech paused, putting a hand on Dr. Richards, and looking her in the eye, a moment of stillness in the trembling. "Michele," he said more affectionately, calling on her first name, "Listen to me. I know that the world is shaking. It is exactly why we cannot be shaken. I need you. Right here. Right now."

Dr. Richards had been in charge of this young medical tech when he first began his employ. She had taught him the routines of the Baja Province's primary medical center. As she looked at the boy—the man—she was moved at how he'd grown. He was leading her. Michele focused on his words.

He went on. "You cannot help all of the Global Union. You taught me that. You can't even help all of New Hispaniola. You can help the Baja Province people. I can't do this alone."

The doctor blinked, took a breath, and then nodded at the younger worker, snapping out of her daze. She shifted her focus to Linda for the first time. The two finished detaching the monitor from her bed and began to cart Linda toward an exit, joining the parade of people moving off this no-longer-safe level of the building. No sooner had they started to move her than the ceiling over the area where her bed sat moments ago collapsed on the med tech.

"Olive! Olive," the doctor screamed to the pile of metal pipes, plaster, and construction innards.

Linda wanted to do or say something, but the mere thought took all her energy. She could only close her eyes again.

The next time Linda opened her eyes, a young woman with thick, straight red hair, big brown eyes, and gray medical scrubs sat at her side. The woman was reading through something on a pad. Linda didn't have the energy to get her attention. Linda's eyes drifted to the woman's arm. It was covered in broad stripes of orange, blue, green, and lavender. There was something different about this tatua. It seemed to reflect the light in a subtle manner, changing as the woman's arm moved relative to the window. Did she have a window now? Maybe she was hallucinating. Watching the colors on the woman's skin dance in the light was hypnotic. Linda tried to reach out, but only the very tips of her fingers managed to clumsily brush the skin of the worker.

The woman was initially shocked. "Oh!" she exclaimed, putting her hand gently on Linda and moving her eyes and fingers over half a dozen tubes and controls, immediately in monitoring mode. "I can get the doctor!"

Linda's head shake meant to stop her was so understated she wasn't sure it was seen, but the worker was attentive. She lowered her pad and Linda thought she could read the name MAYA on her digital nametag.

"Okay. I don't have to leave just yet," the redhead smiled reassuringly. "What can I do for you?"

Linda managed to tap a finger on Maya's inked arm and wrinkle her brow in question.

"It's vee isn't it?" the woman said. She was young. Linda had only heard the newest entry level workers using vee to describe something trendy or exciting. "The GU is doing some experiments on UV-protective skin dying. I'm trying out a few of their colors. Not very artistic, I know. I wish it could be applied in more of a design like henna, but they're testing the effectiveness of the different colors. It could be a real breakthrough. Citizens at sea, in the agricultural provinces? They could all benefit if it works. I'm one of their fair-skinned test subjects," the girl said, admiring the color on her arm. "I do like the lavender."

Linda tried to smile but wasn't sure if it came across with her lips still inhibited by tubes.

"You, too? The lavender would look so pretty on your skin. Do you like Henna?"

Once more Linda tried both smiling and nodding. Neither felt right. It was as though her brain couldn't quite remember how to make these simple movements. The tiny amount of interaction drained her.

"I should get Dr. Richards," Maya said.

Linda heard the young medic rushing off as her consciousness slipped away.

Linda took a deep breath. It felt good, like she hadn't had a breath that deep in months. It turned out she was right. It had been just over two months since her lungs last filled to capacity. They hadn't fully expanded from even the yawns her body constantly sought. Until this very moment, she didn't realize how strong that yearning for a deep breath had been. The sensation was extraordinary, and she realized how often she'd taken it for granted.

"Dr. Richards!" called the young woman excitedly. What was her name? Maya? Or had she imagined that?

Linda blinked repeatedly trying to get her world and her mind to come into focus. She took more deep breaths and each one felt like inhaling some new power.

As she focused on the redheaded girl, Linda wondered if the young man was okay, or maybe he was in a bed like her, or dead. Did she dream about the other losses? The islands lost to quakes? And the tsunami the doctor had spoken about? Her heart quickened involuntarily as an image returned to her mind – the man with the hissing tube hanging from his mouth. Was he real? Was it just a nightmare? It was all a fog.

"She's awake!" The colorful technician called out.

"Well, I'll be damned," the doctor said, and Linda realized Dr. Richards didn't look the same either.

The doctor was calmer, but in a sad sort of way. More like numbness than peace. She was a beautiful woman, possibly Chinese in Earth-Before-the-Melt. Her skin was like porcelain and her hair was black and silken. She was slender and had a healthy glow which Linda imagined wasn't easy to come by in a medical ward.

"Let's get her some ice chips right away, get her drinking on her own again. We'll try broth later," Dr. Richards said to Maya who quickly rushed off to her assignment. The doctor then smiled as she sat in the chair formerly occupied by Maya and addressed Linda in a maternal tone. "Just in time. You won't have to be here much longer."

"Here" was a different room again. There was no window here. The space was smaller, less noisy. The whole world seemed quieter. There weren't as many people around nor as many sounds of alarms and announcements. Even the lights felt warmer, less stress-inducing. She didn't have a core monitor across her torso. She was no longer connected to tubes or wires. She did have some robotic lifts that would move and bend her legs and arms occasionally, but she couldn't see any bandages. She was weak, but not broken; tired, but not hurting.

"What—" Linda began, wanting to ask, 'What happened?' but her voice was barely a cracked whisper and speaking at all felt foreign, a distant memory of something she used to do. And she didn't sound the same as that memory, either.

"Keep trying. It'll take some time to be able to talk again. But the longer you go without using your voice, the harder it will be to get it back."

"What," Linda began again. It was hard and Linda was frustrated. She parted her lips to speak again but stopped just as quickly as she saw her arms rising with the machines to which she was attached.

"It's okay. You can do it," Dr. Richards encouraged. "I know it's hard to ignore the digital lifters. They've been working to keep your blood flowing and your muscles working."

But that wasn't what had stopped Linda. She'd seen a glimpse of herself as the lifters did their work and she noticed lavender-colored henna-like painting on the backs of her hands. She found herself staring at the intricate artwork.

"I hope you don't mind," Dr. Richards said. "It's been a while since we had a full roster, and we were just . . . I don't know. Maybe just trying to bring some beauty into this place. Maya thought you'd like it. It's just surface ink, not the UV-protectant dye, of course."

Linda had never been able to afford the tatua and body painting that was featured on the glamour programs. She had her provincial and aptitude markings, but nothing of artistic value. She thought how ironic it was that she'd finally get to experience such beauty from the bed of a hospital.

"Thank. You. Doc—"

"Michele. We're practically family at this point," the doctor said with a gentle touch to Linda's shoulder.

Linda felt tears welling up in her eyes, but also a need to deflect the emotion, so she made it situational instead.

"What happened?" Linda croaked out through her raw throat. The words caused her to wince.

"You were critically injured in a dreadful earthquake," Dr. Richards continued in formal tone. It was clear she had practiced how to deliver this information. "The Great Quake registered stronger than anything the moment scale had ever seen."

Michele paused quietly – her eyes focused on a different time and place. In the short silence, Linda continued to inhale fully, indulging in the feeling of air in her mouth and nose and lungs.

Eventually, Dr. Richards' mind returned to the conversation. "You've been kind of special to all of us. A bit of a miracle, really. You were the only one in your whole community pulled from the rubble. A wall board fell against you, protecting you from falling objects and providing a pocket of oxygen that lasted until the rescue."

Linda pictured Henrietta in her mind, her favorite chicken spreading its wings out over her body.

"The GU's emergency responders think you must have been knocked out or asleep," Dr. Richards went on. "Your body's muscles were relaxed, so they handled the tremors well. They didn't tense up. You bruised at the times when a body that had tension in it might have broken. Being asleep may have saved your life."

"Asleep," Linda said. The word felt like hot sandpaper was being rubbed up the length of her esophagus and over her tongue.

The doctor watched her carefully after she spoke the word, as if looking for some other explanation. "Of course, you had plenty of other impact injuries to keep us busy," she said as she pulled up a screen on the side of Linda's bed and began to scan through it. "You were absolutely covered in bruises and welts. We laser-stitched your right temple. There was internal bleeding. A nasty concussion and bruising on your brain. A broken wrist. Your identity tattoo was gouged on something, so we couldn't even conduct a palm scan on you for identification or medical history," the woman looked to Linda for an answer to this latest revelation.

Linda turned her left hand over and looked at her palm. It didn't look like her own. Bits of what had been her unique code still existed along their former edges, but the entire center of her hand was smooth and pink like a burn scar. She narrowed her eyes at it, feeling like it wasn't even her own hand, then she turned it back over to look at the lavender henna once more.

Dr. Richards continued to look at Linda with a combination of mourning, exhaustion, and awe even though her patient offered no name. "Your spine was fractured, too. Suffice it to say it's no less than the magic of GU medicine that you are still here. You took quite a beating."

Ignoring the word beating, "You. Said. We. Were. Leaving?" Linda asked in staccato, pausing to swallow phlegm to lubricate her weakened throat between each laborious word.

"There are two planned transports left, Miss . . . what should I call you?" Michele continued to unsubtly probe.

Linda looked at the doctor and blinked. She was still unsure if she wanted to lose her anonymity. A GU administrator paused as he passed by the foot of the bed, his hat and arm band distinguishing him from the medical workers of the facility.

"Or if you need me to check the records for anyone who might be looking for you?" prodded the doctor.

The administrator looked lost in his pad, but Linda felt sure he had an ear to the conversation between she and Dr. Richards. The words, "You're a nobody, now," echoed in her head. She remained quiet.

Michele turned toward the GU administrator and gave a polite smile and nod. He moved on. "It's okay. It will come to you." Dr. Richards said patiently.

"The transports?" Linda encouraged the conversation forward as her speech started to hurt less.

"Yes. Well, we have two transports left and which one you go on will depend on how you're feeling and progressing. You're capable of moving on your own, but out of practice. We need to get you eating again, speaking again, and moving on our autowalks. The second to last transport is in just four days. I think you'll need the extra time waiting for the last one. It will be another two weeks after that."

"Why leave?" Linda managed.

"This is going to be hard to hear," she began. "Just remember. You're through the worst of it. You can get through this, too," the woman brushed the hair back off Linda's face as she spoke apologetically. "The Global Union has decided the Baja Province is unsalvageable. They are evacuating all surviving citizens to locations around the world where they can get reestablished for requisite rations. As many of them as possible will still be in New Hispaniola. They're keeping families together to the best of their abilities. They will find new work and quarters for all citizens of age in the most appropriate land nations. Most of us have had a couple of months to adjust to this development, but you're waking up into it. You have to accept something. We lost millions here." It was the doctor's turn to have a crack in her voice.

Linda moved her arm off of the mechanical lifter in an attempt to offer a compassionate touch to the forearm of the doctor. Instead, her arm weakly flopped onto that of the Michele. The movement snapped the caretaker back to her medical role.

While speaking, Dr. Richards gently lifted Linda's arm back onto the mechanical mover and she tied a stabilizing strap over it, careful not to pull it too tightly over the artwork Maya had left. "And, with the earthquakes still coming," the doctor continued as robotically as the lifters to which Linda's appendages were attached, "they just can't serve this area anymore. It's certainly not safe to work in . . . to live in."

Michele looked at Linda for some kind of confirmation that she understood. She could merely nod.

"Also, unfortunately," Dr. Richards went on, "with those never found at all, those who left on the earlier evacuations before the extent of the damage was known, and, well, people like you, it's going to be some time before we know the real loss. Identification is being done at Global Union processing stations and that's how we'll actually have a handle on—" she paused. "On the details of who made it through this whole nightmare."

Linda took her own breaths purposefully, without the aid of any machines, still relishing the feel of air in her body, like she'd never truly breathed before this moment. She worked on a history in her mind, reflecting back on what she believed to be true.

Lukas was going to kill her.

He finally snapped.

He removed her palm scan so that he could cover it up if she was ever found.

Before he could finish her off, the earthquake killed him.

The earthquakes were happening all over the world, more frequently and at stronger levels, taking the lives of countless GU citizens.

She was found and brought to the medical center, along with however many more who were dying.

She would have died, too, if it weren't for . . . she once again remembered the young man who had moved her medical gurney in the nick of time. What had the doctor called him?

"Olive?" Linda asked Dr. Richards.

"What?"

"How is...."

"He didn't make it."

"I'm. Sorry."

"He saved your life. You're alive because of him."

Alive, Linda thought, nodding to the woman and not knowing how she should feel about that word. Had she ever understood it at all? Lukas gone. Her home gone. The work she'd known gone. The very land she'd always lived in was going to be abandoned – for all intents and purposes . . . gone.

She was alive, though and that had to mean something – something she now had an entire anonymous lifetime to discover.

CHAPTER 4
YEAR 2908

Gubernatorial Grounds Zip Pad
Zoe Baja
Zoelands Concord

Zip choppers had replaced helicopters nearly 700 years earlier. In the mid-2200s, the vehicles became the latest-at-the-time answer to short-distance, small-load, maneuverable travel. While their power efficiencies, distance capabilities, and capacities had certainly improved over time, each upgrade sold as a once-in-a-generation breakthrough, they were as common to man today as they had been when introduced in the 2200s. Powered by just a small electric charge for initial takeoff, they then became nearly self-sufficient, their series of strategically placed and sized propellers functioning as miniature wind turbines, generating power that could not only move them as skillfully as small insects up off the ground, but also directionally guide them. They could go for nearly a full day before recharging, assuming they didn't have a burdensome load, receive damage, or get overpowered by a storm or erratic wind currents.

Once in the air, the speed of a zip chopper's propellers was so fast that the little aerial vehicle would seem to whistle, which is where the crafts earned their more common name by which they'd been referred for the last hundred years. Whistlers had a major renaissance after the era of the Zoelands Concord began in the 2600s. While most land nations relied on a system of pods pre-programmed for various destinations with zip choppers only used for emergencies or security scenarios, Zoelands were typically developed on disconnected, discarded, or damaged lands. These locations lacked the geological infrastructure of Global Union land masses and, along with it, much of the order necessary for an efficient pod system. Zoe Baja, really a promontory between the Sea of California and the Pacific Ocean, was ideal for whistler travel.

Miriam and Inoke stood at the edge of the gubernatorial grounds zip pad awaiting her last tour of Zoe Baja's districts before she left for alliance negotiations.

Heavily, Miriam continued casting glances at her most trusted advisor.

"Out with it, Miriam," he finally said.

"What do you think about all of this, Inoke?" the governor asked. "I mean what do you really think? Don't give me the newsfeed answer."

Inoke looked up toward the sky as if seeking an answer there, and then down to the ground before bringing his gaze back to the governor. "It sucks. I'm not going to lie. The GU operates as a whole unit, different parts of the same machine. You are about to seek a partnership with some of those parts and I think it's going to mess with the order they like to keep. I don't know if that's something that happens quietly."

"Am I trying to be quiet about all of this? Inflation and scarcity have gotten so severe on Baja that we have people living on eggs and water right now, Chief. Shouldn't we be yelling about that?"

"Yes. Yes, we should. But we're inviting snakes into the nest, Governor. Snakes may very well just eat the eggs and we'll have nothing left but the water – salty water at that."

"You sound like Francisco."

Inoke looked at the governor and narrowed his eyes with disappointment.

"Disculpas, Chief," Miriam said sincerely. "I didn't mean that."

Resignedly, "I don't think seeking a partnership is wrong. I don't have a better answer. I just know that there is going to be a cost for working with the Global Union and I don't know what that cost will be."

Miriam pondered Inoke's words as the zip chopper arrived. There had to be a way to work together with the Global Union while still maintaining their Zoe identity. Perhaps being outside of the governor's residence for a bit would help her remember why this all mattered.

Miriam took whistlers to survey her country as often as she could, focusing each visit on the different districts: the northern and southern port districts, the basins where kelp farms and fish nurseries lay on the central east coast between the ports, the power districts made up of both the southern solar farms and the northern wind farms, coastal erosion support which had outposts all around the Zoeland, and the water desalination and production plants on the west coast. The governor's residence was located on the northeast tip of Zoe Baja. Most often, trade took place at the southern port. The southern port was not nearly as far south as it once had been. What made up the original southern peninsula had been immersed almost entirely under water for the last hundred years. A combination of erosion, earthquakes, and ocean expansion had slowly saturated and then quaffed the very land that the Zoeland founders had once called home and, while an occasional year of low precipitation caused former moderate to high elevation areas to peek out on an odd year, habitability was long lost.

What remained of the former Baja Peninsula west of the San Andreas fault line was farther away from New Hispaniola to its east than it had been in its founding days, too. The hundred-years of quakes, which actually took place over 112 years from 2547 to 2659, had driven the divide to expand while the plates beneath the sea were in a constant tug-of-war with one another. The southern points of Baja pulled away from the coastline of EBM North America. The land drifted outward over the Pacific Ocean in an inverted V, while the northern points, at the top of the V, were closer to the large land mass, but long since under flowing water. Stretches of underwater pod tunnels connected the northern Zoe Baja points to New Hispaniola, but satellite views showed what was essentially an island. At the time of the Great Nekros Quake of 2552 that began the Zoelands era, the peninsula covered nearly 140,000 square kilometers. Today the entire strip was significantly smaller and shrinking every year.

Miriam sensed her diminishing land slipping away, or actually sinking away – down beneath the waters. It hurt in a way that felt human and relational, like a lover who was receding while her own passions remained strong and desperate. Her efforts to hold on were met with apathy, the land doing what it wanted to do despite her pleas with it.

She stepped off the whistler to the primary coastal erosion support outpost. The ground below her feet squished like a soaked sponge. Even before hearing the latest reports, she knew how they would read – like an obituary. Each of Miriam's steps gurgled when she put her weight down and then smacked moistly as she pulled her foot forward from the ground's saturated muddy grasp, a suction cup letting go.

Miriam took a deep breath. The scent of ocean rot was heavy in the air at the outpost.

The grasses that still fought to physically hold their ground despite the mostly-washed-away root support were limp yellows and blacks. They were already dead but didn't yet know it . . . ghost grasslands, just like the ghost forests filled with leafless tree trunks and limbs on the northeast coast near the governor's residence. Soon they too would go under, adding to the displacement while also no longer serving the prevention of erosion. It would be a double penalty for her homeland. The triple penalty would be inevitable when their decomposition added to the gases in the ocean, raising its fever ever higher.

The soil losing its grasp on the plants was these days composed mostly of salt and sand. Even worse was that it was fully saturated. When Miriam met with Aaron, she was sure he would only confirm it; Zoe Baja was drowning.

"Governor," said Aaron Ramos in greeting when he met her at the zip pad.

In the EBM world, Ramos would have been Filipino. His perfect smile and high cheekbones below almond-shaped, deeply-set, dark eyes still carried his genetic history. He had UV-protectant dye at one time, but it had faded leaving his skin somewhat luminescent, but not particularly colorful. The neutral pearlescence suited him.

"Aaron," she greeted.

She offered a hug, and he pulled her whole body in closer, tighter, and longer than she'd expected, his emotions on his sleeve. Embracing definitely wasn't Miriam's preference. She wasn't one for touching at all, though she had grown accustomed to handshakes. She knew what it meant for Aaron, though, and it was part of her acknowledgment of who he was, much like the bowing that still came in handy when she visited the easternmost provinces of the Eurasian Collective Land Nation or when she visited the Southeast Continental Indigenous Nation that her dear friend Nina had once called home. It always felt awkward for her, but she knew the prefects and councils appreciated her efforts.

For Aaron, touching was punctuation: a word of concern accompanied by a gentle hand on a forearm, serious information joined by a firm front shoulder grasp while he looked you in the eye, shared laughter came with a rugged pat to the upper back – the bigger and more drawn out the laughter, the heartier the hand to the back. Hugging? That meant you were welcome in his world – you were a part of his family. She learned to appreciate it from him and would honestly be a bit hurt if it didn't come.

There were generations before her and plenty still today that assigned physical contact to circumstances and relationship levels – kisses for intimacy, hugs for friendship, handshakes for business, bows for submission. Miriam preferred to think of the gestures as assigned to a combination of character and intention.

Miriam knew that when Roberto Francisco hugged her, an extremely rare occurrence, she would be leery of what he wanted. Whereas a bone-breaking handshake from Cityship Tatsu's Captain Mik Ridgelin meant he saw her as an equal. The captain's executive officer Kate Murphy rarely shared more than a curt nod, but if she didn't like you, you wouldn't get even that.

There was an instructor who Inoke's sister Sefina had in intermediate school. He would place his hand on her lower back while he guided her through essay questions – Professor Schenk. From some, it could have been a grandfatherly gesture. Schenk's words, his spoken intentions, were those of a caring mentor, but something about him made Miriam's skin crawl. She didn't trust him and, when she couldn't quell her suspicions, she had tapped into her resources to have him quietly investigated. The investigation revealed countless images of his young male and female students. He had synced their images with the human imitation programs of his servebots and engaged in the kinds of acts that actual humans would never have allowed. The unsanctioned "Sefina-bot" had been a favorite of the professor and they were grateful to have stopped him before he transitioned his fantasies from facsimile to flesh. In the rehabilitation center where he was spending the rest of his days, he would be allowed neither.

When Aaron at last released Miriam from their embrace, he held her out and looked at her. Both hands were in firm shoulder grips accompanied by long, deep, sorrowful eye contact. It was very serious. Miriam pursed her lips and sighed through her nose.

"You've seen, then," he said. They turned and began to walk, his arm across her shoulder. One of his botany students handed him his digifile and he let go of Miriam while they continued in an outdoor walk that could just as easily have been a meeting in a conference room. They both knew the reality without being in it. But they also both wanted to absorb every last possible al fresco green and dirt moment of life they could before it was gone. The walking was definitely preferred.

"They're all nekros, aren't they?" she asked. "Our plants aren't okay," she replied. Our was a purposeful word choice for Miriam. She didn't use it with all her district administrators, but she shared Aaron's affinity for growing. She always had.

As a child, she'd worked alongside her dad to plant hundreds of thornless honey locusts and Japanese black pines – the trees that were most tolerant of salinized soil. Jomo Heirlinda kept the Zoe tradition of garden boxes alive for generations as an educator in the Baja's schools. It would have been hard to find a level three student in all of central Zoe Baja who didn't have a Jomo Heirlinda garden box at home.

Miriam's was the first. It was nothing more than a wooden box with stones below the dirt. It was on wheels so that it could move throughout the day and year to take advantage of the sun or shade each plant desired.

Miriam usually started seedlings in her box. Once her seedings grew strong enough, Miriam and her father would add them to the grove and—while there—they would tap the fully grown white and black mangrove trees for their unique syrup. The syrup combined with their crop of sugar beets were a treat. She and her dad would make rock sugar and eat the crystals by the spoonful together.

She'd spent most of her childhood barefoot and with the earth embedded so deeply under her nails that her mother Susan used to paint them just to cover up what she couldn't get out with scrubbing. Young Miriam would talk to the plants, as well as to the worms that she saw as partners. To this day, there was little that made her feel more alive, more human, than digging in the ground. It rooted her as strongly as the most stubborn of plants.

When Miriam was nine years old, she tried to grow a prickly pear cactus. She thought it was such a funny looking plant and her dad had told her they could even eat it, like many of the cacti grown in drier parts of the world. It never quite took to the point that it fruited, though. The plant loved the salt, but also liked ground that had far less moisture than what they had to offer. She was so disappointed because there had been an empowerment that came with knowing she could grow something that actually fed her and helped her grow in turn.

Today, almost nothing of edible substance was being sustained on Zoe Baja anymore. The few crop growers they had left were primarily hobbyists who made what they could for their own families with imported soil. Those who truly farmed professionally had found agricultural work in the land nations of Africa and the Southern Territory of New Hispaniola Land Nation. Grazing animals had nothing of value left either. That industry had eroded as thoroughly as their land, with many of their animals being shipped to parts of the Canadian and Mississippi East Land Nations. Only the ethical poultry farm remained. If Nina Kalua weren't the one running it, that would likely have been exported as well. She stayed mostly because her family was close to the governor.

Modern trade painted a pretty picture of everybody meeting the needs of one another – some with goods, some with services, some with desires, some with necessities. Zoe Baja certainly had a place in that complex machine, but there was a frightening humility in being incapable of producing life-sustaining nourishment for yourselves. Her people had been relying on their trade partnership with New Hispaniola Land Nation to stock their grocery store shelves. The eastern neighbor offered inflated prices to the Zoeans while also over-pricing the salt, water, and battery cells that they imported from Zoe Baja in turn. It was a suffocating relationship she kept for necessity and Miriam was about to deliver it a damaging blow. Her actions could mean they would get out from under the thumb of the Global Union. It could just as easily mean the thumb would be replaced by a fist.

The report from Mr. Ramos wasn't a surprise. There was a finality in hearing it confirmed by one of the world's most renowned botanists, though. It was a wet finger pinching the last spark of hope.

"The decline of the land goes well beyond our inability to grow food, Governor," Aaron shared. Then, immediately more personally, he followed with the bottom line. "Aqli Muqli with all of this, Miriam. My brain is completely fried trying to see a solution, but I don't believe that Zoe Baja can sustain plant life of any kind for much longer. Death is spreading from the shoreline to our highest altitudes."

There was no good news to be shared. Ramos told a doomsday tale for each of the planting zones. The tangle-rooted mandrakes on the shoreline were leaning over the waters, occasionally kissed by the tides and—when it was calm—catching their reflections in their own eventual graves where they would add to the rising waters. Instead of lush green grasses and vegetation, the Zoeans would have to build up their land with stone and sand. Instead of the gray wood and cone clumps of their black pines, their shorelines would need the protection provided by metal nets and concrete. Either they start implementing these manmade answers or the land of Zoe Baja wouldn't exist at all anymore. The next generation of little girls would have stone gardens to tend with their fathers. Miriam felt her throat close around a lump of salt that had nothing at all to do with the saline levels in the soil.

"Shie shie, Aaron," she said when he saw her back to her zip chopper.

She hoped he knew just how much more there was to say than thank you, but her tight throat wouldn't allow her to say it. His job, the impossible task of saving the vegetation of Zoe Baja, would not be around for much longer. At best, it would change to a role of converting the natural earth to something as fake as Professor Schenk's sexbots. Her life's greatest love, and she felt sure his too, was Zoe Baja . . . and it was dying.

She didn't blame him.

She mourned with him.

Before Aaron's report, Miriam learned that the bull kelp forest and fish nurseries fared only slightly better. After the near extinction of kelp farms from the oceans over a period of centuries, the water levels had drastically suffered. These leafy plants that danced in the waves supported a rich ecosystem and were remarkably efficient at carbon absorption. The loss of most of the world's kelp along with other sea vegetation led to significantly increased carbon in the oceans, much warmer water temperatures, and an overall rise in sea levels. Coastal communities around the world suffered, then were abandoned, and eventually were lost underwater.

While Zoe Baja's kelp on the central coast was healthy, and—beneath it—the eggs of the many fish that needed protection, those minor industries were never meant to sustain life so much as protect the long-term health of the world. The reality was that they weren't enough for the Zoeans and certainly not enough for the world's oceans. It was like expecting the contents of a child's fishbowl to provide for a crowd of thousands and miracles of that kind hadn't been done for millennia.

There had been a thought that when Zoe Baja and the other Zoelands began their preservation efforts, the GU would follow suit. It was assumed that they would utilize their own coastlines and coves in the effort to bring health to the world's oceans. The Pacific Islands and Antarctic Land Nations made some changes, but the rest of the Global Union did not. Miriam's one little piece of the world wasn't enough to make the difference Earth needed.

Miriam was zipped to the solar district where the solar-mirrored spheres looked like a garden of ancient light bulbs. It was beautiful in its own way, but also sad as she thought of real gardens. She took in the view as she passed over the central cultural district where she'd worked for years as head of the Zoelands Foundation. During that time, she also managed the Heirlinda Museum's surrounding plant beds and she longed for the simplicity of that work, away from the pressures of political leadership.

After her visit to the southern energy farm, which was working to generate the power for their own land, as well as to charge the battery cells that would be loaded and shipped to other parts of the world, she headed to her final destination. The importance of the last stop Miriam would make before returning north to board the Cityship Tatsu weighed heavily on her. The very existence of her homeland depended on the vital projects unfolding in that district.

The west coast of Zoe Baja was devoted to the desalination plants, an industry as old as Earth-Before-the-Melt but ever more important after it. As more of the world's waterways became connected to the oceans, less of those waters were fresh and consumable. In the case of places like Zoe Baja, the brackishness of their inland freshwater supplies had required the same desalination as the water from the Pacific Ocean. High volume solar distillation was Zoe Baja's preferred process for separating water from the salt and other elements that made it undrinkable.

The by-product left behind after the sun superheated the liquid to cause the separation, was a salty brine. It used to be returned to the ocean at that point, leaving the fresh water to be treated and consumed as necessary. The efficiency had since greatly increased. The brine itself was processed; the salt was extracted. Then, what remained was further refined, separating the different minerals that were valuable to nutrition, medication, and even construction. Every century or so, a new step was added to squeeze every last resource out of every last drop of the sea.

The clean processed water from desalination efforts hadn't been used for anything more than human consumption for nearly a millennium. It was only recently that a second process was added for that product – the production of hydrogen power. The idea of hydrogen power was hardly new, but the west coast research team made some recent breakthroughs that would change the face of power forever.

The largest desalination plants of the world began in this region even before the Global Union existed. Zoe Baja was the dominant exporter of fresh water and the extracted and usable minerals taken from the brine. Now, they would be the only exporter of the very thing that might save Miriam's people.

Miriam shook hands and took reports from the plant's leading scientists and then met with Dr. Jacob Bradley in the newly added hydro plant building to see how their assignment was coming along. The scientist would be joining her on the trip to the Pacific Islands Land Nation, but one last explanation and tour was in order before they left.

"Dr. Bradley," she said as she met him at the end of the desalination wing of the plants. His handshake was firm and intense. "Based on your reports, this is more than I could have hoped for," Miriam said while extracting her fingers from his. "Thank you for all of your hard work on this project."

After greetings and some well-earned bragging rights from his leading team members, the two moved on to an all-white room with several bamboo hooks hanging and storage cubes stacked against one wall. A distinct hum told Miriam that the air filters were running in tandem with sonic cleansers and UV lighting for even further sanitizing. The high-pitched sound drove tension into her neck and shoulders. Or maybe it was just the stress of what this work could mean.

"Are you wearing any jewelry or belts? Do you have any other metals on you?" asked Dr. Bradley.

"No," Miriam replied.

"You'll need to remove your moccasins. I see they have some small grommets. You can use the cotton slip-ons," he gawkishly looked at the ceiling as if uninterested. "We have them for everyone."

"Of course. Shie shie," Miriam said. She grabbed the pair of slip-ons Jacob had indicated and smiled when she saw that they had been embossed with her name HEIRLINDA. She laughed. "You have these for everyone?" she said coyly.

Jacob grinned. "Thought you'd like those. They'll keep your feet warm on the Tatsu, too."

"That was very considerate," she said maternally to Jacob.

"I'm grateful for this project, Governor. I just wanted to let you know how much I appreciate you giving me a chance."

Miriam nodded as she slipped the gift onto her feet and put her own moccasins into a storage cube.

Back to business, Bradley asked "And you don't have any metal body inlays?"

"I'm a bit old-fashioned for those, Jacob," she laughed.

"Lastly, do you have any liquids on you? Hydration bottles, for instance?"

"No. I've just got myself."

"Place your feet on the pad," he indicated a bluish square on the floor. "And stand still, please," Dr. Bradley went added.

He stepped to one wall of the room and keyed a few strokes onto a pad. The room dimmed and a slit in the ceiling opened. Bluish laser rays spilled forth like water over Miriam. The scanner tickled and she twitched slightly from the sensation, an actual giggle slipped out.

Jacob appeared almost embarrassed at having caused Miriam a vulnerable moment. "Disculpas, Governor. I have to be thorough. You'll thank me when you're not giving yourself static shocks all day long."

"I understand," she said sincerely.

When the light scanner didn't produce any alarms, he keyed a few more strokes on the wall pad and the ceiling closed, sucking the light back into itself like smoke as it did so. The room brightened once more. Dr. Bradley placed his digifile into one of the storage cubes and pulled out two pair of silicone safety goggles.

"It is important to protect you, Governor," the scientist said with a small nod that Miriam thought was meant to be silly, but Dr. Bradley looked sternly at her with his golden-brown eyes after putting on his own goggles. He turned paternal in an instant. The trait was quirky on such a cerebral person.

She donned her own pair, and the scientist then opened a door opposite the one from which they had entered causing a pressure change. With a feeling of being in an enormous vacuum, Miriam's ears popped, and a suction sound reverberated throughout the small space.

The two entered a second room, deep gray and the size of a large closet. The scientist pushed the door shut behind them. Her ears popped again. This time they opened back up and she was immediately relieved. After a chime sounded and a light turned from red to green indicating the first room's door was fully sealed, he finally opened the next door into a cavernous workspace. Miriam felt a warm brush, like an insect had just buzzed by closely. The hairs on her arms stood up and her unruly curls rose away from her head.

The room reminded Miriam of a distillery she had visited with her dad when she'd turned sixteen. Large vats of liquids filled the space from floor to ceiling and clean-clothed workers moved about taking readouts from the tanks and dashboards in various parts of the room. It was hot and Miriam immediately felt beads of sweat forming at the base of her neck and across her chest. The massive space was broken into three clearly distinct sections.

"This first space, as you might have guessed from the buzzing and the static, is where we mine the hydrogen through an electrolytic process."

Dr. Bradley's voice was strangely deep for his small frame and it gave him an air of authority. He'd earned such authority, but his youth sometimes overshadowed that fact. The young man had the peach-fuzz facial hair of a teen just starting to shave and his skin was soft and fair. His body moved as though his legs always wanted to run full speed into the world, but he was forced to contain himself to meet some standard of adulthood that said you couldn't move excitedly.

"It's kind of the reverse of a fuel cell," he boomed in the loud room. "The process uses electricity to break apart the hydrogen and oxygen before separately harvesting the hydrogen. We've had decent success here. I'm sure you've read about it in the documents I sent."

"Yes, I have. I must admit seeing it is always a far more invigorating experience, though," she smiled as she ran a hand across her forehead.

"Disculpas, Governor," Dr. Bradley said while handing her a white towel to wipe her brow. "We've all become quite used to the temperatures in here. You're feeling the heat overflow from our other sectors. It is not from the thermal process sector, which you might naturally think. We are phasing that out. We had to use it as a starting point because it was the most common manner of efficiently creating hydrogen, but the heat for that process comes from natural gas and it wasn't realistic for long term renewability, especially as more and more of the natural gas resources have become deep-sea excavation enterprises."

"And you've completed the phaseout of the biological processes already?"

"Yes, ma'am," he responded. "We just don't have the resources necessary to continue that form of hydrogen production, either. As you well know from my reports, we need very specific algae, molds, and other plants for that process and the plant life of this world is needed most of all for nutrition, medicine, and land preservation, not electricity. The majority of the heat you're feeling is from our photoelectrochemical water splitting. Our solar mirrors are creating the necessary temperatures to separate the oxygen and hydrogen...." he trailed off with an upward tone, as though he were holding something back

"But?" Miriam led him on.

"It is by far the most sustainable in terms of what's needed and available. But the process comes with its own problems. The number of solar mirrors necessary at our altitudes requires a massive amount of physical space and that is at as much of a premium as energy itself. More, actually. Wind nets, tidal turbines, better solar access; these are some of the other power sources toward which we'll eventually have to turn. World partnerships will be necessary to utilize those efforts."

"That's why the real innovation isn't the power, which can be captured anywhere, but in the cells that hold it." Miriam concluded.

"Exactly. Governor, our planet has nearly unlimited resources for power if gathered correctly," he said with an oxymoronic combination of scientific stiffness and childlike awe. "That's something I could certainly go into more when we meet with other scientists during negotiations. Would you like to understand them, now?"

Miriam wiped her forehead again and wondered how inappropriate it would be for a governor to wipe her armpits in front of one of her constituents. She decided against it but was keenly aware of sweat beads dripping down her front and back. She hoped she hadn't pitted out her shirt. Her hair grew ever larger in the humidity. "I appreciate your enthusiasm, but let's stick to the major points."

Looking somewhat disappointed as he adjusted his safety goggles, Jacob went on expressively. "This hydrogen power can be gathered and produced in massive quantities all across the globe, and better in many cases, if it's a high altitude or an equatorial region. Storing that power is and always has been the problem. Batteries are heavy, relatively large, and inefficient in terms of the amount of energy they carry as well as in various other inefficiencies that can occur."

"And your solution to this storage issue?" Miriam prompted.

"In traditional power engineering, a number of obstacles exist with hydrogen. As a gas, it takes up a massive amount of space despite the fact that it's lighter than air. Fourteen times lighter to be precise. Handling it in liquid form could be dangerous. As an element in any form, it's tremendously unstable and flammable."

Dr. Bradley said each statement with increased emphasis. He was as passionate about energy as she was about Baja's gardens.

"Throughout the centuries," he went on. Miriam tried not to glaze over when she heard the word centuries. "People have experimented with ways of optimizing hydrogen because it's powerful and it's clean," Jacob continued. "Keep in mind that traditional batteries and resources provide power but nothing else. Or, worse, they leave behind waste and toxins. Hydrogen has the usable exhaust of water." That word perked her back up. Her mouth began to feel dry as the scientist spoke. "We've been looking primarily at Earth-mined resources to create the power cells that hold this energy. We tried to develop something that would allow us to take advantage of the power and permit the extraction of the exhaust."

"You mean that the water will actually be usable, too?"

"Yes," Jacob confirmed flatly. "Not just usable, but sanitized – very healthy. But the instability of the resource has made storage an insurmountable obstacle for centuries."

Centuries. There was that word again. "Until now?" Miriam asked, wanting to get to the finish line. She wondered what the long version of his explanation would have been.

Jacob's thoughts continued to drip out because they were his everyday understanding of his work. His words were robotic but the animation in his face was passionate. "Until Lunar and Martian mining expeditions. Those resources were used. It was a step in the right direction but what we've created here—"

"What you created," corrected Miriam.

Humbly, he nodded. "Yes, with my team. We created something entirely new. We made what we call a tri-stellar compound to house the power."

"Clever," the governor said.

"I came up with that," Dr. Bradley said, more matter-of-factly than proudly, before going on. "Graphene produced right here on Earth is a light and strong material. We combined it with proprietary elements from Mars and Luna. That was the key. It wasn't about the resources of Earth, or Luna, or Mars, but a union of all three."

"A cord of three," Miriam said nodding.

"What?" asked Jacob.

"Something Mik Ridgelin told me once when talking about mooring ropes. It means, basically, that we're stronger together."

Miriam moved into her own thoughts. The double entendre of a cord of three wasn't lost on her as she prepared to create a partnership between Zoe Baja, the flagship of the Cityship Regatta, and two Global Union land nations. She realized she wasn't listening to Dr. Bradley and she tuned back in.

".... the cell encasements that we've termed hydrocells help to stabilize the hydrogen at never-before-attempted pressure levels. We can store more energy in each cell than past iterations could have even imagined."

"And the water exhaust? Where does that come in?" Miriam asked.

"There are actually two chambers in each cell. I've incorporated computer chips that force the switching back and forth between the two cells. When one is providing power, the other is releasing water. There is a constant flow of energy and constant flow of released water. A single cell isn't providing a lot of water, but a block of them would provide a significant amount of clean, simple H2O."

Sincerely, "Amazing," Miriam added.

"Hydrocells are strong, stable, lightweight, renewably sourced power with water for exhaust."

"And how many of these things are needed?" Miriam asked.

"With the pressures at which we can now store the power, a single hydrocell could power this entire facility, the largest draw of power on all of Zoe Baja for more than a full day!"

Miriam didn't look as impressed with that statistic as the doctor had hoped. "Let me put it another way," he said, wanting to pull as much eagerness from the governor as he clearly felt for the project. "Think of a home – an average home with a family and needs for heating, cooling, cooking, cleaning, and living. One of these cells would power an average home for two weeks."

That did it. Her eyes got big as she nodded. She smiled genuinely at Dr. Jacob Bradley. He had been the right man for the job. Still, the pressure of knowing that this little piece of the world could be the hope for all of them was incredibly overwhelming. Could she convince the others that this innovation was worth the more traditional resources her home needed? Would they be willing to collaborate in a partnership that saved Zoe Baja for this hydrocell technology. She wished the job wasn't hers to find out.

"Let's see it," Miriam said, trying to match his enthusiasm but aware that the tension in her body was just as evident in her voice.

She was equally aware of the fact that her clothes were sticking to her body. The weight of the humidity was as great as her responsibilities.

Carefully, Jacob opened a well-padded case in which the hydrocell lay. The small object was so unassuming. Seeing it on the ground somewhere, one might think it just a piece of metal refuse. The five-inch rod with a mere one-and-a-half-inch diameter was unremarkable despite the exceptional amount of engineering time and experience that went into its creation. Computer chips and chambers were concealed, but she thought she could make out where the water would release. Despite her curiosity, Miriam found herself afraid to even touch the prototype. The idea of transporting it across the ocean to the negotiating table was even more terrifying. She was grateful to have the scientist who created it coming along to protect it.

"Here's the greatest part!" Dr. Bradley added, snatching up the hydrocell with a surprising casualness that made her flinch. She suspected he was trying to diminish her visible fear, but the effect was quite the contrary.

"Don't worry, Governor. It has insulation so we can handle it."

"So you don't burn yourself?"

"No. So you don't freeze yourself," he said. "Even a brief exposure could cause frostbite. We lost a worker just last week."

"WHAT?" Miriam exclaimed, but Jacob huffed out a small laugh.

"Kidding. You looked tense."

Surprised at the unlikely humor, "I'm just hot," she laughed as she began to fan herself. She was going to have to change clothes before dinner – sweat continued to drip down her body.

"We're almost done, here. A couple last things for you. Once this cell has been exhausted—power and water drained—we can re-use it! Charge it up for another run. It does lose a fraction of efficiency, but our testing with this particular rod, the latest iteration, has shown that the loss is not measurable until it's been through multiple uses. Our current estimates are that each cell could be used twenty-six times. You see the significance of that?"

She didn't.

"Twenty-six! If each cell lasts a couple of weeks and is good twenty-six times, we get a full year of power before the materials from it have to be recycled. This little thing!" Jacob tossed the rod from one hand to another. Miriam couldn't prevent her huge dark eyes from widening even more. "Just imagine! One in every home in the Zoe!" he exclaimed, using the rod in gesturing for emphasis.

"Not just the Zoe," Miriam added.

"Right?" the scientist agreed energetically, still being overly casual with the hydrocell. "And it will power the world!"

"The prototype exceeds all of my expectations," Miriam said in awe, taking it gently from the scientist's hand and replacing it in the gel-foam bed from which he'd grabbed it. "This case," she said as she closed the lid around the hydrocell, "holds our future, Jacob. This represents life for Zoe Baja. "

CHAPTER 5
YEAR 2552

Baja Province
Northern Territory of New Hispaniola Land Nation
Global Union

Linda gazed at the lineup of patients outside the medical center.

The sight transported her back to her graduation celebration after her mandatory final youth break.

Following aptitude results and the three-month assignment allocation period, the Global Union held huge celebrations at zip ports and docks all around the Baja Province and, Linda imagined, probably all around the world. Each career field represented amongst the graduates was honored, with the highest scoring new assignee giving a one-minute speech about how his or her skill was going to contribute to the balanced GU quality of life.

Agricultural assignees always promised an end to food shortages before they went on to serve in the African Land Nation. The scrubbers and sea life professionals, who vowed to reclaim the fresh waters of the world and turn back the rising seas, stood at the ready for their on-the-job training aboard any number of docked vessels at the southern port. The medical field workers who would train in the Eurasian Collective Land Nation before receiving their assignments were going to predict and prevent the inevitable illnesses that always followed a melt or other toxin release into the oceans and soils of Earth. The botanists and forestry students headed to the Pacific Islands Land Nation were going to see to the health of Earth's natural resources. Meanwhile, research and technology professionals, as well as educators, headed to the Antarctic Land Nation; they would, according to their speech-giver, "innovate, educate, and activate new solutions for the state!" That graduate annoyed Linda.

Some of her classmates were going to feed souls by training in entertainment and hospitality – those aptitudes included food and event fields, as well as sports, music, art, and various other endeavors that would be perfected in the Mississippi East Land Nation. Linda's dearest friend was going there to learn how to run a vice lounge. Even though that work was not something to which Linda was drawn, she still felt a twinge of envy over her classmate's impending travel.

The Canadian Land Nation representatives were eager to bring home trainees in leadership, management, and administration. And then there was the Australian Land Nation. They sent their administrator to greet the new animal preservation professionals. Envy crept into Linda's heart when that group was introduced.

After a while, every high aptitude speech sounded the same. "Part of the intricate design," was a phrase three different students used. "The GU doesn't work without," was another that was particularly popular. And, of course, there was the repeated reminder that "this generation, like none ever before, was facing challenges as a result of diminishing resources." She'd wondered for just how many generations that same theme had been stated.

As many as forty fields were represented in all, each with their own subcategories of the work that citizens would likely fulfill for the next sixty years of their 115-year lives. Some would move on after aptitude training to serve in GU Land Nation outposts around the world, proudly representing their field of study in their assigned communities. Some of them would be forever stuck in the very place they were now headed to engage in their educations. But at least they weren't stuck in Baja. Each was ready to ship or zip to the land nation or sea vessel that housed the instruction of the discipline with which they were tasked for the Global Union.

The pomp and circumstance of the event was huge. Live musicians sang and played the Musical Reimaginings, reworked triumphant classics that were saved for celebratory occasions. Full gluttonous spreads of natural foods were laid out for them to enjoy at will. High level GU officials shook every graduate's hand and presented each with a medallion-emblazoned arm band representing his or her career field and assigned land nation or ship. Most would later choose to turn those arm bands in for the tatua that symbolized their aptitudes and provinces.

At the final station—it felt like station stops to Linda—students received their palm scans. It was a fifteen-second procedure in front of a GU monitor to permanently incorporate the new citizen into Global Union society. Each graduate placed their left hand on a small glass ball. The administrator in charge of monitoring laid a hand over that of the graduate. The gesture was both a traditional offering of familial affection and a practical method of holding the young person's hand firmly against the scan printer. The instrument would read the individual's vitals and map his or her palm print. Simultaneously, a scannable code was imprinted on the palm with a UV laser and blue ink. The last thing felt by the newly initiated citizen would be a tiny prick, like the needle of a cactus. Microscopic chip implants helped protect citizens by tracking them if they were ever lost.

Linda was apprehensive to put her hand on the small sphere that would identify her, even though they'd practiced the procedure a dozen times before the ceremony. Despite assurances to the contrary, she was sure it would hurt, especially when the chip was implanted. She felt a panic rising within herself as the seconds passed. It really didn't hurt, though. At worst, her hand felt warm and maybe a bit numb and prickly, like when a foot goes to sleep and then wakes up again all at once. She barely had time to absorb and process the sensation before the administrator monitoring the ceremony said, "Welcome, citizen," and nodded while removing her hand from Linda's own, indicating that the next graduate should approach.

She looked down at her opened left palm. Linda thought she would have some sort of emotional response. She'd heard stories about the moving sensation that immediately followed scan imprints, how people would discover a feeling of completeness for the first time in their lives. They knew their purposes. It was supposed to be an experience akin to baptism.

Nothing.

She stared at it, longing for connection to the moment. If not purpose, then at least some kind of feeling.

Maybe newfound pride in the Global Union. Or sadness that her fate was set. Or relief for the constant care she would receive. Or satisfaction that she would forever be part of caring for others – part of that "intricate design." It didn't matter what she felt. She just thought there would be something as opposed to nothing. Looking at the code, it felt foreign, like it wasn't even her. Rather, it seemed like something that could simply wipe away. Linda was completely detached from it. She rubbed it and it felt a bit tender, but it wasn't going anywhere.

The graduate behind Linda bumped into her. He'd been staring at his own palm and, both distracted, he'd walked right into her. She hadn't realized she had stopped walking, holding up the line. She put her hand down and timidly began to move forward along with the student behind her. Then, they sat once more for what felt like an eternity before the transport launchings began.

During the leadership speeches, everybody was told that they were essential pieces of the puzzle that made the Global Union complete. An administrator of the province's school gave a heartfelt send-off, filled with "delightful satisfaction" that her students were now GU contributors, that her very life was dependent on the work that this next generation was doing.

Linda had every reason to feel important. The atmosphere, the speeches, the food, the palm scan ceremony, the authentic pride and respect in the administrators and officials; it all fed into what should have been a euphoric moment. But . . . nothing.

Linda was just sixteen and she didn't have an adventure in front of her, not one that she would have chosen to call an adventure, anyway. Everybody was leaving, people she'd known all her life. She wondered if they'd all felt something when they were imprinted. She looked around and observed several people showing their scans or staring at their own with awe. The scans of so many were going to take them around the world. She was stuck in New Hispaniola Land Nation. Stuck in the power industries. She wasn't even off to another territory or province. Linda was average, nowhere near the level of student who would give a speech. She wouldn't have some prominent job in her field. She would be merely a minor subordinate because that's what they told her she could do. There were some classmates she'd thought would be lifetime friends, but they were too excited for their own assignments, their own transfers, to even feign sadness or disappointment for Linda. In farewells, she put on her best smile and let them have their moments in the sun, posing with them as they created pictures for their personalized satellite feed screens.

"It's not so bad," Lukas said to her as she returned to her position after three of her friends left for the Eurasian Collective Land Nation.

He stood behind her as her invited family member because she didn't have any living relatives left on the province.

"We've got the power!" he joked, making a fist, and flexing his bicep.

Then he flashed a full smile, and she was pretty sure his blue eyes actually sparkled. Out of sight of the other graduates, he put his fingers through the belt loop at the back of her formal ceremony uniform and pulled her close – protected from all the other people and feelings that overwhelmed her.

"Smile," he said to her as he playfully tugged her in even closer and she felt comforted by the heat of his body against her own.

Lukas had gone through his ceremony two years earlier and had only recently started his power employ. In fact, he was in a role that might even mean he would ultimately present Linda with her final employ options once she finished training. He promised to take care of her and make sure they would always be able to live close to one another. He talked up all of the many paths she might be able to take and, when he spoke about them, Linda almost believed that they could be exciting.

Lukas took pride in his field and was glad to have Linda with him, staying in the same neighborhood they'd shared from a time before she had any memories at all. He'd helped her study for the aptitudes, guiding her through the power industry questions. Because animals came so naturally to her, he thought it was more important that she worked to strengthen her aptitude in the other areas. He explained that it would probably mean she would have even more options. The Global Union would only place her somewhere that she could succeed.

Thank goodness he'd helped her; the power industries were the only industry that aligned with her skills. If Lukas hadn't guided her during the exams, she might not have qualified for an aptitude at all. Graduates without specific aptitudes were assigned draft numbers for toxic cleanup assignments. It was high-credit work, but Linda was justifiably suspicious of any work that earned higher credits than all the other supposedly just-as-important pieces of the Global Union puzzle.

Lukas reminded Linda of the struggles she would have in a field that was outside of her skills and how grateful she should be that she was going to be able to maintain her employ without failure or reassignment, maybe even to a non-aptitude task. It wasn't his fault that Linda dreamed of working with animals on the preserves or on the ethical farms.

There was a time in human history when animals had been hunted for sport or raised in massive numbers and kept in terrible conditions until they were deemed ready for consumption. That readiness usually came long before their natural lives would have ended. They were slaughtered solely to harvest the protein. But this was the twenty-sixth century. Humane protein agriculture had been practiced for centuries.

Preservationists passively cared for animals for their whole long lives and, when the animals died, as long as it wasn't from disease or infection, they were then processed for food. Invasive species were an exception to that rule. Those were pulled from their habitats to protect the ecosystems that were suffering as a result of their presence. If the invasive animal couldn't be easily moved to a more natural environment, or if such an environment didn't exist anymore, only then were they allowed to be processed for food.

It was always Linda's hope to care for animals. The preservations were especially intriguing to her. They were open-air wildlife centers on huge swaths of land where the animals were observed in their environments and provided for when in need. If a preservationist was lucky enough, she befriended the animals through animal-invited interactions. She would have been just as happy as a poultry merchant, too, if it had meant she could leave Zoe Baja.

Linda had scored very well on compassion and routine, both qualities that were necessary for the animal aptitudes. Unfortunately, she scored low in relationship management and self-protection – other traits sought for preservationists and humane protein cultivation. It was necessary for the caretakers to also be able to care for themselves in situations that may become dangerous. The GU's primary job was to protect its citizens. Linda was considered to have tendencies toward self-neglect, and it was determined that the Global Union animal environments could be dangerous to her.

According to the speech given for what instead became her assigned field, the power industries would "care for others so that they could care for the Global Union." It sounded like compassion. It felt more like lip service.

Everybody cheered with each new citizen send-off. The animal aptitudes were the last to leave. Linda looked longingly after the Australian Land Nation's zip choppers that day as the last of the animal preservationists left for their assignments. Even with Lukas behind her, she wanted nothing more in that moment than to be on that transport. She melted into Lukas like a fallen kite and was grateful he was there to hold her up.

Very few people remained in attendance to celebrate the handful of new power industry workers who would staying behind on Baja Province. Her world became very quiet very quickly. Administrators in attendance gathered the graduates in groups and took them on tours of their training centers. Lukas nodded to her, promising he wasn't going anywhere. She was grateful. He was all she had left.

The sounds of the last transports faded away.

Now, Linda had the chance to get on another transport and it scared the hell out of her.

Looking around, she didn't know any of these people. There were hundreds of them here in lines for the many zip transports. Many of the citizens were in various states of injury and recovery, while others were those who had been stabilizing the no-longer stable province – rescue workers, sanitation engineers, medical professionals, and administrators.

Dr. Richards had left on the earlier transport weeks ago. Even though Linda only had a few conscious days with her, she had formed some sort of relationship with the woman, something she hadn't done in years. She enjoyed a number of at least surface-level conversations. She shared things that she believed seemed friendly, but without revealing any of her true self to the woman: the neighborhood she liked, the tea she preferred, what she grew in her garden box, whether she had a chicken or a goat, her favorite places to use discretionary credits when there were some available to her, the pod routes they agreed had grown too crowded, and—of course—the weather and the earthquakes.

She talked a bit about her aptitude assignment to the power industries, but when Linda felt the questions began to probe, she deflected the conversation back to the doctor. It turned out Dr. Richards hadn't worked in emergency and trauma recovery for long, but the work was growing on her and she liked both the specialty and her field assignment despite the obvious battlefield fatigue the role carried.

Linda had also become acquainted with the new tech Maya. She thanked the redheaded young woman for her henna work, which the tech had touched up twice in the time between transports. The two of them had conversation that revolved mostly around Linda's care, though. Maya was the one to make small talk when checking on her. Right now, the tech was at the other end of the long lot which was being used as a makeshift zip chopper port to evacuate the last citizens from the rubble-laden disaster area that stood in for what was once a bustling society.

Maya was managing a line of those still most critically injured and ill, making sure they were properly loaded and cared for before their transport to wherever it was they were going to start a new life. A dozen other lines stood between the two, each with at least some citizens suffering from their own degree of injury severity. The fact that Linda found herself on the opposite end of the most serious cases must have meant that, despite all she'd been through, she really was okay . . . at least physically.

It seemed she hadn't fully absorbed all that had happened. Not just the evacuation of the Baja province, or her physical recovery, or even the terrible quake and continuing tremors that led to her standing in this line right now. No. It was more than all those things.

Linda was reflecting on everything that happened before the big quake . . . the Great Quake. The deathblow that was supposed to be hers but became Lukas's own undoing. The hundred beatings she took in the ten years before the last one. The fruitless rapes she endured during the eighteen months of their child-bearing permit. The lonely, isolated work she hated. The day Lukas first raised a hand to Linda, and she realized that her one connection to this world was the very thing she hated most about it. The deep hopelessness she felt when her choice about whether or not to board a graduation transport was taken away from her.

Linda's heart began to race.

She had been dazed, lost in her own thoughts as the line in front of her progressed forward toward new lives – lives they hadn't chosen but that would once again be assigned to them – new homes, new employs, maybe even new nations. She was still close to the building at the back of the lot while, out in the open, the other patients and medical personnel closed in on the zip choppers.

She could take a step forward toward the end of the line she'd faded from or she could take a step backward, into the shadows of the hangar behind her. One of those directions was indeed an assignment, but an assignment that would mean she would be protected, employed, and cared for all of her days finally away from the place that—thirteen years ago—she had been aching to leave. The other direction was a choice full of equal parts adventure and uncertainty, neither of which she was sure she could manage.

Linda could not remember the last time she'd had the freedom to choose.

CHAPTER 6
YEAR 2908

Northern Point of Pacific Sea Route
Cityship Tatsu IV
Cityship Regatta
-
Northern Port of Zoe Baja
Zoe Baja
Zoelands Concord

The Cityship Tatsu appeared on Zoe Baja's western horizon. Unlike many of the ships that came into port at the Zoeland's capital city, Captain Mik Ridgelin didn't need to bring the local maritime pilot aboard to aid them in docking. Mik knew the waters of his favorite port as well as the shore workers did. The Tatsu captain stepped onto the bridge of his cityship and puffed up his burly chest. His joy for the impending task of mooring the great vessel was not hidden from his face or posture. He ran his massive fingers through his salt-flecked ginger hair and pulled the working hat of his uniform tightly down. He rubbed his callous-hardened hands together in ritualistic preparation and nodded to the bridge crew that had snapped to attention upon his arrival.

"Don't scunner me, team," he said to them. Don't disappoint. "Let's go and do this, eh?" the captain's heavy accent was most prominent when he was passionately in the labor of navigation.

Without relaxing from their stances, each of Captain Ridgelin's sailors stiffly and quickly took up stations around the complicated room.

Punching in a few buttons on one of those stations, Mik opened their mooring procedures with first contact to the port. "Jambo, Harry, how the hell are you?" he radioed to Zoe Baja's lead longshore worker, while using a tone many times more casual than that he used in any other port he entered.

"Welcome back, Captain," the seasoned worker returned. "I hope you brought something for my boy!"

Harry's boy was Potcake, the mix-of-a-little-bit-of-everything dog that followed the lead dock worker everywhere he went. The rust-colored canine with a black snout had been found hiding in a cargo container as a barely-able-to-stand puppy and Harry adopted him for his own, initially feeding the pup goat's milk from an infant's bottle. Zoeans were known for the keeping of pets, almost in sheer defiance of the GU ways. In the ten years since Harry had rescued the wiry haired mutt, he and Potcake had had lived up to the old adage about man's best friend. They were inseparable.

"Devon picked him out a mickle something, I'm sure," Mik said elfishly.

"It's those little somethings that make you Potcake's favorite ship. He's been whimpering since you appeared in the distance!" exclaimed Harry. "We'll see you in a few hours, Captain," he added, aware of how long it would take before they would actually shake hands.

They ended their radio transmission and Mik got to work. The captain led his crew through the shallow rises and jutting rocks with the ease of an ancient street driver dodging his own neighborhood's known potholes and bumps from behind the wheel of a road-bound vehicle. Today the sun shone brightly, and the wind and waters were still. He almost missed the challenges that bad weather and rough seas opportuned.

Even so, tension filled the air as the bridge team, aft bridge team, small vessel pilots, and mooring parties took up posts that would have to be manned with full attention, readiness, and expertise for the next several hours. And that was if everything went according to procedures.

Mik bounded between his sailors on the bridge looking over shoulders and punching in keystrokes as he dropped by each station. He didn't distrust his crew, but he fine tuned their movements along the way, each time offering encouragement and reassurance that they had done their job well.

"Braw," he said to his port navigator with a hearty slap to the back. "Brilliant!"

The navigator had dark hair and skin with a blue tinge to it. Like many of those on the cityship, the seaman had opted for UV protective skin dye to prevent the sun damage possible when spending months under the unobstructed rays of the sun at sea. Tatsian events were often filled with colorful people in simple uniforms in contrast to the Zoe Baja citizens who tended to wear bright colored clothing over natural skin colors. Captain Ridgelin didn't have skin dying, although his fair skin was known to pick up pink and red hues, never quite growing dark or golden under the sun.

While Mik commanded from his post on the bridge, Kate Murphy relayed orders from the aft bridge to direct the ship's docking teams and line crews. She was Mik's executive officer, or ExO, the second in command for the Tatsu. By the manual, cityships operated with a rank structure, but those ranks were respected more in terms of roles than they were in terms of formality. Outside of navigational duties, the crew and teams aboard the Tatsu called one another by first names, or—even more casually—surnames. There weren't fraternization rules or sharp delineations between lower ranks and officers, nor the civilians who called the ship their home. The organized structure was a requirement of the operational infrastructure of a cityship; but—make no mistake—the Tatsu was a family community, and not a military unit.

The team slid levers and inaudibly tossed various control powers back and forth. A crew member sent a function from one screen to another with flick of her finger and the sailor across the bridge took over for several strokes before he flicked it back. Other workers moved amongst one another like choreographed dancers. It was in a day's work for the crew but maneuvering an entire city to berth in a narrow strip of the ocean without the aid of canal waters was no small feat.

The consequential bridge-team chatter was minimal and low, the hum of sea business creating a deep harmony under the bells, whistles, and moaning metal of the gargantuan ship. The words and actions had been perfected and put into practice more times than they could remember. The largest ship of the Cityship Regatta carried with it the strongest and most experienced crew. A dozen different navigational tasks were carried out with every one of Captain Ridgelin's commands. Even minor shifts of the Tatsu were received by the talented sailors as orders with their own associated procedural checklists.

"Sideships, away!" Mik called over a headset, putting the next of a hundred steps into play. "Tugs only!"

"Drop the tugs!" the fiery second-in-command called out. Her order was repeated by engineers all up and down the port side of the Tatsu.

Kate's headset was squished on top of a hat that barely contained thick, sloppy braids of frizzy orange coils. Her pale green eyes, which stood out beautifully from her fair coral skin, were tightly focused on her digifile as she flipped list after list up into the air above it.

"Full tug fleet, Murphy!" Mik rang out, while simultaneously managing the bridge team.

Cityship Tatsu IV carried its own flotilla of tugboats. The process of bringing in a ship that was more than a full kilometer in length was slow and arduous. Moving at such subdued speeds made it difficult to gain the momentum necessary for changing direction or even making small movements. When large recreation and container ships docked centuries ago, the very biggest of them would use as many as four tugboats to pull and push the large ships ashore. The Tatsu used six.

"Aye, Sir!" Kate called back before quickly correcting herself to, "Oui, Sir," as she punched something in on her digifile. "Mish mushkela!"

Several decks up from the surface of the water, large white panels surrounded the entire ship. On Mik's order and Kate's subsequent execution of it, those panels flipped down against the sides of the Tatsu revealing hundreds of smaller ships. Bamboo nets served as barriers between the ships and the air outside. Without the nets, an open hatch could result in a Tatsian falling to the ocean surface. From the bay deck height, the landing would be no different than falling from a tall building onto a concrete bed. Generically, all of the occupants of the Tatsu's bay deck were termed sideships, but their functions were as varied as their paint jobs.

Some sideships were capable of holding their own staffs or families. Those that held the latter were modern day recreational vehicles known as dayships. Dayship families were free to take their own expeditions while still calling the cityship home. They were the little ducklings to the mama duck of the Tatsu. Dayships followed her as she paddled through the oceans and docked on the bay level as a baby duck would tuck in under its mother's wings.

The ships that held staffs, called workships, were rarely residential. The workships included merchants and commuter ships. Still others were charged with conducting ocean mining or toxic cleanup activities alongside GU or Zoeland scrubber crews.

The last type of ship housed on the bay deck were the tugs. Tugs were manned by Mik and Kate's crew. Pushers were stationed at the reinforced port quarter, port half, and port quarter aft panels of the Tatsu. The pullers, with mechanically launched ropes tethering them to the Tatsu, took up positions at the starboard quarter, forward center bollard, and center stern of the ship.

Once the bay deck hatches opened, the bamboo nets in front of the six tug panels retracted into the bays. Entire teams of engineers manipulated sets of shiplifts, the mechanical arms that would carry workships, dayships, and tugs nearly fifty meters down to the surface of the water. The tug shiplifts conveyed their fully crewed vessels outward, twenty meters away from the sides of the Tatsu.

Then, shiplift operators slowly lowered the tugs to the water. Once each sideship was steadied, the shiplifts retracted, were raised back to the bay deck, and withdrew back into their respective hatches.

"Tugs are out," Kate announced.

It was systems like these, whole lists of protocols accomplished in order, that kept the city afloat and thriving. The greatest ship, with the most advanced technology, was no better than a log on the waves without the structure necessary to managing it.

"Workship launch!" Mik's voice rang out.

In order to prevent obstruction of the labor required of Tatsu's tugs, the dayships that desired to disembark from the cityship would have had to do so prior to mooring. Workship bays were far enough from the tugs that they could be released for commercial activities they had on Zoe Baja. Kate slapped her hand down on a button that withdrew the nets of all workships that had requested departure prior to docking. More than thirty of the smaller boats were conveyed out of their at-sea garages in the same way as the tugs. They sped off, out of the way of Tatsu's tugs, to quickly and easily dock at the commercial piers throughout Zoe Baja's northern port.

With the workships away and the tugboats in position, the slow, steady duty of berthing the Tatsu truly began.

"Devon! Imaging!" Kate ordered an unseen worker.

Two dozen cameras shot off the deck of the cityship and buzzed into the air. Each camera-mounted drone flew a circular pattern at a decreasing altitude that carried it to within a meter of the water's surface. Then it would return to an elevation equal to that of the deck of the Tatsu. All the while, laser imaging captured details ranging from obvious potential encounters such as a nearby ship with a course that could intersect the cityship or its tugs, to the minutia of protected sea life just below the water surface. Each bit of relayed information determined the movements and communications called for by the Captain Ridgelin and ExO Murphy.

Mik directed the movements of the cityship from the bridge, managing twelve rudders and six engines. Kate guided the tugboats to push and pull by following imaging provided by Devon's drones, satellite guidance, and direct visuals coming from cameras mounted at all of the widest hull points on the Tatsu.

Hours passed.

Mik watched as the shore workers began to line the dock, suited up in bright colors, gloves, and protective eyewear. Looking just beyond them, he could also see the governor's residence and he recognized Miriam Heirlinda's zip chopper coming in for a landing on the gubernatorial grounds zip pad.

"Send the drops," he commanded the heads of his mooring parties.

His crew checked that the knotted ends of the ropes, called monkey fists, on the ends of sixteen different ropes, were securely fastened. These bound balls of heavy-duty hemp and sisal rope were as wide around as one of Mik's legs after a lifting session. Each monkey's fist was affixed to a heavyweight auto-flyer launched from the cityship. The auto-flyers carried mooring ropes to the dock and dropped them to shore workers below. It took two to three workers to capture each as it fell. To avoid injury from the weight and size of the massive rope balls, the workers would stretch a nylon fabric between themselves to create a drop zone for the monkey fists. Each drop was guided by visual cues from the on-deck line workers who would relay the "Go" signal to the auto-flyer operators who, in turn, would direct the auto-flyer to release the monkey fist.

Outside of the drone cameras and auto-flyers, the whole process seemed a bit primitive and out of place for thirtieth century Earth. For thousands of years, sailors had been using these same methods and materials to dock large ships. What reconciled the ancient methods to Mik was that they still worked. It was laborious, but reliable.

Magnetic mooring clamps were used by a number of ships, but they had no give, no elasticity to manage the waves and tides. Ropes remained the tool of choice for berthing and mooring cityships and other vessels the size of the Tatsu. Not that any ship on the planet was quite as large as the Tatsu, but plenty still used ropes. All the technological advances humankind had come up with through the centuries could not compete with the sound system of ancient design Mik preferred for the Cityship Tatsu.

Large hydraulic drums released dozens of meters of rope out of sixteen starboard-side mooring locations. Four of the massive woven moorings extended from the stern, two from the breast at the aft of the ship, four total spring ropes aft and bow of center, two from the breast of the bow of the ship, and four more at the head, or bow of the Tatsu. The ropes, meant to stabilize the ship, criss-crossed each other in paths creating a giant, fibrous spiderweb connecting the cityship to shore.

The moorings were then attached to bollards on the docks, but the work was never truly done. Rather, the drum operators and mooring parties continuously released and tightened the ropes to accommodate the movement of the water. A rope that was pulled too taut or that had too much slack carried with it the danger of a snapback and a single punch of a monkey's fist could be fatal. So, even while the crew was anxious for a little time off ship, they were patient. They didn't step one foot away from their posts until they had the go ahead from Kate . . . and Kate didn't give that go ahead until she had it from Captain Ridgelin.

Mik saw a marked pod approaching the port. That could only mean the governor. He was as ready to be on shore as his crew and citizens.

"Good job, ExO," the big captain said with a childlike urgency to Murphy. "Dismiss the crew."

"Oui, Sir!" Kate chimed back and the tension of berthing and mooring the flagship of the Cityship Regatta dropped down along with the gangways.

"Fourteen hours," he said to his right hand. He'd already pulled on his formal cover to replace his working hat and he straightened his uniform.

"Oui, Sir!" she agreed, and she barked the time limit to the gangway monitors lined up all along the deck of the Tatsu.

The captain was the first down the gangway. In every other port, he was the last, if he exited at all, but his ExO took the post at Zoe Baja.

"Harry!" Mik called, his arm extended for a death-grip hand-shake before he even reached the longshore worker. "Good greetin' ye," he inflected jubilantly. Then, nodding at the woman behind Harry who had been a part of the onshore rope team, "Vera, good to see you!"

The woman waved meekly.

"You're dismissed, Vera. Good work, today," Harry said to her.

Potcake gave a deep play bow to Mik while Harry greeted the captain. His tail was whipping back and forth so quickly, Captain Ridgelin joked that the dog could motor one of the Tatsu's side-ships. Potcake's whole body waved with the power of his tail.

"What do you want, buddy?" Mik said to the pet.

Harry's furry friend could barely contain his excitement as the captain patted his head. He bounced on his front paws repeatedly in playful fashion, excited for some surprise gift that always came from his favorite visiting ship. He barked a high, airy, joyful woof.

"Here you go, Potcake!" Mik said, tossing a ball into the air.

The dog tried to capture it, but it bounced high, and then lightly flitted from side to side. The mechanized toy would keep him busy and happy for hours.

"Not much time, today, Harry. We'll get lunch next visit. On my word!" Mik promised shaking Harry's hand a second time.

"I'll be back at the southern port in a couple of days, Cap'n."

"I thought it was strange to have you up north, here."

"Just a short whistler commute. You get on, though. She's waiting for you," Harry said, patting Mik's shoulder heartily.

"And who would that be?" asked Mik with a mischievous wink as he gave a two-fingered salute to the longshore lead and walked quickly away.

Spirits were high.

The Tatsu was at its northern home.

CHAPTER 7
YEAR 2552

Former Baja Province
Former Northern Territory of New Hispaniola Land Nation
Former Global Union

It was dark shortly after Linda watched the last evacuees take off.

She wasn't sure how shortly. In fact, she wasn't sure what the time was at all, and she found that to be a bit disturbing. Life had always run according to a GU-dictated schedule and not having an awareness of the passage of time was surreal and unsettling. That feeling led to the first panic she would experience. It wouldn't be the last.

Her throat closed up.

Her heart quickened.

Her breaths grew short.

Her mind raced, spiraling into negativity.

Her vision went blurry.

She crouched down to keep from fainting.

Following several minutes of forced, deep breathing, the feeling passed.

After waiting long enough for fear to diminish and accepting that she was truly alone, while dusk was transitioning to that rich, timeless darkness, Linda made her way out of the building she had ducked into during evacuations and toward the eastern shore, not more than a kilometer or two from the zip chopper port where the last of the other injured survivors had flown out. A number of temporary tents that emergency personnel had set up during the rescue and recovery efforts were at the docks and several had been left behind. She wondered if they would ever return to gather them or if it was more economical for the GU to simply abandon them . . . to abandon her.

Panic attack number two. She worked to keep her heart and mind at bay, but her breaths were short, and she felt a buzzing sensation in her veins. She balanced herself against a bollard. *'You haven't been abandoned; you chose this,'* she told herself. Eventually, once more, the feeling passed.

Linda wished she'd thought to look for some kind of provisions before dark, although she had been well fed in the clinic, so she wasn't in terrible shape. She'd already eaten the nutrient bar. They gave each patient one of the bars in addition to a small hydration pouch before they lined up for the evacuation choppers. Her stomach growled urgently as her thoughts focused on the bar and water. Panic.

She sat down and sipped on her water pouch. They passed – both the grumbling stomach and the panic. She stopped sipping, realizing she should save some of the pouch for when she really needed it, rather than when her anxiety just made her think she needed it.

The moon was full, and—across the turbulent waters—she could see the flickering lights of the largest cities of New Hispaniola, but those things together didn't nearly provide enough light to be of any use. She zipped open the one side of the tent she'd found and claimed for her first night as an independent woman. She tied back the large flap that faced the water, so she at least had some light in the distance.

Panic assuaged.

It was warm and the breeze was tropical, so Linda would be fine without blankets, at least for now. Her frame was quite small, so she'd been fitted with an older student's plain uniform while she was still in the clinic. The light cotton pants garment was comfortable, if not stylish. Lukas had usually preferred her to dress in more fitted clothing with sheer panels to show off her figure. Honestly, the simplicity was refreshing in its own way. Her body relaxed.

The sudden relaxation caused Linda to flash for a moment on her youth, and also with the same thought, on the young Lukas she remembered from the time she was just a girl. She remembered his smile and his eyes and his confidence. She remembered how he had wanted to protect her and how, somehow, it had all gone wrong. He'd broken her when life had broken him. Linda couldn't remember the first blow that had attacked his human fragility, but for all that was broken—and all that he consequently broke—he paid. He paid with his life. She didn't cry or grieve his being gone. That would have felt insincere at best. He didn't deserve her tears or mourning. Those tears should have been reserved for more deserving victims of the unrelenting tragedies in the world.

Yet, it didn't feel right to be glad for his death, as though she was a victor over an enemy. Instead, in that moment, she decided to set aside all of the hate, bitterness, and regret that came from her life before the quake – that came from her years with the innocent boy who grew into a frightening man. Life hadn't been good to him, so he wasn't good to those in his life, in return. His had been a sad journey. Linda didn't know what the future would hold but she wouldn't invite her past into it to walk beside her. An at-least-temporary peace replaced her panic and Linda realized that she'd been living in the latter for more than the last day. The tension had been in her heart for her entire adult existence.

As the air lightly kissed her face, she smiled. The pungent smells of the medical clinic were a distant, if unforgettable, memory and only the salty air, cleaner than she'd ever known, was reaching her now. She lay across the opening of her little shelter, facing the waters that separated her from the rest of society – from the rest of time. She waited for sleep to come. It didn't. At least not right away.

It was the quietest night Linda had ever experienced in her entire life. The sounds she'd heard for as long as she could remember were suddenly absent: the buzzing of pod cables, administration announcements ringing through the air, workstation shift and release chimes, the high-pitched sounds of the zip choppers overhead, the popping of province lights that came on at dusk and went off at dawn, the compressing metal of ships coming into port. It was all just gone, and—with it—the white noise hum of the wind- and solar-charged batteries that kept it all going. It was all replaced by a silence that made every natural sound stand out deafeningly. As much as the human sounds of Baja had grown quiet, her home was also louder than Linda had ever realized.

She had no idea that the noises of the natural world could make such a racket. The waves crashing against the shore were thunderous. The sea was still stirring from the continuing tremors and aftershocks. Between the crashes were the trickling sounds of the water running off of the jagged rocks of the shoreline that had just been splashed by the tides. The seals on the beaches barked all night long, and their voices carried and echoed as though they were in a cave. There was a chirping sound. Linda wasn't sure whether it was crickets or frogs or birds, but it was an eerie constant. The wind pushed through trees and grasses . . . but also rippled across the rubble of places in which she'd once done life. The breezes caused occasional tumbles of the small stones and pebbles that remained of tall buildings. There was a whistling of the air through the now-empty shells of the very full world in which she'd existed. The sounds catalyzed an erosion of her previous life.

Eventually, the discord of her new world must have formed its own lullaby because, without her remembering how or when, sleep came.

A scratching sound at the back of Linda's tent startled her awake and her eyes snapped open. They were met by a blinding sunrise that reflected brightly on the waters and made the land on the other side of the Sea of California invisible for the moment. The abrasive sound continued followed by shuffling along the side of her tent. Whoever was here was moving around the temporary structure toward the opened front flap. There was nowhere Linda could hide. She sat up, as quietly as she could, so that at least she was ready to run if she had to. She looked around for something, anything, to defend herself if the need arose. A piece of broken concrete, the size of a palm scanner, was all she could find. She picked up the stone and waited. The shuffling grew closer, sweeping along the side of the tent, but nobody was speaking.

Then, around the corner, into the open flap, a small chicken poked its head and let out a single cluck. Linda dropped the stone and laughed nervously at first, but her laughter continued until it became almost hysterical. The response was over the top, but she couldn't help her reaction as emotions of relief, humor, and possibly even joy overtook her. She realized, in that moment, a quieting of the loneliness that had dwelled inside of her for far longer than just the night after the Global Union had departed.

Her morning visitor was a plain chicken, the kind that was pictured on advertisements for domestic animal selections right alongside friendly looking goats.

"Well, aren't you sneaky!" she said to the fowl. "If you'd had a brother, you could have just had him wake me instead of tiptoeing around to where I slept. I don't suppose you do have a brother?"

She paused.

"Yeah. I know," Linda sighed. "We're alone. They must have missed you."

The chicken was quiet. Linda looked at it in silence. She felt ridiculous making conversation with the feathered thing. She looked around, into the empty, dead spaces in front of her. She couldn't remember a time in her entire life when she'd been truly alone. There was nobody around to speak with, but also, she realized, nobody around to judge her. Her conversations with the chickens she and Lukas had always kept were either whispered secretly to the birds as she cared for them, or just in her head. Without such precautions, she would have felt crazy. But with this new creature, there was nothing to keep her from just voicing out loud the things that, in the past, she'd only harbored on her tongue.

She sighed as she looked at the thing. Its feathers were mostly white, nothing at all like Henrietta's. And it was a bit scraggly, too. It's head and neck looked like they'd been partially plucked, and its eyes bugged out in the midst of the pink pimply skin of the thing. The creature looked at her expectantly. This chicken would be her conversation partner because sometimes a person just needed to say something out loud in order to believe it . . . and Linda expected she had a lot in front of her that would be hard to believe.

The chicken walked circles around Linda and paused each time her face was in sight. It tilted its head toward her and clucked. Then it would reverse, cross behind her, and do the same thing again.

"Is this begging?" Linda laughed. "I've never had a chicken beg before. Is that what you're doing here?"

Click-chip-cluck!

"I don't have anything for you!" she said. "Come to think of it, I don't have anything for me, either," she said as the hen continued back and forth in its circles around Linda. "I don't suppose you do. Got a nest around here by chance?"

The chicken cocked its head to one side, scurried away from her and moved to the opening of the tent. Then, it plopped down on its folded legs and stared at Linda.

"Sorry. I didn't mean any offense. But maybe you could work on that? I'm thinking you're at least a few months old, yes?"

No answer came of course.

"Well, I guess now is as good a time as any to get moving around and figure out . . . um, everything," she said to the feathered creature. She was glad to have decided to talk to the animal, even though it couldn't speak back. "You're welcome to join me," she added with no expectation that it actually would.

Linda stood and stretched overwhelmed by the idea of where to begin. She stepped out of the tent and squinted against the morning sun, looking toward the Northern Territory of New Hispaniola Land Nation to her east. Zip choppers filled the sky, buzzing in and out of the shoreline ports to their assigned bearings. Some of the choppers appeared to be surveilling the shoreline. Security personnel, Linda assumed, ensuring that no citizen was hurt or lost. She had never thought about the weaponry on the surveillance zip choppers but wondered about it now. What would they think of her, a citizen who opted out of the life of provision they made possible? Would she be somebody they tried to help, or a person to be apprehended?

Linda turned away from the shore to face westward on the Baja Province. "Holy hell," she breathed as, for the first time ever, she really saw with her own eyes just what had happened to the only home she'd ever known.

The bird clucked and moved around the tent to stand at Linda's feet.

The plucky thing stood behind her legs as if they provided some needed protection. It peeked around her ankles trying to understand the human's reaction. Linda ignored the chicken for some time, unable to focus on anything but the debris field in front of her. Then, it began to peck at her hard-soled slippers, and she snapped out of her shocked daze.

"I agree," Linda said. "We need to find some food."

Linda had no idea what she'd crossed in the darkness the night before. Baja had been gentrified and modern, even by GU standards. Clusters of skyscrapers were gathered all across the province, each surrounded by building groups: the work buildings, circled by the community centers such as those for entertainment, medical facilities, and shopping courts. Those were surrounded further by several sets of neighborhood quarters, each with its own courtyard. The groupings of buildings were connected by intricate pod systems that made for convenient travel for each citizen within his or her own cluster. Zip chopper routes had then connected the different clusters to one another. Additional connections featured walkable routes with occasional man-made recreation areas or parks breaking up the paths connecting the groupings.

Each community cluster took pride in its unique identity and architecture. There were celebrations during which the buildings would be illuminated and contests between the different neighborhoods would determine whose fiberoptic and twinkle drone displays were most reflective of the holiday at hand. Linda had always found it intriguing to look across the skyline and see how each grouping had its own signature of sorts on the shapes, colors, and designs even while maintaining the same basic structure and functionality. It was all beautiful in its own way, if one could look past the noise of it.

As Linda gazed across that skyline now, there was definitely no noise. There were very few clusters left at all. She thought, looking northwest, she saw some buildings still standing, but in contrast to the flattened world around her, they may not have been that tall at all. And she wasn't sure just how far they were, either. The usual landmarks were all washed away or had tumbled down. It was difficult for her to find bearings other than her knowledge that she was on the southeastern shore.

The rest of her surroundings had crumbled from the quakes and aftershocks as easily as if they had been a child's sandcastles washed away by the tide. Large riverbeds of sorts cut crisscross designs throughout the debris mapping out the flooding and mudslides that had followed the quakes, creating as much damage if not more than what had resulted from the initial tremors. The channels cut by the rushes and gushes had since dried up and were now filled with the rainbow confetti of fallen cities; brick, stone, glass, plastic, fabric, metal, and synthetics of all colors that had gone through mother nature's shredder and joined the chaotic current of an entire life being washed away.

Some hundred meters from where she'd camped on the docks, a large ridge of debris was piled up as high as a wall, as if ground clearing equipment had pushed it all backward in a line from the shore. It took Linda a moment to realize that this must have been how far the water had surged into Baja before receding. It dumped all that it had gathered in a pile before pulling back into the ocean.

Linda looked down at her feet; the medical slippers weren't going to last long in these conditions. The sun was already warm. Linda looked up and realized her clothing might not be ideal, either. Then, her stomach growled.

"I guess our first jobs have just been decided for us," she said to the chicken. "Shelter we have for now. Today's mission is clothing and food!"

Linda started walking but stopped a few steps from the tent and turned back. She pulled down the canvas flap and the three ties that she'd used to pull it back. She rolled up the material and wrapped the ties around it on both ends and in the center. She then draped the rolled canvas over her shoulders like a yoke.

"Just in case we don't make it back here tonight, I could sleep on it," she said to the hen. "Now we can go," she nodded, but the chicken didn't move. Linda looked back when she was a few strides ahead. "Well, are you coming?"

The chicken took a single step forward, cautiously. Linda waited, but the stubborn creature didn't move until Linda took another step . . . followed by another from the chicken. Another step from Linda. Another from the bird. In time, Linda just accepted that the scraggly feathered thing had joined her for the journey, always a few steps behind, occasionally pecking at her heels in hopes for her to provide some grain she didn't have. Linda spoke to the hen as though it were an annoyance, but she was relieved for the company, even if that company would only add to her own burden for providing food. In time, if she helped it, it would surely help provide food for her in return.

The two made their way across the flattened province toward the needs she was sure would be found, if not easily, in the debris piles ahead. She had a large amount of ground to cover, and she had to start somewhere. Why not here, near the shore, with nothing but some cotton clothing, hard-soled medical clinic slippers, half a water pouch, and a chicken?

They covered ground far more slowly than she expected. She stepped carefully on the uneven earth and sometimes had to detour in winding paths rather than taking the most direct routes, in order to avoid some fallen dangerous debris, a deep crevasse, or a still churning pool of the washout. Her slippers provided little protection and she could feel the larger and sharper stones straight through the soles into the arches of her feet.

By late morning, the sun's rays were baking down upon her. Linda paused and tossed the canvas to the ground. She took off her top to bare her skin in nothing but the cotton athletic bra that had been issued at the medical clinic. She tied the shirt around her waist.

Olive clucked at Linda . . . she had started calling the hen Olive. Linda figured the name could just as well be for a hen as a human and, as this creature was her only friend in the new world, she thought it was proper to honor the medical tech who had saved her to be able to live in it. Linda knew that, on average, a chicken could learn as many as thirty human words. If she said the name often enough, that could be one of this chicken's words.

"I know I could burn, Olive," Linda said to hen. "But right now, I'd rather burn than sweat and cook," she added as if the bird's initial cluck was its means of scolding her for removing her shirt.

Olive tilted her head and it transitioned from clucking to murmuring. It must have liked Linda speaking to it.

"We should have some water, Olive, don't you think? It's probably been a few hours since the last time."

Linda sat on what looked like an old stove unit flipped on its side and pulled her water pouch out. She squeezed a little bit into her hand and held it out to the chicken, but the bird didn't take it.

"Well, we can't very well waste it," Linda said.

She cupped the water into her own mouth and looked at her surroundings. The closest thing she found to a receptacle was the case of an old, broken, education pad. She snapped off a piece of the case, turned it at an angle to make somewhat of a well in it, and wedged it into the ground so that it would sit upright. She squeezed a bit more of her water pouch into the makeshift miniature water bowl. Only after Linda stood up and stepped back a couple of meters did Olive start pecking at the water. Unfortunately, it made a mess. The hen drank very little and ultimately knocked over the tiny bit that was left. The chicken looked at Linda presuming she'd refill the little container.

"Sorry. That's all I have for you right now. We'll be lucky to get one more drink break today."

Linda picked up the broken case, licked out the droplets that remained and put it into her cargo pocket along with the now nearly empty water pouch.

"Does the neighborhood cluster look any closer to you?" she asked the chicken who was, obviously, quiet. "Yeah. Me neither," Linda said looking in the distance to the still standing buildings.

Linda sighed as she picked up her yoke once more. It felt heavier after having had a break from it. "Shit!" she said, tossing it back down onto the ground.

Cluck.

"Oh, shut up. You try to carry it!" she snapped in frustration.

Linda kicked at the heavy material on the ground. She touched her tender shoulders. She hadn't noticed that they were raw when she still wore a shirt, but her skin was pink and sore to the touch. She wasn't sure she could allow the canvas in direct contact with her sweaty skin. Lifting the material had also taken all of her leg and back strength. Clearly, fatigue had set in. The digital lifters in the medical centers and the physical therapy that followed for the couple of weeks before the evacuation choppers had kept her muscles from atrophying. Still, her strength wasn't where she wanted it to be. Linda took a breath to steel her stubbornness. It would be that mental toughness and not her physical ability which would make her task possible.

She bent down to hoist the canvas up once more when she felt a heavy blow to her back, and she fell onto her face on the ground.

CHAPTER 8
YEAR 2908

Jomo Heirlinda Residence
Zoe Baja
Zoelands Concord

"I couldn't eat another bite," Miriam said clearing the table.

"Leave it," Jomo said while lovingly tapping his daughter's hand to put the bowls back down. "The mess isn't going anywhere. Come repose. Catch up."

"Sir, I have to agree," Mik said while placing salad plates back onto the table. "A fine stew."

"Not every day I get to host the head of the entire Cityship Regatta," Miriam's father replied.

"It'll take the whole regatta to tug me out of here after that second helping," Mik said patting his stomach and picking up his wine.

Nina laughed while making her way to the enclosed porch where all Heirlinda evenings ended. "So, this gourmet cooking is on account of the Tatsu captain, and not the governor, pops?" She shook her head at Miriam's dad, the unofficial father figure to their whole group of lifelong friends.

"My girl knows I host her with the same attention!" he defended himself. "If only she would come around more often," he winked. "I have to sneak in a stop to coincide with her diplomatic missions to get a moment's notice," he said while slapping the back of Mik's arm chummily and scooting past him to his own favorite chair on the porch. He sat into the cushioned seat that was so worn to his shape it was unlikely anybody else could have comfortably fit into it if they had wanted to do so.

Mr. Heirlinda grunted heavily as he plopped into the chair and flopped his arms down onto the cushy, threadbare sides of the seat. His glass of cactus wine splashed and dripped onto the back of his hand. He casually wiped away the drops of alcohol without a thought. He did nothing small. The meals he cooked, the way he moved, the way he talked, and the way he loved were all larger than life. His skin was darker than his daughter's and his eyes were large and of such a deep shade of brown that they appeared nearly black. Jomo's big round face had deep-set lines in his cheeks and around his eyes.

Miriam glanced warmly at her dad. She didn't wrinkle in the way her father had. She and Nina once joked about their different wrinkle patterns and how the lines of age told the story of a person's life. Jomo was a man of jubilance and joy. He always found the silver linings in the darkest and stormiest of clouds. His eyes in old age smiled even when his mouth did not. And, when his face was still, one could make out his dimple. Miriam inherited the dimple but her lines, while far finer than pop's, were forming across her forehead and between her eyes. The corners of her mouth were turned slightly downward in a permanent pout when her face was at rest. The story in her face was one of depressive episodes and concerns both warranted and unnecessary. She was beginning to wrinkle in much the same manner as her mother had before the woman passed.

Perhaps the heavyheartedness came with the weight of being a woman with the name Heirlinda, the name that her parents chose to take when they coupled and had a child. Most families no longer adopted singular names, but—even in the thirtieth century, when the world should have been past such things—many prominent community members continued the formal practice. Miriam's mother Susan carried the name from her father as a matter of tradition. Of course, Jomo took Susan's name – it could go no other way when one partnered with an Heirlinda. When Miriam came of age, she knew there would be just as much scrutiny over choosing a new name as there was for keeping Heirlinda. She decided to go with the devil she knew and accept the matrilineal surname though she secretly questioned whether she could ever live up to it.

Miriam casually sat in front of Nina, who was settled on a floral-cushioned settee, and she leaned against her friend's legs. Nina had thick, silken, dark hair and glowing tawny skin. Her most prominent feature was an intricate tatua that began on her lower lip and continued to the bottom of her chin. She had the markings, called ta moko, since before she moved to Zoe Baja from the Southeast Continental Indigenous Nation. When Nina accepted Inoke as a partner, when the two of them decided to raise his sister Sefina as their own child, and when she took the job as Zoe Baja's head poulterer were all occasions that led her to add to the artwork.

Nina began to rub Miriam's shoulders without thought even while Inoke took a seat beside his partner. It was a natural act, an interaction the women had clearly shared many times before. In this one place, on a tired, sun-faded porch in central Baja, Miriam didn't have to be the governor. Neither did the rest of them have to be any more than family and friends. While they would all be required to pick up the weight of their responsibilities on the front stoop as they left, in these walls they could relax.

"If you're here, who is in charge on the ship tonight, Mik?" Jomo asked the captain as the big sailor sat on the step that led to the sunken porch.

Kate stood behind him, not because there wasn't a seat remaining but because it was typically her preference to stay standing and alert.

"We take shifts," Kate answered for her boss. "I've got my aft-bridge second-in-command on lead right now. He's good. Deserves my job, but I'm not giving it up until I'm wearing Mik's hat," she said with a gentle sisterly tap against the captain with her foot before she leaned against the door frame.

"Hold up, Murphy. You'd drown in my hat. Don't forget I still approve your credits," Mik joked. "I hear there are some openings on a few GU scrubbers if you play your leverage right."

"You know I'm not going anywhere," Kate almost smiled.

Jomo observed the interactions between the captain and his executive officer looking for some kind of insights. "What about you, Mik?" Jomo asked. "Would you ever leave the ship?"

"No, Sir. I belong out there," he said assuredly. "It beckons to me. We call it fernweh."

"It's like being homesick for someplace you've never been," Kate added.

"Exactly," Mik said. "And me? I keep looking for that place. For home."

"What would make it home?" Nina asked

Mik stared out the porch screens to the many garden boxes Jomo had assembled. Each one was filled with its own plants and herbs. Some contained seedlings that were only growing here temporarily. Others contained plants mature enough for harvesting.

"It's like your plants, Jomo," he said. "You have a bit of everything. You have flowers for beauty, vegetables for nourishment, herbs for flavor, and trees that will take root in the soil. This is all of life to you. You can take in this view from outside your porch and know you have all you need. Me? I'm still filling my boxes. The things I need are sea, and sky, and land. Not one of them but all of them. Those are the necessities I crave in my garden boxes. The water that is never still? It reminds me to keep moving forward. The sky? It shows me how big the world is and how little of it I actually know. Land? That connects me to history. It tells me that I'm human."

Inoke narrowed his eyes toward the captain, his mind lost in thought. Then he chanced a sideways glance to Miriam. "And nothing has ever made you want to stay in one place?" he asked wryly.

"Nothing has ever been all of those things at once for me. So, I lead the Cityship Tatsu because it takes me to all of those things and, at least in small doses, I get each of them. I fill all of my garden boxes."

The room was quiet. Mik took a sip of his wine and looked down at the ground, suddenly embarrassed by his vulnerable authenticity.

Finally, "LAME!" Kate said, cutting the tension. "Hey, Jomo, you got any more of this wine?"

"Second cabinet over the sink," he said. "I'll show you," he added while hefting his body out of the seat.

"I could use a refill, too," Nina said as she got up and gently shifted Miriam off of her legs and back against the settee.

"Give me a hand with these dishes, Inoke," Jomo called from the kitchen and Inoke jumped up and left, as well.

Laughing, "Subtle, aren't they?" Miriam said to Mik who had shifted to let everyone else pass by.

"Shite," he shook his head in jest, "Something I said?"

Miriam just rolled her eyes toward the ceiling. She stood up, walked to the screens, and looked out across her land. Mik stood and moved beside her.

After a deep sigh, "I could fail, you know," she said. "I could try to convince the Pacific Islands Land Nation that we need the food that they grow. I could try to convince the Antarctic Land Nation that we need their mined resources. For both nations, I only have an idea to offer them in return. We have a power cell."

"A revolutionary power cell is what you promised me," Mik added. "I for one can't wait to hear more about it."

"I think you're biased," she playfully shoved him. "The others are going to recognize that I'm desperate. Zoe Baja is desperate. My people are starving, Mik. We absolutely must have what these nations can provide. There is no plan B for me. They may have plan B through Z for power efficiency! Is Jacob's hydrocell enough? Or is all of this," she pursed her lips. It was difficult to say the words. "Will all of this be gone?" she flippantly directed her hand toward the garden boxes outside.

Mik put an arm around Miriam, and she leaned into him. He was a pocket she fit into perfectly. He didn't have the words to offer the governor to reassure her, but he could hold her up. She inhaled and it was like he was her breath and she could breathe him back out into her work.

"If it's not enough—the research and the knowledge and getting this hydrocell produced—then we'll have to become Global Union, if they'll even have us. I would have to give up the technology and the hydrocell to them in exchange for our very survival," Miriam exhaled, and then sunk deeper against and into the captain.

"See?" Mik said, as he wrapped his other arm around Miriam. "You do have a plan B after all!"

Miriam wasn't feeling the joke. She continued in a downward spiral of negatives. "Survival has never been enough for the Zoeans though," she said as much to herself as to Mik. "Our nature is an independent one. Will my people ever forgive me if I save their lives at the same time that I nullify their way of life?"

"It won't come to that," he reassured her at last. "It's more than an exchange you're working toward. It's about unity. That makes it a movement. A human unification movement. And joining a movement is far more valuable than joining a trade partnership." He squeezed her a bit closer before releasing her and looking into her eyes as he finished, "I believe in this movement."

Miriam looked up at the captain. His reassurance was that of just one person, but she couldn't imagine one that she desired more fully. The sun was nearly set, and his green eyes twinkled in the amber light.

A crash echoed from the other room.

"Oh no! I'm so sorry, Jomo," Nina called.

Miriam broke off her stare, blinked at the view outside, and said, "We'd better go see if they need a hand. We have an early start tomorrow."

The two grabbed their wine glasses and stepped back into the main house.

CHAPTER 9
YEAR 2552

Former Baja Province
Former Northern Territory of New Hispaniola Land Nation
Former Global Union

Linda groggily sat up.

Her back ached in a way that radiated all the way to her head and caused a displaced headache. It was nearly dusk. She looked around and she was right where she had been before she was struck. The canvas still laid on the ground, rolled up and ready to be carried. As she stood, she took a deep breath and her body ached as a result of the inhalation. Maybe it was a broken rib, but she'd certainly had plenty of those over the years. Immediately, she felt ticked at the fact that a deep breath was painful, just as she had learned to indulge in the sensation.

What happened?

Somewhere nearby, she heard thudding footsteps and the rustling of debris across the ground accompanied by the frantic chirping and growling of a chicken. Her chicken. Linda scanned her surroundings and found a heavy stone. She picked it up and cautiously made her way to the sound.

"Get over here!" came the scratchy voice of a woman. "Now!"

Olive screeched a deafening Bawk-Bagaw in an almost human high pitch.

Linda tiptoed carefully behind a tree and peered around its trunk to the noise, the stone in her hand heavy with more than its physical weight.

"Stupid bird!" the woman screeched desperately.

Linda pulled her arm back as though winding up for a pitch, but she paused as she got a better look at the person she had encountered. She was young, couldn't have been more than twenty. She had scraggly mouse brown hair that was shaven on one side, but it had grown out, leaving her to look like a child who had cut her own hair. The girl appeared as though she hadn't eaten in ages. She was emaciated. Her yellow, tissue-thin skin hung loosely over bones covered by barely conceivable muscle tone. One arm was inhumanly larger than the other and it took Linda a moment to realize it was a mechanized prosthetic. This woman had at least some trans-humanist enhancements.

Linda couldn't reckon with hurting the first human she found in her broken world. She lowered her arm and settled back on her heels, snapping a piece of plastic under her left foot as she did so.

Immediately, the woman stopped running and turned toward Linda. She bounded toward her in the span of a breath while Olive shuffled away in the other direction. Both women found themselves eye to eye, only an arm's length of space between them. Linda noticed that the woman had ink markings indicating her status as an entry-level power industry worker. This could have been her at one time.

"I don't care if you saw it first. I need that chicken," the woman sneered.

"I don't want to eat it," Linda said.

The woman looked back and realized the hen was no longer in her sights. "You lost it!" she screamed to Linda. "You did that on purpose! You distracted me!"

Linda had absorbed close yelling before. She believed she could read when a person was ready to hit versus when one needed to express anger or frustration. She stood her ground.

"I'm sorry. It will probably be back," Linda said.

The woman turned to her agitatedly and the two stood in silence for a moment.

"I have water," Linda said without flinching. "Not much, but you're welcome to it. I'll share."

The woman looked down at Linda's hand that held the stone, then back up at her face. Linda dropped the rock while never breaking her gaze.

"Give it to me!" the woman snapped.

Linda reached into her pocket and held out the small pouch. The woman snatched it from her hand and put it to her mouth, sucking it dry like a ravaged animal.

The woman narrowed her eyes at Linda. "Give me the rest," she said.

"That's all there was. I don't have any more," she said honestly while the woman stepped even closer to Linda, breathing heavily.

"LIAR!" she said as she dropped the pouch and closed the remaining distance between them.

The woman grabbed Linda by the throat with her prosthetic arm. She squeezed with mechanical fingers and Linda could not even gurgle, much less call out. Even if she had been able to do the latter, it would have done no good. There was nobody left to hear her. She scratched and pulled at the woman's fake fingers ineffectually.

In a feverish fury, the woman pushed Linda against the trunk of the tree, squeezing her fingers ever tighter. Linda felt certain her throat would break in the death pinch of the prosthetic fingers. She writhed beneath the grasp of the stranger. Her eyes started to feel puffy, and they rolled back into her head. Her skull felt heavy and dizzy.

Click-cluck!

Olive ran back into the clearing behind the woman. The maniac flashed her eyes toward the animal, and then released her grip on Linda, dropping her to the ground. Linda could only concentrate on breathing, clearing the blur from her vision, and making sure she was still whole. The rock was next to her on the ground. She picked it up.

Linda caught her breath much more slowly than she had hoped. Lifting the rock took every ounce of her strength and she threw it into the circle in front of her. It hit the woman in her natural shoulder and knocked her onto her backside. Olive ran over to Linda and hid behind her legs. It was becoming the chicken's go-to move for self-preservation.

Linda ran into the circle, picked up the stone once more, and stood over the woman who had rolled onto her back and gazed up at her.

"I don't want to hurt you," Linda said, even while she held up the large stone. "If I help you up, I need to know that you will not hurt me." Olive chattered. "Us. I need to know that you won't hurt us," Linda added.

The woman said nothing.

"I know you're hungry and scared. We can work together," Linda added.

Still nothing.

"Do you promise not to hurt us so that we can help one another?" Linda asked.

"You're Global Union? You have food?"

"I'm not and I don't, but I'm sure food is somewhere. We just have to find it," she said.

"Only the GU has food," said the woman frantically. "You can't help!"

"I can," Linda said and—for the first time since she stayed behind during evacuations—she believed it. "Let me help," she said offering her hand to the woman.

The woman stared up at Linda for a moment before taking her hand and getting to her feet. Linda began to back away. She prepared to make her case, a case to this stranger about how they could manage better as a team.

"Listen," Linda started. "I have a few things that I can share and I'm making my way toward— "

"AAAAHHH!" the woman screamed while lunging at Linda.

Linda dodged her and fell back into a large puddle of saturated mud and compost.

Olive was off again, running zigzags around the area while its human tried fruitlessly to talk to the real animal there: the woman.

"I understand how you feel!" Linda shouted as the woman stumbled after her repeatedly. "We really can do this, though," Linda said breathlessly, always one step out of reach of the madwoman and feeling grateful that the stranger's enhancement was an arm and not the woman's legs.

"You don't know what you're talking about! They forgot me! They need to know I'm here. I need to stay strong until they come back for me," she said clawing her way after Linda.

"I can help you do that," Linda reassured as she ran through the area and splashed into a large puddle of something that might have passed for water if it weren't colored with countless chemicals.

The woman stumbled behind Linda and began to crawl her way toward her prey. Then, her mechanized arm landed heavily in the puddle and she just stopped. A buzzing sound filled the air. Linda turned back and saw the woman—the girl—as she vibrated and trembled in the liquid, her mechanical arm smoked and sparked. Her eyes bugged out and veins appeared bulging through the skin on her forehead, neck, and across her upper chest. Linda could only watch, helpless to stop the electrocution.

Finally, after one last full-body twitch and more time than Linda expected it would take, the girl stopped moving. She was dead. Linda dropped next to the saturated ground and worked to catch her breath. Her body was filthy, but it was nothing compared to her mind and spirit, both exhausted by death and its constant close proximity to her.

Olive gently bobbed its way over to Linda and pecked at her hands. Linda stood up and wiped away what she could of the mud on her body before she defeatedly trudged back to the place where the canvas laid rolled up on the ground.

The tents were far behind them. The sky was getting darker and darkness in the abandoned province was a blacker night than she could ever traverse. She wasn't going to make it back to the shore tonight or she'd find herself in this same position tomorrow, starting from zero on her way to the only pieces of civilization that appeared intact.

Linda swallowed her panic, pushing it down firmly before it could surface. She unrolled the canvas on the ground, lay upon it, and closed her eyes. Olive sat down next to her and folded its feet beneath its body. Linda and the hen saved one another. They were family after today.

CHAPTER 10
YEAR 2908

Roberto Francisco Residence
Zoe Baja
Zoelands Concord

Roberto Francisco peered out of Miriam's office window.
The deputy governor cast his gaze over the gubernatorial grounds from the space to which he temporarily laid claim. Night had fallen and the sky was clear. The lights of New Hispaniola's Northern Territory glowed in the distance, an orangish hue formed a domelike effect over the city to the east. It made it impossible for the lights of his own home or the stars above it to shine their brightest . . . and he hated that fact with a passion.

"Lights down," he said aloud, and the office dimmed.

He squinted fixedly toward the shadows of the water in the distance, trying to no avail to make the luminescence of Zoe Baja come into focus. Out on the sea, a spiral of ripples rose from nowhere. His stomach rumbled in echo. He was hungry for more than food.

Frustrated, "Lights up," he commanded the room. It responded obediently. If only all of his desires could be answered so simply.

If he could not appreciate the world by looking out, he would look within. Miriam's office was filled with historical artifacts that had fallen into her hands as an Heirlinda, or possibly as governor, but

Roberto didn't believe she thoroughly appreciated the relics the way he did. He walked around the room pausing before each piece of a photographic narrative of Zoe Baja's History. The poster-sized photos circled the space and, had he wished to do so, he could have pressed buttons at each station to hear a narrator describe what was being depicted. He knew the story well enough on his own.

There were hopeless pictures of a land destroyed following the Great Nekros Quake, cluster after cluster had collapsed. They were left to decompose where they fell, along with whatever humans lay beneath the rubble. After that station were photographs of the Baja Province evacuations. The deputy governor fumed with anger as he viewed the temporary zip port lined with dozens of choppers and hundreds of people. This was the very evidence of the Global Union abandoning Baja for the first but not last time. He could look no longer, so he moved on to the next heirloom.

Francisco stopped in front of a glass case containing a mounted white feather. The bit of plumage was that of a chicken for which Linda herself had once cared. He keyed in a lock code and opened the case. For a moment, he simply stared at it with no re-flective barrier as an obstruction between them. Like a child reach-ing toward a cookie, Roberto touched the very tips of the feather. The sensation brought on a high for him, the drug of Zoe pride rushed through his veins.

He relished being in the capitol building, and especially in this room, the center of all the Zoelands. He stood a bit taller when in the governor's office, despite his having one leg slightly shorter than the other. The leg was one of several physical manifestations that remained following the illness that damaged him and took his sister. While there were surgeries and cloning treatments available to at least aesthetically change the remnants of the disease, he had turned each such treatment down. He declared that his scars were a source of motivation for him.

The most prominent such scar was his mangled right hand. His fingers curled in upon themselves and his thumb was bent at an odd angle. The entire hand was wrinkled – the red skin wrapped around the twisted bones like a child's poorly done artwork. No matter his limp or his deformed fingers though, the real scars of his illness were not ones that could be seen.

A chirping sound broke his meditation and Roberto quickly closed the glass case. He picked up his digifile from the desk. He punched a few buttons. A voice rang out in the room.

"What? No visual today?" asked a woman's voice.

"Or any day," Roberto responded coolly.

"Can you speak?"

"I answered, didn't I?" he said.

"I read Dr. Bradley's reports, Francisco."

The deputy governor waited for more, but it didn't come. He finally prompted, "And?"

"And nothing," the woman said. "There's not enough information here. I've had some of New Hispaniola's top engineers review the written specifications and they are not able to fill in the missing pieces. What are the elements of the tri-stellar compound? What code is used for the programming on the computer chip? And so many other questions. I could send them to you, but the bottom line is that we just don't know enough."

"What about the other engineers? Your people in the Canadian or Antarctic Land Nations?" he sounded desperate.

Before he even finished, the woman was answering, "No. No." Roberto could picture her shaking her head as he heard her words and it infuriated him. A rage grew deep in his chest as she explained. "The two nations are close to one another diplomatically speaking. They always have been. Science before the state. Antarctica is involved in these talks where Heirlinda is headed. They won't touch it, so neither will the Canadians."

Francisco slammed his good hand on the desk with a thwack.

"We knew this might be the case, Roberto," the woman said. "And even if our engineers had conjectured the specs, that doesn't mean they would have been able to replicate it without Baja's resources."

"Couldn't the Pacific Islands facilitate the same processes."

She reminded him, "But we can't approach them before we know how they will respond to the talks."

Roberto shook his head as though the woman on the call could see him.

"Are you still there?" the woman asked

After a pause, "Yes. Of course," he said sharply.

"I don't think we have a choice. We need to bring in a," she paused. "A contractor," she said with whispered inflection.

Roberto stepped back to the window of the office and caught a glimpse of his own reflection looking back at him. His final scar was on full display. The deputy governor's right eye spun counterclockwise in its digitized socket. He tilted his head down and back up, then back and forth as he scrolled through reports that his brain waves read directly from his mechanical eye's signals. The false eye, which replaced his diseased one decades earlier, was a badge of honor to Francisco. A similar enhancement had been operated by one of Zoe Baja's very own historical heroes. Those heroes chose a way of life separate from—he believed better than—that offered by the Global Union. The deputy governor had every intention of upholding that way of life. It was his duty to Zoe Baja.

"What if the talks didn't happen?" he asked the woman as he picked up the digifile and walked away from the desk.

He began a stroll backward through Zoe Baja's history.

The voice sighed. "Buying time? I don't know. Maybe. But your governor departs tomorrow. The Tatsu is already there."

"I have one more card to play," he said as he passed the encased feather.

"And if it doesn't work?" she asked.

Roberto stopped once more in front of the evacuation photos. He saw broken people being loaded into choppers by Global Union administrators, all on the backdrop of an earthquake-destroyed land. He focused on a redheaded medical worker, mindlessly following orders, sending people away from all they had ever known. His loathing swelled within him. He stared more and more intensely at the GU citizens in the photo and thought about their full bellies and their full bodies and their full families and he was disgusted.

"Then we'll do what we have to do," he said. He pushed a button on his digifile and closed the call.

CHAPTER 11
YEAR 2552

Former Baja Province
Former Northern Territory of New Hispaniola Land Nation
Former Global Union

Linda rolled up the canvas she had slept on.

She chipped dried mud off of her body. To her right was the flipped over stove unit where she and Olive had taken a water break before all hell broke loose. She realized that, if there was a stove unit here, there may be other things that at one time had a use for her and somehow still may.

Linda began to dig around in the pile they stood on. It felt fruit-less. Everything was just garbage. A whole society had existed here. It made no sense to her that there wouldn't be anything here to support that society . . . or even just the one person and one chicken left behind from it.

Olive began pecking at her feet. She shoved the hen away. She felt helpless to care for the chicken; she couldn't even care for her-self. Panic returned. Frantically, Linda began to search with more fervor and frustration. The chicken stepped away, watching, but out of the line of fire. Linda continued to grab objects and toss them behind her, making her way deep into a pile of rubble that turned up nothing of use for her effort.

Then, the pile vibrated beneath her hand and Linda stood unsteadily. The ground was shaking, violently. It was strange to her to be in the middle of an earthquake with no administrator's announcement ringing through the air telling her to get to a shelter, to get to low ground, to get inland . . . she looked around and realized there was no shelter, but she was inland, she was low, and there was nothing left around her that could fall. Linda sat with her legs crisscrossed on the ground for stability. Olive ran over and plopped in her lap, its body shaking as strongly as the ground while its head was held stiff in shock and fear.

Linda closed her eyes, cradled the hen, and waited for the tremor to pass. It took much longer than she expected. She folded herself over the bird, protecting it instinctively even though there wasn't anything that looked like it could hurt them. She felt a sort of reverse deja vu while she and Olive sat there long after the world stopped shaking. Finally, feeling that the earthquake, or maybe aftershock, really was finished, Olive hopped back off of her keeper.

Linda opened her eyes and looked around. The tremor had changed the very pile they'd been sitting in. Linda spotted a piece of U-shaped pipe that looked like it had come from a sink similar to one in any typical residential quarters. She picked it up and realized that, in the bend of it, there was a bit of water. She tipped just a few drops of it at first into the broken plastic piece she pulled back out of her pocket. It looked like clean water. She dipped her pinkie into it and tasted the liquid. Satisfied that it was acceptable to drink, she set the container before Olive who was eager for a second serving in addition to being more careful in drinking it. Linda reached into her pocket for her water pouch before remembering that she no longer had it. She drank the rest of the water from the pipe, and then kept the pipe, too, tying it to one of the sleeves of her shirt.

The thought occurred to her in that moment that she and Olive were sitting on a pile that had clearly once been a home. The stove and the sink pipe were standard issue necessities. She didn't have time to be sad or reflective over this fact. Rather, Linda tried to get her bearings in the midst of the former building.

"If this was once a kitchen, however many floors up, then there had to be...."

Linda trailed off, walking the area more methodically this time with eyes open to greater expectation and even, she dared think, hope. She avoided going to the other side of the large tree near them because she knew what was on the other side. But there was plenty more to explore. Her eyes darted around searching for something.

"There!" she said, approaching a splintered wooden box and digging through the mud and dirt in which the planks lay.

She clawed through the debris and Olive came to her side, curious as to its human's actions or what may come of them. Finally, Linda pulled something out!

"I knew it! A garden box! Breakfast time, Olive. Well, and lunch and dinner, maybe, too."

It was an onion.

"I hope you're not picky."

Linda kept digging. Three onions, and a tiny misshapen carrot that resembled what she could only compare to a crooked old man's thumb. She cleaned the produce with the shirt sleeve that wasn't holding the pipe. Then, they ate their root feast, one of the onions and a piece of the carrot. She set aside the other two onions.

"We can't have it all at once," she said.

Linda chewed the two foods together to tame the strong flavor of the onion. It didn't really help. She spit some out onto the ground, chomped into small bits, so that Olive could eat.

"You'll get used to it," Linda said as she also ate the raw onion which, for what it was worth, quieted growling stomach. "Not sure how this is going to settle tonight," she said to the hen while patting her stomach, "But you can't complain since I'm sitting here chewing your food for you."

Then, Linda began to look around. "You know, I used to take care of your cousins. Well, maybe not your cousins, specifically, but at least the same general family. And, when the egg take was big, I would bring them down to the courtyard to trade with neighbors. I used to have...."

She was digging again, re-energized from food, water, and—most of all—a newfound belief in her ability to survive. Linda moved heavy objects out of the way as she went through, not one person's former home, but what must have been an entire residential complex. Her search's success began with a small, wheeled cart including half a dozen closed, mounted crates and one less-than-ideal wheel. She recognized it as belonging to a chicken merchant. When she'd been in her home, her neighborhood cluster's merchant would visit several times a year to claim barren hens for the preserves before they would age out to be processed for food. The carts usually had a lot more enclosures, but those must have been lost in the collapses after the quake. She'd actually been looking for just a single strapped crate that she would use to carry Henrietta down on exchange days for the picky neighbors who wanted to know what chicken their eggs came from, but this was a far greater discovery!

With her prized new tool, Linda gathered more food from abandoned garden boxes. She had radishes, potatoes, more onions, ginger, carrots, turnips, parsnips, beans, a couple bulbs of sad-looking garlic, and even a bit of hearty rosemary that was starting to go to seed, but still had some usable sprigs. The food went into one of the crates. She found an entire box of nutrient bars; it must have been a family's supply for a whole month.

Linda imagined in her head that, of course, this family had made it out. She pulled out one of the fifty bars and put the rest into one of the cart's crates. She found a pair of young boy's shoes which were a bit tight on her, but worth it for the thicker, more protective soles. She put her old medical slippers and her shirt into one of the baskets. She put her pipe and a small kitchen knife she'd found into another.

"Well, I can throw out this piece of garbage," Linda said while tossing away the broken case piece after finding a small metal cup and a new water pouch.

Both went into a crate with the pipe and knife. the pouch was empty, but Linda was optimistic it wouldn't stay that way.

Olive followed her around, pecking at the ground as Linda dropped crumbs to her from the nutrient bar that she munched. By the time Linda had finished stocking her cart, she'd covered what must have been a full neighborhood. In addition to a full stomach, she now had two crates packed tightly full of food; one with various dishes and tools, including a solar-powered flashlight; one for what she considered personal items in which she'd put her shirt, a tube of vitamin- and mineral-infused bandage glue, a packet of shampoo powder, and a sports cap (which she immediately pulled back out and put on her head); and two crates containing linens she thought might be necessary for shade or shelter. One of the two fabric coverings was a coated nylon-like tarp and the other a large cottony sheet, which she had balled up like a nest.

"Look, Olive," Linda said, "I made you a bed."

The chicken didn't listen. She was pecking away at the rubble.

"We need to keep moving," Linda said as she tossed her tied canvas onto the cart with the crates, grateful not to be carrying it across her shoulders which were now showing bruises beneath her raw skin. "I want to get a bit closer to the tall cluster before it's dark."

Still, the chicken didn't move.

"I'll give you more food," Linda bribed, but the critter became loud and obnoxious, refusing to leave the pile of debris at which it persistently pecked.

"You're going to make me come get you, aren't you?" Linda chided the hen.

When Linda reached Olive, though, she recognized a mess of the piled-up bedding she used to use for her own fowl. Eggs, Linda thought. As she pulled away the bedding, careful not to crack any eggs, she realized that it wasn't eggs, after all. The bird had found another chick, this one younger than Olive. It was brown and still had soft, fluffy feathers. It was very weak, barely able to keep its eyes open.

"Oh. I see," Linda said, carefully picking up the fragile creature. "I don't know what's going to happen to...." she paused and flipped the chick over trying to figure something out. ".... him," she completed the thought after sexing the chick. "But we can give him a bed for the night."

Linda carried the frail young chicken and put him onto the sheet nest she'd made in the crate. It was shivering and, when it did occasionally slit open its eyes more fully, Linda wasn't sure if it was intentional or some kind of dying twitch; she'd seen it before in the young chicks that merchants sold cheap. Sometimes they didn't make it more than a day or two. She didn't have much optimism that this new bird would fare any better. She looked down at Olive who now stood obediently at her heel. She had followed Linda back to their cart having accomplished the task of alerting her human about the other bird.

"You were right not to leave him," Linda said.

Then she scanned the rubble again with a look of inspiration. She took her hat off, pushed her hair back tightly, and replaced the cap once more as though putting on a duty uniform.

"Come with me," she said to Olive as she bent down to scoop up the older of her two chickens and wrapped one hand around its tiny limbs.

At first, the bird pecked at her hands, but eventually, she settled into the cradle of Linda's arm. Linda moved more quickly across the old neighborhood cluster when she wasn't constantly looking back to make sure she hadn't lost Olive. She quickly covered about fifteen meters from where they'd started before she put the hen back down on the ground.

"If we can save one of yours, let's find one of mine," Linda said.

Linda began to move with a new purpose through the piles, removing large pieces, and passing up the very things that, just hours ago, she would have been tucking away into her cart's crates. That's not what they were doing now. Olive just stood there – no help other than moral support.

After a while, Linda picked up the hen again and moved to another area, repeating the same scavenging in a new section of the debris. She traced her way around her salvage cart in a clocklike pattern. She kept their treasures in site, and never added to them.

She had no idea how many hours had passed by the time she reached oh three hundred on her clock-pattern search. Olive had only pecked at something one time. It was a protein pack and Linda had allowed her to nibble at it while she searched that area. In this section, Olive was once again of no assistance, but her human continued to rummage through the clutter, nonetheless. The light was getting low by the time something caught Linda's eye and she ran toward it, madly pulling away the broken bits of the building.

When she reached what she'd been looking for all along, she wished she'd never started her search. It was a person, but she certainly had not found a life. It was a hand that had first crossed her vision, but—by the time she'd revealed enough of the former citizen—she realized that the hand itself was rotting and it wasn't attached to much, anymore. The head was missing its eyes and the whole face had sunken, as though all of the bones in it had been crushed or impacted. They probably had been, she realized. She wasn't sure where the body ended, but there didn't appear to be legs further buried beneath the pile or at least not legs that angled out in any normal direction one would expect for a human body. The skin was bloated and filled with maggots that wiggled beneath the bluish tissue-like layer.

It had been months. Of course, Linda thought, feeling both stupid and let down. The only explanation she could figure is that the chicken they'd found must not have been hatched yet when the Great Quake occurred. (She'd heard some people in the medical clinic refer to the recent disaster as "The Great Quake," and she realized it had gained that title in her own mind, too.) She didn't have it all worked out in her head, but—by some miracle—the new bird, the brown feathered creature, had survived.

Linda sat down, defeated, trying not to look at the decaying corpse in front of her while simultaneously feeling a heavy burden for honoring whoever he or she might have been. This was different than the madwoman she'd left behind who tried to kill her, who had no humanity left. This person felt more real somehow. Burying the citizen was out of the question. Even if she could reach and clear a reasonable patch of dirt, she wasn't sure she could gather up all of the body . . . certainly not in any sanitary way that wouldn't cause possible infection to herself. Then there was transporting the remains, and then the actual digging, and finally the burying.

Eventually, Linda settled for dragging a large piece of broken fiberwall back over the top of the person and laid it down in such a way to covered the whole body. She choked back a gag because, for some reason, it felt inappropriate to be sick as opposed to sad.

She took a breath, wanting to say something. She remembered being at her mama's memorial service – her cremated remains were released in the waters when Linda was just fourteen years old. She didn't speak then, either, but several others had shared words, so she didn't feel any pressure to add to the eulogizing. As the only human to know for certain where this person had died, though, she couldn't shake the feeling that this was her responsibility.

"Um, Good Citizen," Linda said out loud feeling kind of silly, at first, before realizing anew that nobody was around. "So, I didn't know you," she went on more confidently. "But I do know about life in the clusters, and I know that you were part of the Global Union. So, I'm sure you contributed to the lives of many other people, including my own. I know that each day, the sun rose for you in the east, over the Sea of California and set over the Pacific to the west. I know that the fog was sometimes thick as smoke swirling over the water and hills. I know you rode pods to and from your employ each day, and that you probably took choppers to New Hollywood in central Baja Province to see if the Entertainment Cluster lived any differently than the rest of us or maybe just to catch a glimpse of the singer Elsie Laurita. She was my favorite, by the way. I wonder if she...." Linda trailed off.

After a beat, she continued, "I know that you either worked in the power industries, were the partner of somebody who worked in the power industries, or you supported the workers of the power industries through your work. And the power industries care for others so that they can care for the Global Union, so you should be proud of that. I know you received rations and credits every month. I know that you probably enjoyed cactus fruit and oranges and maybe water spinach. I know the breezes smelled of salt for you and your neighborhood had beautiful garden boxes and animals and people gathered beneath its pod system. And I guess if I knew nothing else about you, that might be just enough to know your life wasn't so terrible after all."

Linda paused and stood numbly for a while.

"Anyway, I'm really sorry you didn't make it through the Great Quake," she said.

Then, she moved her hand to her heart, bowed her head, shut her eyes, and finished with the standard closing she'd heard at the handful of GU memorials she'd been to or seen broadcast over the years. "Sleep well, Good Citizen. Your work here is done. Peace."

Linda then scooped up Olive and scanned the grounds that would have been the stage for the rest of her recovery efforts.

"We don't have to look anymore," she said resignedly to her chicken. "Let's go."

She walked back to their cart in the dusk light where the little brown bird still shivered in the crate. Linda bundled the sheet all around the thing and cupped her hand over it for warmth and comfort under the cover. She stayed that way until the thing stopped shaking. She checked to make sure it hadn't died and was relieved to find it just asleep. She put Olive into the other crate with the tarp in it. It clucked angrily at first, but then changed to a purring chirp.

Together, Linda and her tiny flock began to wheel their way slowly through the fallen city toward the standing cluster in the distance on the northwest part of Baja.

The three managed another kilometer before making camp with their supplies under the branches of a still-standing orange tree. Linda closed up the crates that kept her chickens so they wouldn't wander off in the night. She pulled her shirt from its crate and rolled it up as a pillow.

Sleep came better on the second day, not because the noises of Earth had stopped so much as the voices in her head had quieted for the moment. Her eyes were heavy, and her body was tired.

"Sleep well, Good Citizen," she whispered to herself as she dropped off into a deep sleep.

CHAPTER 12
YEAR 2908

Northern Wind Farm
Zoe Baja
Zoelands Concord

Miriam and Mik strolled together on the recycled pathway.
The two walked between rows of compact wind turbines on Zoe Baja's wind farm. It had been an uneventful morning departing on whistlers from Jomo's home to their final preparations before their travels. Mik and Kate had slept on couches in the family room and on the porch, respectively, much more like crashing teenagers than the visiting diplomats they were.

Now, the captain and governor were both relaxed from their roles, comfortable in their own skin and with one another, as they breathed the fresh air and awaited greater obligations. The security personnel showed up the moment Miriam and Captain Ridgelin started out in the morning. Deputy Governor Francisco stayed true to his word to keep an eye on Governor Heirlinda until she departed. The uniformed personnel remained a few steps behind the two leaders as they walked for a long time without words at all.

Work on the energy farms usually took place in the night hours to protect the workers from heat exhaustion in the extreme temperatures. The sun was warm, and the humidity hung thick in the air, but there was still something refreshing in the moment for Mik and Miriam. The sounds of the dock were far behind them, washed out by the white noise of the turbines around them, and few people took to the energy farms in the hottest parts of the day—after dawn and before dusk—so it was quiet and intimate, save for the governor's guards.

Miriam never wanted to be governor. She was, if not happy, at least content in her life before politics. Up until two years ago, she worked for the Zoelands Foundation specifically in the Heirlinda Museum, sharing the history of the independent societies that began with the Great Nekros Quake of 2552 and grew into the six full and productive independent Zoe of the Zoelands Concord that existed today. As she introduced pieces throughout the museum, she shared stories of Linda's heirs all the way up through herself, which usually resulted in some gasps from visitors and typically at least one question from a young person about whether she'd ever met Linda. *'No,'* she'd tell them. *'Linda lived 400 years ago,'* she'd say with as straight a face as possible.

In addition to studying and maintaining the museum of artifacts, Miriam also—with her retired educator father—tended to the lush gardens surrounding the building. She found the work to be irenic. Particularly the gardening and artifact cleansing were simple, independent, and peaceful work, even when they were hard. Through the museum tasks, Miriam was a part of Zoe history, while—in the gardens—she was planting vegetation that the next generation of Baja people would enjoy. In the pairing, she felt purpose in being at the pivot point between the past and the future.

Mik had first met Miriam when leading the cityship students on a field trip while docked at Zoe Baja. It had been the Tatsu School's annual Captain's Day event. On the cityship's special day, the youngest students would pick a port at which they would get to spend a whole day with the captain and executive officer. On such days, they acted more as tourists on a trip than they did little learners. The students had selected to visit the Zoelands Foundation headquarters, at the center of Zoe Baja, during the Dandelion Festival. The day had been all about the gardens and grounds of the

Heirlinda Museum, so Miriam and Jomo served as hosts to the young Tatsians.

The yellow flowers, once thought of as weeds, were prevalent in the grassy hills around the museum, so it was a plant the students could pick as many of as they wanted. Walking through the gardens, they had learned about soil preservation and plant pollination, and then had made wishes by blowing the seeds off the dandelions that had turned fluffy and white. They'd enjoyed—or not enjoyed in the case of some of them—dandelion salad and had received over-air-transfers of a recipe for dandelion wine on their digifiles to bring home to their parents. They'd posed for satellite photos that would eventually scroll across the on-ship three-dimensional marquee that was posted on the education deck. They had died fabric with a pigment made from the flower heads. The peak of the day for most of the children, though, had been coloring the backs of their own hands by rubbing the yellow flowers upon them. It was always the simple things that had the greatest impact.

The students had finished their day by making crowns out of woven piles of the dandelions. They'd thought it was fun to make Miriam and Captain Ridgelin into King and Queen for the day.

The governor smiled to herself as she recalled that part of the captain's first visit to her.

"That crown suits you," Mik winked at Miriam. "I don't suppose it unsuits you, too?" he teased.

"Disculpas?" Miriam asked.

"I'll even let you keep it on if that floats your boat while you're . . . on mine," he said with intentional pause to imply his euphemism.

Miriam couldn't prevent the blush from rising in her cheeks. "Do people actually respond to that sort of line?" she asked.

"On my boat, that is. My ship is what I meant of course," he added with boyish innocence, though his intense gaze gave him away. "You do know I'm the captain of the Cityship Tatsu, after all," he grinned.

Neither her father nor the children could hear the comments he was making, but it was enough that she could. On the one hand, she appreciated his aggressiveness, but she was equally shocked that there were still people who spoke in such a chauvinist manner.

"Ahem," Kate cleared her throat behind Miriam and Mik. "A moment, Sir?"

So, not everybody had missed his comments.

"I won't be gone long," the captain said as he stood and took a nearby conference with Murphy.

With Mik and Kate on the perimeter of the garden, Miriam was left to be rained upon by children and their handfuls of velvety yellow flower heads. She laughed and played, tossing the flowers back at them.

Returning to where Miriam was still seated, "So, it's Heirlinda, is it?" Mik nodded deeply and pressed his lips together. "You had the children call you 'Miss Miriam.'"

It was Miriam's turn for a flirtatious sideways glance. "It is my name," she returned the wink he'd given at the beginning of their exchange.

Shaking his head in what appeared to be awe, "I did not realize I was in the presence of actual royalty, Your Highness," he teased.

Miriam just laughed. She peered across the field of children and caught her father looking back at her. It caused her to blush even more deeply.

"Hardly," she said humbly.

"Oh, trust me. I know a queen when I seen one. You, 'Miss Miriam,' are indeed a queen," he said as he presented himself in a deep bow before her.

The children cheered and laughed, glad that the grown ups were playing along with their game. The captain reached out a hand to Miriam. She took it and allowed him to help her to her feet. Before releasing her fingers, he kissed the back of her hand to an eruption of "EEWs" from the students. Ever the diplomat, even for his youngest of Tatsians, Mik transitioned from king to jester in an instant, leading the children through goofy faux-traditional dances.

The Dandelion Festival had been—for Mik and Miriam—a day of managing chaos, as much with the many chaperones as with the children, sharing about one another's lifestyles and histories, and awkward moments of flirtation. There had been adulation for the captain from all of the students and unmatched passion from Miriam for the world's vegetation, a subject that had far less concrete presence for children being raised at sea.

Before Captain Ridgelin had returned to the Tatsu on that visit, he and Miriam already had an understanding of one another. They both had an affection for their homes that could not be matched by what they would achieve with other human beings. For Miriam, Zoe Baja, and, for Mik, Cityship Tatsu, were the eternal sparks in their souls. There was an intense and deep connection between the two of them from the start because of a shared understanding of the unique affinity they each held in their hearts for the places to which they dedicated their lives.

As was always the case after the Captain's Day event, a satellite program interviewed the cityship captain to hear what he thought of the children, of the Tatsu education system, and of the special trip they'd shared. To the last question, Mik had expressed how taken he was with Miriam's love for Zoe Baja, her absolute energy for the preservation of its roots, and her determination to plant the seeds of tomorrow. He'd never met Miriam Heirlinda before that day, but—through her—he understood the strength of the women of that lineage.

It was just standard diplomacy. Mik could have focused on any aspect of the visit, and it was customary to compliment the hosting port. Miriam would have simply taken the well-intentioned flattery if Zoe Baja didn't happen to be, at that time, in the midst of a hotly contested election cycle with weak candidates. The polling for the most likely next governor was barely led at the time by Roberto Francisco whose platform consisted primarily of Zoe exceptionalism rather than any real ideas or issue stances. His big speeches had focused on finding enemies to blame for the problems of Zoe Baja rather than finding solutions to fix them. The Zoeans, by contrast, were seeking hope and inspiration, not anger and accusation.

Mik's unwitting moment of praise, carried on satellite programs all across the Zoe, and combined with the historic Heirlinda name, began the grassroots "Miriam for Governor" campaign. The movement spread more quickly than the autumn wildfires of New Hispaniola. She became a write-in. Millions around Zoe Baja put their thumbprint on the "unnamed candidate" selection and spoke her name into the vote tallying processor.

Partly in jest, as he actually quite enjoyed having someone like her at diplomatic events, Mik apologized a hundred times over, but Miriam could never have turned down the people of the land who had asked her to guide them. She gave up the Zoelands Foundation for a life of leadership. Mik in turn became a comrade for Miriam in the midst of her governing journey. Her role had been chosen for her and accepting it was the only way for her to return love to the home that provided the same to her.

In her role as governor, Miriam shared a great kinship with and affection for Mik. When he came into port, always with his formal cover fixed tightly on his head for disembarking, she couldn't help but imagine that a crown of dandelions still hid beneath the captain's hat, sitting crookedly atop his white-flecked fiery hair, just as she remembered him from the first day they'd met.

Miriam saw the layers to Mik: the one in the starched uniform who spoke with a diplomat's tongue to the satellite programs; the freckle-faced playmate that the children of the Tatsu adored; the coquettish friend full of apology who had dragged her into the world of politics; the hardworking sailor who knew every aspect of his city-ship and reveled in the challenges of life at sea; and the tough-love commander whose crew and governing officials followed with fierce loyalty. He was a chameleon, much better than Miriam at wearing the many different hats required of leaders, and capable of taking the helm in any room with as much natural comfort and ease as he took the controls on the bridge of the Tatsu.

Today, that helm was heavy.

"What's wrong?" Miriam asked.

"How the feck do you do that? I've barely said a word other than about the weather," Mik shook his head while Miriam smiled.

The security personnel exchanged a glance and Miriam looked back at them in turn with a stern expression one would expect from a scolding mother. They slowed their step and allowed Miriam and Mik a bit more privacy in their conversation.

"I just know. You're here, and even glad to be here, but your mind is in a dozen other places."

After an exasperated sigh, Mik's diatribe began. "We have thirty-seven families expecting babies over the next five months, including two sets of twins and a set of triplets. I have four more extended families, spouses and children of Tatsu crew, who have finally finished their transfer paperwork to join their sponsors in on-ship housing. Do you realize I only have six unclaimed domestic sideship leases? All this and our demographics are still quite young, too. Plus, the entirety of our older population is staying on the city-ship. Historically, the ship has been less appealing for some of our older citizens. They typically emigrate to one of the seasteads, a Zoe ally, or even a land nation as they get older. But they're staying and we're just growing."

"That's a great thing, isn't it?" Miriam asked. "You've made it a safe and happy home for them."

"Miriam, our population is growing but the ship isn't!" he exclaimed. "We're just out of room. I don't know how else to say it. We're at capacity. And it's not like we're on land. We can't just build upward. We have balances to maintain in weight and distribution. Not to mention the fact that every new person means new needs for hydroponics, so that level has to expand. It's already delayed, mind you. We should have expanded there two years ago. And it's more than just food. A new Tatsian means another desk in the school, another room in a family's quarters, more energy used, more water used, more food used."

Mik put both hands to his head in exasperation. "Along with all of that, enough new people means adding even more people to provide the services that the new people need," he sighed. "Our growth is exponential and outpacing the needs of our citizens," he finished, and—for the first time since Miriam could remember—he shrunk a bit in his posture appearing inches shorter with the weight of the words he shared.

There wasn't much Miriam could do or say at this point, but she offered an ear and an expression of empathy. She would put her arm around him if not for the security team a few paces behind them.

"What are your plans right now?" she offered, ever the pragmatic one.

"I don't have any. That's half the problem. I can't rally anybody to fix this one. I don't want to go the old child-permit route. I know the GU land nations take turns rolling those plans in and out, but who am I to decide who can have kids or when?"

"And that's the only thing you can think of?"

"My go-to is publicity. This time, I can't create a media frenzy to generate a message that will change the situation. What would I say? That the Tatsu is not a good place to live? Some have suggested a new ship, but that's what? Colonization? Of the sea? I don't like the idea of that at all."

Mik threw his big, workman's hands up in the air frustratedly. "I don't see how the quality of life does anything but go down from here for Tatsians. More crowding, less resources, fewer services. It won't be the same," the captain said. "About a fifth of the ship is dedicated to energy storage, and another aft half of a full deck to water sterilization. Between weight and volume both, we're just plain out of room. "

"So, you need Dr. Bradley's power solution to alleviate the weight and volume issues associated with energy and water, as much as I need it to alleviate our food shortages."

"You've been coy about this, Heirlinda. If it weren't you, I wouldn't even be a part of these talks. I know you're looking for an energy partnership, but none of us have even seen the prototype yet."

"That's why we're meeting with your officials first. I know you'll understand the scope of the project . . . the movement. And together, we're far more likely to get buy-in from the Pacific Islands and Antarctic Land Nations."

Mik looked at her for something more, raising his eyes in a way that was begging to be let in on the whole picture right then.

Miriam answered by shifting her eyes to indicate the people walking behind them. "You understand that I've had to work a bit discreetly. It's radical to bring people together for anything more than a credit-based trade scenario, so I didn't really want to be giving too many details over public channels."

Mik sighed acceptingly, before making light in the conversation once more. He chanced an elbow to nudge her even while he looked forward on the path. "You know you could always request a private channel," he insinuated the double entendre with a smirk.

Miriam playfully leaned his way. "Well, maybe you ought to come into port more than every couple of months!" she teased back.

"What difference would that make?" he encouraged.

Miriam looked behind them. The security team had closed the distance once more. They stepped back. Mik joined her glare. The guards took yet another step back and straightened their march.

Clearing her throat and returning to a formal business tone, "Well, the most significant work was completed in the last quarter. Let me get you up to speed because, as much as this is something Zoe Baja needs, I think the Tatsu may need it even more," she began.

Miriam covered the public-worthy bullet points of the new hydrocells as best as she could without Dr. Jacob Bradley there to add his enthusiastic scientific flair. Before she dug into the necessity of the partnership she sought, they both stopped in their tracks as an ear-splitting siren poured out of the northern port's sonic amplifiers. The unnerving sound was joined almost immediately by booming announcements coming from the governor's own residence in the voice of Roberto Francisco.

"Zoeans and guests, we are under a tsunami warning at this time. Tsunamic defense will be activated at our southern port. All coastal outliers should make their way inland or to your designated flood protection elevated shelters. The threat is code yellow. Please do not partake in water business or recreation."

The announcement was placed on repeat, intermixed with the siren. Miriam and Mik were quickly swept up into the whistler they'd taken to the wind farm. It wasn't panic, as TD activation wasn't incredibly rare in recent times, but it usually was preceded by great preparations, so they did have to move quickly.

While still in the air before their first stop, the governor's residence, the captain tuned into his team over his earpod.

"Full disembarking, Murphy!" he called over the sound of the whistler and the sirens that were only growing louder as they got closer to the northern port. "Yes, the sideships, too. Have Devon send their drones out with the message."

Miriam, meanwhile, was in communication with her Zoe water safety team. She would receive confirmations. Mik would then relay the information to his crews onboard the Tatsu.

"Just the southern port?" the governor asked. "And how are the sideships and tugs of the Tatsu?" Miriam said aloud in her conversation.

"No, Kate," Mik spoke into his own comms, picking up on the governor's cues and passing along what he could to his executive officer. "Looks like they're just engaging the tsunamic defense at the southern port. We should be safe."

"The waters are going to be rough, but no tidal waves expected, then," Miriam nodded in relief as she passed the positive nod onto Mik.

"Look," Mik went on. "It seems like this may be an abundance of caution, but the waters are going to be rough. Nobody wants to be banging around on the Tatsu. Just get them to the high elevation port shelter."

"Do we even need the defense system?" Miriam shouted, barely even hearing herself over the chaos.

In response, Mik continued to his team, "Murphy, they may not even activate it. I just want the Tatsians safe."

The whistler made its landing at the gubernatorial grounds zip pad to release the governor. Mik had no further details coming from Miriam to pass along.

"I'm coming into port. I'll be there in two minutes," the captain finished, closing the comms as the zip chopper took off once more to bring him to the northern port. Mik continued to his destination while looking back at Miriam crossing the grounds in front of the governor's residence.

After hopping off the whistler without another word to Mik, Miriam walked incredibly quickly with her escort toward the capitol building. In such cases as urgency was a necessity, running was almost instinctual. Her diplomatic training, though, held her feet back from moving into a bounce. She had never gotten over the fact that governors were not supposed to run except for fitness – and she hated running for fitness. Miriam's gait was at a pace that had the security officer next to her joining in a jog. For him, it was allowed.

Miriam entered the public side of the residence and headed directly into her office. There, Deputy Governor Roberto Francisco had already made himself at home in her chair, at her desk, in front of her three-dimensional screen, ready to press the launch button for tsunamic defense.

CHAPTER 13
YEAR 2552

Former Baja Province
Former Northern Territory of New Hispaniola Land Nation
Former Global Union

Each morning, Linda began her day with breakfast and breath. She had an orange, and she and her chickens ate a combination of roots and nutrient bars throughout the day as they clumsily moved with their cart over the grounds. After a few days, Olive even laid an egg on her nylon tarp bed, and this became more and more routine as Linda cared for and fed the creature. Food wasn't an issue for the moment. The oranges did well to quench Linda's thirst along with more water she'd found in other neighborhood rummaging sessions, but she knew that better hydration would be a need very soon.

Every day, Linda filled up their crates with items of necessity they came across as they cut through the remnants of the GU province. She found tooth cleanser and box of shave strips – the hair-melting product New Hollywood stars advertised on the feeds. Although, she couldn't imagine a need to be bare-skinned without having Lukas to please. She had a magnesium lighter which helped make fires. She wasn't very good at building her first fire, but she assumed, with necessary practice, she'd get better at it.

In what must have been an education center, she found a backpack containing an intact digital pad with a small charge still remaining. She tried to open satellite news programs, but it wasn't connected to the GU network, so she couldn't figure out how to find anything. She kept it but made sure it was powered down completely so it would be ready when she needed it. She also had several additional water pouches she discovered in the same vicinity. She tried not to think of the children the items had once belonged to or what might have happened to them.

Another day, she found a jar of fruit preserves, canned nuts, and a tin of tea. After a light rain late one morning, she captured enough water that she didn't feel guilty enjoying the steeped beverage with the gourmet goodies. After her time spent in nature's detoxification, the tiny amount of caffeine in the drink was almost dizzying.

The forward progress each day was frustratingly slow at times, and it wasn't until days of traversing the debris of Baja that Linda finally felt as though the distance had closed between her flock and their destination. But she also had a more realistic understanding of just how far away she had been at the beginning of her journey. Linda wondered what they would do when they got there. It made sense to find a goal toward which to head, but she didn't actually have a plan for what life would be like once she arrived. For the moment, she just kept her feet moving forward.

At the start of her second week of travel, the fog was thick, and the building cluster was invisible in the distance. Because of the large swaths of debris and carved out trenches from the water, she sometimes had to walk around the straight line toward her destination. She feared she could lose track of her direction, so Linda opted not to travel at all that day since she could not see where she was headed. The humidity was suffocating, so it proved a good day to rest to preserve her energy and fluids. Linda did nothing that day but lie on her canvas, with a pillow of salvaged clothing, while she watched her chickens roam in the flattened clearing they'd found.

She looked at her left palm and ran her hand over the soft, smooth, pink scar tissue. Her body was tired, and she remembered with resigned humility that she was still healing from a lot of physical trauma. She enjoyed just lying, listening, resting, and eating her fresh food and nutrient bars. On that day, she'd found a bed of fescue grass on which to make camp, so it almost seemed luxurious. It still felt strange to her to go to the bathroom outdoors, but all of the other activities alfresco were very gratifying to Linda. Her body felt like it was healing – growing stronger and more purified by being separated from the digital and mechanical world she'd always known.

Linda would end up with one other rest day – it was a day on which she'd found an apple tree. The tree's timely appearance was ideal because the orange supply had been growing low and some of those that remained had gone bad in the stifling heat. After a couple of weeks of nutrient bars, roots, and citrus, the apples tasted like pure candy.

Unfortunately, she had another, less relaxing no-progress day when she'd lost the new bird. He had wandered out of sight after they set out and she'd spent the entire day looking for him. Once she found him, she spent most of the dusk hours working to trap him safely. She felt a desperate need to keep her little flock together. At least he was healthy now. That much was good. Olive was angry with her when Linda returned. The chicken squawked alarm at her person because, while Linda had searched during the day, Olive had been locked into a crate. Linda was fearful the hen might also disappear while she sought the young rooster. When Linda and the brown fowl returned, Olive clucked madly at them.

In all, it had taken more than three weeks for Linda, Olive, and Hank, the name she'd finally given to the young rooster, to make it to the edge of the standing neighborhood cluster. When Linda had spotted the tall buildings on her first morning alone on the province, she had thought she'd go there and return to the shore in a single day. She had no idea the journey she'd bitten off. Some days, between gathering supplies and managing the heavy cart that didn't roll easily with a broken wheel over the uneven terrain, they barely covered the length of a city block. Other days, they couldn't move safely because of continuing tremors, heavy fog, or sweltering heat.

One day, she came to a wide waterway that she had to go around and, by the time she was headed back in the proper direction, two full days of travel had passed, and she was just barely to the other side of where she'd begun.

It was almost dark, so Linda decided she would wait until morning to explore the streets. The anticipation carried a thrill for her, and she didn't want the feeling to pass just yet. Thunder began to clap bassily in the distance. Hank, who had continued getting progressively better, started to shake with fear.

"Let's put you guys to bed for the day," Linda said as she looked out at the ominous sky that was dark as much for the rolling storm clouds as it was for the impending night. "You guys have to share a room, tonight," she said as she put them both on the sheet and stretched the tarp from the second crate out over her head, fastened to a branch and a bit of debris. She strung her canvas material beneath the large tarp, a cot-like bed she'd climb into when it was time.

The air had grown even more humid over the last couple of days and Linda hoped that the storm might break the heat. The wind gusts whipped across the land. Another clap of thunder, followed by a nearby strike of lightning, and the sky opened up. She quickly dragged her cart beneath the tarp to protect her birds and supplies. As the water fell in sheets, Linda stepped back out into the pouring rain, tilted her face up toward the sky, and drank in the water.

Then, Linda grabbed every receptacle she could find and secured them in the ground so that they could all gather water. The rains quickly soaked her, and she stripped out of her clothes. She put her shoes, finally stretched out enough to be comfortable on her feet, under the cot. Next, she washed her clothes with some shampoo powder between her hands in the downpour. She scrubbed her own body and hair, too, with the pure water of nature's shower. Her pungent scent from weeks of travel had failed to hide itself even from her. She did not truly recognize it until it washed away and was replaced by the fresh scent of the powder.

"Sorry about that," she laughed back to her chickens. "I had no idea!" she smiled to them.

The clouds continued to dump down on Linda for nearly an hour and she soaked up every minute of it dancing, splashing, and singing like a child. Eventually, the storm slowed to a steady, but light drizzle.

Linda's cot was sheltered under the tarp, but she stretched her feet outside of the makeshift lean-to. She'd hung her pants and undergarments from the back of her canvas bed where they dripped down onto the ground beneath her. She sat up on the canvas, kicked her legs out in front of her so that they were exposed to the storm, and washed her feet in the rain to clean away the mud. When she felt sufficiently refreshed, she lay naked in the hammock – clean, and full, and feeling prosperous with water. The sound of the rain drops on the tarp brought her the deepest sleep she could ever remember having had. She smiled into dreams of what the buildings ahead might hold.

Linda awoke to Hank and Olive chattering away, including what was a sad attempt at Hank's crow. Maybe because he was young, or maybe it was his early-life injuries; but he just didn't have a very hearty sound, certainly nothing like the "Qui-Quiri-Qui" she would expect of a rooster.

The three of them must have slept in until very late in the morning. It was unbearably hot, even while she lay there nude, as the sun was already high. Linda reached back to her clothes. They were still a bit damp, but not soaked. She could certainly wear them again. She looked at her hands and realized how little of Maya's lavendar henna remained after weeks of digging in the rubble, sweating, burning, and then washing up in the storm. Suddenly, she had a frivolous thought. She dug through her tool crate after she let the chickens out for the day. She pulled out the shave strips she'd found.

"We're going to the city today, kids!" she said to the birds. "Mama's getting glamourous!"

Linda pulled her hair back in a braid tied by one of the straps from the canvas, and she dressed in her storm-washed clothes. She rubbed citrus peels on her wrists, pulled from the last remaining morning orange before feeding the picked-apart peels to Olive and Hank. She pulled her braid through the back of the cap she'd found, rolled up the sleeves of her cotton shirt, and knotted it in front to reveal her midriff. Then, she cuffed her pants up to the middle of her shins. Her shoes were still a bit wet from the storm, but the cluster didn't look quite as bad as what they'd already come through. She put the young boy's shoes on top of the cart to continue drying and she pulled her hard-soled medical slippers back out in the hopes that they would provide enough protection to her feet.

"What do you think?" she asked her chickens as she struck a pose. Olive clucked. "Well, see what you can do with nothing but a cart of recycled materials!" she said.

After gathering up their water receptacles, sealing and saving as much of it as possible, and enjoying a breakfast of fruit, limitless water pulled from the sagging roof that was their tarp, and an egg (thank you, Olive) cooked very slowly over her very weak fire, Linda set out into the neighborhood cluster with childlike giddiness.

The streets of the northwest cluster, as Linda had referred to it in her mind, were hardly untarnished. Cracks and rubble filled the walkways. The buildings that, from a distance, looked pristine were clearly much more damaged now that she drew close to them. One full side of the tallest structure had collapsed. The other buildings leaned at odd angles, including one that was still upright only because it had fallen against the side of another building. A fire had obviously burned out one of the structures as the roof was gone and the windows all along the highest floors were missing their panes and charred black. The pod systems here had collapsed as fully as those near the southern part of Baja where Linda had begun. Large cables crossed the land as prominently as the mud-slides had crossed the earth further south in the province.

Linda found several crates and added them to her cart, but—in reality—she wasn't sure how much more she had the strength to pull. This cluster was supposed to be a place of rest, a kind of light at the end of a lifelong tunnel . . . a place to make a home of some sort. She felt foolish for having had the thought. Of course, this place was destroyed, too. The Global Union would never have aban-doned it if they had been able to recover these people or their homes. She looked at her cart of rubbish and wondered if this was all she'd ever have. It felt like so much blessing when she had been wandering the apocalyptic wilderness, but not now when at the destination where she dared to imagine a future.

Linda's walk along the paths reflected the complete devasta-tion by which she was surrounded. Her emotions orchestrated her sluggish footsteps. There was something about seeing the neigh-borhood clusters in a state of only partial collapse that was more impactful than the total destruction through which she'd already trudged. When she'd been digging through and dragging her cart over the completely flattened neighborhoods, they looked like nothing more than community compost and recycling centers. She couldn't even picture them for the lives they once held. This was different. Seeing buildings that still resembled buildings and homes that still resembled homes, while neither of which could serve its purpose any longer, brought the weight of this tragedy down on Linda with tremendous force. For the first time since the Great Quake, she really cried.

She didn't just cry; she bawled, openly and without abandon. Olive and Hank wandered off, out of her line of sight, and she didn't even follow. She surrendered completely to her breakdown.

Linda's body shook and the sobbing continued deeply and un-controllably. She collapsed to the ground, leaned against her cart, and wept for a timeless length. Every time breath came to calm her, images took over again, dragging her back down.

She saw all of the people who had been in her life, the faces of the people she'd never really known but who were part of her routine, and she agonized painfully over having lost them. She remembered the neighbors with their annoying goats and how they felt the same pride for sharing their milk as she did for gifting them eggs. She thought of the administrator who helped her learn her job. She saw the people she commuted with, the residents of her cluster, the manager at the vice lounge where Lukas would get a drink and place his bets on the springball tournaments . . . and a thousand other faces flashed through her memory. They were faces she didn't even realize she remembered until they appeared in her mind as vividly as if they were standing before her now. She regretted not knowing each one of them better.

Linda pictured Olive . . . Olive the person . . . the young man who saved her life. Then, she imagined a boy wearing the very shoes she had used to hike across the ruins of Baja Province. Finally, she conjured up an image of the man with the hissing oxygen tube from the medical clinic, and another of the starved woman with mechanical enhancements, and another of the decaying body she'd found.

It was a flood of faces followed by the flood of her tears. She couldn't bring any of them back to life as she once had done for Henrietta in her mind. Instead, a parade of the dead marched through her thoughts leaving a dark stain across her brain.

The endless funeral procession of her mind brought grief and desolation. She'd been dancing naked in the rain on the graves of her fellow citizens, on the mass grave of an entire province, and she felt shame and despair over it all. Linda rested her head on her arms, over her bent knees, feeling a sense of overwhelming panic and pain mixed together in an intoxicating tonic that filled her lungs and body completely.

"What am I going to do?" she said to herself.

The last thing she expected was a response.

CHAPTER 14
YEAR 2908

Governor's Residence
Zoe Baja
Zoelands Concord

"Stop, Roberto!" Miriam said firmly.

The governor stepped into her office with a natural flourish. "You knew I was close. Tsunamic defense is a governor's call."

"I just didn't want to worry you, Miriam, with all of your preparations for the negotiations," Roberto replied.

"Negotiations you could have ended if you had activated!"

"Governor," Inoke said, running into the office. "I have Tsunamic Defense Coordinator Doug Beamer on comms for you."

"Shie shie, Inoke."

Miriam grabbed the digifile from Inoke, tapped the screen a few times and projected an image above the handheld device. A light-skinned, slender-faced man with long hair and a goatee appeared in the air.

"Doug, I want to talk about this. Where was the quake?"

"Ring of Fire of course, Mid-Pacific, Governor Heirlinda. No land masses were affected; that's why we were a bit slow in reporting the warning. Had to wait on enough of the sea-floor sensors to confirm location—ground zero for the possible wave origin. Strength is not yet determined, but there is a chance for a tsunami."

"How big a chance?"

"I didn't announce a level red—" Deputy Governor Francisco jumped in defensively.

Miriam held up a finger to quiet him while keeping her eyes on the projection. Inoke did his best not to nod harshly with smug satisfaction at Roberto at the same time. After all, he was going to have to report to Francisco until Miriam returned.

"Doug?' the governor pressed.

"Seven percent."

"Seven! Why would we activate with a seven percent chance of a tsunami when we've made no preparations? I'm assuming you must mean seven percent chance of one that is so large, its damage will be insurmountable."

"If it comes, it could be as much as a meter high."

"Seven percent chance of a meter of water. This does not warrant an activation of TD, Beamer!" Miriam's voice could not conceal her anger. She knew that the conductor of this great orchestration was not Beamer, though. It was Francisco.

"Understood, ma'am."

"Shut. It. Down." Miriam ordered.

She put on quite a show. Nobody would have ever guessed that her stomach was knotted. Miriam abhorred confrontation, but not as much as she accepted the need to lead with conviction in conflict.

"Yes, Governor."

Miriam tapped a button that collapsed the projection, and she handed the digifile back to Inoke before turning to face the deputy governor. Roberto looked coldly at Miriam, refusing to allow his expression to indict him in wrongdoing. His numbness infuriated her.

"What the hell were you thinking?" she grilled him.

He was ready with duplicitous fast-talk that a newsfeed might find believable. "I was just acting in an abundance of caution for our Zoe Citizens. I would think that you would want that."

"Don't turn this around, Roberto," Miriam shook her head. She was not the newsfeeds. "If that system is activated, while we have the Tatsu here, it could radically delay the energy negotiations with the Global Union. It took me months to get us this far, and we don't have that much time again. You want to be cautious for our citizens? Guess what, Francisco! Those citizens are starving! And those negotiations are the only way I have left to save them. Not to mention how many of their livelihoods could have been lost by not evacuating the ports first. Imagine the damage!"

"I...." Francisco began, "I hadn't thought of that," he finished, but his tone didn't seem to agree with his words. He was clearly concerned about something, but Miriam questioned if it had anything at all to do with the chaos he nearly caused.

"Get out of my office. You'll be sitting in here soon enough. Inoke," she continued, ignoring the Deputy Governor as he slinked out, "Get me Captain Mik Ridgelin. And coordinate with our safety directors to make sure that our people move inland just in case this seven percent chance yields something. I really do want to protect the Baja people."

The door to her office slammed shut and the loud steps of Francisco were heard walking away as Miriam collapsed into her chair.

"Oui, ma'am, of course you do," Inoke affirmed, typing away on the digifile. "I've got Mik . . . uh, Captain Ridgelin."

"Governor," Mik's face said as it appeared projected over the digifile. "I am getting conflicting reports all over the place. What's going on?"

"We're going to have some choppiness coming, but not tsunamic defense. Standard precautions for turbulent waters."

A tone was interrupting their conversation, "Hold yourself a moment, Miriam. Let me get Kate in here!"

A few more tones blended into the mix and Kate's face joined Mik's, projected into the air.

"The docks and ports are going to be a bit rough, we may be expecting higher than normal waves, so we'll be a bit delayed in getting out, but nothing serious," Miriam assured the captain and his executive officer.

"And certainly nothing like the delay we'd have had if Beamer had activated TD," Mik acknowledged. "So, Kate, just make sure our people are on land now if they want to come ashore and away from the docks and shoreline. If they stay on board, central decks, midship is best, antinausea patches for those who want them. Get the crew on distribution for those."

"Oui, Sir, ordering it now," she said as she began keying away on a control panel while continuing in conversation with her captain and the governor. "But I don't really understand. Won't their tsunamic defense prevent the waters from being dangerous? Why not just use that and we can keep our brief-visit schedule and get back out?"

"That's not exactly right," Miriam jumped in. "Yes. The system is designed to keep the most violent and deadly of water disasters from becoming as dangerous as they could be, but short of an actual tsunami, the technology is its own kind of disaster."

"She's right, Murphy," Mik said. "Do you know how it works?"

"Only in theory," she admitted. "Sound waves, pumps, nets. Sefi is in the midst of a whole course on it at University. But reading isn't the same as understanding."

"It's a five-part defense against the waves," Miriam began.

"And you're right about some of the mechanisms, but they have a specific order and purpose," Mik added. "First there are the pumps, only activated on the shore most likely to be affected by one of the waves."

"Historically on Baja, that's the southern port, but we have the capability to activate TD around the entire Zoe," Miriam said.

She and Mik easily spoke together in a single explanation to Kate.

"Those pumps pull in water from deep in the ocean." Said Mik.

"It almost looks like a large underwater canal . . . millions of liters," continued Miriam

"That works to counter the tidal wave pulling the other direction," finished the captain.

"Not that we could ever come close to the power of Mother Nature," added Miriam.

Mik shook his head dramatically. "Not a chance! That's where the next pieces come into play. Every quarter kilometer, beginning at two kilometers from the land mass, large poles are raised, kind of like really tall luxury gates."

"Like the ones from ancient mansions and castles?" Kate asked.

"Sort of," said Miriam. "Only made of steel and titanium. And immense. And stronger. And filled with technology. So, sort of. But not quite. They're actually called sea gates, so Mik's description is perfect."

"Thanks," Mik said, flattered. "Well, there are eight of those. Two kilometers, one-and-three-quarter kilometers, one and a half kilometers, and so on, all the way to a quarter kilometer from shore."

"And at an eighth of a kilometer from shore, we have a twenty-meter-high mesh net. It's flexible, so it moves freely with the water. The water passes through it, of course, but gets broken apart to a certain degree. It's the last physical defense."

"Those sea gates, though" Mik took back over, "They aren't just there to break up a wave, although they help with that. They actually send sonic waves out into the water against what could become the tsunami or tidal wave. All different directions. Each pole of each gate has thirty signal emitters. The effect causes the water to almost looks like it's boiling."

"It does, doesn't it?" Miriam said. "I never thought of that."

"What about the pumps?" Kate asked.

"Well, I guess that's really the last defense, to correct myself. When the wave hits the mesh, depending on where it hits and whether it is still considered a danger, the pumps then push the water back out full force, doing our best to use the ocean's own power to our advantage. We compel the sea to backfire against itself."

"So, the initial water pull fights against the pull of the tsunami," Kate's image over the digifile moved in and out of view. While she spoke, she must have been pacing the room where she stood. "The sonic waves break up the water across a whole plane. If the wave still comes, it runs into eight sets of gates to further dispel it, followed by a mesh net that essentially shreds it. Then, it faces a full force gush of countless millions of liters of water being spit back at it all at once."

"And," Miriam added, "if that all works as it should, and it has in the past, the wave will still come, but lives can be saved."

"It's not like we can really stop a tsunami. That thing is coming with the force of almost fifty million kilopascals," Inoke contributed.

Nodding, Miriam offered some light. "But, when we do use it, we've bought ourselves some time. I can get my people to safety and our scientists diminish its power enough to lessen the damage, which also shortens the recovery time. It doesn't have to be a global event anymore."

"Plus," Mik chimed in, "the early detection system incorporates oceanic movement scales placed along the sea floor. Those have made a drastic difference in the effort to deescalate tsunamis' effects, too."

"I know about those, of course," Kate said. "We collect those readings along our route. I just didn't understand how small a piece of the puzzle they were."

Encouragingly, Miriam said, "Even if it's just to let us know that we'll have to activate tsunamic defense, they are an important piece of that puzzle. With the early detection system, we're able to get people off the water all within that two-kilometer distance around the threatened land mass. Ideally, we have enough time to direct them around the specific tsunamic defense being activated, so that they are out of harm's way for both the tsunami and tsunamic defense."

"Sailors know that nobody operates TD like Zoe Baja; they've never lost a ship."

"But" Kate concluded for them, "putting this thing into play when there is not an actual threat is a pretty big deal."

"Very!" Miriam exclaimed.

"Deadly," added Mik. "Think about it. Imagine you're on a ship that has passed the two-kilometer point. You're trapped in a blender. The sea level sinks, a steel gate shoots up behind you if you're lucky; it could shoot up right through you. Then, you have less than twenty minutes before the next one is up."

"Something like that happened to the Cityship Tchi, right?" Kate asked. "They opted to turn sideways off the northern coast of the Australian Land Nation, put themselves between two of those sea gates."

Mik shook his head no while he said, "Yes. But the Tchi is half the size of our ship," he said. "Imagine getting the Tatsu to ninety degrees between those gates quickly enough! And in the midst of water that is as choppy as a pot of boiling water."

"Feck!" Kate said as she stepped back into the visual frame to be captured by the digifile communicator.

"And, if you managed to do that, now you're about to be sandwiched between two waves, one pumped out by man," Inoke said, "and one driven by nature."

"I don't see how anyone gets out of that alive," Kate said.

"We do have a manual release to deactivate TD to allow a ship to pass safely through, but only a handful of people even know where it is."

"Cityship captains, governors, or in the case of land nations, prefects, and usually the lead longshore worker of a port are the only ones with the codes to execute the land-side releases. Of course, a few of the fleet families are in the know, too."

"Is that so, Captain?" Kate said to Mik with narrowed eyes.

"That's what I've heard, anyway."

"And even though you were already in port, today," Miriam said, "Those rough waters don't die down quickly. We usually shut down all Zoe water traffic for several days following tsunamic defense deployment. And there can be damage to the ports, too. It's not something to be taken lightly."

"Why ever use it, then?" Kate asked sincerely.

"2873," Mik said, and Miriam nodded.

They didn't need to say any more to indicate the great tragedy that had taken place thirty-five years earlier. Kate wasn't even born yet when tsunamic defense was activated off the southwest coast of the Eurasian Collective Land Nation's Southern Territory. The Cityship Niu, which had an eastern sea route in the Indian Ocean, went down against the resulting violent waters, and every person aboard perished. But it was estimated that one point seven billion citizens survived as a result. Today they would not need to lose anybody. At most, the Tatsu would delay its departure a few hours while they determined whether any wave would come at all.

Miriam couldn't help but wonder if humans would ever figure out a way to save lives without simultaneously costing others who become expendable by comparison.

CHAPTER 15
YEAR 2552

Former Baja Province
Former Northern Territory of New Hispaniola Land Nation
Former Global Union

"Are you okay?"

Linda jumped so quickly to her feet and away from the voice that the sudden movement didn't even feel human. She'd have thought she was fully mechanical if her heart wasn't in her throat. Her crying stopped as abruptly as if she were a satellite program that somebody had directed to pause. Words eluded her while she studied the man who had approached her.

"I'm not here to hurt you," he spoke gently, and he held up both hands in submission as he stepped backward from her to reduce the threat he imposed.

Linda's eyes involuntarily darted to her cart.

"I don't need your things either. I just.... I heard you. You were crying."

"Who are you?" she managed. "How are you here? What are you doing here?"

"Same questions," he retorted while attempting a friendly smile. She didn't return it.

The man's complexion was a dark olive tone, though some of his color looked like it came from time in the sun. His unkempt hair was black as licorice and stick straight. He was thin and his skin was wrinkled, but he didn't look old. He had the appearance of somebody who had gone through an illness and lost weight too quickly.

Linda said nothing to him.

"I'll start, then," he said. "I'm Uru. I live . . . or, lived . . . or, well, I guess I still live here," he said indicating the tallest building in the midst of the mostly-fallen cluster behind him.

"Did you miss the transport?" Linda asked.

After a pause, Uru replied, "Something like that. You?"

"Something like that," she answered cautiously. "Where is here?"

"New Hollywood," Uru said.

Linda did not want to take her eyes off of the man, but she did raise them to the shattered skyline behind him. Even though it was just a chopper ride away, she'd only ever seen the city on satellite programs, and it was held up as the height of luxury. As she scanned behind Uru, she began to truly visualize the buildings for the first time as something other than some random distant destination. She started putting them back together in her head, cleaning them, straightening them, surrounding them with people, and recognizing them for what they once were.

The silver and mirrored tubular tower was the Top-of-the-World Building. It had once spiraled up to the sky and boasted glass-bottomed stages that stretched out from the superstructure every thirty stories. Now it was a pile of rubble recognizable only by the once-mounted letters of the building that were fallen next to the reflective scrap. The Set Stadium, once a skyscraper with the largest footprint in all of the Northern Territory of New Hispaniola Land Nation, was now a hill of the synthetic red brick from which it had been made. Before the Great Quake, it had housed classic style sets of actual building facades and structures in lieu of the computer-generated backdrops used in most modern entertainment. The outdoor amphitheater, the bowl for springball tournaments, and the building-sized screens that used to show live theatre and concerts all fell into place in Linda's memory. Then, beyond what had been the center of New Hollywood, she spotted the quarter buildings. The stars and athletes who once lived there had made their ways into her own life on screens at home and in virtual entertainment rooms that she and Lukas occasionally visited. The quarter buildings of the cluster were dust. Fame did nothing to protect the household names from the Great Quake. Linda's heart fell out of her throat and plunged into the pit of her stomach.

"I'm going to sit," Uru said. "Is that okay?"

Linda made eye contact with the man again and nodded curtly. Uru took a couple of steps backward. He sat on the trunk of a fallen tree that laid over the remnants of what had likely been another mudslide. While he did so, Linda took a deep, calming breath and wiped her face on the sleeve of her shirt, not wanting to be any more vulnerable than she already had been in front of the stranger.

Carefully, she pulled her cart closer to herself and sat on the platform of her little home on wheels. A couple of meters stretched between the two and so began what she believed was surely humanity's longest and most awkward staring contest. Except, not staring, exactly. They sized one another up. From the looks of it, Linda assumed she had fared better than Uru had in the aftermath of the Great Quake. She thought of the girl who attacked her early in her journey. If it turned out this man wanted something from her, she believed she would be able to fight him, or at least outrun him. She leaned back on her cart, kept her eyes on the man, and smugly nibbled on an apple she pulled from a crate, projecting a far greater confidence than she actually had.

"I still didn't get your name," he finally broke the silence.

Linda parted her lips as if she was about to share but closed them again. She took another bite of her apple.

"I have a scanner at my . . . at . . . where I've been staying. I would hate to have to go get it," he joked in a manner far more friendly than she was ready to accept.

Linda's eyes narrowed. She opened her left hand and held her scarred palm out in front of her to show it to Uru.

"The chip, too?" he asked.

She raised her eyebrows in positive reply.

"Oh. No scannable ID, then. I guess you didn't want folks to know who you are."

Carefully, "I'm not the one who removed it," she said.

"Well, if you do tell me—your name, that is—who exactly are you afraid I am going to share it with?" he asked.

Linda smiled. Uru smiled bigger, proud that he'd finally broken her, only he hadn't. Just beyond the man, over his shoulder, Olive and Hank had appeared. Uru noticed that Linda's eyes weren't quite on him anymore, so he turned in the direction of her glance and jumped with a childish yelp at the sight of the other life. Linda huffed out a small laugh. She made a clicking sound and pulled out a nutrient bar that she crumbled for her chickens. Both shuffled over quickly to peck at the ground by her feet.

"You have pets?" Uru asked startled.

"I have chickens," Linda replied. "This is Olive, my hen, and the fiercely masculine rooster, mister Hank!" she smiled genuinely.

"So, their names you'll share!"

She swallowed and looked at Uru. "Linda."

"Thank you, Linda," he nodded. "Nice to meet you."

"You, too," she said, and it surprised her that she meant it. "Do you want an apple?"

"I do actually," he said.

Linda pulled out another apple and walked it over to him, holding it out while still keeping an arm's length away. He took it, careful not to touch her.

"Why are you still here?" he asked while she returned to sit.

Her birds crowded near her in a way she chose to believe was protective but was more likely because she was the provider of their crumbs.

"I'm not really sure, to be truthful," Linda answered while still also pondering the question. "I could have been evacuated, but I just didn't get on the transport. I don't know if I have a better answer. You?"

For the first time, the cordial man lost the light in his eyes.

"My family is here."

"Your whole family?" Linda asked as she sat up, suddenly wondering if she'd let her wall down too soon and she was about to be ambushed. "Where?"

"They didn't make it," he said.

"Oh." Linda said wishing there was something more to add, but there wasn't. The words "I'm sorry" would have felt trite.

"My wife and three children all perished."

"Three!" Linda exclaimed and immediately was upset at herself for it. That was hardly the impactful thing Uru believed he was sharing, but the idea of a family who had three children was akin to being told they had magical powers.

"A long story," Uru smiled, but his smile quickly dissipated.

Unlike Linda, Uru was an open file, not just willing, but seemingly eager to share his journey. It was almost as though he were waiting for somebody who could simply listen. He spilled forth for the next hour and a half about the way his life unfolded on the day of the Great Quake.

Uru punched a few buttons and the sounds of a brass band erupted in the room.

"How about this one?" he asked the curly-haired singer.

"It kind of forces your toe to tap, doesn't it?" she responded. "'*Mister, why'd you call up, what you doin' tonight?*

Hope you're in the mood because I'm feeling just right
How's about a corner with a table for two?" she started reading out loud. "Not sure I love the lyrics for today's music. What's it called?"

"*In the Mood*," Uru answered.

The singer bit her lip and shook her head questioningly. "Let me think about it. I'm not even sure if I want to do another twentieth century collection. What about the Arab arrangements from the 2300s? Let's pull up some of those again."

Uru walked away from the computer bank where he and Elsie Laurita had been researching, and he led them to a different digital music collection. Just as he was about to pull up a new song, a voice called out in the room.

"Mr. Mageo, your family is here to visit you. They are waiting for you in the gift shop."

"Oh!" he said looking at the time on the projected wall clock, "Thank you," he said aloud to the overhead voice. Then, to Elsie Laurita, "I didn't realize it was that time, already."

"Neither did I," said the singer. "Tell Kim and the kids 'Jambo' for me," Elsie said. "I have to get out of here, anyway. I have to meet my studio band at the zip port."

Elsie grabbed her pad full of the latest recommended listening and exited with Uru. After they left the archives of the entertainment complex, the singer turned toward the exit and Uru went to giddily greet his wife and three children in the gift shop on the main level.

"Dada!" Alice said when he appeared, and she ran into Uru's arms laughing.

"My little giggle monsters!" Uru said back as he squeezed Alice who was joined by Grace and Andy.

Kim kissed her husband, leaning over their children as she did so. "Lose track of time, again?" she teased.

"I was in the twentieth century recordings!" he admitted knowing that it would more than serve as explanation for his tardiness.

Kim knew him well enough for that much. She didn't really mind, either. His wife adored the passion Uru had for music and historical entertainment. He often brought home old two-dimensional movies or massive metal or vinyl discs that contained music. Their home was decorated with the replicas of masterpieces by artists whose work had disappeared with the melt. Most citizens weren't even aware of the painters and photographers who existed in Earth-Before-the-Melt, but her home was brimming with their works . . . and she loved it. Their little family found great joy in these cheap forms of entertainment while the rest of the world partook of vice lounges, gaming complexes, and mixed reality literature.

"Dada!" Grace smiled. "Let me show you!" she said, pulling Uru along by his pinkie finger while her brother and sister clung to him.

Grace was breathing quickly with excitement. It was almost as though she had to let out some air in order to release the pressure off of her childhood enthusiasm valve or she would just burst. Kim rolled her eyes playfully at her husband as their three children pulled their human jungle gym over to a display.

The gift shop shelf included an assortment of figurines of human animal hybrids and, if you pressed the belly buttons of the creatures, they would play a song. There were also little pieces of children's jewelry and fake tatua depicting characters from the children's musical group, "Fluff & Tumble." Grace pointed at a small bracelet with such awe that one would have thought she was picking out a piece of jewelry constructed of platinum and black diamonds.

"That one, Dada!" she said. "It's my turn, right? Alice and Andy picked something last time!"

"Okay, okay," Uru said as though it was painful to him, but he enjoyed being able to bring smiles to the faces of his children with his archive discount.

Uru stepped up to the automated checkout counter, scanned the little bracelet, and then placed his palm on the scanner to pay for the trinket.

"They have been talking about visiting you all day," Kim said as her husband clasped the bracelet onto

Grace's wrist. "I don't get a tenth of that enthusiasm when they come to my workplace," she said.

"That's because you're the real grownup between us," Uru joked. "I get to play all day!" he said as he put his arm around his wife and placed another kiss on her lips proudly. The family of five walked out the front of the building to enjoy lunch together. They saved their GU recreation time to take turns visiting one another and sharing a meal once a month. They knew that they wouldn't have many more of these family visits as the children grew and made their way into the education centers and schools.

"What was my biggest kid playing with today?" Kim joked to Uru.

"Maybe another song selection project, but I'm not certain yet," he sighed. "The GU hasn't determined if it's time for another classic work. We have to wait and see if Elsie can earn one of the allotted entertainment release slots."

Leaning into her husband, "And if she doesn't?" Kim asked.

Uru shook his head. Organizing and reorganizing the archives felt completely purposeless when he wasn't assigned an actual project. It was as though the Global Union had found a place to put him and they no longer had to think about him. He believed people needed, not just a credit deposit, but fulfillment from their work. He would move one storage bank to another and back again when he didn't have a project. It was futile.

"It would be a shame for my client," he said, not admitting that the loss would be just as much his own. "She has some great selections."

Kim looked at Uru and was sure by his expression that he didn't have confidence in his entertainment project earning the permit.

"Well, I'd love to hear the selections if you want to share them," she encouraged.

Uru smiled at his wife. "Yes?" he asked. "I could go get them."

Kim nodded and Uru bounded back into the building. He ran down the stairs to the archives to grab his storage pad. When he was two steps from the shelf where the pad laid, it fell from the shelf. The floor trembled beneath his feet, and he fell to the ground as the Great Quake arrived with a violent appetite. Before he could stand, a large light fixture collapsed and knocked him out. He didn't wake until the worst had passed.

"All four of their bodies were recovered nearly ten kilometers away from the archives where the mudslides swept them up," he finished with deadened detachment. "I could only identify Grace by the Fluff & Tumble bracelet she still had on."

Linda had listened sympathetically, only occasionally asking something for clarification or to encourage him to continue on out of an overly emotional moment through which she was not yet ready to comfort the man.

Following the quake and mudslides, Uru stayed behind. At first, he was in shock. He sneaked in to help aid in the recovery efforts of any in his neighborhood who could have survived. He worked with no emotion or maybe in defiance of it throughout the operations. Without the proper certifications, though, rescue and recovery professionals would not let him continue to assist. He'd lost two other friends and a neighbor who were alive beneath the rubble following the initial disasters, but not long enough for the certified rescuers to reach them.

That was when he gave up.

He stopped eating and drinking, but his willpower eventually failed him in that area and survival instinct took over. He tried other ways of ending it all, ways he could not bring himself to describe to Linda other than to say that they had occurred. Each time he attempted suicide, something stopped him from being able to follow through.

After giving up on giving up, he began going through the motions of survival in spite of himself. He assumed there must be some reason he couldn't just die. He found himself back in as much of a routine as was possible. He kept up his garden boxes; he had three of them where he was staying. It was the same number he'd had in his quarters in place of having any animals or animal shares and enough for the rations of a full family. He powered up his old work building with a couple of solar panels and chargeable battery packs he had squirreled away, initially for his workshop back when he led operations there, but then they became very helpful for after the GU's final shutdowns of all non-medical facilities on the province.

Fourteen of the archive's lowest floors, on one side of the building, out of the original ninety-eight, survived the quakes and aftermath. The GU declared it, and the rest of New Hollywood, unlivable and condemned, but he'd avoided them each time they came to clear out various inventories. He had made a home of sorts there.

Yet life remained empty for Uru.

He eventually reverted back to his wish to end his existence. He began to seek out possible slide zones following each storm, aftershock, or earthquake, in the hopes of going down in a mudslide to join his family, but he continued to survive, despite his best worst efforts. The last death attempt had been the night before, in the heavy storms, when he thought a slide might come. He had lain down in a bed that he'd seen flooded as many as fifteen times since the first slides occurred months earlier. Only, this time, it didn't fill.

After he finished telling his aftermath story, Uru fell quiet for a long time. Linda didn't want to say anything, either. She thought empathy to a stranger might not feel sincere. Words of inspiration would seem like nothing more than platitudes. Some random comment on suicide might feel like judgement. None of these were what she wanted to convey. So, she waited for Uru to provide the closure. After some time, he did.

"I stayed so that I could die," he confessed to Linda. "And then, I found you here."

Linda felt an unrelenting compassion for the man that she'd never evoked for another human, always lost so thoroughly in her own hidden depression. Behind the kind smile of Uru was a deep and dark sadness. In her own way and for her own reasons, that was something she understood.

"I didn't know until just now," Linda began. "Why I stayed. Honestly, I felt like I may have made a really big mistake. In fact, I still feel that way from time to time, but I have an answer for you," Linda said. "I know why I'm here."

Uru looked up, grateful to be pulled from his pit.

"I think I stayed so that I could finally live," she said.

Linda walked over to the man. He stood up and looked at the woman a foot shorter than he was. He nodded.

For now, it would be life.

"Okay, then. Come this way," he said.

Linda grabbed her cart and followed him. For the man who wanted to die and the woman who wanted to live, it was a new beginning.

Linda and Uru didn't exactly make a family, or even a team. It was more of an alliance than anything. She shared eggs and he shared fresh food from the garden boxes. She showed him how to properly rummage, and he showed her how to adapt the old GU materials to outfit the building as a home. He tried to teach her how to make the plants thrive and she tried to show him how to find the eggs that Olive had a knack of hiding. Those efforts resulted in them deciding Uru should manage the greenery and Linda should manage the animals. Linda's obligations now also included a couple of fertilized eggs, courtesy of Hank, that would eventually add to their little flock.

By day, after waking to Hank's ever-growing crow, they survived, pulling Linda's cart through the old-looking streets of New Hollywood, and loading it up. She always had Uru manage the actual city roads or collapsed buildings of the cluster. She worked through the beds of washouts to prevent him from having to think about the people lost in the slides.

They didn't have a lot of power, but any power at all was more than she than that with which she had managed while making her way to the cluster from the southeastern docks – a distance she'd learned was nearly fifty kilometers. They used the power for a bit of light at night, an atmosphere fan when the heat was unbearable, and refrigeration to extend the fresh life of their food.

Conversation was light, focused more on needs of the moment than on what the future held. That was something Uru seemed to understand was important to Linda. She knew it was important to him, in turn, to let him share long stories about his wife and children. She respected his enduring love for the family he'd lost.

The two slept protected in the entertainment archives. Uru showed Linda to a floor of the building that appeared to be administrative offices, and he excused himself to another level. The implication was that he was gifting her this space, but the other was his. Linda was certain Uru didn't realize his crying carried through the vents at night. And, after the crying, the pacing. She wasn't sure if he ever really slept.

In time, they developed something other than a friendship. It was a realization that the other would always be there and that they would always take care of one another. Theirs was an agreement to live with what life had dealt them. The important thing in that was just to live. For Linda at least, that shared pact was perhaps the greatest love she'd ever experienced in her life. She began to look at Uru with a new perspective.

CHAPTER 16
YEAR 2908

Northern Point of Pacific Sea Route
Cityship Tatsu IV
Cityship Regatta
-
Northern Port of Zoe Baja
Zoe Baja
Zoelands Concord

"Hey, Cap?"

Mik looked away from Miriam as Kate's voice sounded in his ear. He held up a finger to let her know that he was managing another conversation she couldn't hear through his earpiece.

"I'm here, Murphy," he responded.

"We have a bit of a situation here. Could you make your way to the aft-bridge?"

Miriam and the captain were at the docks with Inoke, Dr. Bradley, and Harry, waiting to board the Tatsu for the negotiations. Harry's assistant Vera stood with them nervously. She was already clothed in the heavy gloves donned by the onshore docking parties. The look was a bit quirky given that it would still be a couple of hours before they could leave as they waited for the rough, though not tsunamic, waters to die down, the evacuated cityship to reboard, and the launch procedures to begin.

"Miriam?" Mik said, looking for permission to depart, giving her a glance while tapping his earpiece.

She smiled. The man led the flagship of the Cityship Regatta. He did not need her permission. "Go ahead," Miriam nodded in understanding.

Mik took the gangway in four large strides and moved into a quick-paced gait toward the back quarter of the ship.

"Inoke," Miriam said turning back to the other gentlemen on the dock, "I'm counting on you to keep Harry in the loop. The quakes will come, but Francisco can't have an itchy finger on that TD button every time there's a tremor. He was going to hit that activation sequence before we'd even sent out the drones to warn ships within the two-kilometer range. People could die. Harry knows the manual release locations and codes. You two are my safety net."

Potcake let out a breathy woof and Harry shook his head. "Power hungry piece of...."

"Deputy Governor, have you come to see the governor off?" Inoke jumped in as Roberto approached, saving Harry from his own words.

Miriam rolled her lips in and pressed them together to contain her laugh. Inoke was such a gem.

"Well, I was, but I understand Captain Ridgelin isn't ready?"

"The entire ship needs to be reboarded because they evacuated when it looked like tsunamic defense might be activated, SIR," Harry said, his voice gruff and implication not-even-slightly veiled. "He'll be out of your hair in plenty of time. I run an efficient port."

Vera put her face down behind Harry. She looked so lost in the midst of the leaders.

A digifile drone appeared in the middle of their small circle, settled low, and flipped over, landing on the ground between them. A screen popped up over the top of the digifile mounted on it.

"Governor, I was hoping that's where you still were," Mik said. "Stay there. ExO Murphy and I will be down soon. Deputy Governor, you, too."

Miriam nodded while Francisco looked offended at taking an order from the cityship captain. The projection closed and the drone returned to the ship.

"What the hell do you think that's all about?" Harry asked.

Miriam looked burdened as she processed the thought without answer. Dr. Bradley awkwardly stepped aside, separating himself from the diplomats.

Inoke spent the next several minutes going through a shared checklist between the Governor and Deputy Governor to ensure the hand-off duties between the two leaders were in order before Miriam left the Zoe. With each new task, Miriam would place her thumb on his digifile to release control of the checklist item, followed by Deputy Governor Roberto Francisco placing his thumb on the digifile to accept control of it. The two didn't make eye contact with one another when Inoke read out the tasks related to tsunamic defense, an item he read with as little inflection and as much speed as possible. The final thumbprint exchange finished with Inoke ensuring them that Governor Miriam Heirlinda was set to leave, and primary government control of Zoe Baja was securely in the hands of Deputy Governor Roberto Francisco.

At that moment, Mik and Kate approached with a man dressed in a well-worn Global Union uniform with a Transportation Industries logo emblazoned on the breast. He held his arm and wore a bloodied bandage across his face. Two cityship security personnel flanked him and his wrists were in coded magnetic restraints. The man and his security escorts stayed on the dock directly at the bottom of the plank while the others stepped a few feet from him and spoke in low tones to remain out of earshot.

"He stowed away when we docked with New Hispaniola's Mexican Province. He was injured here in the port as a result of the turbulent waters," Mik said.

"Just the turbulence?" Miriam asked in a low tone, implying that there may also have been some coerced questioning going on.

"I swear it," Mik said, and his eyes told Miriam he was sincere.

"REFUGE!" the man shouted toward them.

Dr. Bradley took a couple extra steps back, feeling sure he wasn't supposed to be there, as part of this political business.

"What's your name?" Miriam called back to the stowaway, who appeared to be in his early thirties.

"Hemi," he said. "Hemi Mauga, Transportation Industries, Pacific Island Land Nation, Samoan Province."

"Rather soldierly," Inoke said under his breath.

Deputy Governor Francisco glanced at Inoke, but quickly back to the group. He wasn't sure he'd heard anything at all.

Kate's eyes narrowed to slits as she looked at the bandaged man. Then, to the group, "Our medics cleaned him up, but I think he should be examined at your clinic, too."

It wasn't unusual for GU citizens to make their way to Zoelands, in an ask for refugee status. Not that people didn't also leave the Tribal Regions, Zoelands Concord, or Cityship Regatta, either, but those places allowed freedom of movement and travel, so leaving wasn't a clandestine operation. Leaving the GU meant leaving a hole that would need to be filled. Applications for such an exit were possible, but often took unreasonable lengths of time to process.

Miriam shook her head thinking of this one more thing to add to the list for while she was away.

Inoke could read her mind, "It makes sense, Governor," he said. "He can't very well go with you to the negotiations."

Sighing, "See that he gets a shower, clothing, a good meal, and medical attention," Miriam said to the deputy governor.

"You're leaving him here?" Francisco asked in shock.

"Without knowing more, we can't bring him on the ship," Miriam said echoing Inoke's concerns.

"But" Francisco started.

"I agree," said Captain Ridgelin. "My own team can question him further when we return."

Appealing to his need for authority, "You're in charge, are you not?" Miriam asked Roberto.

"Of course, I am," he said before adding, "in charge of Zoe Baja citizens. He's . . . he's GU."

"He's a man who's been hurt and who's asking for refugee status. Find out his story and take care of it, Roberto."

"Citizens are still making their way back," Mik said, assured that the matter was resolved. "I should get you and Dr. Bradley to your quarters."

"You know how to reach me," Miriam said. She directed her gaze toward the small group and Francisco was very aware that Inoke was receiving the instructions more than he was.

"Sailors," the captain said to the two security personnel. "After escorting Mr. Mauga, get back aboard. We'll need your incident report by twenty-two hundred hours UTC."

"Oui, Sir," the two men said in unison.

"Calm waters to you," Harry added in farewell.

"Harry," Mik responded in salutation with a firm grip goodbye to the longshore worker.

Captain Mik Ridgelin patted Potcake on the head, and then he, ExO Kate Murphy, Dr. Jacob Bradley, and Governor Miriam Heirlinda boarded the Tatsu while Deputy Governor Roberto Francisco and Chief of Staff Inoke Kalua led the two security personnel and Hemi Mauga to the capitol building.

"I'll get it out of the way," Roberto began as he spoke to Hemi in a small, informal interrogation room on the east wing of the public side of the governor's residence. "I don't trust you. I don't trust anyone from the Global Union. You're a bunch of cogs in a machine that your government uses to strongarm the rest of the world."

Cleaned up, the stowaway looked solid. He had facial tatua and hair that was shaven on the sides and pulled up into a bun at the top of his head. His eyes were slightly sunken, surely the result of being in stowage.

"I understand your feeling," the man said, unsure what else he could offer to the conversation.

"Did I say you could talk, Cog?"

"No, Sir. I just meant...."

"Did. I. Say. You. Could. Talk?" he repeated each word threateningly as he closed in on Mauga.

The man didn't respond.

"Your . . . union," Roberto spit out the word. "What's its motto?"

The man stayed quiet.

"You can talk, now. I asked you a question."

"Every citizen's contribution collected toward every citizen's care provided—the whole is greater than the sum."

"Except you're here asking for refugee status. So, you must have some care that's not being provided for. Some need?"

"Not exactly. I do have all of my physical needs met. The GU takes care of its own," Hemi said.

"Its own fellow citizens, anyway. So, what then? Slaving away like a prisoner for those needs? No time for rest?"

"I have allotted recreation time plus credits for personal well-being."

"You're not helping me much here, Mr. Mauga. You don't sound like a man who needs refuge. You make this place sound idyllic."

"On file, it is. The GU is not a bad home. It's just not right for me. Not now, anyway," he said. Then, in an effort to win over the deputy governor, he added "I'm not a cog."

"Still human then, are you?"

"We're all human, Sir. We're not enemies," the citizen said. "We just have different approaches to life. And I think the Global Union approach might not be right for me. I've spent my whole life in the Samoan Province. It's not a lot to have seen. I want to change that while I still can."

"So much so that you'd risk injury aboard a cityship? Seems a bit extreme. Why not just apply for non-GU visitation? You a criminal?"

"No, Sir. It wouldn't be processed in time. They'd have to fill my role. That might take as much as eighteen months."

"Is there a lover who may leave you before then? Is that it?"

"Not happening for me," he sardonically laughed. "I made my bed with Chloe. I just want to lay with her in the world for a while before she puts me to sleep."

For the first time, the smug expression of the deputy governor dropped away. Chloe was the latest named virus from the melt. Internationally, they were on the second time through the standardized alphabet with named viruses. Most of the illnesses that appeared when they escaped the ice and came to life again in the warming—the microorganisms and bacteria that spent entire epochs safely frozen away—had localized, seasonal, or minor effects on human life.

Romeo, eleven years earlier, was devastating to animal populations across the Australian Land Nation after becoming an epidemic. The Zhu had patient zero for the Mahmoud Pandemic twenty-nine years before that. Chloe first appeared three years earlier and it was technically a pandemic in its global reach, but its human casualty numbers were relatively low and—even while its victims suffered and would eventually die after ten to twelve months—they could not pass the illness along easily. Too many factors needed to be in place for transmission of Chloe to keep it at the front of most people's minds. Transmission required either a prolonged exposure to Chloe-infected body fluids or a fluid-to-fluid exposure such as through a blood transfusion. If that much were to occur at precisely the right temperature and humidity levels to not kill the virus and during a very short time period following the original Chloe patient's infection when the virus was most virulent and if the two individuals had a shared blood type, only then could it be transmitted.

For those who were infected with Chloe, the microorganisms took up residence in their brains tackling each of their senses first, followed by speech centers, and then it took a seemingly random trip through each individual's brain, taking down system after system, until the person eventually just stopped functioning. For some, they stopped breathing. Others suffered heart attacks or organ failure. Some lost their minds and took their own lives. By the time the virus, which looked a bit like a jellyfish in magnified depictions of it, was caught by medical scans, it was too late – too invasive to be removed without simply killing the patient even sooner. As far as medical technology had come, the human brain was still such a fragile mystery.

"How far has it progressed?"

"No sense of smell. Touch has gone in my extremities. Taste is less defined. My words get confused. They say sometimes speech and senses can go together."

"This still doesn't sound like a refugee situation."

"It was my only option."

"So, you've come here to die?" the deputy governor asked.

"I came to the Tatsu. Then they brought me here."

"To die, though." Francisco confirmed.

"Eventually, yes. I left my country with a plan to die."

Roberto stepped to a window in the small room that looked out over the port. To either side of the window, the Zoe Baja and Zoelands Concord flags hung limply in the humidity. In the distance, Cityship Tatsu IV was steadily working its way through its launch.

"I'll have Inoke set you up in quarters, Mr. Mauga. We may yet get you to the Tatsu."

CHAPTER 17
YEAR 2552

Former Baja Province
Former Northern Territory of New Hispaniola Land Nation
Former Global Union

A storm was rolling in like a wave across the eastern sky. It was the middle of the day, but it would be as dark as a starless night soon enough. Linda gathered her chickens and brought them indoors. She hadn't seen Uru in hours, not since they'd set out that morning. Linda went back outside and called to him to no avail.

They'd thoroughly salvaged through more of New Hollywood than she ever imagined they could. Their little building was stocked. Today, they had been starting their second pass and he should have been within earshot of the archives where they slept.

Thunder boomed in the distance, but much closer than she liked without knowing where Uru went. Linda returned to the building. The few steps up would take her to the level where she and the chickens stayed. A floor beyond that was the garden boxes soaking in the sun and occasional rain of the open side of the building. Maybe Uru had gone down to the level where he spent his nights.

"Uru?" she called down but got no answer.

Linda began to walk down the steps to what had become, in her mind, a sort of forbidden level, like a secret magical realm from an ancient tale. Her heart quickened as she entered the open floor below. Linda gasped. It was a collection of stages. Camera-and-light-mounted drones sat scattered on beams that lay across the top of the platform, ready to stream the sessions that went quiet months ago.

Linda had seen all of these sets before. They were the concert stages where vocal and instrumental performers were recorded for the satellite programs and it was the one type of entertainment that she and Lukas had both agreed on, able to set aside the tension in their lives for a couple of hours while they were carried away to youthful fervor and innocence on the notes of a song.

It was strange seeing the stages dark like this, but the child in her was still awestruck. She touched each one as she walked around the room, then paused in the center of some of the performance spaces and closed her eyes in a daydream. A wardrobe rack stood beside one of the sets and it made her laugh to look at the different animal costumes she recognized from the jungle fusion recordings done by the popular children's group, Fluff & Tumble. She hadn't even known they recorded in New Hollywood. Rather, she assumed they worked out of the entertainment headquarters in the Mississippi East Land Nation. Because she had no children, their music wasn't something in which she often partook. That said, the blend of natural animal sounds and drumming for which Fluff & Tumble was known, was having a commercial moment that went beyond young citizens. Certainly, the group was a part of daily life. Their tunes infected everything from advertisements to fitness programs to random people imitating their hits in the pod exchanges. As she touched one of the costumes, she remembered Uru's daughter and the gift shop bracelet by which he had to identify his dead child. A somberness came over Linda and she moved on.

As she turned toward the next stage, something caught Linda's eye, and she couldn't help but run to it. It was a gown she'd seen a dozen times as she watched and rewatched Elsie Laurita's Centennial Recordings. The singer had her own version of the

Reimaginings. While digitized instrumental classics were common for ceremonial purposes, Elsie Laurita was known for finding lyrical pieces from history and making them current. Each recording session covered a different century of remarkable music, and she went back as far as her music producers and available source materials allowed. The vocalist covered Chinese elegant music from Before Christian Era, traditional African music that used to be played with iron bells in the fifteenth century, early AD sacred music, sixteenth century Italian opera, twentieth century jazz and blues from the Americas, twenty-first century Latinx fusions, new concertinas from after the melt, and the Global Union standards.

Linda had loved all eight of Elsie Laurita's sessions and here she was touching the gown that the singer had donned in the performances. Taking in the garment, she could picture the woman who'd worn it: her dirty blonde curls and hazel eyes, her petite curvy frame that somehow managed to produce a sound bigger than her body should allow, and the way the singer would tense up her arms and face when she was really wailing, like she was giving her whole body to the performance. The times spent watching her sessions on the program feeds were those when Linda had felt most human.

The top of Elsie Laurita's dress was a fitted bodice of turquoise lace and partially pearled stones formed into a pink floral mosaic. The skirt was made up of layered silks in blues and greens, and a strip of rose-pink lighting had been wired along the entire shape of the dress and up along both sides of a thigh-high, geometric slit. She took the dress off of the rack and was shocked at just how light it was. She fully expected it would have a weight as exorbitant as the design, but it was airy by comparison to those expectations.

Like a child who couldn't resist the cucumber ice served at province picnics, Linda eagerly hungered to put the dress on. She hung it back up and stripped out of her clothes, dropping them right there onto the floor where she stood. Then, she took the dress down, stepped into the gown, pulled it up onto her body, and began to seal the snaps along the back, as high as her hands allowed her to do so. When her hands could reach no further, she was surprised to find other fingers there to help her finish. She froze, allowing Uru to help. Linda had only ever felt his fingers when handing him eggs or taking something else from him. One time, when planting carrots, they'd brushed one another. She didn't realize it until now, but this was the only time, other than those instances, that they ever touched. This touch was the first of affection. And yet, Linda knew the feel of his hands and fingers. They were already familiar.

Feeling ashamed, she turned to face Uru.

"She was my favorite," Linda said, running her hands along the dress that hugged her body, her way of sheepishly trying to explain why she was wearing a gown from the forbidden floor.

Uru looked at Linda. He was sizing her up in a very different way than he had when they'd met on that first day and he couldn't figure out what that way meant. His cheeks flushed. Suddenly and unexpectedly, Linda took his breath away. He quickly bolted from her and ran over to one of the stages. He pulled back a curtain to reveal a full-length mirror, turned to Linda, and smiled to beckon her over.

She hadn't seen a complete image of herself in months. In scavenging, she and Uru had found items to have makeshift dressing rooms and one of those items was a small mirror she used to wash her face, put her hair up, or brush her teeth, but this mirror reflected her entire body and in the kind of attire that she never would have worn even in her life before the Great Quake.

Linda had put on weight since the day of the evacuations, but she carried it well. Her arms were strong and toned. Her power industry tatua did not stand out as strikingly as it once had because her skin had darkened from exposure to the sun. Her curves were refined and alluring. She blinked at herself and was a bit embarrassed at realizing she had been staring before that moment. She found beauty in the mirror's image and she wasn't alone.

Uru stood behind her, staring just as intently. When she blinked, it pulled him out of his own daze. He took Linda's hair down and draped it over her shoulders. Instead of holding onto the hair tie, he pulled his own hair into a bun on the top of his head. With his thick hair out of his face, his strong jawline and dark eyes were both accentuated. He too had put on healthy weight since they had met.

He rested his hands on Linda's shoulders and she could not prevent herself from tracing back from his fingertips to his body with her eyes. He was strong again. Her heart fluttered.

"You look so elegant," he said sincerely.

Linda laughed nervously.

"Elsie had the most glamorous wardrobe," he added as though it was the dress and not the woman wearing it who had drawn his gaze. He dropped his hands and sat on the edge of the stage. "She was my favorite performer, too. And she was very kind."

"I keep forgetting that you knew her," Linda said sitting next to him.

"I helped her find all of her music, not just on that day of the Great Quake. Well, not the music that she would record, but the stuff she used to make it. The recordings from the original centuries. Or, in the case of the really old compositions, the written music . . . digitized files of it, anyway."

"That's so vee!" Linda said and winced as the word escaped her mouth. She was acting like a teenager.

Smiling, "I'm the archive guy. It's what I did. She was my biggest job. It was a nice break from my usual entering of all the Earth-Before-the-Melt files."

"I love her centennial recordings. Especially the Chinese and American recordings. Oh! The GU standards, too."

"You probably just named her three most diverse sessions"

Laughing at herself, "I know. It's just that she could do anything with her voice."

"She made it out after the quake. She went to the Mississippi East Land Nation. Before the evacuations, they played endless broadcasts. It was a huge spectacle the way the GU evacuated the New Hollywood survivors. Didn't you see any of the newsfeeds?"

"Mostly, I was in a medical center until the evacuations."

Shaking his head at himself, "I'm an idiot."

"It's okay. It's so great to know that Elsie Laurita will still get to perform!"

"You know she didn't actually want to be a performer?"

Slapping Uru's arm puckishly, "What? That's crazy."

"Don't get me wrong. She loved the music, but she would have been perfectly happy just sharing that with a small community or her family. She wanted to work in the hospitality industries or in botany – wanted to go to the Pacific Islands. The GU selected her for entertainment."

"Well, they knew what she could do for the world. It's where she belonged to make the greatest impact." Linda didn't even realize when her statements were direct quotes from Global Union propaganda.

"Maybe," Uru said not wanting to dismiss her. "She just didn't feel it was the right impact for her."

"Sometimes," Linda added, "others see the value in us that we fail to recognize in ourselves."

At these words, Uru just stared at Linda. He pondered the value she perceived in herself.

Bashful under his gaze, "I can't imagine the Reimaginings without her," Linda fumbled.

Teasingly, "That's a mouthful," Uru smiled.

Linda shook her head and rolled her eyes.

"She definitely did her research to put her own spin on the music. Want to see what she chose from?" he asked.

"You mean the Earth-Before-the-Melt music?"

"Yeah."

"Is it weird?"

Laughing, "I don't think so. I think, when you hear it, you can sort of understand from where all the sounds in her songs came." Uru stood and offered a hand to help Linda up, as well. She took it as they began to walk away from the stage, and he continued in his musical education. "There's not really anything new in music or writing or anything creative, really," he said confidently as he was clearly in his element. "It's just new artists putting new spins on it so that the people of their day can relate to it and connect with it."

"Won't we have to use our power to hear the music?"

"We can afford it. We don't need the atmosphere fan today with mother nature's wind out there in the storm. What do you think?"

"Yes," she said. "I want to hear it. All of it!"

Uru took Linda behind all of the stages to room after room filled with the digital records of music, sports, art, and entertainment from the history of man. Thousands of artifacts from the EBM world were recorded on digital drives. Footage from great sporting events throughout history, concerts, plays, paintings, two-dimensional movies, and so many more things than Linda ever imagined could still exist.

They walked to different banks of files marked with dates and flags of countries that no longer existed. Some of those countries were lost to the melt and others fell as all political civilizations eventually fall. At the marked posts between banks, Uru would key in a few strokes to pull up a song from the classical era, the republic era, and so many other periods in time. The song would explode in the room, filling every echoey crevasse with melody. The music was vastly diverse and yet, with Uru's guidance, Linda found herself hearing similar instruments, tunes, rhythms, or other musical features that she'd always thought were unique to the music she knew from today.

After the digital archives, they came to another room that stopped Linda in her tracks. What she saw was not merely digitized saves of Earth's creative and artistic history; they were the actual objects and relics saved over time. Books printed on paper, paintings on real canvases, round discs of different colors and sizes, some of them with ridged lines on them, and all of which contained music, comedy, or stories. Hours passed as the two strolled through the creative history of humankind.

"I know it's materialistic, maybe even selfish, but I just couldn't leave it all. The GU didn't come to salvage it after the Great Quake. I just sort of stayed and this stuff gave me something of the world we had . . . the world I had."

Linda turned to look at him. He was still broken, and she had a longing to help put him back together. Thunder boomed heavily and the room faded to a dark gray, drawing any remaining light away from Uru in his depression. The storm was raging on outside of their walls, and the drops pounded heavily onto the partially collapsed roof of the building.

"I have something!" Linda said suddenly and she ran past Uru, holding up the length of her gown as she moved so as not to step on the fabric.

She flew up the stairs, dug through her crates, and returned to Uru shortly afterward.

"It's an education pad," she said proudly and slightly out of breath. "I found it on my way here. It still works and you could fully power it. It won't hold the physical things, but you can probably fit most of these other files on it. I know power and storage pretty well and most of this stuff in here has a tiny file size. They didn't used to have dimensions or interactive programming," she continued speaking as plainly in her knowledge as Uru had been in his. "Terabytes were considered colossal back then. Could you imagine? Anyway, what you have here," she indicated by gesturing toward the digital files, "it's all pretty small."

Linda held the pad out to Uru. He grabbed it, leaving his hand on hers for some time before taking the device from her. Once he had it, he looked down at the pad and began to tremble. He broke into tears and collapsed to the ground, hugging the device to his chest.

The reaction was unexpected following their afternoon of amusement. Linda cautiously put her hand on his shoulder as a gesture of comfort.

"I was in the riverbed," Uru whispered between tear-filled, painful cries. "I'm so sorry. I knew the storm was coming. I thought it might flood. I'm sorry. I'm so sorry."

At first, she was confused, still tying his emotion to the gift of the education pad. It took Linda a moment to understand what he meant. When she realized it at last, her face dropped. It was his guilt that was being expressed. He had almost broken their unspoken agreement to live.

"It's okay," she said. "You came back."

Linda sat next to him and pulled his head against her chest. He cried and he curled up on her like a child.

"Shhh," she said as she stroked his head affectionately.

Linda lay back and kept Uru's body against her. His sobs grew quieter and further between until her friend fell deeply asleep, possibly for the first time in months. She held him close, long past the time when her arm went to sleep, through hours of slumber, afraid her movement would wake him from his much-needed rest and, more importantly, peace.

CHAPTER 18
YEAR 2908

Pacific Sea Route
Cityship Tatsu IV
Cityship Regatta

Travel to the diplomatic level of the Tatsu was an adventure. It took a combination of ladder-like stairs, elevators, moving walkways, and long walks to weave through the ship to their assigned quarters. Dr. Bradley was brought to his door, then Miriam was led to what would be her room for the next few days. They would be taking a leisurely pace to the capital of the Pacific Islands Land Nation.

Her assigned quarters were decorated in a simple, but elegant manner. She had small, oval-shaped windows that looked out to the other ships in the port and would eventually look out to the Pacific Ocean. Her linens were white and fluffy and made of natural fabrics. She had a bureau in which to store her clothing and a bio-safe for any important items. A small box contained delicacies made on the Tatsu. Most preciously, there was a colorful art piece, created by hand, not digitally, by Tatsian students, welcoming the governor to their city. It was a watercolor painting depicting dandelions of yellow surrounded by whisps of white floating through the air.

Miriam was quite impressed by the writing and art of the students who had created this gift, and even more so once she realized, as she read through some of the comments signed on the back, that these weren't just any students. Rather, they were the very students who had met her two years earlier at their Captain's Day event. They would all be a little bit older now and their work made that fact abundantly clear. She found the special touch to be very moving.

Miriam had some time to pass before the launch procedures finished, so she put on comfortable walking shoes and ensured that the sound and projection features were active on her digifile to let her know when the captain was available to begin their formal itinerary. She pulled on a light pair of sleeves that Inoke must have slipped into her tube. He knew her well. The ship did feel cool to her. Miriam smiled as she headed for her door. Immediately outside her quarters stood a sailor assigned as her escort. She snapped to attention as Miriam stepped out.

"Governor," she said. "May I escort you somewhere?"

"Yes. I'd love to see more of the ship."

"Where would you like to start?" the sailor said, before reminding Miriam, "All of the operations areas are off limits during launching and mooring, but we could go anywhere else."

"How about your day? Walk me through it, please."

"Oui, Ma'am," said the sailor.

Miriam nodded knowingly at the response. The five known fleet families of Earth were organized crime cartels with territories on the waterways of the world. They chose the languages spoken aboard their vessels, typically an EBM language that they kept alive. The cityships, on the other hand, shared common terminology. The French "Yes," was typical language for GU, Zoe, and cityship sea workers across the globe. Because French-speaking Canada was one of the first places in the world to be lost to the melts, they were also first to make existence on the water a chosen lifestyle. They brought their language with them and all who followed adopted it. Hearing the word "Oui" out of the mouth of the crewperson who greeted Miriam was a treat to the governor's ears. There was another accent mixed into her speech and listening to her speak even that single word was melodic.

The sailor was a tall, slender woman with high cheekbones and tight, closely drawn curls of a black as dark as her skin. Her uniform was perfection at every crease, button, and lay of a seam. Her cover was tucked neatly under an arm and, unlike the other crewmembers Miriam glimpsed, she wore sharp gloves of white with the Tatsu flag embroidered on one and the Cityship Regatta emblem on the other. The palms of the gloves appeared to be digital, likely to read the scans of visiting Global Union diplomats, a system they'd used for hundreds of years in some shape or form. The sailor managed to move with both precision and grace.

"What do I call you, Sailor?" Miriam asked while walking briskly to keep up with the stride of the leggy crewperson.

"Ensign Aida Bintou-Keita," said the sailor proudly, even as Miriam's eyes involuntarily widened upon hearing the name of one of the world's five fleet families.

"Yes, they are my family," the ensign added shamelessly. "No one can rewrite where they came from. Nor should they." she added.

"That, Ensign Bintou-Keita, is something I understand," Miriam said.

"I thought you might, Governor," she paused for effect, "Heirlinda."

Miriam started her tour with a smile. Her escort took her to the cityship center, where Aida got her morning breakfast with other security team members in a "downtown" of sorts that was as bustling as any she'd seen on land. They dodged the ensign's fellow runners who were doing laps on the health deck.

"Morning, Aida!" called one as they ran by leaving behind a rush of air.

The same deck also housed fitness facilities, medical offices, nutritionists, and other specialty wellness centers.

They passed through a museum of sorts on the way to the education complex. The history of the Cityship Regatta covered the walls in panels of projection screens. Three-dimensional photos of

Tatsu Mageo and his eventual ExO, Peter Kimathi, a tribute to sea-mining vessels, visual recordings of the treaty signing that united the twelve cityships and two seasteads into the Cityship Regatta, and dozens of other artifacts. In the center of the room, enclosed in a well-lit display case, was a glove of rubber and silicone with some wires showing through the well-worn fabric.

"What's this?" Miriam asked.

"A credit-copying glove. Came from the first cityship. Nobody's sure whose it is, exactly, but probably one of Tatsu's own crew aboard the Mining Vessel PS-1707."

"What's a credit-copying glove?"

"To put it politely, ma'am, it's a theft device."

"That is polite?" asked the governor. "What's the politically incorrect term?"

"DCA glove."

"And DCA means?" Miriam prompted.

"Dead Citizen's Account, Governor."

"See? We can speak plainly with one another," she teased.

"Yes, ma'am. Same technology, give or take human and engineering advances, is still used by the fleet families."

Miriam flinched again.

"So I hear," the sailor said with a perfectly straight face and Miriam wasn't certain if she had built some sort of humorous rapport or if Aida was being serious.

Ensign Bintou-Keita showed the governor where she took her son to school each day. At every level of the education complex, there was a fully staffed and occupied learning center. They had breakout areas for children from age four to sixteen and advanced teaching through age twenty-two, though many opted out at age sixteen to go into fields of study not taught aboard the Tatsu.

The cityship's entertainment district included interactive theatres, virtual gaming clubs, pubs, restaurants, and live performers. Another deck was dedicated to their teams for soccer, lacrosse, cricket, and springball, each with its own field or court, as well as seating for crowds. There were work centers, and government offices, and facilities maintenance, and crew management areas.

There were houses, and service providers, and retail locations. There were gardens, and playgrounds, and recreation centers. While she'd been aboard cityships before, it never ceased to draw awe from Miriam when she realized their names were appropriate. They really were cities – entirely functioning economies and homes and communities. Nothing about Cityship Tatsu was any less a civilization than what she led on Zoe Baja.

"And Aida just randomly gets assigned as her escort?" Kate said in a loud whisper.

"So?" said the captain.

"Ensign Bintou-Keita?"

"I've got nothing to hide," Mik said as Governor Heirlinda entered the visiting diplomats' lounge.

"Governor," ExO Murphy nodded as she exited with a glare to Captain Ridgelin.

"Afternoon!" Mik chimed. "How are you feeling?"

"I'm a bit dizzy. Are the waters still rough?"

"Not terribly, to be honest. Some turbulence expected later tonight, he said. I can have my medics hook you up with an anti-nausea dissolving patch if you like. Might make you a bit tired but could help strengthen those sea legs. Don't need you getting boke," he said.

"Boke?'

"Yea. I don't want you throwing up on the negotiating table."

Miriam's expression showed her momentary consideration of the offer, but she responded, "I don't think I'd better opt for the patch but shie shie. I need my wits more than my legs. Maybe I should visit the water closet before the sessions begin."

"Tell you what," Mik began as he used a keypad to open a door for Miriam. "Captain's head. You can get into any one of these you find across the ship. Just type in 1-7-0-7."

"The mining vessel, right?"

"I see you've been visiting my museum."

"I figured it was only fair," said the governor. "You saw mine, after all."

"You show me yours; I show you mine."

"Something like that," she said.

Once Miriam returned, "Care for some lunch before we have to be diplomats?" Mik asked.

"I think it better be something simple," she said with a hand to her stomach.

"I wonder if Workship Pan has docked," Mik said typing something on the display in the room. "They have," he said, pleased. "Allow me to bring you to the bay deck, Governor," he said as he offered his arm.

Miriam and Mik made their way to the bay deck. It was surreal seeing all of the sideships encircling the entire level of the cityship. It appeared much like a port, except that, below and beyond the workships and dayships were the hull and foundation of the Tatsu.

The civilian side of the deck had an appearance much like that of a neighborhood on land. Each of the family dayship bays was decorated like a yard would be in Zoe Baja. Lights and chairs faced inward toward the center of the Tatsu and the track-like pathway connecting them. Miriam could picture the families gathering and joining in conversation with one another at the end of the day. Several families had their seaside nets dropped and their bay doors opened to let in the fresh air. Some were enjoying lunch in those settings and Miriam equated those meals to a Baja cookout.

The workships were more like the restaurant and commercial districts of larger cities. Bright colors and signage stood out on the vessels used for everything from eateries to water taxis to cargo shipping. While the workships did much of their business on the waters of the Pacific, they were just as likely to conduct their activities right on the Tatsu.

A lovely, pink-skinned woman waved Captain Ridgelin and Miriam to her bay, "Fresh scallops, Captain," she beckoned. "Recent harvest came of age."

"Aye...tempting," Mik said with thickly accented affection. "Introducing me guest to the Workship Pan, though, today," he said.

They continued to walk past other storefronts until they found themselves in front of a ship that looked nothing like the others. It appeared to be made of wooden planks, the likes of a ship many generations older than any other in the Cityship Tatsu's flotilla.

"Madam Governor," Mik indicated the ship with a welcoming gesture to the old vessel, "the Workship Pan."

As the two of them entered the bay, Devon Cas was exiting.

"Captain," greeted the green-hued drone operator of the cityship.

"Devon, are you on schedule for our retrofitting project with the sideships?"

"Oui, Sir, mish mushkela," Cas replied. "Tugs are done. Started the workships last week."

Devon, Mik's nonbinary lieutenant who led audiovisual operations, had chosen a green tinted UV protectant dye for their skin. They had hair of the same color with blue tips. Their clothing was typically black and utilitarian to allow quick and flexible movement throughout the ship without showing the grease that inevitably found its way onto clothing while in those many nooks and crannies.

"Devon here is working their arse off getting the Tatsu fully equipped with specialized drones," Captain Ridgelin bragged to Miriam.

"Doesn't the ship already have drones?" she asked

"The cityship does, sure. But not all of her sideships," they responded. "And these drones," Cas continued, "Are going to be programmable. If we need them to be cameras, scanners, lasers—"

"Lasers?" Miriam questioned.

"For cutting away obstacles," Mik said with a nod to Devon.

Cas paused before going on, "Of course. Well, whatever we need, really. We still have the Tatsu drones, but by equipping all of the sideships with them, too, we really expand what we can do."

"How long will it take to finish an undertaking of this size?" Miriam asked.

Devon looked at Mik, who nodded his approval to allow them to answer. "Ten years was the proposal, but I'm aiming for less," they said. "I have a goal of seven."

"What do you recommend today?" Captain Ridgelin asked, changing the subject with a hand gesture indicating Workship Pan.

"Sweet potato bread. Rich and hearty," they smiled. "Disculpas," Cas saluted as they began to walk away. "No rest for the AV Ops Lieutenant looking to shave three years off their work!"

"Don't let us keep you," the captain saluted back. The gesture felt more friendly than it did formal.

A dark-haired woman exited the workship at that time.

"Let me guess," she said, "they recommended the sweet potato bread?"

"How did you know?" Mik said.

"Devon has a habit of recommending what I've just run out of!" she laughed. "Any chance I can interest you in squash cakes instead?

"Are they portable? I'm bringing the governor to the aquarium."

"I can package a couple up for you, Captain," she said.

Miriam and Mik walked the length of the Workship Pan as they waited for their food. The vessel barely looked seaworthy.

"How on Earth is this thing still floating?" Miriam asked in awe.

"Nothing but the sheer will of its owners if you ask me," Mik said. "I offered to have it updated for them. They are a big part of our community on the bay deck. But they insisted this ship would last as long as it was meant to last and if it ever went down, it would be while working for the Tatsians aboard this ship."

"Proud people," Miriam said.

"Stubborn more like," Mik sighed.

"I heard that, Captain!" the old woman said as she exited the Pan with a brown paper bag.

Mik pulled out a digifile to pay her, but she swiped it away.

"You know your credits are no good here!" she exclaimed while presenting her cheek.

Mik kissed the woman's cheek, and she gave him the bag of goodies with a wink and a nod at the governor. She didn't care that Miriam had seen the gestures.

After the bay deck, Mik took Miriam deep into the belly of the Tatsu, and past all of the workings in the mechanical rooms. It wasn't the first time that Miriam had seen the aquarium of the Tatsu, but it took her breath away every time.

A fifty-yard portion of the bottom two decks of the port side of Cityship Tatsu IV was a stretch of clear glass. They called it the aquarium, but—unlike the enclosed ecosystems of wildlife hundreds of years earlier—the ship was the enclosed ecosystem, and the wildlife freely swam outside of it.

The captain and governor sat on the floor, enjoyed their small squash cakes, and watched as the Tatsu moved through waving plants and colorful schools of fish. A large stingray floated past them, much further off the bottom than the creatures usually swam. The entire scene was serene, and it was just the calm Miriam needed to carry her through the first part of the negotiations. She leaned against Mik restfully and the two let the time pass in silence.

The rest of the leaders' day was spent in meetings with Captain Ridgelin's ministry team. She met the Minister of Power, Christina Feldman; Minister of Housing, Danielle Soto; and Minister of Ship Architecture, Shawn Klementa. In addition, there were a handful of other names and titles Miriam couldn't keep straight. She didn't need to so long as she remembered their roles and allegiances.

Dr. Bradley expected everybody to share his enthusiasm for the unique hydrocell engineering, and he wasn't accustomed to the level of convincing required for more traditional politicians.

Feldman initially expressed an interest in the new battery, but then shared his fear at the number of jobs lost in loading, securing, maintaining, and unloading the older, larger batteries. Klementa believed that, while they could reclaim a huge portion of the ship for rebuilding, a full restructuring and reordering would be necessary and the construction, though ultimately good, would actually be a hindrance on the ship for months or even a full year. Soto was concerned about the tight housing during construction, as well as retrofitting the new hydrocells in their oldest quarters. Then, the Minister of Travel, Miriam had forgotten his name – Raji or Ravi or? Where was Inoke when she needed him? He was wondering what the cityship's part was in all of this. Would their route be affected? They preferred to be the benevolent neutral party between the GU and Zoe, and this could change all of that. Would they still be welcome in GU ports if they were part of a Zoe-led alliance?

In short, the ministers all saw dollar signs and votes where Jacob Bradley saw only human advancement. Miriam helped diplomatically where the scientific details weren't convincing to them all, but—by the end of the day—the normally energetic engineer was spent with frustration and exhaustion. To Jacob, it all made such perfect sense. It did not compute with him why the rest of them weren't getting it.

Miriam excused the scientist from having to join her for the formal Unity Dinner being held that evening, and the man's relief was immediate. The introvert in him, his true character when the subject wasn't one he knew well, gratefully returned to his quarters to rest and turn in early. He would have to present all over again when they met more leaders at the Pacific Islands Land Nation.

CHAPTER 19
YEAR 2552

Former Baja Province
Former Northern Territory of New Hispaniola Land Nation
Former Global Union

Linda was making tea when Uru joined her in the morning. She was wearing a simple t-shirt and cotton pants with a pair of hiking shoes they'd salvaged from the wreckage.

"Good morning," she said when he appeared in the doorway, exiting the archives. She smiled at him from beside the fire and held his gaze for just a moment before looking away uncomfortably.

Uru continued watching her form move in the morning sun, maternally going about the day's tasks as if nothing had changed between them.

Everything had changed.

At last, "You took off the dress?" he asked.

"Not exactly practical. I put it back on the wardrobe rack next to her stage. Care for some tea?" she offered.

"That would be nice. I stored all of the files on the pad. Thank you, by the way."

"Already? You work fast."

"I woke energized," he replied with a smile.

She nodded in understanding as she passed him a cup of tea.

"And each full block of files has a single download code. It's a quick task. I just needed the one missing piece and you had it."

Qui-quiri-qui! Hank crowed.

"Oh hush!" Linda said. "He's up, already. We know you can crow. Good for you!"

Uru laughed. "How long will you keep talking to them like people?"

"Does it bother you?"

Shaking his head playfully, "No. I like it, actually."

"We have a lot of stuff, now," Linda started tentatively. "I was thinking that maybe we should make some sort of plan. Like, what do we do with all of our supplies? Should we find a pod to try and explore more of the province? That sort of thing."

"I know where there's a pod. A few actually."

"Why didn't you say anything?" she asked.

"Because I don't know anything about them. I can power up my floor with a couple of high-efficiency solar panels and charge my batteries. That's something I'd been rigging up for years. But I'm no good with pods."

"But I am! That's what I did! I worked with pods as part of the power industries. Not that it's been of much use these days."

She realized now that she'd often done most of the listening, while rarely sharing about her own past.

"What good is a cable pod with no cables?" Uru asked.

"Because every pod comes equipped with surface wheels. It's a failsafe." Linda shook her head thinking of the absurdity of the design. Then, as if it dawned on her for the first time, she added, "I guess maybe they always knew that there was a possibility the cable system could collapse."

"I don't find that comforting," Uru said.

Shaking off her own negative thoughts. "It's very comforting. The GU really tried to think of everything. They learned from so many civilizations before them."

"Well, that's a load of waste," he retorted.

"What are you talking about?" Even as she said the words, Linda wasn't certain whether they came from her own mind or they had been trained into her. "All of our needs are met by the Global Union. Food, shelter, work. It didn't used to be that way. Life before the collapse of One Net, Earth-Before-the-Melt, I wouldn't have even had work. I'm not qualified to do anything."

As Linda spoke, she seemed to shrink.

"That's insane!" he exclaimed. His temperature rose, and his skin turned red. "The very fact that you believe that is proof that you're a victim of GU brainwashing."

Linda pursed her lips and swayed her head back and forth vigorously. "You're just saying that. I didn't pass the aptitudes for anything else. I'm lucky I wasn't assigned to toxic cleanup efforts."

Uru put down his teacup and stood to face Linda. "You lived without power and traveled across fifty kilometers of rubble by yourself!" He stepped right in Linda's path. "You!" he exclaimed, putting his hands on her arms. "A woman the GU had convinced she couldn't do anything. A woman who apparently still believes it!"

"Some people really can't do anything, though. Before the Global Union, did you know that people could actually starve in the streets! And think about it! That's when they still had paper and metal money instead of credits. Citizens could actually pass a person dying on the street and not even drop him or her a yuan to make it to the end of the day."

"I'm not trying to fight about intentions, Linda. I think everybody would agree that part of EBM is pretty messed up. But if you're such a Global Union cheerleader, why did you stay here?"

Linda paused. There were times she still asked herself the same question. "It wasn't so much the GU. It was me," Linda poured more tea into their mismatched cups and sat back down, compelling Uru to do the same.

"Tell me more."

"My mom died before I even took the aptitudes. Dad, he wasn't very good to her. And when she died, he took it pretty hard. He'd already been so messed up, so taking it hard meant he decided to change. He did something different. I don't know. Maybe he'd dug himself so far down that he finally reached bottom, so the only option left for him was to start climbing up. He stopped going to the vice lounges, became a hard worker, and turned things around. Then he had a chance to transition to a new employ, but he had to leave Baja Province. He told me that sometimes you have to leave a life behind in order to fully commit to a new one. He needed a new geography. It was my aptitude year, so the neighbor family, Lukas's family, they took me in to finish my schooling and my Dad left."

"I'm sorry."

"Don't be. It was right for him. He's still alive, I think. He was doing well and became a great contributor the last I heard from him."

Linda realized that she may never know if her Dad continued to do well. He probably assumed she was dead. The last time they spoke was more than a month before the Great Quake.

Blinking away the thought, she went on. "He was right about one thing, anyway. You can't make a new life in an old place. When I sat there at the zip chopper port, looking at all of the evacuation transports, I realized that the place I'd always known was actually not the one where I was standing, but the one that was getting on those choppers. All of the people and systems and networks that made me who I am were leaving."

Linda bit her lip as she reflected inward. She fumbled to make her words relay her thoughts.

"I understand what my father meant. He needed a new landscape to be a new person. For him, that meant a new place as a new home. For me it's a new perspective in my old home. Maybe, I can be somebody here."

Gesturing dramatically to the air, "There you go again! I have mentioned that you walked, and sometimes probably crawled, all the while dragging a broken wheeled cart, across half of the province all alone, right?"

"I had my chickens."

"Chickens you rescued!"

He calmed his body language and made eye contact with her. "Linda, you already are somebody."

"But remember how you found me?" she asked. "I was a mess."

"You were stronger than how you found me. You rescued me, too, Linda."

She swallowed her tea and pondered Uru's words. Maybe she was already a new person for the new place. Now, it was time to figure out what the hell they were doing with the new place.

The trembling jerked all of them from their sleep. Linda instinctively snatched up the crate containing Olive and her two incubating hatchlings in one hand. She scooped up Hank in her other arm while she ran down the steps. She nearly tripped over Uru who was running up from his level. He had the education pad in one hand and an overstuffed bag in the other. Together, they all bolted from the building as it shivered in the quake. Linda didn't remember the Great Quake for comparison, but this one was by far the strongest she recalled experiencing.

Uru helped her up as she tripped over the debris skitting and scatting across the ground like dice in a cup. She returned the favor just a few strides later. The two dropped beneath a wall of rubbish, protected from the stones and panes of glass that fell to the ground around them. Then, a rumbling boom, like an explosion, echoed in the air, followed by the whoosh of a cloud of dust so mighty it pushed them to the ground. Linda landed on Olive's crate. Then two more explosions occurred, and another after those, each followed by its own rushing dust cloud. One final boom, larger than all the others pushed her body like a tumbleweed along the ground.

Her ears were ringing, and her eyes burned, when she finally rolled back over. She must have passed out. Uru sat next to her with the chickens in his lap. All of them were beside the pod hauler they'd brought back to their site days ago. The large vehicle had provided some protection from the collapsing buildings. A full load of private pods was on the large transport bed. They'd outfitted the hauler with mountain-terrain wheels and solar batteries.

"We lost one of the babies," Uru said, predicting Linda's first question.

She looked at Olive's crate and saw one egg cracked with bits of moistened down poking out. Uru held Olive, Hank, and the other fertilized egg in his lap. Olive's feathers were coated with dust, making her appear light brown in color. Hank fared a bit better. Either that or his plumage was better at camouflaging the dirt. The two chickens pecked at one another like parents picking crumbs out of a child's hair. Uru was coated in dust, as well. His raven black hair appeared gray, and the dirt had settled into fine lines on his face. The sight helped Linda imagine what he might look like as an old man and, if this view was any indication, she hoped to see the real thing one day. As she looked upon him, she noticed a small droplet of blood making its way out of his hairline and down his forehead. Her eyes widened and she reached out toward him.

Waving her hand away casually and pressing his fingers into his head. "It's nothing. I already checked," he said. "Everyone else is okay, other than some scrapes and bruises. I had to move you and you seem fine, too, but I imagine you have a bit of a headache."

Linda sat slowly up, making herself aware of her whole body as she did so, assuring herself that she wasn't injured. She opened and closed her mouth to attempt to force a yawn because sounds were a bit muffled. Then, she turned to peer at the scene behind her, looking under the bed of the pod hauler and between the pods on top of it. New Hollywood looked the same as all of the other clusters she'd been through. Piles of rubble. Nothing more.

She turned back to Uru who gave a half-hearted nod, "I guess we'll see if you're right."

"About?" she asked, then pushed her hands against her ears. Everything was quiet.

"Me, too," Uru said, pointing to his ears. "It'll pass in time. Happened to me a few months ago when the cable system fell. That was one hell of a boom. I thought I was deaf. One day, my hearing was just back. I listened to Elsie Laurita in the archives that day."

"What will we see if I'm right about?" she shouted.

"New place, new life?" Looking at the fallen buildings, "If that wasn't a sign of goodbye, I don't know what could be."

Linda looked at Uru for a moment and allowed the stifled words to set in. Until the ringing in her ears stopped, her hearing was just a few beats behind the conversation. Finally, she smiled to him.

"We'll talk when we hear better!" he shouted pointing to his own ears.

Linda nodded deeply, as if trying to turn up the volume of her nod. Uru huffed out a laugh.

He gently took the chickens off of his lap. He secured Olive in an unbroken crate with the good egg set into the enclosure with her in a makeshift nest. Hank went into a second crate. Linda stayed seated on the ground for the few minutes it took to stow the birds. She stretched and rubbed her body, ensuring everything bent and worked the way it should.

When finished with Hank and Olive, Uru helped her up and they each wiped the other off. Linda moved slowly over Uru's arms as she cleared away the dirt, subconsciously feeling his muscles as she traced over them. When she dusted the dirt from Uru's face, she found herself mesmerized by the lines of his cheeks and forehead and felt a sudden rush of affection wash over her. She realized she was staring at him, and she allowed her eyes to travel to his, where she discovered he was staring back. Uru had paused over parts of her body with the same attention as that which she had allowed for his shoulders and biceps. They held the glance for a moment. Then, Linda nervously laughed and put her hands into his hair. She ruffled through it, sending dust down on both of them and Uru joined, doing the same to her head. They finished cleaning one another off and permitted the carnal thirst to pass.

The rest of the morning was spent loading what was salvageable and finished with Uru's large bag. Eventually, their hearing had returned to a point that conversation was less awkward.

"Well, I haven't seen the coast," Uru began, "and, based on the fact that the GU kept the southern docks operating longer than any other area, that's probably as good a place as any to make our way toward. Some higher lands up north, but not great for year-round growing."

Uru shifted his eyes along the length of the pod hauler and nodded affirmingly at the hefty tires of the vehicle. "I figure we travel east to the coast, continue southward all along the shore, and set up at the port down there. We've stocked every one of these pods on this hauler.

"I know," Linda said, but she was sure he was saying these things out loud to justify the departure for himself and not for her.

"We've got food, clothing, batteries," he went on, nodding with each item he checked off his mental list. "We have a handful of solar panels, supplies, your pets."

"My chickens," she said smiling.

"Your chickens," he laughed back. Then, he looked at Linda. "And each other."

"And each other," she repeated.

"So, let's figure out what the new world looks like, shall we?"

Linda climbed up into the driver's seat of their hauler. She was the more experienced of the two with vehicular management. She waited in the seat while, behind her, taking in the flattened skyline of his former home, Uru searched for words that never came. Good-bye had happened long ago. This was just the acceptance stage. He was quiet when he joined Linda in the cab of the hauler. She didn't ask anything. He took a deep steadying breath, and they began to drive eastward.

Linda's eyes were fixed forward, and Uru's never looked back.

Most of their travels toward the southwest docks, the long way around by going first to the east coast, revealed the same discoveries they'd already experienced in all of the other areas of the province. Primarily there was debris with an occasional useful treasure. They grew their flock of chickens and even found goats to add to their farm stock in their travels. By the time they reached the southeast docks, they would have a full farm. And that had better be soon because transporting all of the critters in pods on a hauler was getting more and more difficult. All the difficulty felt worth it, though.

The two former citizens shared stories of their lives in the GU, childhood memories, and their favorite tales and jokes. When their power allowed, Uru charged the education pad and introduced Linda to his favorite music, the originals that had inspired Elsie Laurita's Nineteenth Century Centennial Recordings. The blues and jazz of Duke Ellington, Ella Fitzgerald, Tommy Dorsey, Glen Miller, and Billie Holiday at first felt too raw for Linda, but eventually they grew on her.

There were hard times when Uru spoke of his children and wife. And just as hard when Linda talked about the way she and Lukas had fallen into disarray and she had ultimately fallen into abuse.

Linda got better at growing things and Uru got better at managing the chickens; including the fertilized egg that had survived the final New Hollywood quake. She became another hen they called Elsie. The others had names that Uru had decided were interchangeable as he couldn't ever remember them, and Linda mixed them up like a parent calling the wrong child's name.

They made plans to move into the zip chopper hangar when they reached it. They would travel a bit each day on the hauler, release two of the pods—one for each of them—while the hauler and other pods charged, and then return each night with some stories and supplies. Occasionally, one of them would find an alcoholic spirit that they would enjoy while they shared those stories. Of course, their tolerances had waned significantly since the Great Quake, so those nights were often followed by rough mornings.

One night, Uru didn't come back before dark as he'd done every other time. Linda returned her pod, took one of the others that was mostly charged, and made her way in the direction he had set to explore that day. After several kilometers, just as she was about to turn back, she spotted a fire burning in the distance. She exited her pod and made her way toward the light. The sight before Linda washed away all their plans like a mudslide.

CHAPTER 20
YEAR 2908

Pacific Sea Route
Cityship Tatsu IV
Cityship Regatta

Miriam was not a person who got girlishly giddy.

It simply wasn't her style to gush or giggle. But, when Mik arrived at her door in his full-service uniform ready to escort her to the Unity Dinner, her heart leapt, and she felt certain that the flushing in her wide-eyed face had given her away as surely as though she had done both. The fitted uniform made the captain positively cotisuelto. It accentuated Mik's muscular physique and presented him with an air of power.

"Ensign," Mik said, "You're excused. I'll contact you when you need to resume your security for the governor."

"Captain," Bintou-Keita curtly nodded while her feet snapped to attention. "Governor," she said in salutation to Miriam before exiting in a stiff march down the corridor.

Once she was gone, Mik was able to become Miriam's down to earth friend once more. "Feck, this thing's itchy. I doubt the buttons will last past the meal. I could do for a girdle right about now."

She laughed heartily, which beat gushes and giggles every time. For all his complaints, Mik looked good . . . and Miriam sensed he knew as much. She fought the urge to touch his form and pull him back behind the closed door of her quarters. The clean-pressed white dress uniform had crisp seams and gold button accents on the pockets and shirt cuffs. Across his chest was a sheer gold panel with the Tatsu emblem subtly screened on the fabric in navy blue. A small pinpoint of light traveled through the emblem, tracing the route of the Tatsu.

For Miriam's part, she wore a two-piece purple and white gown that showed off her toned shoulders and Mik's eyes did their own bit of widening – which she pretended not to notice for the sake of his comfort.

"Miriam," he said, catching himself in a stare. "You look," he paused. This would normally be the moment when Mik made either a joke or a filthy comment. Instead, he shook his head, unable to come up with either. "Ravishing," he said, allowing his eyes to travel down and back up her body again. "Completely fecking gorgeous."

Smiling confidently, "Take my arm, Captain?" she offered.

Clearing his throat and tucking his hat beneath his other arm, "My pleasure, Governor," he said. His fingertips brushed the back of her arm as he moved to link arms with her.

While she expected it, Miriam still felt uneasy when all eyes turned to she and Mik as they entered the formal hall. He was better at it than her – the smiling and shaking of hands. The schmoozing and boozing and remembering of names. All of it. He could act as much like one of the politicians, as one of the crew, as one of the Tatsian civilians, as the captain and elected leader of the Cityship Regatta's flagship. Miriam envied his ability to blend and also felt special that she might be the only one in the room who knew which personas were an act and which were the real Mik shining through.

Because she'd met with many of the ministers formally already, Miriam was able to exchange niceties with the spouses and significant others of most people in attendance by dropping some random fact she'd learned that day. She appreciated a fellow weak small talker in Aleksey Ivanov who was also in attendance. He was the head of the Tatsu's hydroponics gardens and the ex-partner of her own green thumb, Aaron Ramos. Ivanov and the governor were able to chit-chat about things she understood since he'd spent a good amount of time on Zoe Baja. They passed much of the social hour on the fringes of the engagement merely pretending to be in deep conversation.

In a constant pace around the perimeter of the room was Kate Murphy. She was clothed in the same formal dress attire as Mik, complete with the sheer golden chest panel. She had let her voluminous strawberry curls down out of their braids. Without reaction, she moved past the heads that turned to gawk at her full bust through the uniform. Kate was never one to choose the modest option. Young sailors' libidos would be satisfied in dreams of being on that pinpoint light route across the panel of her dress shirt tonight. It was obvious, though, Kate was not here to mingle, imbibe, or see any of those dreams come true.

Her eyes darted about, looking for signs of trouble and not so casually turning an ear toward characters or conversations that would be helpful to her captain. While the personalities and dynamics were clearly different, Miriam could see that Kate was every bit to Mik what Inoke was to her. They were a team.

Aleksey left Miriam's side and a momentary panic set in, but the space around the visiting governor quickly refilled. Miriam found herself standing in a cluster of dignitaries discussing who knew what? The weather? The latest quake? The invitation procedures for the arrival of the Pacific Islands delegation? No real work was being done here. The words themselves rarely mattered at these events as much as the fact that the people speaking them were present at an important social function.

Miriam stood amongst the politicians courteously, her drink poised in her hand like a prop. She dropped the occasional "Absolutely!" or nod whenever it seemed appropriate, and even asked a question here or there – something that was bland enough it could be used in any scenario. She wasn't really engaged. Even her smile felt like part of the evening's uniform or maybe her choreography in this great political dance. Like a schoolgirl, her mind drifted to the feel of Mik's hand on the back of her arm when he'd first greeted her. The memory made her skin tingle.

Without even knowing she was doing it and with her costumed smile still absent-mindedly spread across her full lips, she found her eyes taking in the rest of her surroundings. Through the center of the room, there was an unintentional blank space – a tunnel in which there were no gathered people. Miriam looked down it, away from the ongoing conversation around her, and she caught Mik peering admiringly back from the other side. She was pleasantly surprised that he showed no shame in being caught. He didn't break his gaze but intensified it, and Miriam's smile suddenly became genuine as she held him just as intentionally in her own sights.

For the space of a breath that felt like paused time, the room was quiet and still. The other people shifted out of focus. Miriam felt herself inhale while her chest rose and fell in the beat that stopped the room, the beat that none but two noticed. She winked one sparkling eye at the captain and, as spontaneously as the moment had come, it was gone again. The murmur of the crowd returned, the stillness washed away, and the tunnel closed.

Miriam's smile remained authentic, though, like she was the only one who knew a secret truth. A silken sheet of passion was forming beneath the warm blanket of familiarity she shared with Mik. She couldn't decide if that secret was scary or exciting.

For the most part, Miriam took the opportunities afforded by the Unity Dinner to observe, listen, and take note of the other leaders. She was grateful to hear the tone of the evening change as more and more leaders were sharing their enthusiasm for the hydrocell as if that had always been the stance they'd taken.

When the painful social hour finally passed, they all sat upon molded carbon chairs around white-linen-draped tables and enjoyed a feast on crystal dishes with real silver utensils. The dinner began with ginger-marinated albacore on a bed of water spinach. Miriam realized that it had been the ginger scent that was lingering in the air and, while it should have been settling to Miriam's stomach, she actually found the intensity of it to be nauseating.

Served with the tuna was wild rice and turnips, the latter grown in the ship's own hydroponics gardens. The meal was accompanied by mango-infused dandelion wine. For dessert, which was served with mint tea, they partook of a cinnamon turmeric goat cheesecake with candied citrus slices.

Miriam politely nibbled throughout the dinner and moved food around her plate to make it appear as though she had eaten more than was the reality. She was still queasy. The mint tea was her one saving grace.

Following the dinner filled with as much pompousness as pomp, the leaders enjoyed live entertainment from the Tatsu's performance troupes. Until the evening's shows, Miriam hadn't realized that the walls of the room were screens. They had appeared like simple white walls with recessed lighting. However, once the performers came into the room, the walls and ceilings took on a new appearance. A starry sky for one performance, a rainbow beyond storm clouds for another. The entire room was programmed for the event as acrobats and contortionists performed choreographed moves to the reborn music of long-gone sea-faring societies.

Once the formal program completed, musicians took up posts around the room and the walls changed once more to make the entire space look as though it was a nineteenth century pub. Kate was even pulled into a traditional dance to an ancient fife and drum number. The dinner attendees all cleared the center of the room, pulled the tables out of the way, and stood in a circle to enjoy the routine.

When Miriam joined the spectators, she felt the sway of the boat far more than she had before the meal. Mik took notice right away and discreetly came to the governor's rescue, holding her up while making it appear that he was merely offering to escort her out for the evening once the dance finished.

"Still working on those sea legs?" he said under his breath as they awaited the completion of the song.

"I swear to you, it's not the wine. I nursed a single glass all night," she returned in equally low tones.

"Whatever you say," he jabbed.

At the appropriate time, the two leaders made their way out of the Unity Dinner with polite handshakes and waves. Miriam kept her mouth in a pressed lip, forced smile to hold back the vomit she felt churning up from somewhere deep in the pit of her body. Within steps of the view of his government officials, Miriam removed her tall wedges and Mik undid his top shirt buttons.

"I think I might be able to use one of those anti-nausea patches, now," said the governor, putting one hand to her stomach and the other to the wall in the corridor for balance.

"It takes practice to dine like a sailor!" he joked back, taking the governor's shoes for her, and putting his hand on her lower back for support.

Miriam began to laugh, but the rocking overtook her, and she had to pause in the middle of the long hallway.

"You going to make it?" Mik asked concerned.

"Will we have rough waters, tonight?" she asked while she steadied herself. "I really do think I should lay down."

"Unfortunately, yes. Let's get you back," said the captain in a gentlemanly manner.

Moving again, "I think I'll be just fine if I can stop the rolling for a bit."

"That and maybe just let it happen. A good puking always steadies the land flies."

"A fly? That's what I am?"

"Both of us. Not that I'm comparing you to an insect. It's more about whether you are accustomed to land or sea. Sometimes I feel like I have to puke when I first step off the ship."

"Mik, please stop saying 'puke.' I beg you."

"I like begging."

Miriam felt incredibly vulnerable. She definitely did not have the energy for flirtation.

"For what it's worth, Captain, the dinner worked," she changed the subject. "I think you convinced your leaders that this alliance is a good thing tonight. Helped quell the questions they still had after meeting with Dr. Bradley."

"Talking out my arse is what I did!"

"Maybe so, but I really do think they believe in hydrocell power. They said it. I guess they just needed to hear it from," she attempted a smile, "a sea fly."

"I can't take credit. They believed it already when Jacob was talking to them. They just each had to get on-record with their objections before anything becomes real. Dr. Bradley's a passionate speaker."

"I'll be sure to tell him. It will ease his mind before the next round."

"Do that. He should know it was just a little bit of classic cover-your-arse politics. Been going on since Rome in Earth-Before-the-Melt."

Breathing heavily, "Sometimes I think it's the only thing we all have in common," Miriam said.

"Nah. There's also greed, a desire for power, lust, all sorts of other things we share."

"What are we trying to save again?" the governor huffed out an attempted laugh as they reached the door to her quarters.

Miriam straightened up as much as her nausea would allow and faced the captain.

"For starters," Mik said while he began to lean in, "all the sailors who get to walk someone to their quarters for the first time."

"Mik?" Miriam said meekly. "I—"

Before she could finish, the governor bent over and threw up all over the captain's perfectly shined shoes.

"Well, he said awkwardly, it wasn't all over the negotiating table, at least."

CHAPTER 21
YEAR 2552

Former Baja Province
Former Northern Territory of New Hispaniola Land Nation
Former Global Union

Linda was certain her ears were fooling her.

She arrived upon the scene where she found Uru. She heard voices, and not just one or two voices, but many, and not just any voices, but the voices of children.

She crept up to the edge of a fire that was burning, and she peeked around some barrels stacked in a ring around the gathering. The group of children looked like animals. They were thin as rails with wild hair and tattered clothes. They all ran about and screamed at one another. Two of the children were hitting each other. It looked as though they were playing, but it was so close to the flames of the fire that it made Linda gasp out loud.

"Can I help you?" asked a young voice behind her. Linda jerked around and found herself face to face with a teen boy.

"Hi, there," she said in a friendly tone, but the boy held up a knife and, despite his size, he suddenly became a menacing threat.

"Walk," he said.

Linda put her arms up in surrender and walked toward the fire with the boy at her back.

"I found another one!" he called out as they came into the light around the fire.

A dark-haired girl, slightly older than the teen with the knife, but still childlike, exited a mostly fallen structure and rolled her eyes at the boy. "Julian, put that blade down!" she said with parental affection.

"But you said I got to be guard!" the boy said, suddenly sounding like the child he was.

"Go play with your cousins," the girl scolded, and Julian scampered away.

"Are you Uru's partner?" the dark-haired teen asked.

"He's my friend. You are?" Linda answered cautiously.

"I'm in charge of this lot," she said as various kids darted about. "My name is Mercy."

Linda nodded. "Do you mind if I see my friend? Is he okay?"

Suddenly an off-key belted song erupted from out of the structure and Uru exited with three young children draped on him.

"My turn! My turn!" said a tiny one hanging on his arm.

Uru held onto the child and spun her 'round and 'round while he sang. He stopped when he spotted Linda at the fire.

"Your girl finally got here!" said Mercy.

"Linda, I knew you would come," Uru said. "Which pod did you bring?"

Confused, "The black one with the good ground wheels."

"Perfect. That's where I put the nutrient bars!" he exclaimed to the cheers of the children.

"He said you could feed us," said Mercy. The girl stood tall, not relaxing her toughened stance. She was small, but she wanted to be certain Linda understood that she was the one in control of the situation.

Breathing deeply and still uncertain, "Okay. I'll just go get the boxes, then," Linda said standing up.

She tried to glance at Uru to see if he had anything else to communicate to her, but he was lost in play with the littlest children of the group.

As she started to walk away, "Stop," Mercy said. "Dee, go with her. She'll need help carrying enough for all of us," she directed, her meaning clear. Linda had better come back. Dee was watching her. She'd better bring the food . . . and only the food.

Folding a group of what turned out to be twelve children into the life that Uru and Linda had been growing proved to be difficult. They had spent two nights outside of the shack where the children had been sleeping. Linda traveled back to the pod hauler for food and to check on the chickens. There was an unspoken and uncomfortable understanding that, because the children outnumbered the adults, they were the ones in charge.

On the morning following the second night, Linda told the young group that she and Uru really had to continue in their journeys to the southern port and Mercy—the girl at the head of the miniature squad—tried to make a show of her control.

"You can't go," she said, and Linda wasn't certain if it was a threat.

"We can't stay," Linda said, standing her ground, as well. "This is no place to build a life."

Uru looked at Linda and at the brood of children and at the shanty where they were barely protected from the elements.

"And what are we supposed to do?" Mercy asked, trying to be demanding, but her fear was peeking through her tough facade.

For the first time in two days, the gathering grew quiet. The children clustered around the two women who faced off, unshakably moving from their positions.

"You could come with us," Uru said at last, breaking the tension. "You could come along. We have room in the pods for you each to sit while we continue our salvage route down to the port."

Both Linda's and Mercy's expressions softened, as if they hadn't considered the option of joining together, and it was the first day that the two sets of survivors became one.

Over the course of the remaining travels, tensions between the group of children and Linda and Uru relaxed. Slowly, the power struggles disappeared and were replaced by a familial structure. Mercy accepted help with the youngest children who were now being fed and given more attention than she could manage on her own. Uru and Linda became de facto parental units to the eleven youngest former GU orphans and Mercy—in time—allowed herself to become one of the children, again, too, though she was still slow to warm up to the adults.

By the time the group reached the southern port, the children were well-nourished, Linda and Uru kept the unit together as a single family, and they looked at the former zip chopper port as a settlement to be claimed and made into a house.

"We're here," Linda said to Mercy as she woke the teen who had fallen asleep in her pod on the back of the hauler during their last travel day. "Come look at where we'll be building."

One-by-one, Uru and Linda helped the young ones out of their pods. They all looked at the large hangar on one side and the open water on the other side of where they would live. There was a pier on the water where boats could dock. The grounds outside the hangar included a large grassy area that wasn't even cluttered with rubble or fallen buildings. It was like looking at the seedling of a society; the elements were present, but they needed tending. Something about the place felt hopeful in a way that even life before the Great Quake never had.

With tears in her eyes, Mercy grabbed onto Linda and sobbed. She could finally rest. They were home.

CHAPTER 22
YEAR 2908

Southern Port
Zoe Baja
Zoelands Concord

"**W**hat is it, Potcake?" Harry said to the mutt. His boy was running back and forth along one of the darkened piers with the low breathy "woof" he saved for greeting unknown sailors and navigators.

"All shut down for the night, buddy. No more ships coming in," the lead longshore worker added with a pat to Potcake's head even as he looked out into the open waters beyond the port.

It was as black as the bottom of a dead volcano in the distance under the clouded sky that hid the stars from reflecting on the sea. Only a fool would sail without lights on a night like this, and all Harry could hear was the splashing of the water against the docks.

"Let's get home," Harry said, assured that the work of the day was done.

He turned with a jump as he found himself face-to-face with a drone floating at head-height.

"Son of a—! Devon! Leaving one of your drones around here again! You're not as clever as you think," Harry said to the drone. "But I give you credit for getting one down here to the southern port. What did you do? Leave it behind to have somebody launch it down here for you?" Harry laughed while staring right into what he believed was the camera of the drone.

Except it wasn't a camera. The red light simply marked its target, and Harry felt no pain when the close-ranged laser knife shot right through his eye, and he collapsed to the ground dead.

"Weigh him and drop him," said a man stepping out of the shadows.

"What about his dog?" asked Erik, one of two other men that had joined him.

Li Fang looked at the dog that had lain down on the pier as his owner was rolled into the water and began to sink. Potcake whimpered, staring into the water as if he hoped Harry would jump back out of the deep with a new toy.

"Leave him. He won't be a problem."

"What did you do?" Vera asked coming out of hiding from behind one of the massive bollards. "I didn't know you were going to kill him," she cried. "I never would have agreed to that," the dock worker shook her head.

Fang walked over to the trembling woman and looked down on her. "Give me your hand," he growled.

Vera shook her head even as the other two men with Li Fang appeared over his shoulders. Fang snapped his fingers. Erik grabbed Vera's left wrist and George, the other man, yanked off Vera's glove to reveal a Global Union palm scan.

"You agreed," Li sneered as he pulled on a digital glove and gripped Vera as if shaking her hand, "To one hundred thousand GU credits."

He released her hand, removed his glove, and handed it to Erik. "And now you've been paid," he smiled before stepping even closer to the woman and saying, "Now disappear."

Vera stepped backward slowly at first, but then turned and ran out of sight as quickly as her legs would carry her.

The current head of the Wang Family Fleet was fully hairless, without even eyebrows or eyelashes, as a result of toxic exposure he'd experienced as a child. Scarring on his arms had been blended into white ink tatua that covered his entire body and head. He had black opal inlays on his face in the shape of a jagged wave. Diamond nail tips were at the end of every finger, and he incessantly tapped them on each surface he passed.

The fleet family patriarch signaled a small patrol ship, not his lead vessel, to come into port and a light appeared in the darkness making its way to the Wang Family representatives waiting for her. Once the patrol ship was tightly tied in, a slender woman with raven black hair stepped off the boat, looking far more refined than her brother.

"It's no good coming to shore like this," Li Ju said.

"It's Zoe. They trust everyone," Fang said. "Besides, we're invited."

"Did Francisco invite you to do that, too?" said Fang's sister, indicating the still whimpering dog.

"He had the codes. He had to go. This was the easiest way."

"You have no tact."

"I have the fleet. I don't need tact. Now, let's go."

As though they'd done nothing more than accidentally bumped into a person, the group of four, Fang, Ju, Erik, and George, stepped onto a whistler to make their way to the deputy governor's home.

"Calm down, Vera! This is an open line," Deputy Governor Roberto Francisco screamed at his digifile.

As Vera continued to babble, "Shut up! Shut up!" he exclaimed. "You are in this, now. There is no turning back. I'll take care of the rest," he said before slamming his fingers onto the digifile to end the communication.

Roberto stood up and began to pace the room, occasionally rubbing his face or wringing his hands. He only had a fifteen-minute window in which security would be cleared out. He used his handicap to advantage, requesting certain times of the day when he did not have to be under watch. He claimed modesty and declared a need to get changed out of his day clothes with no guards or cameras on his home or on his body. Nobody dared question him.

Finally, Francisco heard the distinct high-pitched sound of a whistler. He moved to the window and spotted the passengers as they stepped off the zip chopper and made straightaway for his side entrance.

"Privacy, blinds," he commanded the room and mechanical shutters snapped down over every window of the room.

"I didn't ask you to kill him!" Roberto said in a whisper shout when he opened his door and quickly pulled Li Fang inside by his jacket.

Fang put his hand on Francisco's wrist and, with threatening calm, removed the arm from his body. "You said he couldn't be around when you activated tsunamic defense," the family patriarch said. "I can promise you now that he won't be around. Don't tell me how to do my job."

Pulling the door shut behind the rest of the Wang Family members, "This was supposed to be discreet!" Roberto exclaimed. "If you want the rest of your money, you'd better make sure that—"

"If?" Fang cut Francisco off. "We will get the rest of the money," he said with one of his sharpened fingernails at the deputy governor's jugular.

"Just do the job," said Francisco.

Roberto went to his desk, put away the official digifile on which he'd been speaking to Vera, and pulled out a second device from beneath a false bottom of his desk drawer. He pressed his thumb to the secure digifile and held it out to Fang.

"Ju," Fang nodded to the woman.

His sister stepped forward and pushed her thumb onto the device.

"Why not your own print?" asked Francisco.

"Because" Li Fang said, closing the distance between himself and Roberto, "I was never here."

"You have half of your credits. You get the rest when you finish the job. I need the hydrocell and I need the man who developed it taken care of."

"And by 'taken care of' you mean?" asked Erik.

Fang flashed a fiery glance at his men, and then returned his gaze to Roberto, "Just to be sure we're clear."

"You know what I mean," said the deputy governor, "He's far more valuable than Harry. Without him, there is no hydrocell."

"We'll take care of it," said George.

Roberto looked at the henchman and smiled slyly. "I like you," he said to the man. "I admire your loyalty to your own people," he added. "It's not as common of a characteristic as you might think. You would be surprised at just how many people forget their roots. They forget who shaped them. Not you. You stand with this man because he's Wang Family Fleet and so are you, no matter who else you might have been in the EBM world. And who would that have been?"

"My family was Egyptian," George answered, but only after Li Fang nodded indicating it was allowed.

"And you?" Roberto asked Erik, who's skin was so fair it had a blue tinge to it, as though it wasn't thick enough to conceal his own blood vessels. The man's eyelashes and eyebrows blended right into his skin.

"Norway," he said.

"Well, we don't use those ancient titles anymore, do we? You two know that, though." He looked at them with a posture that somehow expressed both respect and disdain. "You are a family. Zoeans are a family, too."

"Enough of this," Ju Fang rolled her eyes.

Roberto looked embarrassed at having been cut off. He had clearly rehearsed his speech about family.

"I won't pay until I know that the Tatsu is within two kilometers of Zoe Baja," he said curtly. "You and your men have to stay and watch for their return. Is that understood?" he asked, directing the question to Li, and ignoring the woman in the room.

"If we didn't understand the job, we wouldn't have taken it."

"You have to protect family," Francisco added unnecessarily. It must have been another line of his practiced monologue. "Don't screw up," the deputy governor finished.

Erik and George assumed intimidating stances once more in response to the tone, but Li waved them off.

The Wang Family members turned to go, but Ju looked back with a sigh. She was giving a closing line opportunity to their employer. "Why would you do this to your own people?" she asked.

"They are not my people. Not anymore. I'm Zoean. I am protecting those who truly want to remain Zoean. My . . . governor," he spit out the word, "is becoming something else. Becoming *global*," he said the word with a bitter pucker as though he could taste it. "And if we're global, we are not us, anymore."

The Wang family left with the same arrogant bullying with which they'd come. Roberto released the privacy blind on one of his windows and watched their shadows cross the grounds to the whistler. He didn't fool himself into thinking they were his partners, but at least they didn't pretend to be, either. Self-service, no matter how ugly it was, was at least something he could trust. Fang placed a hand on the back of Li Ju as she stepped into the zip chopper's pilot chair to take them back to the southern port.

A pain pulsed behind Francisco's sternum – a loss as present today as it had been almost thirty years ago. That's when he last saw his own sister. The Mahmoud Pandemic began innocently enough. The first patients to contract it were working in the Hudson waters. There was even a rumor that the Zhu had manufactured it in an attempt to create an anti-viral super-vaccine to trade with the Global Union, but it got out of hand.

The ship's citizens began to develop rashes, as innocuous as anything a worker in the cold saltwater of the Hudson might expect after a hard-day's labor. The illness progressed quickly, though. It moved from rashes to open wounds, from open wounds to blood poisoning, and from blood poisoning to mutilation and dismemberment as medical professionals amputated and cut out parts of the body little by little, each time hoping the virus had been irradicated. Those who survived, not that there were many, resembled human pinecones. They were given robotic implants and replacements, as well as silica-surgeries and cosmetic laser repairs, but they never looked or moved like themselves again.

Roberto Francisco never looked or moved like himself again.

The illness did not become airborne, but it survived on surfaces for weeks, so it didn't take long for it to spread throughout the globe and make its way from cityships to the Global Union and, from there, around the world. It arrived in ports on packages and food and building materials and medical supplies. If it shipped, and everything in the world shipped, the virus shipped with it. It shipped from Global Union to the Zoe's oldest allies, the cityships, who betrayed Baja and the other Zoelands with their part in the pandemic's spread. Mahmoud shipped to Veronica Francisco on the back of a birthday gift from her older brother. She was twelve years old.

The Global Union – the great spreader of the viral murderer – came up with a treatment that had a large enough supply for all of the GU. Everybody else, even the little sisters of up-and-coming young diplomats whose hands they shook and to whom they promised partnership, needed to get in line. In time, the GU cured the world . . . first the Global Union, then the cityships—their partners in crime—then the Indigenous Nations, and finally the Zoelands. But not Veronica. It was too late for her.

Francisco removed his dark gray suit jacket as his anger caused a fever to flare up in him. He caught a glimpse of his own mangled hand as he undid the coat's buttons and decided he couldn't stop there. Madly, he undid his shirt next, revealing a pinecone-scarred chest. He angrily ripped off his shoes and socks. He undid his belt and ripped it out of his pants. He yanked his pants off of his body and threw them across the room. He projected one of his shoes and his shirt and his coat to the different corners of the room and grunted loudly as he picked up the last shoe and turned, catching the full view of his pocked and mutilated form in a mirror on the other side of the room.

He paused, panting in fury as he stared at his hideous body in nothing but his underwear.

How was he supposed to shake the hands of GU prefects when they didn't care about any of the non-GU hands lost to Mahmoud? How was he supposed to trust the cityship captains when those were the people who made the virus that took away his sister? The thought of working with all of them made him physically ill. How could he trust anybody else to care for the Zoeans the way he wanted to care for them? The way he failed to care for his own sister. There was a disgusting monster in the mirror and the Dr. Frankenstein who made it was equal parts GU and cityship.

With all of the power that his broken body could summon, Francisco screamed out loud and launched his shoe into the mirror, shattering the glass and, along with it, any humanity that Roberto had left.

CHAPTER 23
YEAR 2553

Pacific Sea South Of The Former Baja Province
PS-1707 Mining Vessel
Global Union

“That's completely out of the way, Captain!”

"All of these mussels will go bad by then," Wang Wei, the anchor room engineer went on.

"You will still get your standard rate. Feel free to complain to the higher-ups."

"That's not right and you know it," said the frail framed man with greased back hair, possibly with actual engine grease mixed in with the grime and sweat of his working day.

Behind him stood Erin, who had fair, pocked skin, and dirty brown hair. She was fast and strong, so she was a good worker, but she was known to be arrogant. Beside her was Randall, a man so bland, you could call him vanilla if his skin weren't so dark. Randall was a nice enough crewman, but was easily pushed around, letting Erin and Wang dictate most of his positions rather than taking an initiative. Clearly, the two had elected Wang to speak on behalf of the crewmembers who, Tatsu suspected, also went to Wang for their chemical fixes. They were less understanding of their captain's struggle to go on about their activities as if nothing had changed.

"The men and women on this ship are accustomed to our bonus runs," Wang went on. "The standard rate doesn't stretch as far as it used to."

The captain just shook his head. He was sure the standard rate would be okay for this run if Wang skipped the vice lounges. He liked to play big man on crew and buy rounds of fermented cannabis spirit . . . amongst other poisons . . . for his own squad within the crew: Erin and Randall, as well as Josh, Adam, Darius, Carrie, and Mari. Most of the time, the squirrelly nature of his engineer, Wang Wei, was just a minor annoyance the crew had to deal with. He was a weasel, but usually at least an amicable weasel. And, while his predominant trait was to be self-serving, that trait often helped the crew to find secondary markets for their goods. Wang knew all of the illegitimate black-market connections at the ports where they simultaneously did their more legitimate business.

Like most sea-scrubbers, the common name for mining vessels similar to the PS-1707, they were assigned a specific list of materials to mine, a specific set of coordinates at which to mine, a calendar, and a delivery route. Many of the northern vessels, for instance, were recyclers stationed over the long-underwater cities of the EBM world like Edinburgh, Venice, and New Orleans. Those miners scavenged skyscrapers or smaller buildings for their components and resources: glass, metals, and synthetic materials that could be processed and repurposed. Then, there were the natural earth miners around the world who mined what the GU called origin-source materials, the raw resources that still existed beneath the surface of the world's waters. Refuse scrubbers were stationed throughout the world's oceans. Some were assigned to excavation of underwater landfill mounds and others filtered the polluted waters. The netted collections of refuse scrubbers were sent to processing for the reusable fragments of life that generations before had once discarded.

Refuse scrubbers were the lowest-entry jobs for seafaring work, but just barely above them were ships like the PS-1707 captained by Tatsu Mageo. His ship was assigned to invasive species. The crew cleaned them from one area, then sometimes transported them to other areas where they could benefit the ecosystem, and other times processed them for use in the products necessary for daily life in the Global Union.

The PS-1707 cleared invasive mussels from what remained of reefs and other natural areas in the Pacific Sea. The chalky black and pearlescent shells of the mussels were crushed into a dust that could be mixed into a sludge-like paste, molded, and used in the construction of flooring, countertops, public walkways, and bottling. That was the official business of the vessel Tatsu commanded.

The official business.

Relatively known and usually ignored by the GU, most mining vessels had a side hustle. They all did it; nobody talked about it. The ships on the northern seas were known for coming up with quality bottles of alcohol that withstood time and water pressure, remained intact, and went for a decent number of credits to the right buyer. Refuse scrubbers came across any number of lost historical treasures on which individuals or municipalities wanted to get their hands.

Because scrubber work was hard on the body and dangerous, it wasn't uncommon for a crew to lose two or three workers every season: radiation poisoning when working a contaminated ocean zone, falling overboard in a storm in a sea under constant threat of extreme weather, untangling scrubber equipment under the water, or getting lost in former cities . . . there was no shortage of ways to die horribly as a scrubber. And because a lot of those who chose the scrubber way of life didn't have people waiting to mourn them at a home port, the GU didn't always hear about those deaths. As a result, "dead citizen accounts" were basically an entire shadow economy for at-sea workers. If a scrubber lived long enough to retire one day, he or she usually did so with a collection of digitized palm scans, the dead citizen accounts of all of their former crewmates.

Tatsu himself had three such scans and, to keep those accounts padded, his ship moved one of the most sought-after commodities of all: food. The GU only wanted the shells of the mussels that the PS-1707 mined, leaving all of the meat to be discarded or, as his crew quickly discovered was preferable, traded for credit to a dead citizen account. If their schedule was tight, they'd sell the whole lot as bait to a fishing vessel working under the radar. When they had time, though, they would sell smaller portions at each delivery port.

Natural protein sources were valuable, and they not only kept the workers of the PS-1707 living better than their way of life should have allowed, but they also enjoyed more than their share of the seafood, eating like the kings of their day. The typical take from a single black-market mussel meat trade was the equivalent of two months' worth of standard GU wages. Work on a sea scrubber carried neither glory nor ease and most that chose the assignment did so because of the great unkept secret of bonus runs.

"The rest of the crew knows what you've lost. We'd be willing to share even some of our cut from the protein trade, to make this easier for you," Wang pled like the addict he was.

The weasel just needed his fix and Tatsu was not endeared.

"This isn't about credit Wang! Do you really think a few extra credits in my dead citizen accounts will make this any easier? That's my brother I lost," the captain shouted, easily substituting anger for his pain. "Not to mention his whole family! My nieces. My nephew. You've met them, too. His wife used to cook for your sorry ass! Millions drowned or crushed and those who didn't die lost everything! The GU sent them all to other parts of the world. Whole communities gone. Does that mean nothing to you?"

Tatsu looked beyond Wang to Erin and Randall.

"To ANY of you?" he asked, knowing they were as much a part of this greed plead as was Wang. "I am going to pay my respects even if we lose the entire fucking shipment. Do you understand? And you ought to have a wish to do the same!"

Captain Mageo was built large from years of hard labor at sea. He stood up to his full 6'7" height and faced Wang with a look of power. His decision was final.

"Of course, Captain. Oui, Sir," the man shrunk back from his request.

"Now, call in our recon ship. We're going to Baja Province!" he barked the order.

"Oui, Sir," the man said, off to recall the small vessel assigned to the PS-1707.

While Wang skittered away, and his minions followed meekly. The captain slumped back over the edge of his ship, becoming smaller than his frame should have allowed. He somberly looked northward toward the Baja Province fearing what his return might mean – finality.

The sun shone on his deeply tanned leathery skin. Tatsu wore his curly hair cropped short, and he shaved his multi-colored facial hair with sharp-edged shapes to create designs he often changed. Single-ink and laser tatua covered most of his torso, but he usually hid the skin tapestry with a contrasting fashion statement of pastel, water-colored, cotton button-downs. The fun, short-sleeved shirts reflected his personality far more than the stereotypes applied to his career path or body size. Today, he wore a sleeveless, plain blue work shirt, nothing at all to soften his appearance.

Decades ago, a snapped pulley had thrown a fastener his way resulting in the loss of his right eye. Rather than restore the sight, he chose to have it replaced with a programmable optic monitor. If you looked at him, unless you knew he had only one working eye, you would never have guessed it. Tatsu would tap a pattern on his temple and, through the optic monitor visible only to him via signals sent directly to his brain, he could manage his ship's operations, handle communications with ocean administrators at Global Union headquarters, and enjoy incoming entertainment and headline programs.

Even while transmitting, the color-matched mechanical replacement looked and moved like his real eye. Only occasionally, in the midst of challenging operations, would he appear to be distant, focused elsewhere. Today, one might look at him and think one of those operations was occurring, but Captain Mageo was distant for a completely different reason.

It had been months since the most recent major earthquake notices had come across the headlines. New Hispaniola suffered extensive losses in Mexico City and the Baja Province. He wanted to go immediately to help in the recovery efforts and even riled up all of his women and men to desire the same, but they were turned away, blockaded by the GU because they didn't have the right certifications and licenses to participate in rescue efforts.

The entire crew of the PS-1707 had waited at the southern port of the Baja Province for over a week, begging daily to help and knowing that more hands could mean more lives saved. Their frustration was palpable as they were repeatedly prevented from helping by what felt like arbitrary regulations. Eventually, they had to return to their route and wait, along with the rest of the world, for the victim and refugee lists being announced on the daily headline programs.

All day and night, tremors and aftershocks continued along with the occasional tidal wave that followed. Most of the latter were too small to do any damage but some that reached the shores of various land masses were full-blown, devastating tsunamis. Every morning, Tatsu would scan the access code to the latest released refugee list and run a search for every imaginable name or spelling of a name that would have been recorded for those in his brother's family. The same reports were coming in from the lost islands of the Pacific Islands Land Nation including: Lanai, Japan, and more than sixty percent of the Philippine Province, nearly five thousand of the islands in the beloved Pacific archipelago. He checked those lists, too, just in case they'd been evacuated to one of those Land Nations.

In the days and weeks that followed, the captain continued to hold out hope that his family would be found and identified at a Global Union processing station. New Hispaniola had six such stations marking the arrival of Baja Province and Mexico City evacuees. Not one of them listed his brother or his brother's family. Another dozen existed throughout the Pacific Islands Land Nation, and he checked those, as well, more out of thoroughness than optimism.

The pattern of new storms, new lists, and new prayers continued until Tatsu finally heard that Baja Province itself had been fully evacuated. The hospital evacuations were the last before the province was abandoned as many could not be safely moved until they had time to heal. When the names of those from the medical centers had been added to the final lists and he hadn't found his family, Tatsu had to accept that, just like the tens of millions of others around the world, his loved ones were buried under rubble, swept away in the waters, or dead in a medical center that never identified them.

There were no more lists.

Now that the Global Union had evacuated Baja Province and they no longer cared about their old metropolises, Tatsu could finally return to say goodbye without somebody turning him away. There was also a part of him that needed to see it for himself, see the places he'd been with his family and understand why they didn't make it. He needed to know and accept that he really was alone in the world before he could decide what that would mean to him.

Seven years ago, Tatsu thought he'd met the woman with whom he would spend his life. She was his lo'u loto. His heart. His love. The woman's Global Union assignment was located in a different part of the world. Though they could have tried to make it work, Tatsu didn't feel it was fair to her. He chose the bachelor's life at sea, the scrubber life. No matter how much he wanted to—he never looked back.

He got a tatua of the woman after they said goodbye, not because he wanted to remember her, but because he wanted the reminder that he should never go back there. He wanted to physically walk with that person until he was ready to leave her behind. And he did eventually leave her behind entirely, obscuring the tattooed face with a new design of an opened mussel shell. Only then did he allow his crew to truly become his family . . . along with the family he helped his brother to have.

Tatsu could have held onto his rights to paternity but his older brother had been coming up on the maximum allowable age of procreation. He opted to give up his own permit, a practice that was frowned upon but not strictly illegal. It allowed a family to have additional applications in the annual drawing for child-bearing permits. It was how he himself had a brother. A close friend of his mother's had donated her annual permit application and, combined with his mother's and father's permits, the three chances led to their ballot being drawn and his parents were able to reproduce a second time. He couldn't imagine life without his older brother. He didn't think twice about passing along his own permit for the chance to share the love of siblings with a new generation.

His brother already had a son, but deeply desired a second child. Against the odds, and with Tatsu's permit application surrender, his brother won the drawing to have another child. When his sister-in-law, Kim, had healthy medical scans, against even greater odds, his brother's wife became pregnant with twins, a fact she swore to without evidence. Kim insisted she could feel two children growing inside of her and her husband took her hunch very seriously. The two put off their initial maternity examination as long as possible. The Global Union would have forced abortion of one of the two children in-utero had her medical scan proven her intuition correct. That is why Tatsu's sister-in-law joined him on the mining vessel, one of her certified employs, until her twin daughters were born.

His brother's family declared it a happy accident and, without proof otherwise, the GU merely told them that they had to make it work without any Global Union ration or employ increases and, if they couldn't, they were welcome to surrender the spare child as a ward of the GU. She would be given rations and raised until she was a full adult according to the greatest needs of the union. After that time, they would consider giving the child citizen status, but that consideration was rarely realized.

GU rations and quarters for four would not stretch easily for five, but Tatsu's brother and sister-in-law could not imagine having to choose a child to give up. It was only then that Tatsu accepted credits in dead citizen accounts. Unlike many of his crew, it wasn't why he'd come to sea, but his access to them allowed his brother to care for the girl that the GU had designated "a spare." As an uncle to three great children, Tatsu felt his family had a chance at a legacy, and at a picture of what family could look like in a world where adding to the population increase was discouraged.

Now, they were gone. All of them. His brother, the mother of those three children, his nephew, his nieces . . . his family. And with it, his legacy.

The mining vessel operated like an entire egalitarian society linked together by the struggle of working on the ship.

"You're an asshole," Peter shouted from his post.

"Yeah, well, you steer like shit, kid," Khalil called back to great guffaws from Justin beside him in the rotor room, all while they navigated a flawless docking procedure.

Tatsu watched it unfold through his optic monitor and heard it through his comms as they smoothly made their way into the abandoned southern port of Baja Province. Despite the circumstances that had brought them here, he couldn't help but laugh with his crew.

'There's always a flower in the pavement,' his grandmother had once told him. *'Find the flowers in the street cracks and beneath the pod paths. There's beauty somewhere. You have to look hard for beauty. You may only be shown the pavement, my Tatsu, but you? You need to find the flowers.'*

He didn't have to look too hard for flowers, today. The docks and piers of the southern port were being reclaimed by Mother Nature. Until a few months ago, Tatsu would have waited in a long queue of vessels trying to deliver their GU cargo of mussel shells to New Hispaniola. Today, they were alone, coming alongside long-neglected piers. While they normally would have been greeted by hundreds of workers, today another soul was not in sight. The docks were usually bustling day and night. Instead, an eerie quietness hung over the land in the lowlight of dusk that was quickly becoming dark.

"Motor down," Tatsu called over his mouthpiece while he robotically directed his crew through the taxing mooring and berthing procedures required to dock.

As, one-by-one, each major component of the PS-1707 went through its shutdown procedures, the world grew more and more still until the only movement was that of small ripples of water breaking against his mining vessel. Tatsu turned off his mouthpiece and comms. He tapped his temple in a pattern that fully shut down his optic monitor, allowing his right eye to go blind. Life was muted. His gaze shifted and adjusted to single-eye vision and Tatsu stared out alone to an abandoned dock from an abandoned deck.

His crew joined him after a moment of silence. Stacy Pi and Amy Elm, his deck team, put out the gangway connecting Tatsu's ship to the docks that were so familiar, and yet so foreign at the same time. He knew he could count on them to guide him through this process.

"Captain Mageo," Stacy said, "the crew won't depart until you do."

He turned to his second in command, a freckled, fair-skinned woman whose hair had bleached to white blonde from the sun, though her genes may have cast her as a light brunette. Her skin was a pinkish red, the closest to tanned as her fair complexion would allow. Stacy had genuine concern on her face and a maternal expression, even though she was all business. She was an intellectual and a natural leader . . . and exactly what Tatsu needed in that moment.

"We've gathered your women and men," added Amy in a naturally hoarse voice. Amy was a petite woman with short curly hair and a strawberry-shaped frame that turned heads, but she gave no notice to such things.

Beyond the two women without whom this ship would have suffered, Tatsu saw his entire crew lined up all the way to the gangway. Peter stood at the front, just behind Tatsu's leadership team. After him, leading up to the gangway to which Amy and Stacy walked, stood Khalil, Justin, Patty, Davina, Samantha, Marquis, Allen, and Cairo. Wang led a line of his squad to the other side of the gangway, probably intentionally so as not to have Tatsu pass by them.

"Do you want somebody to walk with you, Captain?" asked the sixteen-year-old kid, fresh on his first year of employ.

"I'd like that, Peter," Tatsu said to the boy who was now the closest thing he would ever have to a son. He felt tears well up and not fall, but he wouldn't let his crew see them. He allowed the gentle breeze to dry his eyes as he pulled the young crewman alongside him. He squeezed down on the boy's shoulder with a grip more comforting to the captain than to the boy

'If you feel something, feel it!' he heard his grandmother say in his mind, but he pushed it out for the time-being.

The two men stepped onto the dock and Tatsu realized he didn't know what to do next. He'd dragged his entire crew here, sacrificed their bonus run, the second one since this whole disaster began, and he didn't have a fucking clue what he was supposed to tell them next. How was this whole paying respect thing even supposed to work? He had taken them to hell without a plan, much less a prayer. He turned to address them as they gathered in a semicircle around him on land. Tatsu was unsure what he planned to say, but didn't have to find the words because, just as he opened his mouth, they all heard a crash of empty crates twenty yards away and there stood a petite doe-eyed girl with straight raven hair clumsily breaking the silence for them.

"Ope! Well, shit. I guess here I am," said the teen.

For a moment, they all just stared at her, not sure what to say to the unexpected appearance of another person. She wore what looked like a student's uniform of plain colors and utilitarian design. But she'd clearly adapted it, colored it, tied it, torn it, and created something unique and eclectic. It was a strange combination of a grandmotherly outfit with a teenager's appeal.

"Welcome?" she offered before making a ridiculous smile, pulling her chin in to her neck. The expression couldn't help but make them all laugh, albeit nervously.

"She's not right," Wang said to Erin's laughs.

"Not bad looking, though," said Adam as Wang narrowed his eyes at the young thing.

Finally, feeling a glimmer of hope mixed with his confusion, the captain approached the girl. He crouched down and reached out his hand gently as he tiptoed toward her.

"It's okay," Tatsu said. "I'm not going to hurt you. Trust me."

"Um, you do know I'm not a wild goat, right?" she said sassily as she furrowed her brow at the huge man.

Peter burst into laughter and Captain Mageo, a bit embarrassed, straightened up and tugged at the bottom of his shirt. "Well, we didn't expect a young . . . um—" Tatsu stopped mid-thought.

"We didn't expect anybody," Peter finished peering around his captain and smiling with his bright white teeth at the girl who blushed a bit in turn.

"Neither did we," she said shrugging.

"We? How many of you are there? There are other survivors?"

"Not many here. At least I don't think so. I only know the fourteen of us, but Linda and Tunes did a lot of the exploring without my cousins and me," the girl said as she started to walk and, without really knowing why, the whole crew began to follow. She had that effect about her, leading without telling anybody she was doing so.

Captain Mageo, still marching forward, looked behind himself and gave a gesture of, "Hell if I know!" to Stacy and Amy. He thought what a strange sight it must have been, seeing this tiny pixie of a thing leading a parade of twenty adult scrubbers through the remnants of the newly formed ghost town like a mother duck and her ducklings traversing a haunted house.

"You live here with your cousins?" Tatsu asked.

"Everybody else left on the zip choppers, but we don't have our scans yet, so we didn't think they'd miss us. Well, I was going to get mine. Just finished the aptitude tests. I was going to teach. But I couldn't very well leave my cousins, especially Ziad and Sofia who are the youngest, and they all voted to stay. They're all younger than me. And they're not really my cousins. None of us have parents. We were in the GU children's home. The home's administrator didn't make it. And Linda and Tunes got their own reasons for staying I suppose. We don't talk much about that."

"So, those are the registered citizens? Linda and Tunes."

"Sort of. Linda's not registered. She doesn't have a scan anymore."

"Anymore?"

"We don't ask."

"And Tunes?"

"Oh, that's not his real name. We all just call him that because he's always singing."

"Oh," Tatsu smiled at the picture that came into his head.

"Does he sing lullabies to your younger cousins?" asked Stacy who had caught up to the front of the duck line.

Laughing, "Yee, I hope not! That would cause some nightmares. He's kind of terrible, but it doesn't stop him from doing it. Anyway, his real name is...."

"Mercy!" came the panicked call of a woman frantically dodging between abandoned pods in a search pattern. "We didn't know where you...." Linda stopped upon seeing the parade of people coming behind the oldest orphan. "Get over here, Mercy," Linda said as she grabbed Mercy's wrist and gently guided the girl behind her own body. "URU!" she called, keeping her eyes fixed on the sudden crowd of twenty before her.

Upon hearing the name, Tatsu's eyes immediately began darting around until he finally caught sight of him. He was a little worse for wear, a few more wrinkles, a bit more sun-kissed, hair a bit longer and scragglier, but there was no mistaking his brother.

"Uru," Tatsu said in a whisper to the man as the two stared at one another in shock.

His brother was alive.

"You know this man?" Linda asked in disbelief, still hiding Mercy behind herself, along with her own little gaggle of ducklings who had gathered behind her when they heard the ruckus.

Uru didn't answer but continued approaching Tatsu as if in a trance. The two men didn't say anything. They felt each other's faces and studied one another's eyes until, at last, Tatsu—knowing words could never suffice—pulled his brother into a breath-stopping, tight embrace. Uru was the first to cry, followed by Tatsu, and the two collapsed into one another. Uru laughed madly. Tatsu bawled uncontrollably. Both allowed the contrasting hysterical releases to stand in for all the thoughts, feelings, and words that neither could manage in the moment.

CHAPTER 24
YEAR 2908

Pacific Sea Route
Cityship Tatsu IV
Cityship Regatta

Mik was speechless.

He was caught somewhere between shocked, laughing, and disgusted as he looked down at his shoes covered in sick.

"I am sooo sorry," Miriam said, shocked a bit herself.

"But you feel better, don't you?" Mik chuckled.

"Actually, yes. I believe I do."

"Congratulations, Governor. You've got your sea legs" He patted her shoulder chummily but let his hand rest there a bit longer than he would for just any sailor, his fingers drawing circles on her skin.

"Let's get you a towel," Miriam said, opening her door while Mik followed her in.

She grabbed one of her linens and began to wipe off Mik's shoes.

"I can do that," he said, helping her to a standing position and taking the towel from her. "There is something very wrong about watching a woman clean up her own vomit."

"I should probably be mortified right now," Miriam said. "But I really am just glad to be feeling better."

Mik continued to find the whole scene amusing as he finished cleaning up and putting the towel into a small, provided hamper in the room.

"Remind me to request bonuses for the cleaning crew after this trip."

Mik looked down at Miriam, now standing fully upright and appearing far closer to her deep-golden-brown tone than the greenish gray she'd been just moments earlier. The two fell silent again, any sense of awkwardness between them long gone. He started to lean down toward her when Miriam quickly shot a hand over her mouth and backed off.

"Oh no. You do not want to do that right now," she laughed. "Let me just, um. Why don't you give me a moment to get cleaned up? And you go back to your quarters and do the same. I know you're dying to get out of that suit."

"There's more than one way to do that," he winked.

"Still. I just need a moment and then maybe I could drop by?"

Before Mik could answer, alarms started blaring throughout the ship.

"Is that for turbulence?" Miriam asked.

"I don't think so," said Mik. "I gotta go," he said with a squeeze to the governor's hand and a kiss to her cheek before bolting out of her quarters.

Miriam looked after him down the hallway. Apparently, it was fine for cityship captains to run. She closed her door, swished some mouthwash, and threw on some casual attire to follow. When she opened her door, Ensign Bintou-Keita had returned.

"Damn, he's fast," Miriam said. "When did he call you?"

"As he was headed to the bridge, Governor Heirlinda. Is there something I can help you with?"

"I'm going to the bridge, too."

"I wouldn't recommend that, ma'am."

"Well, I'm going. You can come with me if you like. And I'd like to run, please."

"Yes, Ma'am."

The two women arrived just a few moments after the captain by the time they made their ways to the main control center of the Tatsu. Miriam was breathless, but not at all surprised to find that Aida was unfazed by the fitness.

"What's going on?" Miriam asked.

"What's she doing here?" Kate interjected. She was still wearing her formalwear from the Unity Dinner.

"I couldn't stop her, ExO."

"I don't suppose you could, eh?" Mik said smiling.

"It's a fishing flotilla, Governor," Kate said. "They've blocked the way."

The executive officer shot a look to Ensign Bintou-Keita who narrowed her eyes at the comment.

"How many?" the ensign asked.

"Thirty," Mik said. "Get me the damned captain of the fishing vessel off my port bow, and I mean now!" Ridgelin screamed into comms at some poor soul on the receiving end.

"Flying flags?" Bintou-Keita asked.

"None," said Murphy.

After tense moments when everybody else seemed to be either running madly over buttons, looking around anxiously, or staring at Captain Ridgelin, a voice finally poured in over comms.

"Away and bile your head!" Mik yelled to the fishing boat captain in a brogue Miriam had only ever heard him use in jest before when sharing a drink with Tatsian citizens.

"We're just fishing, Sir. We mean no harm."

"You're talking mince. That ain't what this is and if ye don't get your arses out of my route, I'll run 'em over."

"Isn't it possible...." Miriam began in low tones to Aida.

"No, ma'am," the ensign started to answer her.

"This isn't an accident, Governor," Kate cut in. "Something's happening."

"But what?"

"That's what we're trying to figure out."

"Captain Ridgelin, the respected Cityship Tatsu certainly wouldn't do harm to...."

"Yer off yer feckin' head if ye think I'm falling fer that. You and the rest of yer flotilla git out of me way!"

There was a long pause before the fishing captain answered this time. Finally, he returned with, "We didn't mean to stop your progress, Sir. We'll be on our way, now."

Mik turned back toward Kate, Ensign Bintou-Keita, and the governor who, it seemed—for just a moment—he had forgotten was there. Before he could speak, Li Ju entered the Bridge of the ship guiding Dr. Jacob Bradley with a small bullet thrower held to his throat.

"It could be quick for him, or he doesn't have to die at all," she threatened.

Miriam looked at him and, by the time she looked back at the Tatsians, Aida Bintou-Keita had her hands on the built-in glass bullet launcher in the forearm of her uniform. Mik had pulled a sidearm that Miriam hadn't even realized he was carrying. Kate had grabbed the weapon of another sailor who was on the bridge. All three were aiming at the woman.

"No!" Miriam said. "We can't hurt him."

"We don't have to hurt him," Ju said. "I promise. I just need him to unlock something he says is being kept on the bridge here. After that, I'll leave."

"I'm so sorry, Governor. I had to tell her where the hydrocell was," Dr. Bradley said, his pale complexion even more ghostly with fear.

"It's okay, Jacob. It's okay. You did the right thing."

"Those your boats?" Mik asked. "Slowed us down so you could get aboard?"

"Awww. You caught me. Pretty smart for a...." she smirked, "....cityship captain," she sneered with narrowed eyes that indicated a deeper secret. "Move away from that panel. I know it's a safe," she said.

The captain nodded and, with hands still on their weapons, the crew counter-circled with Li Ju and Dr. Jacob Bradley. The latter still had the bullet thrower held at his throat. At the panel, Ju forced the doctor down on his knees as a shield in front of her, and she lowered herself behind him. She kept her eyes on the weapon-holders, and she opened the safe as easily as if it was her own.

"I see I'm due for updating my security," the captain said.

"We can't all be the best at what we do. Some families are just better than others," she said as she tossed the hydrocell case on the floor in front of Dr. Bradley.

"You bitch!" both Kate and Aida said in unison. Miriam got the sense there was even more going on than she understood and what she understood was frightening enough.

"Open it," the evil woman hissed.

Dr. Bradley looked at Miriam who nodded. "You can do it, Jacob," the governor said. "Your life is more important."

The scientist stood with the woman, opened the case, and Ju snatched the hydrocell. The intruder then dropped a smoke grenade and ran. When she got to the edge of the ship, she paused and tossed a small drone in the air. It cut through the gas and cleared a path between her and Dr. Bradley before it stopped right in front of his face. He ducked instinctively.

"That's a—" Mik began and before any of the rest of them could react, Miriam dove in front of the doctor's head, the drone dropped, and—through the clear tunnel between Li Ju and Bradley—the intruder shot. Miriam collapsed, the weight of her body bringing Dr. Bradley down with her.

Foggily, Miriam saw all three Tatsians running to the edge of the ship, weapons firing nonstop. Li Ju jumped over the side and launched a small chute that would carry her safely down to the surface of the water. She was yanked upward by the chute's opening for a split second before she began to fall, and she was hit with a barrage of glass bullets. Li Ju was dead in the air. Her limp hand released the hydrocell.

As her body floated down, Kate, Mik and Aida closed in on the edge of the ship. Mik began to lean over to look at the water when Aida pushed him back.

"No, Sir!" she exclaimed. "It can't be you."

"You think I give a flying feck? Let them see me! Let them feck-ing see me!"

"She's right, bro!" Kate screamed, pulling him back. "It would be war!"

Ensign Bintou-Keita stared over the edge of the ship and stood tall, holding her weapon high in the air. She made certain she was seen as the aggressor. Li Ju's body landed on a vessel manned by Erik and George of the Wang Family Fleet. The hydrocell sunk below the surface of the black water and the boat sped away to catch the entire flotilla that had already raced out of sight.

"Somebody, help!" Dr. Bradley called. "It's the governor!" he screamed.

Kate ran back to the bridge to find Miriam passed out from pain as she bled profusely, and a small glow burst from her shoulder.

"Holy hell!" Kate called, running over to the two and tearing the corner of Miriam's shirt to further expose her wound. She wiped the blood on her top. "Give me a hand here, Sailor," she said to the dazed crewman whose sidearm she had used.

The sailor stared at Kate's bust as it showed through the sheer panel of the formal uniform. He was more shellshocked than he was gawking.

"Help!" she said again before realizing he was staring at her breasts. "There!" she grabbed the sailor's hands and pressed them against her tits. "You good now? Because I'd kind of like to save the governor's life if that's okay with you!"

"Yes, ExO," he said, finally seeing her eyes and snapping out of his shock.

Kate let go of his hands and he took them off of her body. The two worked to stabilize Miriam.

"I can't do this here, Mik!" she screamed.

"Get her to the med bay," he responded. "Now."

Mik looked ill as Aida, Kate, and the sailor grabbed Miriam and began to carry her off the bridge. The idea of losing her on his ship was unfathomable to him.

CHAPTER 25
YEAR 2553

Former Baja Province
Former Northern Territory of New Hispaniola Land Nation
Former Global Union

It didn't take long.

After just a few days, the extended family, Tatsu's crew, joined ranks with Linda, Uru, and the children. The PS-1707 had nearly two months of time left before their next scheduled mining operations, having made their mandatory runs in record time. Normally, that earned flexibility would have allowed them a full extra bonus run, but the dead citizen accounts weren't going to grow this season. Instead, the crew voted to spend the time at Baja Province to allow Captain Mageo to reconnect with the brother he thought he'd lost. Wang Wei and his squad disagreed, but in a vote of twelve to eight, begrudgingly, they all determined to follow the majority and stay.

It took just a couple of days for Tatsu to get the lay of the land, at least the little piece of it that Linda and Uru had adapted for use, along with the twelve children they'd found en route to the chopper hangar. A tour of the newly formed Baja Province structures they had put together as a home at what was now left of the southern port showed an almost luxurious life of space and community.

Garden boxes overflowed, full of flourishing produce that had been left behind as mere seedlings until nurtured to maturity; three of four fat goats provided milk and the fourth led to one of them looking pregnant. Eight chickens, including two roosters, further rounded out their little family. The livestock and gardens were more than enough to sustain the big misfit collective.

The animals ran around in an outdoor pen that had been assembled with the large cables of fallen pod route lines wrapped around the no-longer-powered outdoor charging posts to create a fence. The outer perimeter of the fence was lined with drying racks for fish and other sea life. The makeshift farm sat on a bed of grass and dandelions growing wild and lush where, months ago, a much less alive city park had been. In one corner of the former park was a small grove of fruiting trees, adding even more to their food supply. Tatsu laughed at India and Tono, two of the children, who hung from the lowest limb of one of the trees throwing apples down for the goats.

Then there was the abandoned zip chopper hangar. It was protected from the elements and was a ground-level reinforced structure capable of withstanding most earthquakes. As it was, the tall buildings nearby had all collapsed, so they didn't serve up much of a threat to crumble further or fall on any part of their own structure. The hangar had become their home base where they shared meals, attended school using a curriculum that Linda and Uru had designed for them, tended their family farm outside, played, and expressed their creativity.

Vehicular pods had all been converted into sleeping quarters for the dozen orphans, decorated as each child saw fit, with any number of odd objects that had been found around the province. The pods lined the longest wall of the hangar and it didn't go unnoticed by Uru that Tatsu counted the room-like additions. There were fourteen of them.

"I care for her deeply," Uru said of Linda, as if reading Tatsu's mind. "But she's not Kim. And I care for all of them, too," he said, indicating the children running around with his brother's scrubber crew outdoors as the two men walked out of the home. "But they are not my Andy, my Grace, or my Alice." Tears welled up in the bottom of Uru's dark eyes.

Tatsu felt a lump in his own throat. "Look what you have here!" he said to his brother with a large pat to Uru's back.

He was providing distraction from another breakdown. They'd shared many in the days since finding one another again. The men walked to one side of the building where the family had affixed several compact solar panels to south-facing walls of their residential building to charge batteries that appeared to have been pulled from the electric pods. The charged batteries brought them light and allowed them to use two recovered refrigeration units and stove units that were inside.

"Looks like you're the one who will be treating me from now on, brother!" he laughed.

Outside of lighting and food storage and preparation, they really didn't use power at all. Education was managed in primitive manners not employed for hundreds of years. Oral sharing, hands-on practice, and non-interactive literature took the place of digital notes, mixed reality literary experiences, and GU standard tests.

Uru brought cultural studies, introducing them to the music, art, theatre, and sculptures of the past. What he chose to cover was based on whatever he had salvaged or could remember from his employ in the archives of the entertainment complex.

Linda cared for the animals and taught the children to do the same. They now had a number of animals that they'd seen birthed, and others that they'd found in their travels or that had joined them once they settled.

Dee and Julian were the oldest girl and boy after Mercy, both just a year out from their own aptitude tests had they still been with the Global Union. Julian taught fishing. He had been hoping to serve on a ship one day. Dee was able to help her cousins continue in science and math. And thirteen-year-old Juan excelled at gardening.

There was only a single electronic pad for their reading. Mercy—who loved storytelling with her cousins and would have been going into teaching based on her GU aptitude test—used reading samples from the archives of the entertainment complex. Uru had a large bag of physical artifacts that he'd taken out before the final quake in New Hollywood and, in addition to the art, it contained more reading materials. The cousins shared the singular copies of the old-fashioned, physical books amongst themselves and Mercy supplemented with countless stories from history that were saved on the educational pad.

They had paper-printed copies of The Complete Works of William Shakespeare, language resources from around the world that preceded Post Babel Global Tongue, along with sample fiction from various origin cultures, the great spiritual books of the past including the Quran, the Torah, the Bible, Tao Te Ching, The Vedas, the Book(s) of Life (and Death), and a dozen other mystical works from the religions and philosophies of Earth-Before-the-Melt. Plus, they inherited the revival works of Anderson, Grimm, Laura Ingalls Wilder, Samuel Clements, Miguel Cervantes, Isaac Asimov, Jules Verne, Lady Rowling, and L.M. Miranda. Their educational pad included the original bot-writings of the twenty third century, the world's nonfiction historical recreations written in the twenty-fourth century and adapted with indigenous influence, and the children's short legends of the Global Union provinces, to name a few.

Thousands of years of humanity sat in a single pad and a collection of books barely large enough to fill the three standard garden boxes that had been emptied, turned on their sides, and affixed to one another to create a small shelf. Mercy treated the relics with the care of a protein shipment. They were delicate and precious. She was making her way through the texts at nearly the pace of an adaptive reader, the digital library pads used in job training that read, summarized, and provided comprehensive notes for full teaching manuals.

With Uru and Linda, the four oldest children took pride in the care they provided to Ziad and Sofia, as well as in the education they brought to Tono, India, Hector, Ibrahim, Salma, and Mary. The strange family had indeed made a life on top of death. It was at once the most primitive and the most advanced little society the scrubbers had ever seen.

Together, the crew and the—they didn't know what to call them—the people without a country? Who were they? New Baja, old Global Union? Whoever they were, they shared meals and stories and jokes with Mageo's women and men. Stacy and Amy chased the youngest children who were thrilled just to have new playmates. Khalil and Justin acted as human playgrounds for Hector, Ziad, and Mary. Randall and Erin didn't bond much with the kids, but they worked to help where they were needed which was surprising in its own way.

Mercy showed off her knowledge of literature to Peter, and Peter, in turn, explained the mechanics of the mining vessel and his many inventions. His favorite invention was a new type of glove for collecting palm scans.

"So right now, if we want to collect palm scans, we have to get the citizen's data on a traditional palm scanner. First of all, those are hard to come by. The GU doesn't just hand them out like rations. But it's more than that," the boy went on.

Mercy didn't much care for engineering, but the big-eyed boy with the dark, chalky black skin could be talking in one of the old dead languages and she'd still have feigned interest just to keep him speaking. She watched his eyes light up and tried to listen for key words that she could ask about just to keep spending time with him.

"The palm scanner is connected to this whole GU network and we'd have to hack into the code to pull that data out. Not just the palm's biological print—the actual skin—but also all of the vitals of the person, the signal of the tracking chip, and the laser and ink imprint that the scanner made on the citizen's palm. That's a lot of places where the information can get fragmented or corrupted."

"Why do you need the scans, though?" Mercy asked.

"Well, you see a lot of people when you're a scrubber. People all over the world. And, even though they have homes and food, sometimes they need something more. A new recording release because it makes them feel joyful. Or, this one woman I remember, her partner was dying. They'd been together for forty-five years. All she wanted was to wear her union ceremony dress for her partner one more time, but of course she had recycled that decades earlier. So, she needed a new one, but their credits went to just living. We use the scans to get credits and we use the credits to help people like her."

"But who gives you their scans?"

"People who don't have anyone left to take care of. Old scrubbers, mostly."

"And everybody just uses those credits to help other people?"

"Well, no. But not everybody in the GU uses their recreation credits for good deeds, either. Some people waste them on vice lounges or – well – just on vices. Still, I think the positives outweigh the negatives."

"And this glove will help?"

"Eventually. It has a silicone palm that can copy the palm's biological print. That's actually unique. It's an ancient identification technique but it works when combined with the rest of the palm scan. The glove also has a light scan to get an image of the imprint. Once recorded, the reads can go back to neutral, too, so it's meant to be able to hold a dozen or so scans that somebody could rotate through. Getting the chip signal and a read on the vitals, though, that's tough. Plus, I have to program it so that there is some fluctuation in the vitals. Like, after every six months, there are tiny variations, so it seems more like a real human. A fifty-year old wouldn't have the same readings as when they were first scanned at sixteen."

"And that's the part that's giving you a problem?" Mercy asked.

"Well, that and the fact that the readers in the silicone palm give a pretty severe electric shock to any skin they come into contact with at this point!" Peter laughed and Mercy joined him heartily, leaning up against him as she did so. "I'm really close, though. I think just a tweak or two and I'll have it figured out."

Linda observed the two from a distance but kept mostly to herself. She was polite, but resistant to connect with the newcomers at more than a hospitable level.

Tatsu and Peter worked with Uru to strengthen some of their structural integrity in and around the hangar. The youngest PS-

1707 crewmember was small. Wang and some of the more seasoned crew loved to pick on him – the scrubber whose aptitude should have had him in engineering design, rather than practical application on a mining vessel. They wanted to toughen him up.

"Bring that toolbox over to Captain Mageo," Wang ordered Peter one afternoon.

The boy, not totally unaware of the smirks on the faces of Adam and Mari behind Wang, grabbed the box's handle and walked, but it stayed in place while his arm yanked backward. Laughter ensued as the magnetic clamp kept the box fastened to the deck.

"No. Pick it up from the bottom, kid. Go be a good table. Captain wants you to hold it for him."

Peter put both hands under the box and lifted with all his strength, but Wang released the magnetic clamp holding it to the deck at that moment and the boy nearly flung the whole kit, and himself with it, overboard. Not wanting to give Wang the satisfaction, he didn't react.

Peter went into the hangar where Tatsu and Uru worked, and he stood beside them holding the box as directed. The two kept grabbing tools from the box and tossing them back in while they worked. Uru threw in a clamp that caused a bolt to bounce up out of the box and catch Peter on the top of his head.

"Ouch!" called the boy.

"Why are you still holding that?" asked Tatsu while Peter's arms and legs shook from exhaustion.

"You can put that down now, son" Uru added.

Peter attempted to put it down gently, but it spilled out onto the floor of the hangar. Off in the entrance, Wang cracked up.

"Get out of here, Wei!" shouted Tatsu.

"He's not worth your scars, Peter," Uru offered.

"Scars come from the stories that make the person," the boy responded while picking up the tools.

"We've got it," the captain said, taking over. "I think Mercy's at the shore."

Peter ran out quickly without looking back.

Three weeks passed, each day leaving the scrubbers and the New Baja people feeling a little less like GU citizens and a little more like a family community. In the evenings, they sat around a fire enjoying food and friendship, the terrible singing of Uru and Tatsu, and a moment's reprieve from having to figure out what it all meant. The youngest children were asleep in their pods, most of the crew had turned in, and just a handful of them remained. Those were the times when a song or memory would bring Uru back to the reality of his human losses and anyone left would find excuses to leave.

"I'm going to give you brothers some time," Linda said, as the last one still around the fire with Tatsu and Uru. "I need to find where Mercy wandered off to, anyway."

As she walked away from the fire, Uru followed her with his eyes as long as the light of the flames touched her body.

"She's really great, you know," he said to Tatsu. "She's okay with me . . . with my brokenness. She accepts it. Accepts who I am now."

"And who are you now, big brother?" asked the scrubber.

"That's a loaded question," he said laughingly with a playful shove, hoping to brush it off, but Tatsu held a straight face letting his brother know that not answering was not an option.

Eventually, after a deep breath, Uru said, "What else can a person do if he can't do what he did before? Everything I'd done, everything I'd lived for was my kids. It was the first identity that wasn't assigned to me. To have that taken away from me . . . it broke me. Sent me down a dark path. Anxiety. Depression. Despair. All of it."

"I should have been here."

"I don't think you could have been. Even if you had been physically here, I still had to go through all of it alone, or that's what I believed, anyway."

"I understand that," Tatsu said as a bitter expression briefly crossed his face.

"I'm sorry, bro. You went through it alone, too."

"I think I'm okay with it. I know now you were going through something so much more difficult. I can't blame you for not letting me know. I don't even know how you would have told me if you wanted to. I got at least part of what I lost back."

"And I lost all purpose, too," Uru said. "Everything turned inward, and I shut down. I was a mess for a long time. I kept thinking about Grace, Andy, and Alice, how they were a part of me. I loved Kim, too, love her, but losing the children? It was like having my soul forcibly ripped from my body. I experienced the physical sensation of my own spirit becoming untethered."

"But now? What changed?"

"I was mourning the dead but realized that the dead weren't mourning me. They were gone. I'd like to think at peace but certainly, from my life here, gone. Meanwhile, I couldn't have life… while carrying their dead weight."

"Zoe life."

"Yeah," said Uru. "Zoe life. That's what Grandma called it."

"Life to the full."

"And, as painful as it was to think of it without my family, I wanted it. I had to piece myself back together, and with different pieces than I had before, different shapes and sizes and colors."

"And names?" Tatsu prompted.

"Mercy, Dee, Julian, Juan, all of their little cousins...."

"And Linda," the younger brother added.

Uru lowered his head, lost somewhere in the emotional abyss between guilt and pain and longing.

"One night, this was before we found the kids, she and I had slept in the cab of the pod-hauler instead of making camp," he said. "We were just so tired. Anyway, in the morning, the sun was coming up and it started shining into the ground-vehicle. It was so perfect. Pink and glowing warmth just poured in and filled the space and I thought she was awake, too. I wanted to comment on the sunrise, so I turned to her, but she was still fast asleep. I looked at Linda, laying in the sunlight, and I got this overwhelming sense of hope. I don't know where it came from. It had been so long since I'd felt anything at all but, in that moment, I knew I would have meaning in my life again."

"Let me ask you something. What are you doing, here? Are you staying? Is this where you live now? Apart from society? Apart from the Global Union?"

"Well, I can't say I can imagine going anywhere else."

"So, this is home?"

"I think so," Uru nodded like he was realizing this truth for the first time. "Yes. I think it is."

"And, in this home you're making, who will you be with?"

"Linda and the kids."

"So, you plan to spend the rest of your life with these people. They are your family, now, right?"

"The kids may leave as they grow up. We'll have to figure that out. But who knows what this all will look like then? Maybe they'll come back. Maybe even with others."

"And if they didn't, it would be just you and Linda?"

After a pause, the resigned older brother said, "Would it be wrong?"

Then, Uru dropped his head into his hands, feeling shame for so deeply yearning for the life that was in front of him now. He felt unfairly and abundantly blessed in the midst of tragedy, gifted out of the graves of many, including those of his own wife and children. He was unwilling to come to terms with and accept anything of beauty that could impossibly be growing out of the rubble of his homeland. He was overcome with the conflicting emotions of gratitude and loss. He desired an end to the punishment of survival but sought—just as much—the permission to accept its end and take hold of a new beginning.

"You love them, Uru. You loved Kim and your children. And now you love these new children. And, my brother, you love Linda," Tatsu said, emphasizing each word and offering that lifeline, that permission to be okay. "She is lou loto. It's not the same love, but it's love, all the same. Love is one of the only things in this world that is pure and true and human. And love is not wrong."

CHAPTER 26
YEAR 2908

Pacific Sea Route
Cityship Tatsu IV
Cityship Regatta

"**D**o not move," Kate said to her anesthetized patient.

Murphy continued, deep in concentration, "I had to use a local because we didn't have much time, so I need you to be still."

The ExO's hair was hanging down in wild red curls from the formal event earlier that evening. She had pulled a medical coat over her dress uniform.

"It's a phosphocyanide bullet," she said as she worked both hastily and delicately in the open wound on Miriam's shoulder.

"What's a phosph—" began Miriam weakly.

"For starters, it's just a bullet. It does it's blunt, gory work," Kate's words were accented by her own bloodied hands. "But the outer layer of the bullet is phosphorous-based, and it begins to burn when it comes into contact with a combination of oxygen, like the air, and moisture, like say—"

"Blood," Miriam finished.

"Exactly," then, "HOLD STILL!" she scolded.

For a moment neither spoke while Kate concentrated on completing very precise movements. She would peel back bits of flesh, then immediately pack the newly revealed portion of the bullet, smothering each new ignition.

"The thing is," Kate went on while she got the bullet in the teeth of her medical tool. "It's not the burning you should worry about. It's when the burning stops. That phosphorous layer is the only thing between your bloodstream and the cyanide that is at the core of the bullet," she finished as she plucked the triple-threat weapon from Miriam's shoulder and dropped it into a metal bucket that she slammed shut. She took a shuddering breath before turning back to Miriam.

Miriam continued to bleed and after the pause, Kate turned back to the governor. "I'm going to have to seal this wound," Kate said as she poured a liquid antiseptic onto the shoulder. Even with the local anesthesia, Miriam had to clench her teeth through the pain. "It's not a small wound, either. Thanks to the burning, it went all the way through even though the bullet was still lodged in you. You'd be dead if it wasn't your shoulder. As it is, you're going to have a hole in your body going forward."

"I take it there's no bedside manner training for the cityship crew?" Miriam said weakly.

"Damned bullet launchers. I should have seen it coming. I should have seen all of it coming. It was too late by the time I called Mik."

"Not your fault."

"It is," she said. "It's my job to protect him. And anyone he's close to, regardless of how careless the relationship is."

Kate sprayed Miriam's shoulder with a liquid that caused her blood to immediately clot on both sides of her body and through the center of the hole the phosphocyanide bullet had left behind. Miriam cried out.

"Liquid cauterizer. It's going to look nasty for a couple of days," she said in response to a question Miriam hadn't asked.

"Where's your medic?" Miriam asked.

"I know what I'm doing," Kate said. I've taken care of Callum and my other brothers from the time I was ten."

"Callum?"

Kate shook her head, realizing she hadn't meant to speak so plainly with the governor about her family but, in the stress of the moment, her guard was down. "Um. Yeah. He's my big brother."

"I wasn't questioning your ability, but it's not supposed to be your job, is it?"

"Mik wanted to keep this one off the books," Kate said. "And we needed to work fast," she added as she prepared an automatic injection machine, filling the mechanism with fluid bags.

"It's hard to be responsible for others," Miriam said sleepily.

"You got that right. Sefina wants to be out here, you know, on a cityship. She doesn't know what it's like. They teach about storms and quakes and tsunamis. They teach business and government. But formal school loves to just pretend the fleet families don't exist," Murphy said angrily.

"You think that's what this was?"

"That was Li Ju, Li Fang's sister."

"The Wang Family Fleet."

"Yes. The one that gives a shit name to the rest of them."

"Aren't they all outlaws?"

"They're not all the same," she said. Kate shook her head and Miriam almost thought she looked hurt by the suggestion.

Five fleet families claimed territorial waters. The Wang Family worked across the whole Pacific, so they were the water mob that most often was known to bring hell to Zoe Baja's trade partners and ships. Reports of their activities were common to hear. Whole shipments disappeared and, beyond that, so did whole ships and their crews. The Morozov Family worked in the Arctic waters. The Atlantic was led by Finlay McMahon's McMahon Family Fleet in the North and the Bintou-Keita Family in the South. Last, there was the Ali Family in the Indian Ocean.

To Miriam's knowledge, it was uncommon for any of the families to hit official targets. It was primarily the civilian and commercial vessels that reported incidents.

"You couldn't have known," the governor said to Kate.

"It's my job to know. And it was my job to protect you and the doctor and your power cell."

"He can build another. We saved Dr. Bradley," the governor said, her eyes getting heavy.

"You. You saved him."

"And now you're saving me," Miriam drawled sleepily.

"I'm going to put you out, now. You could use some proper sleep," Kate said.

Miriam's eyes were already closed.

Miriam was groggily waking up to the voices in the room.

"Aye, Captain," Kate said as she was leaving the room.

"That's 'oui,' ExO," he snapped back.

"Really? Do you think the secret's not out?" she said slamming the door to the med bay.

"Everything okay?" Miriam whispered.

"Hey," Mik said. "Look who's up. I didn't want to wake you," Mik said sitting at Miriam's bedside. "You almost became nothing but a drop in the sea."

She smiled.

"That's funny?" the captain was confused.

"That's my name," Miriam said. "A drop in the sea. That's what my name means. But my dad always said it meant bitter water."

"I like that. Not the bitter part, the drop in the sea part," Mik said. "Maybe you're meant to be at sea, after all," he tried to tease.

"No. My parents meant it to honor Zoe Baja. My home is a drop in the sea."

"What's in a name?" Mik smiled. "I meant to take my mother's name. Ask me what it was."

"What was it?" she sleepily asked, energized only by the presence of the captain.

"Longridge. LONGRIDGE! Could you imagine me trying to get respect with my lot with a name like Captain Longridge?"

Miriam huffed out a weak laugh. "I can hear the jokes about standing at attention, now."

"I modified. Only Kate knows about the change," he said shaking his head. He wanted to make light of their situation, but that didn't change it. He sighed, Then, after a pause. "Well, I'm glad that you didn't become just a drop in the sea, Miriam," Mik finished.

The captain held her hand. Then, he kissed it, much as he had on that first day when they'd met at the Dandelion Festival.

"What did I miss while recovering?" the governor asked.

"It's been a day. We've managed to keep everything under wraps. We have the sailor who helped Kate on lockdown. Dr. Bradley is completely okay, thanks to you. His quarters are guarded by some of my top security, now, and Devon has placed one of their drones outside his bullseye window."

"Shie shie," she nodded.

"And you had a personal call from your chief of staff, but we haven't had any official communications. I wanted to wait until you were ready."

"I feel good. It's okay. He called on unofficial channels? Interesting. I should call him back. I want to get out of this bed, anyway," she said while sitting up. She was wearing a light cotton gown and scrub bottoms.

"Hold on," Mik said, steadying Miriam on the bed. "Sitting up is fine, but you can call from right here. I brought a digifile predicting that you'd want to reach out to him."

The captain tapped a few buttons. A projection of Inoke appeared in the air above the device.

"You're okay, governor!" Inoke said, relief in his voice.

"Inoke, what's going on?"

"That's what I want to know. Francisco's been acting strangely. I mean more than usual. He's expressing concern for your safety at sea because, and I quote, 'scary things happen out there.'" Inoke said making quotes in the air with his hands. "Francisco worried about you? Just because? It all just sounded off. And now he's been meeting with Doug Beamer, and you know how he's been itching to use tsunamic defense. And I can't find Harry who is the only guy here who can stop TD if it is activated."

"Strange is right. I don't know what to make of that." Miriam said, an expression of concern on her face.

"Hold on," Inoke said. His eyes darted around, and Miriam could tell he was taking in the whole image on his own digifile. "Are you in a medical bay right now? You are! I see the equipment. What's going on, my friend?" he said, sounding much more concerned than he had been and that had been quite a bit.

Instinctively lowering her voice, "Is this a secure line?"

"Not yet. Hold on," her chief said as his eyes moved over characters on his screen that she couldn't see. "It is now. I encrypted it."

"I am in a med bay, yes."

Inoke's eyes immediately widened. "That's why I couldn't reach you in the last day? What the hell happened?"

"I'm fine, Chief," she smiled at her friend. "We were attacked. It may have been a fleet family."

"It WAS a fleet family," Mik added, popping his own head into the view so that Inoke knew of his presence.

"What? That's insane!"

"I'm okay, thanks to Kate. They just wanted the hydrocell."

"Okay this is getting even odder. Francisco said, when he was worried about you, he wanted to make sure the cell was secure."

"Anything else?"

"Remember that defector who was asking for refugee status?"

"Of course."

"Can't find him either. And that's all I know. I'm out of the loop, Governor. Francisco wants me to check on you and make sure the hydrocell is fine because he knows it's the lynchpin to the negotiations. And that's all."

"Okay. Let me think about this for a second," the governor considered the new information. She got off of the bed and began to pace the room.

Even in hospital garments and still slightly medicated, she managed to be commanding. She never appreciated it about herself, but Mik could see nothing more. She drew people around her who couldn't help but trust and support and want to join her vision of the world. She was smart and relational and exactly the sort of person that a human unification movement needed.

"Listen, Inoke," she continued, carefully selecting the words of each point of her message, "tell Francisco that you checked with me, as he directed. Tell him I said we had losses that I was wary of discussing over the air with you. Tell him we are no longer going to the Pacific Islands Land Nation," Miriam directed each point thoughtfully. "Tell him that you were not able to speak with Dr. Bradley at all. And tell him that I was very concerned about all of it."

"He didn't ask about Dr. Bradley, though."

"I know. Say that part, anyway."

"Is this all true, Miriam?"

"Yes, Inoke. Which makes it perfect. And one other thing?"

"Yes, Governor?"

"Find Harry. I hope I'm wrong, but I think we'll be needing him."

"Yes, Ma'am," he said submissively, immediately followed by, "Be careful, Miriam," in a tone of familial tenderness.

After the call, Mik took the digifile back and looked dismally at Miriam. He held one of her hands and had placed his other on the edge of her wounded shoulder.

"Not going to the Pacific Islands? Obviously, we have to turn back, now," he said.

Gently, Mik pushed the shoulder of Miriam's hospital wrap down, and he looked sadly at her scar. Kate had laser-stitched the wound after cauterizing it rather than leaving the hole in her body.

"No," Miriam said. We need these talks now more than ever."

"But I thought you said to Inoke...."

"We're holding the talks. Here. Send two ships and bring Prefects Chen and Phillips here, to us."

Sighing, "And I don't suppose I could talk you out of it."

"You couldn't."

Mik kissed Miriam's shoulder, letting his lips rest for just a moment on the fresh scar before he pulled the corner of her hospital garment back up.

"Okay, then. I'll make it happen."

CHAPTER 27
YEAR 2553

Former Baja Province
Former Northern Territory of New Hispaniola Land Nation
Former Global Union

Tatsu Mageo made Wang Wei's blood boil.

The captain was so damned self-righteous. He made his own personal family the crusade for all of them. He manipulated votes and consensuses with emotion. That damned man just pulled out a locker room speech every time he needed to get the scrubbers on board with whatever stray for whom he felt called to care.

This crew had worked harder than they ever had before to earn a longer time off between mining runs, and then that time was wasted – spent with people who could spend nothing on them in return. Protein was not the only thing Wang was accustomed to running and he wasn't even sure if he'd be able to keep control of his other unsanctioned runs after disappearing the way he was forced to do with the mining vessel crew – a crew he should have been running. He didn't sweat his ass off in the anchor room to play charity administrator to a bunch of losers who couldn't figure out how to work the system for themselves.

Wang walked around the hangar while his captain sat in the middle of another one of his sob fests with his brother at a firepit they had built. They made him sick – both of them. They claimed incorruptibility like a badge of honor, as if there was some prize at the end of their long ugly lives because they hadn't figured out how to find the prize in the life they had on Earth.

The Mageo brothers of the world tried to make themselves nothing so that the world saw them as something. Maybe it was a hero complex. The Wang Weis of the world didn't hide their importance. They branded themselves with it. Then there were people like Erin and Randall. The underlings of the world were easy to control. They didn't want to be important. They merely wanted to get by until it was over, numbing their pain along the way. The two of them were addicted before he'd ever arrived on the '07. A few others had followed. He was close to turning the crew – almost halfway. As long as he kept their supply of hallucinatory patches fully stocked, they kept his accounts fully stocked and, more importantly, they kept his secrets.

Now, with no visit to a vice lounge for months, his patch supply had dwindled. So would his control if things didn't change, and soon. He needed a port. And he needed a drink. And he needed to see what sorts of goods were making their ways into the underground market. And he needed—

Wang stopped as he came around a corner of the massive former zip chopper building. He stood near a pile of construction materials they had gathered for the charity cases. Pipes and wires and plastic and wood remnants cluttered the ground. As he stood in the midst of rubbish, he spotted Peter who was sitting in the shadows with the orb eyed orphan girl. Peter – the scrawny black boy with no understanding of what he could make with his little inventions if he had any mind for business at all. The junior engineer was another one following the Mageo brothers' model, ready to squander his future for the sentimental captain's latest lost cause.

As Wang watched his crewman showing off his little glove project to the young woman, the anchor room worker felt the heat rush up through his chest and into his neck and face. His heart began to race with rage as he watched that child Peter brushing the back of his fingers on Mercy's cheek, laughing like a schoolboy, and tickling her sides. The boy chanced a hand on the girl's leg and Wei could see the desire in the dark-haired girl's body language. He could taste her thirst. Peter was oblivious to it.

Wang put his hands to his pants and undid his belt and fly. He had become hard, and he put his own hand to his cock as he looked at the raven-haired young thing with his crewman. Peter glanced down at the dead citizen's account project in his hand, more interested in his toy than the fresh flesh in front of him . . . a far greater toy. More waste. Wang's chest rose and fell with a yearning that he could no longer hold back. The boy wasn't looking. Wang picked up a pipe, charged the young couple and struck Peter on the back of the head.

Mercy had jumped backward, and her legs had fallen open. She was too shocked to move at first, but Wang was sure the heat was still in her and, unlike Peter, he was a man who knew what to do about it. He lunged toward Mercy.

"YOU LITTLE BITCH!"

In barely the time it took for Tatsu and Uru to recognize where the voice came from, Wang Wei appeared at the fire with Mercy following quickly behind. Wang's cheek had a bright red, hand-shaped welt across it with blackish blistering at its center. His face twitched. Mercy panted heavily, her eyes were burning coals, and her clothing was disheveled.

"That child," Wang said gesturing a finger toward Mercy, "is psychotic! She fucking electrocuted me! I could have been killed!"

Linda and Peter had made their way to the firepit to stand on either side of Mercy in a protective huddle. Tatsu took in the group and noticed Peter's credit glove prototype on Mercy's hand. Then he looked at Wang. Stacy and Amy joined the fray, not sure whether they should stand by Mercy or Wang. Amy loyally took a stance next to the captain while Stacy moved to Peter's side.

"Are you okay?" Stacy asked Peter, who was holding a hand at the back of his head.

"I was with Mercy and then, I didn't even see what hit me," the boy said dazedly to the maternal figure.

"Captain, do something," Wang demanded of Tatsu.

The captain stepped toward Wang and narrowed his gaze at the man. Wei shrunk a bit – a flinching reaction he attempted to hide. His eye continued to twitch. In a low whisper that was directed at Wang but was audible to all, a growling threat seeped into Tatsu's voice.

"Maybe, the next time you try to accuse a child, as you call her, of abuse, you'll remember to put away your sad little pecker and close your fucking pants first, you sick prick," he said as he closed the distance to within an inch of Wang's weasely face.

Wei looked down, knowing he was caught as his now limp dick hung sadly out of his fly.

"If it were me, I would have shocked your shriveled little member right off," Tatsu punctuated with spit.

Tatsu held his stare down of the crewman until Uru shouted out, "YOU MONSTER!" and leapt toward the man.

Tatsu pulled his brother back, but not until he allowed Uru to crack his rock-hard fist against Wang's jaw, making the man dizzy with pain. Randall and Erin, who had joined the commotion, flanked their dealer like stray animals.

Tatsu held a hand up to his big brother, preventing further violence from erupting. In the midst of the ugliness, he was filled with satisfaction because, for the first time in months, Uru had found his strength again – his passion. As Wang straightened up, the Mageo brothers stood side-by-side in front of him and formed a brick wall.

"Amy," the captain said. "Take this shit excuse for a citizen to the brig. We'll drop him at the next GU port."

"Oui, Sir, Captain Mageo," she said.

She led away the disgusting man while he awkwardly closed his pants. Erin and Randall followed.

Feeling out of place amongst those who remained, "Let's get you taken care of, too," Stacy said to Peter.

Stacy looked at Mercy, unsure of what to say. Peter hugged the young girl and then relieved her of his glove. Before he was out of reach, the oldest orphan squeezed Peter's hand with her own and nodded to the boy to make sure he knew he did what he could.

"I'll help with Peter," said Tatsu. "Cairo and Marquise just finished setting up an aid station in the hangar for the family."

Then, they were alone. Linda, Uru, and Mercy wordlessly embraced one another by the fire for a long time, a place of unquestioning safety and comfort. Mercy assured her adoptive parents that she really was fine, that Wei didn't actually hurt her at all, and that she was quickly able to stop him with the help of Peter's glove. When Linda and Uru felt certain this was the story of prevented violence, and not of a successful attack, they allowed her to leave them for her bed.

Everyone drifted to sleep, and Linda did so while laying on Uru's chest. His arms were wrapped around her as though afraid to ever let go.

"I can't believe you're really getting married!" Mercy said to Linda as she came into the hangar pushing a small crate on wheels. "Archaic much?"

"Some parts of the world still believe in it," Linda smiled.

"Do you, though?"

"I believe in Uru."

"You guys are so the opposite of vee!" Mercy rolled her eyes, but the corners of her mouth were turned upward. "Anyway, I have something for you," the young woman said as she finished crossing to Linda. "It's from Tunes."

"A present?"

"He said you'd want it for today."

"I can't imagine what else I could possibly need today. I have everything I want," Linda smiled, stroking Mercy's cheek.

"Yee! Mushy," said the girl pushing the hand away while simultaneously leaning into Linda. "Just open it," she added.

Linda took the lid off of the crate that Mercy had wheeled into the hangar and her eyes immediately filled with tears.

"Oh shit," Mercy said. "You okay? You don't cry. Don't cry. This is not a crying day. Not today," she scolded, holding back tears of her own.

Linda nodded while lipping, "I'm fine."

In awe, she pulled Elsie Laurita's gown out of the box. The bag Uru had pulled from the archives before the New Hollywood quake – Linda assumed it was only books and art, but, somehow, he managed to save this, too.

"Help me get into this," the bride said.

Just as much as the first time she saw it, Linda eagerly hungered to put the gown on. She stripped out of the much simpler dress she'd sewn together from uniform fabrics provided by Amy and Stacy, and then dropped it right there onto the floor where she stood.

"Can I have the other dress?" Mercy asked as Linda stepped into the light layered gown she wore the first time she and Uru ever touched.

"That would look nice on you," Linda said while beginning to close the snaps of the Elsie Laurita dress.

Mercy held up the clothes Linda had removed, "Well, after some adjustments, it will."

Mercy finished closing the snaps of Linda's gown and helped take the woman's hair out of her usual braids. She lovingly placed wildflowers into her mother's locks before giving her a bouquet of dandelions from their field.

The ceremony was simple. Tatsu blubbered through it more openly than either Uru or Linda. Uru wore Tatsu's formal uniform, the one he normally donned when coming into GU ports at province capitals and other important cities. It was still a scrubber uniform, but it was clean and pressed with polished black buttons. It was a bit large on Uru, but still the finest clothing in which Linda had ever seen him.

Following an exchange of vows, everybody enjoyed a feast of seafood and freshly grown produce. Then, they danced all night long to a music library comprised of Elsie Laurita's greatest hits, as well as the original music inspirations of her twentieth century American sessions.

All of the children, from two-year-old Ziad up through fifteen-year-olds Dee and Julian laughed and danced and ate with all of the scrubbers, with the exception of Wang who was obviously not in attendance. Peter and Mercy clung closely together, hugging more than they were dancing, and savoring the last time they would have together before the PS-1707 had to ship off once more.

The crew, and the orphans, and the widow, and the widower were one large family. Linda felt, for the first time in her life, that she was truly alive, and Uru was sure she'd breathed some of that life back into him, too.

"Captain!" Khalil came running into the celebration while holding a bloodied bandage to his head. Khalil had been the first to leave the wedding festivities to return to the ship to man the operations. These days, that just meant caring for Wang in his cell of the brig.

"He's gone. Wang Wei. Got out when I was bringing him his meal. He took the 07's recon ship and sped off headed east. I couldn't stop him. I ran back here as fast as I could."

"It's not your fault. Did he say where he was going?"

"What do you think?"

"Disculpas. I'm sorry. Damn," said Tatsu at a loss.

"Should we go after him?" Justin asked having walked over and tuned into their conversation.

Captain Mageo looked at his crew, together as a family with the former Global Union citizens at a joyous occasion. Most hadn't even noticed Khalil's approach and certainly wouldn't miss Wang Wei either. In the years he'd known the scrubber, there was seldom an initiative for anything other than a quick fix or a long high. He'd probably just gone to the closest random port to get in some vice lounge time before the GU read Tatsu's reports. It was not as though there was anywhere that the weasel could run that the long arm of the Global Union could not reach.

"It's dark," Tatsu said. "We don't know where he went. This is my brother's wedding. It can wait until morning."

Morning would come much more abruptly than any of them had expected.

CHAPTER 28
YEAR 2908

Pacific Sea Route
Cityship Tatsu IV
Cityship Regatta

They forced prefects of the two GU nations to come to them.

Calling leaders of nations to the middle of the Pacific was a risky move with regard to winning them over. But it was necessary. Mik had sent his two fastest government ships to retrieve the delegations of the land nations and they would be arriving soon. Instead of the beauty of the Pacific Islands, they would be holding their talks in the diplomatic offices of the Cityship Tatsu.

Miriam remembered the first time she visited the Pacific Islands Land Nation. While they were Global Union, there was a different feel to the culture there than in New Hispaniola or the Canadian Land Nation, her neighbors to the east.

After the second melt, countless refugees found their way to the volcanic islands, secure in their longevity and safety, at least until the volcanic reduction projects. The origin cultures of the Samoan Islands, Hawaiian Islands, and others in the region managed to seep through the seams of the Global Union fabric. Warm hospitality emanated off the people there. They wore bright colors and greeted everyone with smiles and what felt like genuine affection.

Miriam had taken in a fire dancing performance which felt both ancient and impressive at the same time. The foods were simple things from nature, fish and fruits and nuts. But the plant-based displays used to present them were themselves decadent. Each dish looked like a piece of artwork. She didn't know if this had been done for her sake, presenting plants beautifully by the Global Union nation in charge of botany. But she didn't think so. There was authenticity to everything she experienced on the Pacific Islands Land Nation.

She was sad not to go back because it was that nation which gave Miriam hope for true partnership with the Global Union. The people she'd met there were people who seemed to share the Zoeans' affinity for nature and the inevitable fluidity of life. Their lives were less rigid, and their people appreciated beauty – be it that of other people or that of the earth. Those shared values were, to Miriam, a type of freedom.

By contrast, she knew very little of the Antarctic Land Nation other than the fact that they led the Lunar and Martian mining operations, a history she didn't understand as thoroughly as she should. She knew of course, as everybody did, about the multi-centennial space work ban after the Global Union began, but that was about the extent of her knowledge. Because she didn't particularly love the cold temperatures, Miriam somehow always managed to send other diplomats in her place to in-person meetings being held there. She often participated via satellite or virtual presence. She liked Lilibeth Phillips, a headstrong woman who wasn't easily swayed by politicking. Prefect Phillips had the respect of many in the Global Union, as well as amongst other world leaders such as those from the Zoelands Concord, Cityship Regatta, and Indigenous Nations.

"Jambo, Jacob," Miriam said to Dr. Bradley as he joined her in the meeting room. "How are you doing?"

"I'm—" he paused, looking ill. "Honestly, Governor? I was making a power cell. That's all. And I'm proud of it. And I know it will make a difference. But I wasn't prepared for the rest of this. I'm a scientist, not a satellite program action star! Attacks and diplomatic events and . . . and murder threats!" He looked up at Miriam. "Governor! I could have been killed! You saved my life!"

"Breathe, Jacob. You would have done the same for me."

"I don't think so. I mean, not that I wouldn't, but I don't think I could have. You literally took a – what even was that? – a fire poison bullet? – for me, Miriam. Oh no. I just called you 'Miriam.' I'm losing my mind," the doctor's wide eyes were shifting back and forth, and the absorption of tension was stiffening his whole body.

"You can call me Miriam. We've been through enough for that," she said as she put a hand on his.

"How are you so calm?" he exclaimed. "I don't even have the prototype, anymore!"

"We don't need it. We have you. After today, hopefully you can go back to your labs and the hydro plant. You just have to hold it together for a few more hours. That's it. You just talk science. That's all you have to do."

Jacob nodded and then, at the governor's direction, sat down so as to look more comfortable than he actually felt. He thought he would have to stand up and greet people, but it turned out world leaders didn't tend to notice the person they'd never heard of when in a room full of high-powered individuals.

Prefect Phillips arrived first with her delegation and she was far more beautiful than Miriam realized from having never seen her in person.

"Lilibeth Phillips, you've met Miriam Heirlinda," Mik said as he escorted the prefect into the room.

"Never face-to-face, though. Good to finally change that," she said as she shook hands with the governor.

Pleasantries were exchanged with all of Mik's ministers and with those from the Antarctic Land Nation. Enele Chen arrived just as all of the possible small talk that could be held by a group of diplomats was exhausted. He was a fit man in perfectly tailored business attire that would have made Inoke jealous. He also wore many layers, a show of Global Union opulence in the face of re-source shortages that extended even to clothing in many parts of the world. Simple talk and greetings continued again until, as if a switch had been flipped in the room, smiles and handshakes were replaced with stoic expressions on individuals with interlaced fingers.

"I want to thank you all for being so flexible with the change of location for the talks." Miriam began.

"It's our fault, really," Mik took the hit. "The Tatsu was stalled."

Miriam noticed his choice of words, appreciating how he wasn't exactly lying.

"And it was just simpler to send secure vessels for you," Kate added – the two always spoke in the same kind of natural flow together as Miriam did with her father and friends.

"We all know why we're here," Miriam said. "There is an energy crisis. Except, it's not a crisis of quantity. It's a crisis of storage. Meanwhile, Zoe Baja is in, well – I'm just going to say it. Zoe Baja is experiencing a famine. We have a way to fix all of those problems."

"We don't really have a problem," Prefect Chen chimed in.

"That's true. But you could be thriving even more than you already are," Miriam corrected herself cautiously.

Doctor Bradley then presented all over again, this time with far less enthusiasm, but with much more breakdown of how things worked. He tried to include answers to the questions that had been posed by Captain Ridgelin's ministers, anticipating that others might have similar concerns. He spoke to show that he'd thought through some of the obstacles and ideas beyond just the science of his hydrocell.

"What it comes down to is that the hydrocell works. It will eliminate weight and space which, while those issues are very big on a cityship like this one, are realistic concerns around the whole world right now. It will provide power and water and—to a certain degree— return to all of us the luxury of space."

"Can we see it?" asked Prefect Phillips.

Dr. Bradley's presentation of the actual prototype was meant for this moment, but instead he pulled up a three-dimensional visual projected out of the digifile built into the center of the conference room table.

"Oh," Phillips said with genuine excitement. "That's ideal!"

Miriam was amused at the simplicity of a digital prototype. Why hadn't they thought of that from the start?

Jacob walked the room through the power cell while keeping the proprietary information secure. Lilibeth Phillips, a scientist herself before going into government, asked many technical questions that Jacob answered perfectly and with great detail. She continuously looked to her delegation with big eyes, hungry for the gift being presented.

"And the designs?" she asked. "They are...."

"In my head, ma'am," said Dr. Bradley. "Different engineering teams have worked together on each component, but I'm the only one at this point who is aware of the full scope of the project."

"I don't know how you feel, Enele, but—for the Antarctic Land Nation—this is very promising." Phillips said.

"I agree this is well-done," added Prefect Chen. "But could we see the actual prototype."

Without missing a beat, Kate interjected, "It wasn't safe to bring it on the cityship. It was too important."

Another truth, Miriam realized. If the full story ever came out, they'd have said nothing false. Kate was proving uniquely gifted at the craft of deceit.

"What I'm not really understanding is what you need with all of us." Chen prodded.

"Honestly? Food, Prefect Chen." Miriam said. "We have the science for this project. You have food to provide our nation in exchange for hydrocells. My people are surviving on the fringes of famine. Our food is almost entirely imported, and it is taxed at levels we can no longer sustain. We need nourishment out of your nation's abundance."

Turning to the leader of Earth's southernmost nation, Miriam continued in her proposal. "Prefect Phillips, the Antarctic Land Nation has the raw materials needed for construction of the power cells – the tri-stellar compounds unique to its design. In exchange for the completed hydrocells, we are asking for those raw materials."

Miriam stood and walked over to Captain Ridgelin to present her last point. She knew that standing beside Mik would present the image of a partnership that they were joining rather than a charity case they were helping. "The Cityship Tatsu, on its route, would be able to not only ship these things back and forth—the food, the raw material, the hydro cells that would be moving between our three entities—but they would also check on the tidal turbines and wind nets throughout the Pacific." Miriam nodded to Dr. Bradley to pull in the science again.

"Eventually, the initial power we collect to store in these cells," interjected Dr. Bradley upon receiving his cue, "Will have to be collected at sea and not on Zoe Baja."

"And the Global Union in all of this? Why have these individual GU nations represented here but not bring in Sovereign Donte Harris?" asked Prefect Chen, referring to the leader of all of the Global Union land nations.

"We don't need the other nations." the governor said plainly, allowing her meaning to sink in.

"But the other Cityships?" Minister Feldman asked.

"They would serve a purpose in that they could also eventually be power collectors along their routes."

"You aren't seeking our alliance," Prefect Phillips said, the reality dawning on her at last. "You're seeking our defection from the Global Union."

Miriam said nothing and her silence said everything.

"Captain!" Lieutenant Devon Cas came over comms. "Sorry to interrupt, but my recon drones have caught something that I think you all need to see.

A projection popped up over the center of the table in place of Jacob's digital prototype. The live news feed showed a building collapsing in Zoe Chile.

Miriam sat in shock as she viewed the images. "A quake?" she asked the obvious question.

"Yes Governor," Devon returned. "Tsunami warnings, too."

The governor looked at the images of her fellow Zoeans, many of them probably dying as this footage was being broadcast. The tectonic plates finally brought their fist fight to the surface. She found herself staring hopelessly at the feed. Mik saw her and took over as the diplomat once more.

"My esteemed colleagues, it looks like these talks will have to be cut short. We will get you quickly and safely back to your homes," Mik said, taking charge immediately. "ExO Murphy, get our top navigators on those government vessels."

"Oui, Sir!" she called.

The delegates began their exit. At the door, Phillips turned back to the room. "Wait," she said, taking a deep breath and exchanging a glance with one of her people, "I won't speak for the Pacific Islands, but the Antarctic Land Nation is in."

Feeling the pressure, Enele Chen looked at the governor. "You'll have our answer before you reach your home, Governor Heirlinda," he nodded.

In moments, the room was cleared, and Miriam was left alone with Dr. Bradley.

"How did I do?" the nervous scientist asked.

Miriam turned to look at her countryman even while her mind was now on her fellow Zoeans in Chile. He was so singularly focused, and he needed her approval.

She smiled to him. "As well as any of us could have," she said. "Now, we wait."

CHAPTER 29
YEAR 2553

Former Baja Province
Former Northern Territory of New Hispaniola Land Nation
Former Global Union

It was just barely after the appearance of the dawn light.

That was when, outside the hangar that served as home to Uru and Linda, the distinct sounds of Global Union authority boat engines growled loudly in the nearby waters. Initially, Linda thought she was dreaming because the sound was one she hadn't heard in so long. Eventually, she opened her eyes and realized the rumbling was real. Her husband on whom she lay had wide eyes as well, and the two of them sat up.

Following a late night of as much imbibing as dancing, Linda, Uru, their children, and the crew of the Mining Vessel PS-1707 were just rousing and were completely unprepared to react to the arrival of Administrator Luis Fredrick of New Hispaniola Land Nation, even if they had known what it meant.

The administrator approached the hangar home filled with Linda and Uru's family and surrounded by Tatsu's crew. With him were several officials with electronic pads and portable palm scanners, as well as medical personnel, including one woman who was very familiar to Linda. Linda put her head down and felt her panic rise in a way it hadn't done in months.

"Captain," Luis said in a cool greeting as he came upon Tatsu, the first adult he reached on the grounds outside the converted zip chopper port. "I'm surprised to see you here."

"We have a week before we have to be at our next mining location, Administrator." The captain recognized the man from inspections his ship had undergone throughout his tenure.

While the administrator's official role was global logistics management, the responsibility had created in the man an attitude of products and processes over people. He managed logs and inventories as precisely as the official atomic clock that kept the world's coordinated universal time, all with no regard for the circumstances of Earth and humans that might trifle with his ledger. Administrator Fredrick once seized a single kilogram of crushed mussel shells Tatsu's crew had over-delivered to the Pacific Islands Land Nation to ensure the nation's citizens wouldn't grow accustomed to the increase. While it had been Amy who ran weights and measurements at that port, Captain Mageo claimed it was his mistake and a letter of reprimand was added to his digital file. Too many of those and one could find himself on a refuse scrubber or toxic cleanup assignment.

"So, you just decided to drop by a disaster zone for what? A little down time?"

"Our unscheduled route time has always been ours to manage, Sir."

"It has, indeed. The Global Union has been generous enough to pay for the fuel you consume during that unscheduled time, too, regardless of my personal recommendations on resource distribution," he said.

His nostrils flared as he stroked the fine moustache over his thin lips. The man's face could have been chiseled from stone it was so angular. His skin was dark, a contrast to his tight platinum curls, eyebrows, and even the fine hair over his lip. He had white eyelashes, too, adding to the hollowness Tatsu felt when he stared at him and, when Administrator Fredrick spoke to Captain Mageo, he always stared directly at him, like a searchlight trying to locate a target.

"You certainly seem to have a lot of that unscheduled time from what I hear," he drawled. "Perhaps we need to assign a more complex route or larger payload," he finished as Tatsu saw Wang Wei peering from behind one of the other officials.

So that's where he'd gone.

Tatsu clenched his fist and chanced a sideways glance to Uru. Linda had her arms wrapped tightly around him as they stood in the hangar entrance. He wondered if the administrator was aware that she was serving as a human restraint.

"My people work hard and fast in order to earn their down time," the captain said directly, preventing the administrator from glancing around too thoroughly.

"Well, I'm sure you'll be getting on your way, soon, now that I've returned your crew person to you. Mr. Wang has informed me of some pressing concerns. He claims he was attacked by a noncitizen."

"And you believed him?" Tatsu exclaimed, shaken.

"Not to worry. He's agreed not to press any charges but wanted to make sure that we checked on these noncitizens to ensure they received care. Surely that's why the young woman attempted to assault him. She must need help." He said smugly.

"You maggot," Tatsu said vilely to Wei. Then, to Fredrick, "I assure you, Administrator, you have it backwards."

Nonplussed, "I would be happy to address a complaint from any Global Union Citizen after my more pressing matter, but I'm not really here to question you, Captain. You and your crew, including Mr. Wang, are welcome to board your mining vessel at any time," the administrator finished, clearly offering a suggestion more than a reiteration of the regulations.

Barely containing his rage, "I think we'll stay for the moment," Tatsu said.

"That's your prerogative," Luis said flatly before looking down at his pad. "I'm looking for Uru Mageo!" he called out. "Uru? Uru Mageo? Global Union Director of Entertainment Archives, Northern

Territory of New Hispaniola Land Nation, Baja Province? Former spouse of Kim Mageo? Former father of Andy, Grace, and Alice Mageo?"

"I'm still their father," said Uru, stepping away from Linda and the hangar entrance.

"Oh! There you are! You must be Uru."

"Yes. And I'm still their father."

"Excuse me?"

"Andy, Grace, and Alice. They are not alive anymore, but I am still their father even though they are not here with me."

"My mistake. No offense was intended, of course."

"Of course. What do you need from me?"

With a sickeningly sweet tone that nobody present believed, Luis continued, "Not from you, good citizen. It's come to the attention of the Global Union that we unintentionally left one of our own behind and, as you know, the GU cares for its own. 'Every citizen's care provided.' Do you remember that?"

"I do, but I don't need anything from the Global Union."

"Are you sure about that?"

"Yes."

"And the others with you? We heard there were others. Would you at least allow me to have our medical team look them over?"

"Why?"

"Well, you're a full citizen, but most of them are just children if I understand correctly. Wouldn't you like to make sure they are in good health?"

Uru looked behind him and spotted some of the children. They were well-fed and healthy with the light of the sun on their skin and hard work for exercise. He couldn't imagine a child appearing healthier than any one of the orphans he and Linda had adopted as their own. He was ready to turn down the offer when he spotted Linda with a concerned expression on her face. He thought about the daily vitamins the GU provided at schools and work sites, as well as the annual inoculations they underwent to protect them from global virus outbreaks. Mostly, though, he thought about what Linda might want.

Against his better judgment, "Can they examine them here?" Uru asked. "At the hangar?"

"I don't see why not," Administrator Luis said while waving a finger in the air to the team behind him who efficiently descended upon Linda and the orphans. All of them had made their ways the hangar bay doors. "We're only trying to make sure that you all are faring well. The tremors have been strong and unpredictable and you're a man trained in entertainment history, not survival."

"Thank you," Uru said to the man, but his tone made it clear that his mind was definitely not thinking the word "Thank."

"While they are being examined, you and I can talk."

Linda watched as Uru and Administrator Fredrick sat on the large, overturned buckets they used for seating around the outdoor fire. His other officials began walking the grounds, making notes in their pads.

Meanwhile, medical professionals pulled each of Linda's children, one-by-one, to the area that they'd been using as a dining gathering in their home. The team performed physical and digital examinations of them, asked questions, and recorded information in their pads.

Linda tried to keep all of the children in her sights as she continuously scanned the room back and forth, and occasionally glanced toward the happenings outside of the home. She observed through pursed lips as one of the younger doctors flipped over Mercy's left hand while reaching down toward the portable palm scanner. Then, with disappointment, the doctor's face fell, she released Mercy's hand, and excused the teen. Dee and Julian were checked for palm scans, as well. Linda was disturbed by the thought of what the GU would have done if any of the children had been full citizens. Would they dare to take them from her? Panic swelled inside her chest. She regretted allowing the children's examinations. Distracted by her own spiraling negative thoughts, Linda was suddenly startled by the familiar woman stepping into her field of vision.

"I'd like to examine you, too," Michele said to her.

Linda nodded, while holding out hope that Dr. Richards wouldn't recognize her. It had been over a year since she was brought to the medical center. She had been laid up and recovering along with countless others who were under the same doctor's care. At the time, Linda had been weakly thin, her hair was unkempt, and her skin had been out of the sun for far too long. Plus, she had only ever been clothed in hospital garments.

Linda spoke as little as possible as she followed Dr. Richards to the temporary examination area. Her checkup was routine, even with Linda keenly observant for anything that might seem suspicious. At the end of the exam, just as had been done with the three oldest children, the doctor took Linda's left hand and turned it over. It was too late for Linda to withdraw her palm. She was discovered. She simply kept quiet and waited. Michele ran her fingers over the smooth flesh of Linda's scar.

"I knew it was you," the doctor said softly. "I even hoped it was you."

Michele's eyes darted about the area and unfallen tears welled up in the bottom of her almond-shaped, golden eyes. The doctor blinked them away and took steadying breaths.

"You hoped?"

"You're Linda Schmidt," she whispered.

Lowering her own tone to ensure nobody could hear, "I never told you my last name."

"You told me enough. The pod routes you took. The tea shop you liked. I knew where you had been found. It was enough to discover the rest on my own," Michele said.

Another medic passed by, and Dr. Richards picked up a device she had already used on Linda. She pretended to continue in the examination.

While repeating each step of the exam, but with no actual readings, "You are a Baja Province pod battery installer for the power industries," the doctor said. "You were partner to Lukas Schmidt . . . who is deceased. When you were seventeen, you adopted his family name. You're Linda Schmidt."

Wincing at the name, "I don't go by Schmidt, anymore."

"Mageo, is it, then?"

"No. I'm just Linda."

Michele paused and Looked at her former patient. When Linda had come to her, she didn't have a hope in the world that her patient would make it. The broken person in her memory was nothing like the woman before her—the woman for whom she made certain to be assigned to Fredrick's medical team. The woman she desperately needed to believe had made it.

"Linda, then." Michele smiled. "Nice to meet you."

Linda didn't say anything back. She was still unsure of the situation.

"Can I ask you something?" Dr. Richards said. Then, after a nod from Linda, "How did you do it?" Michele asked.

"Do what?"

"Survive," the doctor said. "Not even just survive," she added looking around. "I mean look at all of this. You weren't even supposed to make it. I wanted you to make it, but I didn't expect it. And now you have a whole community here. You have—" Dr. Richards couldn't keep the cry out of her voice even while she kept her tears from flowing. "You have a family."

Linda looked around and the youngest children were already back to playing. They were unaware that today was any different than usual. They just had more friends with whom to play.

"Tell me the story," Michele said and something in the woman's eyes said that Linda could trust her.

In as brief a manner as possible because they could only pretend that this exam was continuing for just so long, Linda recapped life after the medical center. She talked about staying behind during the evacuations, finding the chickens and making her way to New Hollywood. She described what it was like to begin working with Uru and told Michele about the New Hollywood earthquake that drove them to return to the south. She talked about finding the children and later meeting Uru's brother. With every new chapter of her last year's story, Linda spoke about events with the casual tone one might have used for picking up monthly rations at a GU distribution center. Yet, nothing was ever as simple as that for the former Baja people. They collected their own power and foraged for their own food. They sewed their own clothing and developed their own educations. They cared for their own animals and—in the midst of earthquakes and extreme weather—protected their own home.

"You've overcome so much," Dr. Richards said in awe. "You've done more and become more over the last year than most citizens who live their full, long, hundred and fifteen year lives. You don't even realize just how amazing you are."

Michele took Linda's hands into her own, feigning some sort of medical scrutiny in case another GU person may believe her to be showing affection.

"Linda," Dr. Richards said with sudden urgency, "they're going to ask you to go. There's another way. You don't have to leave."

"What do you mean?"

"Ask for nekros status," the doctor added, aware that their time was growing short.

"What's that?"

"On file, you would be dead to the Global Union." Linda looked at the doctor, stunned, but Michele just went on. "Do you remember when I told you that I wasn't always in trauma? That trauma was my secondary medical field?"

Linda recalled some conversations, but not really the details. "Why is that important?" she asked.

"I started in reproduction."

Michele put her eyes to the ground, dropped Linda's hands and took a deep breath while pretending to dig in her medical kit. "What could be more beautiful than to bring life into the world, right?" She shook her head shamefully and bit her lip to prevent its trembling. "I mean, that's what I always believed, but the reality wasn't what I thought. Not everybody can have a child who wants one."

"Of course not. The world's population is too large. That's why the GU takes care of us by having us apply for permits. Partnered women aged eighteen to twenty-nine and partnered men aged twenty-two to thirty-five."

"I know the application requirements, Linda. That's not what I mean."

"What then?"

"Not all of the permits get fulfilled, do they?"

A rush of fresh shame flashed across Linda's face, however unwarranted. "How did you know that about me?"

"I'm getting there," the doctor said.

Linda's mind raced through a short movie of single-frame memories: her father beating her mother, her dad leaving for another province, her one-time love forcing himself on her while she clenched and screamed, Lukas falling to his death. She swallowed away the pain.

"I wasn't meant to have a child," she said.

"You don't know how true that is," the doctor said.

Linda looked confused, but said nothing as Dr. Richards resolved, through shuddered breath, to share.

"If all of the granted child-bearing permits were fulfilled, there would not be enough resources, enough employs, enough room in the world. And, if the permits fulfilled included low-aptitude or no-aptitude citizens, then those people are taking up the resources, employs, and room that could be occupied by high achieving Global Union citizens. By people who the GU believes can make a difference."

Linda was hearing the words and feeling a great offense build up in her, but Michele took her left hand in her own once more and spoke, not with judgment, but sympathy.

"So, imagine that a way to manage that reality would be to make sure that a majority of permits went to those low-aptitude or no-aptitude citizens."

"That doesn't make sense at all."

"Except it does," began the doctor as her voice cracked and her eyes filled with tears of shame. "It does if the Global Union, if they, if . . . if I and people like me . . . were to make sure that those permits never got fulfilled."

Linda shook her head. None of this was making sense. She thought about the medical appointments she had every month when she was on her permit. She thought about the examinations, performed by numerous GU medical persons, which always showed her in perfect health. She thought about the nutritional training and fitness recommendations to keep her in peak condition for childbearing. She thought about the prenatal vitamin-and-mineral-infused injections. Her mind stopped on the thought of the injection. As a permit-holder, she had a small device adhered to her soft tissue skin and, once a day, the prenatal supplement blend was pushed into her system. The memory caused her to experience the pricking sensation on her lower right abdomen, just above her hip bone, where she had opted to wear the device.

"The injections," Linda said as it became clear to her.

"Weren't pre-natal care," Michele finished. "You were never going to be able to conceive a child, Linda. You're infertile."

Incredulously, "And you did this?"

"Not to you. No. But to so many others," Linda dropped the doctor's hand "Very few, even in the medical community, know," Michele continued. "It's done at the DNA level. You have eggs just like any other woman, but they are . . . dead. I discovered, when I was treating you, that you were, what we called, a 'dispermitted parent.'"

"You're talking about eugenics. About the practices of people before we were all made equal by the Global Union."

The doctor looked at Linda knowing she could never truly apologize. Linda could not accept on behalf of all of the barren parents of the world and, even if she could, it would do very little to alleviate the burden of remorse Michele felt.

"How many of us?" Linda asked.

"I don't know how many I injected. I only know that I couldn't do it anymore."

"And they do this to the people who have permits?"

"More than half of them. Limited applications, limited permits, some of what nature just took care of on its own, and," she paused before finishing, "dispermitted parents. Combine all of those things and population growth isn't a problem. And the Global Union picks who can be a mother or father," the doctor said. Then, after a pause, "...and I was a part of it all."

"They didn't think I could be a mom?" Linda asked.

"They were wrong," Dr. Richards said, looking up at Linda with eyes that had renewed strength behind their dew. "I was wrong."

Linda looked around the zip chopper port. On the grounds outside, the youngest children, oblivious to any meaning applied to these new visitors, played with Tatsu's crew. Dee and Julian sat with Mercy by their bookshelf studying, or maybe just pretending to study as they repeatedly glanced over at the doctor with their adoptive mother or out to the administrator sitting with their adoptive father.

"If they could see what I see, they would know," Michele went on with a plead for empathy in her voice. "Who are they to say you can't make a difference? To say your children can't make a difference?"

One of Dr. Richards' team began to approach the two women. Their time was up. Michele quickly stood, shutting down her medical files.

"She's in good health," the doctor said professionally. "No palm scan on this one."

"The children are also all in good health. Perfect, in fact."

"I'm not surprised," Dr. Richards replied. She gave a nod of acknowledgment to Linda in recognition of her care for the children. "I'll inform Administrator Fredrick," she said as she exited the home.

In a trance-like manner, Linda followed Dr. Michele Richards out of the hangar toward Uru and Administrator Luis Fredrick. Tatsu sat protectively near the two. Dr. Richards reached the men and handed her pad to the administrator.

"Everything looks in order, Sir. We give them all clean bills of health," she finished as Linda stood next to Uru, who took her hand. "No citizens among this group, Sir."

"That's okay," said Luis. "We would be happy to care for you all the same. I was just telling Mr. Mageo here that we are more than prepared to offer assistance to your entire family. The children, included. You are all welcome to board our boat and take a nice trip over to the Mexican Province. We can get you registered for rations and get these kids into school or, for the older ones, GU training."

Uru looked as stunned as Linda felt. Their little utopia was coming to an end.

"And you, young lady," the administrator said, pointing to Mercy who Linda hadn't seen follow her out, "I understand you've already taken your aptitude tests? Want to teach? Is that right? No better place to get trained than with the Global Union."

"No thank you," said the girl with certainty and Uru couldn't help but smile at her sass.

"Excuse me?" the administrator asked.

"I said, no thank you. We're fine here."

Mercy's unapologetic nature snapped Linda out of her own daze, and she grinned down to Uru. The two glowed like the proud parents they had become. After looking at her husband, Linda took a deep, deliberate breath, feeling the tension release in her chest for the first time all morning. She squeezed Uru's hand to share the peace.

"Well, I don't really see as you have much choice," Administrator Fredrick said aghast. "You need us!" he exclaimed, for the first time dropping his faux nonchalance and showing contempt in its place.

"We do have a choice, actually," Linda said, and the administrator snapped his head toward her. "We'd like to claim nekros status," she said while straightening up as tall as she could

"How do you," Luis began before stopping mid-thought.

He narrowed his eyes, looking around at the people on his team, but nobody gave any indication that they were a part of Linda's request.

"Do you understand what that means?" asked the administrator.

"Dead. It means our status is dead," Linda said. That was all she knew, and she hoped that he didn't ask anything more.

"Exactly. Dead to the whole Global Union. We erase your citizen accounts. No credits. No rations. Nothing."

"We have all we need," Uru interjected.

"You're sure about that?" the administrator asked.

Uru looked at his wife with a smile, gripped more tightly to her hand, and stood up, beside her. "We're vee," he said as both looked down on the man. Mercy tried not to laugh out loud at his word choice.

Administrator Fredrick stood up and gestured for his team to follow. He surveyed the grounds, taking note of both the mining crew and the former Baja Province people.

"I will be working from my vessel to get the files ready for status declaration. I think you're making a mistake, though," he said before following the rest of his team back onto the Global Union Authority boat. "I don't think you understand what it is to become no one."

"I've been no one, before," Linda said. "It's not as bad as you think."

It was hours before Administrator Luis Fredrick finally exited his vessel once more with his lead official. Wang Wei followed them like a fly on a trail of stench. The rest of the administrator's team stayed aboard the boat, though Michele stood on the deck looking out toward them.

"Here he comes, my wife," Uru said. "You ready?"

"Well, my husband, you wanted an adventure, right?" she smiled before kissing Uru and taking his hand.

The administrator approached the newlyweds with a look of exhaustion on his face and a pad in his hand.

"Uru Mageo, as the only citizen found on the destroyed grounds of the Great Quake, your palm scan alone, and no other, will be required to legalize the status change of your citizenship as one requiring Global Union care to that of nekros," Luis read from his pad. "You understand that, by placing your palm on the portable scanner," he indicated his official who held up the device, "that the Global Union is not required to provide for your needs, be they financial, nutritional, physical, educational, medical, recreational, or any other defined necessity at present or in the future for as long as you live. Is this an accurate statement, Mr. Mageo?"

"Yes, Sir," Uru said.

"You further understand that, upon scanning your palm," Luis once again pointed to the official behind him who once again held up the portable palm scanning device, "you vow sole responsibility for the additional thirteen former citizens of the Global Union present on the Great Quake destroyed lands."

Uru smiled to himself at the word "vow." This was quite a different set of vows than those he had made just the day before, but it would be these, as much as the ones spoken at his wedding, which would truly define the life he and his family would make.

The administrator added, "These citizens include one adult female with no identification, in addition to six minor females with no parental claims nor Global Union identifications and six minor males with no parental claims nor Global Union identifications."

"Yes, Sir," said the older Mageo brother.

"You understand, Mr. Uru Mageo, that the additional thirteen former citizens will also have nekros status, meaning that they will not be eligible for Global Union care or provision. Is this correct?"

Uru looked at Linda who gave a small nod to him. Then, he looked at all of the children. Mercy held Ziad on her hip while Julian sat on the ground at her feet with Sofia on his lap. The other eight children stood amongst them like a portrait of strength. He knew that strength came from his wife.

"I understand, administrator," he said.

"And last, you further understand that, upon scanning your palm, the Global Union lands that were destroyed by the Great Quake will also be declared a nekrosland and the Global Union has no obligation to provide care or resources to any who determine to call Nekros Baja their home. Is this correct?"

"Yes, Administrator Fredrick."

"Your responses have been recorded, Mr. Mageo. Please place your palm on the portable scanner."

It seemed all at once too easy and also too overwhelming. Uru squeezed Linda's hand tightly with his right hand while he placed his left on the device held by the official. He expected to feel something as he had decades ago when he'd first received his scan, but this wasn't injecting him with anything or creating a new imprint; it was merely reading his scan.

Before he met Linda, Uru had spent months trying to die and now—without preparation or planning—it came easily. It came with no attempt on his part at all. It took less than one second to go from living to dead.

The administrator turned to his official. "Please relay the message to the Global Union that its citizen, Uru Mageo, has been re-statused as nekros and that Baja Province has officially been declared a nekrosland. Preparations to clear Nekros Baja may proceed."

"Yes, Administrator," the official responded, and he turned his back on the nekros people.

The two began a march back to the Global Union Authority's boat.

"What do you mean clear Baja?" Linda asked after them.

Without looking back, "Do the dead talk?" Administer Fredrick asked.

"No Sir, they do not," said the official as the two continued walking.

"Mr. Wang, you may rejoin your captain," Fredrick said.

Tatsu looked at Uru, but he realized that he was now the only citizen who could take charge. He blitzed after the GU Authority team. "Fredrick!" he exclaimed, and the administrator turned around, clearly annoyed at not being addressed by his full title or simply "Sir."

"Yes, Tatsu," he said, intending the informal first name to be an insult.

"What about processing the complaint against Wang Wei. Who on your ship can help with that?"

"Did he attack somebody?"

Infuriated, "That young girl!" Tatsu screamed, while pointing back toward Mercy.

The administrator looked around the mining captain's large form to the family behind him. "I see nothing but a graveyard, Captain Mageo. I'm sure you understand that the Global Union cannot waste legal resources on processing the claims of the dead. We have the living to consider," he spat. "As I stated, feel free to leave. I imagine you won't want to stick around here for much longer."

Wang smirked and started walking toward the '07. The sound of boat engines suddenly filled the air, but the mining vessel hadn't yet been started. Michele, aboard the GU Authority Boat, suddenly jerked and turned eastward. Countless ships were charging into the southern port of Nekros Baja.

"What the hell is going on?" Tatsu said, running to his ship. He tapped on his temple, bringing his optical monitor to life. "Satellite!" he commanded a screen that only he saw.

"Fuck me!" he shouted.

"What is it?" Amy called up to him.

"They're everywhere. Not just here. Hundreds of them! No, thousands! Baja is surrounded!" he said frantically as he tapped his temple repeatedly in varying patterns and his eyes were focused, not on his own surroundings, but on the new madness erupting throughout the waters surrounding and the airspace over Nekros Baja.

"Little bro!" Uru yelled, having made his way to Tatsu's vessel. "What's going on?"

"Get the kids. Get Linda. Get whatever you can!" he shouted. "They're clearing it. All of it."

"What? What does that mean?"

"They are wiping it out, Uru! Everything. The entire land is being cleared. These ships are filled with ground pushers and composters and crushers. They're taking it all."

For the next ten hours, all around Nekros Baja, thousands upon thousands of work vehicles cleared the land, compacted it, and loaded it onto Global Union ships to be hauled away.

The youngest children wailed while Mercy and Peter consoled them as well as they could. They crowded together on the deck of the PS-1707 where they'd taken temporary refuge.

Linda and Uru were joined by Marquise and Cairo as they worked to save the animals. All of their goats with the exception of their pregnant nanny had been loaded up. She was too stubborn, running off every time a citizen came near her. It must have been her maternal instinct. Olive and Hank were spared only because Cairo had hidden them in his quarters.

Administrator Fredrick, meanwhile, led a team of individuals who picked up the fallen fruit from their trees before directing equipment conductors to knock down the trees themselves.

The hangar was demolished with the family having saved nothing more than the contents of the bookshelf. The education pad was gone, though.

Then, the piles left behind were crushed and loaded. Linda threw up when she saw the delicate fabrics of Elsie Laurita's gown, her wedding dress, flitting out of the side of a compost cube.

The entire experience was so much worse than even the most violent of quakes or storms because the intensity never decreased or changed or let up in any way. It was chaotic corruption from start to finish – loud and messy and unpredictable and uncontainable and unimaginable and utterly insurmountably complete destruction. The emotional height of it continued for the full ten hours, draining them all – the children, Linda and Uru, the scrubbers. It was as though all of them together were trying to outrun a rushing river while standing in its bed.

Then, like a tornado lifting away and dissipating in the sky, they were just gone. All of the GU ships fled as quickly as they had descended and what they left behind truly was . . . empty. Her family home was raped as she once had been raped and—also for the second time in Linda's life—the Global Union made Linda barren.

From pure exhaustion, the children had each eventually fallen into slumber except for Mercy who regarded herself as one of the adults. In a small meeting room on the mining vessel, Tatsu, a handful of his crew, Linda, Uru, and Mercy sat numbly. It was almost dawn and none of them had spoken for a very long time. All of their words and pleas and pain and anger had been expressed futilely during the entire ordeal and now they had nothing left but ache and emptiness. Silently, they drank weak coffee while they waited for the first day to break over what was now officially called Nekros Baja.

It didn't seem like it should, but the sun did rise, and it was beautiful in its way, spilling out across what was now a plain. Little by little, the family exited the mining vessel onto the foreign-seeming lands that they had chosen as a home. It was brown and flat and empty. No plant life was to be seen. Olive picked at Linda's feet as she had in those early days before Linda ever found Uru or the children. She truly had nothing to give to the hen. The nanny goat wandered aimlessly in the area that once was home to their garden boxes and farm.

Linda sat on the ground, unsure what words of wisdom she had to spread over this mess she'd gotten them into.

"They really took everything," she sighed.

"We saved the books, some of your animals, a couple cases of nutrient bars ...." Amy encouraged before realizing she wasn't getting through.

"And that leaves us enough supplies for what?" Linda said defeatedly. "An overnight camping trip perhaps?"

"We built it once," Uru said. Perhaps we could again?" he made it a question. "They had to leave the one pier where Tatsu was docked, so I could bring supplies that way. Maybe build a boat."

"With what? Hopes and dreams?"

"I have some things," Peter offered. "Not a boat, but a tent. I use it on the deck to keep warm when I have the night shift. And I have a solar flashlight."

"That belongs to the '07, Peter," Erin said.

"It's MY ship!" Tatsu yelled at Wang's most loyal crewmate as he got to within an inch of his face.

"She's only saying," Randall defended his cohort, "that if the Global Union can take what's theirs from Baja, we can't give them things that belong on a GU mining vessel, either."

Tatsu huffed through his nose like a bull, but he knew the scrubber was right. Giving his brother's family things for survival that belonged to the Global Union would just set them up to be pillaged and plundered all over again.

"Well, I own a flashlight," Khalil chimed in. "And it's not GU. It's my own," he sneered at Erin.

"I have a crate of potatoes," Stacy added.

"Cairo," Marquise began, "don't Davina and Allen drop fishing nets when we're off the Pacific Islands Land Nation coast? They could spare a couple, don't you think?"

The two men jumped into action, followed by other crewmembers who each had a contribution. In time, a dozen members of the PS-1707 provided items from their own supplies and resources to help the Baja people.

"Thank you all," Linda said. "I mean that sincerely. But it's still not enough. I'm so sorry. Your generosity is beyond anything I could have imagined and I'm grateful. But we spent months gathering countless supplies. And we had power. And we had food. And shelter. And the chance to grow and turn it into something even greater. This, as kind and thoughtful and beautiful as it is, won't do that. It's charity, but it just won't keep a family of fourteen. And I think you all know that, too."

There was a long silence when the spark that had been growing amongst them slowly flickered out.

"I'm sorry I let you down," Uru said to Linda, pulling her close. "I'm the one who let them scan my palm and now I've fated all of you. I'm the one that allowed Baja to be called a nekrosland."

He held his wife, and a pained expression came over his face. He had no answers.

"That's it," Tatsu said. "That's it. Uru, you solved it. That's it," the captain said excitedly and with a hope that none of them could understand in the moment.

"Solved what?"

"Nekrosland! Baja isn't the only one. The Global Union has given up on all sorts of land over the years. Well, and some of it isn't even land. We pass them all the time."

"Wait a minute!" Stacy chimed in. "You mean the Pacific Trash Vortex?"

"The what?" Mercy asked.

"The trash vortex!" Amy said. "Of course! For literally thousands of years, the discarded life stuffs of people, not just the Global

Union, but even way before them! People get rid of what they don't need anymore, and eventually it just ends up in the trash vortex."

"You're telling me that people throw their trash in the Pacific?" Uru asked.

"It's not quite that simple," Tatsu said. "Yes, trash ends up in the waterways. But sometimes it comes from landfills that ended up under water, or it's washed into the waters from shorelines—

"Or the space junk!" Stacy added.

"Yes," Captain Mageo agreed, gesturing to Stacy. "Or that! Or it blows there, or storms stir it up. Eventually, human garbage piles for countless generations end up getting caught in the Pacific currents and pulled to this central area. The Global Union calls it the Pacific Nekros. It's basically an island now. Some parts have even become their own ecosystems with moss and fungus growing on the debris."

Stacy continued, "whole flocks of birds have even made the place a home."

"There are even rats and insects there," Amy said, "all floating on a pile of human stuff."

"An island full of resources that you could use," Peter added.

The group all looked at Linda and Uru, begging their response to the question they didn't have to ask.

"What do you say, Uru?" Linda encouraged. "Want to bring this place back to life?"

CHAPTER 30
YEAR 2908

Pacific Sea Route
Cityship Tatsu IV
Cityship Regatta

Miriam looked around her neatly organized quarters.

The governor was at a loss for activity. The farewell dinner had already been enjoyed with all of the Tatsu Ministers and their families in attendance: the heads of hydroponics, education, housing, shipping, routing, safety, and Mik's crew. The Pacific Islands delegation reached out to share their "yes," to the human unification movement. The tsunamic danger from the Zoe Chile quake had passed. She had already sent all of her formal communiqués and even had a chance to prepare a scheduled video message for Inoke that he would receive in the morning – a list of needs for when she arrived at the southern port. She looked forward to hearing his feedback from her time away without the veil required when they used official channels. By all accounts, the negotiations were a success.

Her tube was already packed, except for the same travel clothes that she'd worn on the initial trip. Without specific duties for the return trip, she didn't need to dress formally until she arrived at Zoe Baja. Done with the rigid attire and shoes of politics, Miriam already changed for the night into the embroidered cotton slippers she received before leaving Zoe Baja. Going home would take only a day's travel when the high-speed engines were brought online. She wasn't ready to plan the meetings that would take place with New Hispaniola. That would require some time to scrutinize their response to the new alliance.

For the moment, the first one like it in quite some time, there were no fires to put out. She could do nothing but rest for the entirety of the next day. She was no good at resting.

The walls of Miriam's central quarters, simultaneously high off the surface of the water and deep below the deck, not to mention far from land, felt like they were closing in. When she had been busy or in the midst of crowds playing the role of governor, she had been distracted from her own sense of claustrophobia, but now it pressed in on her.

She couldn't work. She couldn't sleep. Once their journey began, at their return speeds, it would be miserable on deck for the most well-trained of seafarers. It would be an outright impossibility for Miriam. She decided she had better take advantage of a bit of fresh air while she still could.

She threw on the orange feathered sweater Inoke had gifted to her. He meant it for style, but she appreciated its warmth most of all. It provided stark contrast over her far plainer pajama set of gray blue palazzo bottoms and a peasant top. Reluctantly, she grabbed her digifile and transferred her connections and securities from it to her passive communications wristlet. She really wanted to be fully disconnected, but that wasn't responsible. She stepped into her slippers and walked out of her room, feeling some of the tightness release from her chest as soon as she entered the larger hallway.

"Governor," greeted the security officer outside her door.

Miriam found it interesting that Ensign Bintou-Keita had been replaced. The new sailor stood up from his chair and dropped his hand that was holding a digifile and on which he was watching some sort of gameshow program.

"Disculpas, ma'am," the sailor said apologetically. "I didn't know you'd be going out again tonight. Most people on this deck have turned in."

"I just need some air," she said as she stepped past him to walk down the hall.

"Would you like me to arrange an escort?" he said out of obligation after her.

Miriam turned back to him and smiled. "I really wouldn't if that's okay. As you said, most people are asleep, and I think I'd like just a bit of solitude in the alfresco air. I have my wristlet programmed. I can be reached in an emergency."

"I understand, Governor."

"Shie shie," she said, then turned to walk again before adding, "Actually, there is one thing you could help me with."

"Yes?" he responded, quickly snapping to once more.

"To the deck. I go past the primary school, up six levels, left through the market strip, and up the last two levels?"

"Well, yes, that's one way. That would take you aft, near the stern. The engineers are prepping for the voyage, though, and calling in our sideships. A lot of action there right now. If you really want to be alone, Governor, you could turn right and go past the crew quarters instead of through the market. Keep on past the offices. They'll all be quiet this time of night. Then, go up to the deck. You'll be at the bow. It's about three quarters of a kilometer that way, ma'am."

"The walk will do me good. And you'll know where I am if I'm needed," she added as she held up her arm displaying the communications wristlet.

"Have a nice evening. I'll be right here, ma'am," he said awkwardly.

Miriam followed the path she was given and felt more kilograms of imaginary weight lift off of her with each level she rose in the ship. When she reached the deck, her whole body relaxed. Everything below her was closed for the night. There were no residences behind her for a quarter of a kilometer. There was nobody around. She was completely alone and in the open and it felt invigorating. She walked the last ten meters to the very front of the Tatsu.

A large wall of garden-like gates crossed the bow before its point. She tried to pull open the gates, but neither one would budge. Behind those gates was privacy and solitude and she wanted it. She looked around for a way through but found nothing to either side; she couldn't even see around them to the tip of the Tatsu, so she began to examine the gates themselves. Finally, she found an entry pad for a digital code with a scrolling notice that read: EXECUTIVE – ACCESS – ENTER – CODE.

Oh, she thought. What was that? The mining ship. 1-7-7-7 she typed in and pulled. Nothing. 1-0-0-7 she typed. *'Damn,'* she said to herself. *'The Mining Vessel . . . Pacific Mining Vessel . . . oh! Pacific Sea! Yes, the PS . . . PS . . . PS . . . PS-1707!'* she thought aloud. She slowly and deliberately typed 1-7-0-7, and immediately heard a small click come from the garden gate. She pulled it open, a heavy job, then—once she assured herself that a digital pad existed to allow her to exit when it was time—she pulled it tightly closed behind her until she heard the click again.

At last, she thought. Alone!

It was almost like an actual park behind the gate. Real grass planted on what must have been twelve to fifteen centimeters of real soil. Gratefully, she slid her feet out of the slippers that Dr. Bradley had given her, planted them in the miniature lush green lawn, and closed her eyes. She could smell the plants and dirt. It felt like youth and life and freedom.

Miriam opened her eyes and stood on the planted deck of the ship peering out over the darkness. They would soon be headed out of the southern waters in order to get in front of the rough seas. They should make it back to Zoe Baja long before the aftershocks from the Chilean earthquake – before the ripples morphed into white caps and then into chaos. The Mid-Pacific storm nets would slow the pending waves, but not stop them. Human beings never could figure out how to overcome Mother Nature.

For now, between the subtle rings on the water's surface, where unseen insects above it and marine life below it made their presence known, were long stretches of inky glass under the moon and stars. It was hard to tell where the sea ended, and the sky began. They floated out on the mirrored world, a navy-black pool dotted with twinkling lights. If she turned her head to put her ear toward the sea and concentrated fully, she could even remove the sounds of engines with her imagination. Miriam focused on hearing only the water as it fell away to the port and starboard sides of the Tatsu, gently folded open by the bow of the ship as it glided forward at a pace not even a fraction of what it would achieve under power.

Being on the deck of the ship was the opposite of claustrophobic. The world was a bellow and she a mere whisper in its midst. She pictured the mining teams from the Antarctic Land Nation looking down as they continued up in orbit. She illogically imagined them moving away from her as she became an ant on a log, that became a stick in the sea, that became an ocean among many, until she was nothing at all. The Tatsu was nothing. The Zoelands were nothing. The Global Union was nothing. Miriam wondered what it must be like for the extra-orbital miners, the oxymoronic combination of tightly efficient quarters in the vast emptiness of space where the whole of Earth was just another speck in the distance.

For a moment, Miriam envied their perspective, desired to be away from the crowded and messy world to a place where it all melted into a water painting of blues and greens and tans covered in a film of white wisps. Her own reality kicked in then, and she felt a momentary panic. The idea of being away from land, from a safe harbor, was too foreign to grasp. Instead, she would settle for the much more temporary open peace of the Tatsu at sea, a respite before the next wave of madness from storms and humans descended on the home she vowed to protect. She stared out at the horizon, letting the sky and water blend together.

A loud rustling noise sounded behind her. "I thought I saw your shadow moving past the crew quarters," came Mik's voice, sounding almost foreign in the quiet. "It's really something, eh?" he said while pulling closed the gate behind him.

Miriam stood up from peering over the ship's edge and turned to see the captain. "I hope you don't mind. I sort of used your access code."

"I'm glad you realized it has more perks than just the captain's head! It's a bonnie garden. It only gets used a few times a year. A shame, don't you think?"

"It certainly drew me in," she returned as she leaned her side up against the rail.

"Kate doesn't like it. Think's it's a waste of observation space. If she's ever captain, the garden's the first thing to go," he told Miriam.

"Too bad. I think it's my favorite part of the ship," she said.

"Ready to trade in for some sea legs?" he asked.

"Not quite. I like my toes in the dirt. I mean, dirt that's not floating, anyway. But the quiet is nice. The water doesn't seem to care if you're GU or Zoelands. Speaking of Zoe Baja, though, shouldn't we be turning back?"

"We will. There's something I wanted you to see first."

"What?"

"Not yet. You'll know."

"I guess I'll wait then. The view's not bad," she smiled flirtatiously at him as she allowed her eyes to move very obviously up and down the captain's form. Perhaps her brush with death had made her bold.

"Agreed," Mik said, looking directly back at Miriam just as obviously before changing the subject. "I always wanted to lead a city-ship," he recollected, looking out over the same waters Miriam had been admiring. "I'd have settled for a cleanup ship or even a transport, but this was the dream. Of course, no matter what, I was going to be on the water."

"What do you mean, 'Of course?'"

Mik paused and looked at Miriam, as if he were trying to read something deeper in her words. He took a step toward her, and Miriam felt herself take in a quick involuntary breath. Her heart jumped into her throat for a short second, flushing her face. She was grateful for the cool breeze. Mik didn't close any more distance between them in that moment, though. Instead, he leaned against his elbow on the rail, mirroring her. He took air deliberately in through his nose and blew it out through puffed cheeks, readying himself for a more personal conversation.

"It's the family business," Mik finally said. There was more, but Miriam could see he was choosing his words carefully. She was patient. Diplomacy had taught her that much at least. "You're an Heirlinda. You had to lead. You have Zoelands in your blood. Even when you didn't run for office, they wrote you in and you led, anyway."

"But we aren't talking about me."

"No, but it's the same. Some things are destined. We make some choices, and we stumble upon some luck in our lives—good or bad—but other destinies are decisions that were made for us, long before we had a say. You could have tried to make any number of choices, but you had to lead. It was expected of you. Well, I was expected to be on a ship. There are long lines of captains that had their decisions made for them and I'm one of them. I chose a city-ship, but I didn't choose captaining."

"I suspect you've made a few other choices of your own, too."

"A few." The words felt like an invitation. His eyes narrowed and half of his closed mouth lifted in a searching smile.

"Have I ever shared with you that I have all of the original records of Linda and Uru," Miriam interjected, letting him off the hook.

"I may have heard this story a time or two . . . or a dozen," he grinned, playing their storytelling game. "Of course, I do love the way you tell it."

"I mean, it shouldn't come as a surprise. I headed up the Zoelands Foundation and, as you say, I am an Heirlinda after all. But most people don't really know the detail that is in those files. One of their children, Mercy—

"Mercy Heirlinda," Mik encouraged her on.

"Very good. I've taught you well," Miriam teased. "Mercy is actually something like my great to the eighth power grandmother . . . anyway, Mercy was a true historian. She kept track of all of the things that Linda and Uru did while developing the Zoe. Everything from big historic impacts like interactions with the Global Union, to personal stuff like how they found the children as orphans and then treated them as their own kids, how Linda and Uru grew a fondness for one another that was love, but it was this practical and respectful and honoring kind of love. They were one another's loto. Their love was somehow even stronger and more meaningful than . . . than a...."

"A fiery romance?" Mik offered while the flame flashed in his own eyes.

"Mercy was the fiery one. She and Peter are the ones who sat down with Linda and Uru individually and captured as many of their personal stories as they could before the founders were gone. And the two of them made sure that everything was physical as well as digital so that it couldn't be lost like the pre-Global Union data when One-Net crashed."

Mik looked affectionately at Miriam, enjoying her storytelling. It was like listening to a favorite teacher who was passionate about a subject, except it was somehow even more engaging coming from her. She made the story personal for you, too. She would light up and look directly into your eyes, drawing you into the narrative. Even with the generations between Miriam and the Zoeland Founders, the story sounded like it could have been her own, like she knew Linda and Uru – had a relationship with them. He didn't know anyone who more deeply personified Zoe life than Miriam and, even though his own existence had always been, would always be, seabound, there was something beautiful about being intimate witness to another person's truest self.

"Most of the Zoelands history that we study in school today—" Miriam began.

"—came straight out of Mercy Heirlinda's notes," Mik finished with a toothy grin. He knew the story but raised his eyes to lead Miriam on in its telling.

"Just like everybody in the world," she continued, "we had units to study the great civilizations throughout our schooling—the Mesopotamians, the Egyptians, the Chinese—"

"—the Greeks and Romans, the era of the colonists and republics, the Global Union," Mik chimed in.

"And tribal resurgence, too," Miriam said. "The GU sometimes skips that one. And then, we spent almost an entire year of primary school on the Zoelands."

"And that era led right up into the Cityship Regatta and the five fleet families," Mik finished.

"Of course. You would know that, obviously," Miriam added with a sideways glance to Mik as she brushed his hand. She paused before adding, "I always enjoyed the stories of the real Tatsu. The moving picture books. What were they called, again?"

"Young Uru and Tatsu at Sea," Mik smiled. He said the title with the gusto of an inspired child.

"You know them, too?" Miriam asked, surprised. "What am I saying? Of course you know them. You captain the latest Tatsu. That was just an auto-response because I know they've actually been banned in some schools. They don't show the GU in a very good light."

"Anyway," she went on, "at the end of the Zoelands unit, we would spend two weeks creating our immersive family trees. We had to program the holographic images of our ancestors as far back as we knew them. It kind of sucked for me if I'm honest because the records for my family went back with a lot greater detail than most of my classmates.

"And if you chose to skip out on part of the work, undoubtedly, somebody would correct you," Mik poked his finger into her side as he said it, like a little boy picking on a classmate.

"Exactly," Miriam said, grabbing his finger and keeping hold of his hand playfully. "But at the end of the project, we would walk our classmates through our virtual reality program and introduce them to some of the family that came before us. For those two weeks, I was the most popular girl in class. I mean, not just an Heirlinda, but the last Heirlinda."

"So, it's true?" Mik asked. "You really are the last Heirlinda?" He looked at her with a reverence, as though she was somehow above him and he didn't deserve to even be in her presence. But she just shook her head and rolled her eyes at him, immediately putting him back at ease.

Miriam thought about the question, though. That's how she was always presented in the world, and it had come to be how she saw herself, too. She had a few distant cousins, though none actually were Zoeland citizens anymore. Some were working in different land nations. Officially, they were refugees to the Global Union. That was just how the GU had to label them in order for them to be folded into their society. Some had been land nation citizens for a few generations, already, and might not even have known they had Zoe blood.

Then, there was the son of one cousin who was working on a deep-sea city miner. He had been stationed over the remains of what was once New York City for as long as she could remember. None of her cousins, though, had the name anymore. After eight or nine generations, a name is just one of those things that was rare to maintain. There were, to her knowledge, a couple of families who called themselves Heirlinda in the African and Antarctic Land Nations. But, as far as she knew, they weren't actually related. The name was one that was just symbolically picked up during the independence uprisings of the 2700s, and somehow it stuck. For them, her name became a movement while, for her, it remained an identity.

"Well, she said, I'm not the last, I guess. But I am the last with the name, who is an heir, and who is still a Zoeland citizen. And I realize as I say that out loud that it sounds really qualified," she laughed.

"But back to the story," Mik pulled on Miriam's sleeve and also dragged her a bit closer to him.

She accepted the invitation with ease.

"As for the story," she breathed, losing concentration for a second before continuing. "I really got into the Mercy Files, as they were called. And, most of all, I kind of related to Linda. She was a little cynical, maybe a bit more than I am based on a pretty hard life, but I sort of understood her practicality. Uru was the romantic, the idealist, a bit of a dreamer. At least, I think it was Uru. It might have more so been his brother Tatsu."

"That's what I always learned," said Mik.

"The two kind of blend together in the stories for me if I'm honest," Miriam shook her head. "I mean Uru was technically the Founding Father, but Tatsu was there for all of it, and he was the founder of the cityships even though they weren't today's twelve routes and two seasteads until—"

"2848," Mik contributed.

"Really? That late?"

"Yeah. Now you're talking about my history."

"Wow. Okay. I'm busted at not knowing better. I always thought it happened around the time of the Zoelands Concord."

"They did become official in 2625, so you're not far off. It just took some time to grow into what the regatta is today."

"Anyway, it's not really the point," Miriam smiled. "There was definitely one Uru story that I've always remembered. I used to share it with the children who visited the museum when I was still working for the foundation. The story goes that, when they first started rebuilding the Zoe with the nekros scraps, Linda regretted staying behind."

"She did?" Mik asked, actually looking like he was hearing that part of the story for the first time.

"Maybe regret isn't really the right word. She was scared. I mean, all she ever knew was the Global Union. The GU had provided for her. They met the physical needs of everyone equally."

"Physical needs are important," the captain said as he moved even closer to Miriam. She understood his meaning, but still wanted to continue with the story. She was building to something. "And the GU had told Linda that she had the right aptitude for all sorts of tasks that were these somewhat mindless chores and those skills, as they worked to make Baja into a livable home, no longer mattered."

"So, Linda felt like she'd thrown away...." Mik interjected.

".... everything she ever knew. Everything that was safe and solid. Everything that, even though it had never been fulfilling, was comfortable and familiar." Miriam took a deep, reverent breath as she paused. "Well, I mean, there were no electric pods anymore. She used to replace batteries in them. That and chickens is all she knew."

"Okay," Mik encouraged. "I don't see where this is going."

"It's not just that GU life was all she understood, but because she had also been in this horrible relationship with an awful person who never saw her worth, she literally did not even know if she could do anything else. But when she and Uru began working together...."

"He was always the one experimenting and trying things for which he'd had no training?" Mik asked.

"Exactly! Well, and he was always reminding Linda that she was doing the same but didn't realize it." Miriam beamed at him as they played push and pull through the narrative. The two spoke as though they'd shared this very story together dozens of times. They had. "The thing is," she went on, "it made her very uncomfortable. She worked alongside him, but completely without confidence. I mean, she was always secretly insecure, but, while they worked," Miriam laughed, "Uru would sing."

"Sing?"

"Yeah. He would sing all the time. And I guess he was really bad at it, too, but that didn't stop him.

"How do you know he was bad?

"Well, it's not as though we have any recordings of it, but that's what the Mercy Files say."

Mik joked as he authoritatively exclaimed, "Trust the Mercy Files!"

"You'd better!" Miriam giggled. Giggled? Who even was she right now, she wondered?

"Apparently he told Linda once that he'd always wanted to be a singer, a musician, or something musically related. Her response was, *'Did you pass the aptitude for that career?'* And he said, *'Oh fuck no!,'* Mercy's words, not mine," Miriam added. "Her files are actually full of that kind of language!"

"Really?"

"Absolutely. She would have fit in with your saltiest crewmember."

"No kidding!" Mik laughed.

"And I promise I didn't quote her directly when I used to teach this to kids."

"It might have kept you out of office!" Mik joked.

"Then maybe I should have," she smiled. "The thing is, Linda couldn't even understand the idea of doing something outside of her aptitude test," Miriam paused.

"What do you mean?"

"She asked Uru why he would want to do something that he didn't score well on during his exams. The Global Union tested them and presented career options. And this is the part that I remember. This is the part that really stuck with me, so I know I've got it right.

"I'm all ears," Mik said with a slow stroke of his finger down the back of Miriam's own ear. He looked with intensity deeply into Miriam's eyes.

Miriam pushed through her flustering to finish the story, "*'Not all of the options,'* Uru had told Linda. *'You chose from a list of employment opportunities that the GU needed done as a part of their machine and that they assumed, based on your aptitude test taken at the ripe age of fifteen, you would be able to do. That's not a real choice. You weren't looking at the whole menu.'*"

"You know the exact quote, do you?" Mik teased.

Smiling knowingly, "I'm paraphrasing," Miriam said. And I'm also paraphrasing Linda who said back, *'But if I did something else,'*–"

"*'I could fail,'*" Mik finished Linda's quote.

Miriam was moved, her voice cracking just slightly as she tapped into a value deep in her own heart and said, "Yes. That." This was definitely one of those moments when history came across as something very close to her.

"So what?" Mik chimed in.

"Well, that was kind of Uru's point, too. *'Then fail,'* he said. *'Fail gloriously and have the experience. Do what you must and let the outcome be what it will. Be a human for a change and not part of a machine!'*"

"So?" asked Mik.

"So? SO that moment, that foundation set by Uru, determined the course for Zoe culture – a culture in which we have many needs, but we count on individuals to determine how to meet them without being slotted into the role that's most convenient for us as a governing body. SO, we work to meet needs beyond physical. SO, we became a nation of people who tried and a nation of people who sometimes failed, all in the name of choosing from the whole menu."

Miriam was full of spirit now, words dripping with passion as she shared her Zoe pride. Mik saw the woman her people had no choice but to elect to represent them, and she wasn't done.

"SO, a domestic abuse victim from the Global Union becomes the founding mother of the Zoelands. SO, a widower mourning the loss of his three children becomes the founding father. SO, a sophomoric, black-market capable scrubber starts the first cityship—"

"Hey!" Mik rolled his eyes.

"Did I mention he was also endearing?" Miriam added with a punch to Mik's arm. It felt like a rock. Miriam paused and pulled herself back to the present from her tale traveling.

The child left her eyes and the level-headed governor returned. No. Not the governor. Someone else. His dear friend. No. Not that either. Definitely something more than a friend. She locked onto Mik with her gaze and relaxed her playfully fisted hand before laying it on his shoulder for a moment. Then, almost coming out of a trance, she moved her palm to his forearm and rested her fingers gently on him. It was Mik's turn to catch his breath.

"So," she breathed heavily, "I may very well fail miserably at government, but I will be fully human while doing it and," she paused, "So...." Miriam panted from the sprint with her words.

"So?" Mik Prompted.

"So even the son of Finlay McMahon, head of the McMahon Family Fleet, can become a respected cityship captain," she finished with a flourish. She looked directly into him. Then she waited. Patiently.

He blinked, trying to absorb the reality of what he'd just heard. Then, his face fell, but not because he was surprised or disappointed, so much as he wished he'd been the one to reveal his identity to Miriam.

"How long have you known?" Mik asked.

"Not long," she said, leaving her hand on his arm and even squeezing a bit. "I mean, I always knew you weren't the typical diplomat. But I didn't actually put the pieces together until this trip."

"What gave me away?"

"For starters, you seem to know a lot about fleet ops . . . even fleet history as you've shared here tonight . . . and I caught glances or bits of communications here and there between you and Kate."

"I thought I was careful."

"I was perhaps more curious than most."

As she grew more comfortable, Miriam allowed her hand to slide up Mik's arm again like they were an old couple. Maybe they were in their own way. At least as much as either of them had apart from their true loves—the Tatsu and Zoe Baja. Mik felt a sense of relief that someone else was in on his secret. The tension in his body released at her touch and he wanted to continue to melt into this moment and into Miriam.

"What I don't understand is, the Wang family, the communications, that was all before we finalized negotiations."

"I know. And?"

"Why did you keep . . . I mean we could have . . . I mean you didn't say anything, did you?"

"Why? If I did, are you going to have to kill me?"

"No. Not yet anyway!" he teased.

The two of them closed the distance between themselves, both with hands on the other comfortably, naturally, like it had always been that way. They felt one another's breath when they laughed together, felt the warmth of words being shared in the cool night air. It was easy and normal.

"But if it comes out, it could delegitimize all of the work that you've done."

"How so?" asked Miriam.

"Well, you know."

"No, I don't," she replied, her words soft and low now—not the child and not the governor and something more than his friend— this was a new person, one that he sensed nobody else knew but that she chose to show him in this moment.

There was a connection between them, one that had been there all along that they were just now realizing. When he came into port, it was Miriam he longed to see. In politics, he felt drawn to back her, confident in her goodness and intentions, never questioning them. He felt empowered to demonstrate that same difference-making mentality when she was at his side. She had always been more than a diplomat, more than a colleague, more than a friend. Why had it taken him so long to embrace that reality?

"What is the flagship of the Cityship Regatta?" Miriam asked, moving one of her hands to his chest, beckoning his answer – and more.

"Cityship Tatsu," Mik replied, feeling stronger, prouder than he ever had.

"And who is the captain of the flagship?"

"I am," he said, and he put his hand on Miriam, resting on her uninjured shoulder, dreaming of lower. What was happening?

"That sounds pretty damned legitimate to me." Miriam said, closing in on him so that only their hands on one another kept their bodies apart. She breathed heavily and he felt her chest rise and fall with her aggrandizing words, her skin lifting to fill his hand and drifting back away with each breath. "That's all that mattered. That's all that will matter."

"Shie shie," he said, his own voice low and whispered, now.

"Nothing to thank me for."

"You know you can't tell anybody though, right?" he said and immediately hated himself for it. There was a trust of touch between them, and he was an idiot for suggesting otherwise.

"I wouldn't dream of it," she said without judgment. "As long as you don't tell anybody I'm faking at this whole governor thing." She moved a hand to his face and traced his jawline in a gesture that set him on fire.

"That's not how I see it," Mik said.

"It's all selfish! I just want to keep Zoe Baja around." She wasn't looking at his eyes anymore, but his lips, his neck, her hand on his chest.

"Oh," said Mik, "that's not going to change." His words were truthful and intellectual, trained through years of political conversation and nuance. They came out of his mouth as muscle memory while his brain was checked out of any thought of negotiations. His mind and mouth kept moving forward while the cravings in his heart slowly overwhelmed his consciousness.

"The Global Union could never reabsorb Zoe Baja," his trained words flowed out as his eyes drank Miriam in, seeing her softness with a growing desire to confirm it. His mouth began to water and the heat he felt was becoming an inferno he had to quench. "Even if they reabsorbed other Zoelands, it wouldn't be politically advantageous to erase the original." He cupped his other hand to the side of her neck, no longer able to hold back the urge to feel even more of her skin. He immediately sensed her warmth. Her pulse quickened and it forced a race into his own.

"That's not what I mean," Miriam breathed, her thoughts just as autonomous from her emotions as Mik's were. She moved her hands into his hair, and she ran her fingers through it before retracting back down to his solid torso. "I know we are not in danger of losing our independence, I'm far more concerned about us losing our very existence." She knew the words didn't match the moment, but she didn't care. She didn't have to pretend with Mik.

Miriam slid her arm down his chest and around his body. She explored each inch of him with her fingertips as she did so and ultimately joined them to the fingers of her other hand that she had traced around his waist. The distance between them was gone. Mik pulled her against him, not wanting to release her, wishing that they could become one, that their skin could melt into each other, the hunger for an even deeper closeness unyielding.

"You'll live forever," he said.

Damn, he thought. The autobot for making language had given out. What the hell did that mean. You'll live forever? Think of something. Say the right thing, he thought. Before he could, Miriam's lips were on his and both of them collapsed into the passionate kiss that erupted beyond lips to earlobes, and necks, and, as articles of clothing were torn away, to Mik's chest and Miriam's breasts. They began devouring each other.

Everything was right with the world. They dropped to the deck and found one another over and over again with hands, and fingers, and lips, and tongues—their internal heat overcoming the brisk of the night as each fabric layer fell to the deck. The duality was such that every touch was slow and deliberate at the same time that it was mad and frenzied. Soft fingers that held on tight – plump lips that pressed hard – opened bodies that tightly, heatedly, passionately closed around each other and squeezed closer and more firmly into one another.

They consumed one another, lustfully quenching needs and wants as a singular feast that was served up ferociously and repeatedly and without abandon. They whispered heavily to one another in one moment and uninhibitedly yelled out in another, years of relationship and friendship and flirtation and desire becoming even more all at once. They were commanders and lovers. They were fully human and fully animal. And they continued shamelessly in their secretly shared time and space until their spent bodies trembled and flinched to the touch.

Finally, the two lay exhausted and relieved and fulfilled . . . more themselves than either had ever been alone.

Miriam felt like clay laying on her back on the deck of the Tatsu, Mik on his side next to her, unable to stop looking at and touching her. Then, the sky filled with waves of sparkling green mist streaked with shades of blue.

"The southern lights!" Miriam whispered aloud, unable to keep the awe of a child from returning to her voice. It made Mik smile adoringly through his afterglow. "I've never seen them live," she said.

"I thought that might be the case," said Mik. "Did you know that, until a few hundred years ago, these actually used to be the northern lights."

"But the magnetic poles flipped," Miriam finished.

"Yeah. That's right," He wasn't surprised she knew. Nothing about her knowledge surprised him, anymore.

"This is the thing you were waiting for," she said. "The reason we hadn't left yet."

Mik slowly drew a finger across Miriam's collarbone to the laser-stitched wound. He gently traced the line on her shoulder with his finger, a sandpaper pointer that became a feather's touch on Miriam. Her scar was like a fault line that tried to break the earth, but somehow made it stronger. This woman was as unyielding as the Zoelands history she held dear. The glow of blue and green shone on the light brown of her skin. She was one with the sea and the sky and the land, a map he could imagine exploring all the days of his life . . . his garden boxes were full.

"Yes," he said. "This was the thing."

CHAPTER 31
YEAR 2553

Nekros Baja

The crew of the Mining Vessel PS-1707 was boarding.

They had made sure that Linda and Uru's family had enough supplies to last them until Captain Mageo returned and they were prepared to launch. Only Tatsu and Peter remained on land.

"You won't be gone long, will you?" Mercy asked Peter, kissing him all over his face and neck between each word.

Uru tried not to look.

"A week. At most. I hope," he said. "It'll give me time to finish my credit glove. It's almost done but you make it really hard to concentrate on the work."

"Who me?" Mercy asked coyly with more kisses.

This time, Linda looked away and caught Uru in a glance. She threw a wink his way and he merely shook his head.

"I'll be back soon," Tatsu said, forgoing any semblance of machismo and pulling his big brother into a suffocating hug. "As for you, Linda," he said hugging her just as tightly, "We're family now, so I won't let you down, either."

"Captain!" called Amy from the ship.

"Let's go!" shouted Stacy completing Amy's thought.

Tatsu stepped aboard his vessel, pulling Peter along by the scruff of his collar, "Come on, Loverboy!" he said.

Stacy ruffled Peter's hair as he passed, and the boy attempted unsuccessfully to put away his ear-to-ear smile. As Tatsu began to enter the bridge, he found himself face-to-face with Wang Wei. That erased Peter's expression.

"I know what you're planning to do. We have a say in our plans. You can't just take this ship anywhere you want on a whim," the scrubber arrogantly stated, standing his ground.

Tatsu stepped up to him, but before he could get a word out edgewise, Peter cold cocked the greasy crewman. Captain Mageo stood stunned for a moment, then looked at Peter.

"Sorry," said the boy.

"Don't be," Tatsu returned. "Randall!" he called. "I know you're right around the corner. Take this compost heap to his quarters."

Randall and Erin both slinked around the corner, picked up Wang, and shuffled back below deck like the rats Tatsu now realized they all were.

Wang started to shake off the punch and rubbed his jaw, "I have a job on this ship!" he exclaimed. "You need me."

"I'm forced to have you on my ship, but nobody said I had to use you. As far as I'm concerned, you can spend the remaining days of your employ rotting in your quarters on rationed sustenance. Get him out of my sight," Tatsu commanded.

Erin and Randall continued to drag him away. Eventually, he flipped their hands off of him and they simply followed as he led the way to his own quarters. Peter began to continue past the entrance to the bridge.

"Where do you think you're going?" Tatsu asked. "You I do need. Randall will be covering Wang's position, so you've just been promoted to the bridge."

"But I'm not trained," Peter protested.

"Training I can teach, son. Character I can't."

As the PS-1707 approached the floating debris field at the earliest light, Peter let out a gasp.

"I had no idea," he said. "How big is the garbage patch, Captain?"

"2.1 million square kilometers. It was nearly double that size before cleanup efforts of ships like ours. The refuse scrubbers got it to this size and then the GU left it because they needed to concentrate their efforts on the waterways near their land masses."

"They just abandoned the work?"

"Not just here. There are other vortexes, too. They stopped work on those, as well."

"They just left them? Left all of this here?"

"One thing you'll learn as you get older, Peter, is that humans get really bored really quickly. Some other tragedy caught their attention."

"Is it safe?" the boy asked as the captain navigated his way slowly through the swirling mass.

"For whom?" Tatsu said sardonically.

The crew shut down the '07's engines at a northcentral point that they were able to reach on the vortex.

"Randall," Captain Mageo said over the ship's communications, "I need you to drop the stabilizing anchors. The standard drop won't suffice if we get rough waters while we're here."

"Yeah," Randall returned unenthusiastically.

The lack of decorum ticked Tatsu off, but the argument wasn't worth his breath.

The mining vessel was a compact vessel compared to many in the GU's armada of scrubbers. The top deck of the ship was roughly the size of a soccer field. It had crew quarters for fifteen but, as was the case with any Global Union employ or home—and the PS 1707 was both—it was overcrowded and often double-bunked. Each of the quarters also had its own separate storage unit. The ship had a mess hall, a small recreation space, a single bridge, an anchor room, and an engine room. All of the remaining space was for their assigned cargo and the equipment necessary to gathering it.

"Stabilizers won't drop, Captain," Randall announced after a few moments. "I tried Wang's code and it doesn't work."

Tatsu had forgotten that he disabled all of Wang's access. Of course, Randall couldn't follow through on the task.

"Shit, that's right," the captain said under his breath. "Peter, I'm sending you with my code. Get to Randall's station and key this in so he can deploy the stabilizers."

Tatsu tapped a pattern onto his forehead and temple, enabling the programming necessary to send the command codes to Peter's pad.

"I'm on it," Peter said upon receiving the sequence.

On orders, the crew suited up in dive gear and stepped out onto the deck awaiting the plan. Much of the area would allow the scrubbers to simply walk across the water. There was such a vast amount of trash floating on the surface that it didn't feel much differently than walking on a ship.

"What are we even looking for?" Adam asked Wang more than the captain as others began to secure the mining vessel in place.

"At one time, this all served a purpose as part of a culture or society somewhere. It needs to again," Mageo addressed them ignoring the fact that some of his crew were looking to Wang. "We need to find anything useful. Wire, pipes, and solar panels are particularly valuable. The entire ocean floor underneath all of this is rubber and tires, too. That's great material. We'll gather that with some of the mining equipment later. Not safe to do that by hand. Use your imaginations. I know you got 'em. What does daily life look like for you? And what do you see here that can make that daily life possible for the people who all just treated you as family for weeks? Invited you into their lives? People just like you and I, looking for a little piece of freedom. We have ours on the water. Let's help them find theirs."

Peter finished putting on his dive gear and, while he waited with the rest of his '07 family to make his drop to the oceanic wasteland, he continued fiddling with the credit glove. It was distraction more than anything. It was one thing to join a scrubber crew, already one of the toughest occupations, but quite another to go rogue with that crew to an unstable trash island searching the unknown for the unknown. His stomach churned.

"Listen up," Tatsu said looking down at Peter. The boy tucked the glove into his wetsuit. "You didn't sign up for this." The captain expanded his gaze to include the whole crew. "If anyone wants to stay on the ship, I won't think any less of them."

Wang Wei, who still sported a fat purple and yellow cheekbone, unzipped his wetsuit, peeled it off, and dropped it to the deck. He was followed, one-by-one, by the seven men and women who had been loyal to the disgruntled crewman from the start.

"You'd rather stay behind on this ship getting high together than see what's out there?" Tatsu unfazedly directed the question at Erin, and the pale, pocked woman looked shocked that Captain Mageo was aware of their recreational activities.

"All of you, is that your choice? Because this could be the day that you choose better. You could make a difference from this moment forward," Tatsu said again as Wang's group walked away. Their minds and bodies were too far gone to do any more than follow their supplier to the recreation room.

Tatsu was somewhat relieved not to have to lead the malcontents through the difficult and dangerous tasks ahead. He didn't particularly like them, but he no more wished to feel responsible if one of them died from the latest high. He felt certain that fate awaited each of them one day.

The captain looked over his remaining team and debated asking one of them to stay behind with the others in case things got ugly when the drugs came out, but that didn't feel fair. He saw the strength and love of each crewmember as they prepared to do good works for others.

"Okay, then. It's the twelve of us. Perfect for pairing off. Be careful. Don't go anywhere alone. Work in your assigned pairs. If you go down, it's not a clear path back up to the surface. That's for damned sure. Don't carry much at a time. It's early. We have all day. And maybe more days after that. We'll bring it back to the holds and we'll sort through it later."

Before they got to work, Tatsu explained their suits to them. If they went down, they needed to punch a button on their left breast. It would immediately close a mask over their face, expel the water from within it, and turn on their air.

"These are the latest in protective dive gear," Tatsu shared. "If you have inhaled water or are incapacitated, but you or your partner manage to get the mask release pressed, the suit will detect your state and begin life preserving methods. This might mean forcing air into the lungs of the person wearing the suit, shocking a diver's heart, or—as a last effort—injecting epinephrine. It's the next best thing to having a doctor in the suit with you. The only thing you have to remember is to press the damned button. That's it. And if you can't do it, your partner can. BREATHE!" Tatsu finished by patting himself below the button on his left breast to indicate they should do the same.

"BREATHE!" the group repeated in unison, confirming they'd understood their most important training.

The right breast button would launch a laser-mounted drone the size of a mandarin orange over their position should they need help. Much more visible than its size would indicate, it would continue to both project an audio signal and flash until a fellow crew person reached it and deactivated it.

"Breathe," Tatsu said, pantomiming punching the button on his left breast. "It's your heart, get it? Your heart only works when you breathe," he said. "Call your right-hand man," he continued, pantomiming punching the button on the right breast of his suit. "Breathe. Right-hand man. Breathe. Right-hand man.

"Breathe. Right-hand man. Breathe. Right-hand man," the others repeated both the words and the pantomimed gestures.

"Stacy, I'm so sorry," Peter said as he continued in the pantomime. "It looks like we swapped dive suits."

Stacy looked down at her own suit and noticed Peter's name badge on hers. "I guess so. I put them into the lockers last time, so I must have mixed them up."

"Does it matter?" Peter asked.

"Nah. One suit's as good as another," she waved off the concern. "I'll try not to pee in yours."

Peter laughed as they continued to refamiliarize themselves with the suits. They only ever pulled them out for training exercises, so it felt good to be putting them to proper use. They had readouts for oxygen levels on one wrist of their suits, as well as a keypad. On the opposite wrist, they could scan an object over the screen to learn what its composition was and determine whether or not to salvage it. They also had long cords of rubber tubing that connected them to their partners and a digital signal to direct them back to the '07 should they lose their way.

"Oh, and there are water and ration bars around your waist, too. We're going to be out here a while," the captain added.

Tatsu led the expedition, climbing down to the vortex first with Amy. Justin and Khalil followed. Then Davina and Allen followed by Marquise and Cairo. Patty and Samantha went next leaving just Peter and Stacy to finish their descent and bring up the rear. The boy took a calming breath and proceeded after his partner.

"You got this, kid. I'm right here with you," she encouraged.

Peter nodded but didn't speak. He was afraid that, if he opened his mouth, he might just throw up from the nerves doing somersaults in his gut.

Moving was slow and collection even slower. The pairs of partners walked wide, to keep their weight dispersed. Each step was taken in two beats, one to feel the surface, and a second to step down, sometimes after having to move to a more solid placement. Stacy's right, followed by Peter's right, followed by Stacy's left, followed by Peter's left.

When they found something of worth, one person would lie out across the rubble for stability while the other scanned, collected, and ultimately stored the item in the wetsack. The work was tedious. From the comms connecting the full team, it seemed to Peter that everybody else had filled their wetsacks while he was holding Stacy back, moving less confidently than the seasoned scrubbers across the unstable surface.

After about an hour, they came upon a massive object. It was clearly not going to fit into their wetsacks. "What is it?" Peter asked as he looked at the gargantuan piece of equipment.

A giant gold compartment was mostly submerged at the center of the mass. Wires and antenna stood out from it at odd angles. Connected to the metal chunk in the middle were what looked like gigantic broken white dinner plates. The object had huge wings, as well. One was bent and broken, a twisted metal framework that had long lost whatever it once held. The other was filled with hundreds of mirrored rectangular plates. Some were shattered or missing, but others were still intact. The entire piece of equipment was blackened in a cone-like pattern.

"Space junk," Stacy said matter of factly. "The old satellites, stations, probes, telescopes, the failed dyson sphere program . . . all of it . . . it ended up in the oceans during the space collapse."

"You mean when One Net failed?" Peter asked.

"When the damned world failed, Peter," she shook her head. "And we still haven't cleaned this shit up. This one's a satellite, I think. Or it was. Lot of valuable stuff here if we can use the equipment to break it down and get it back to Baja." Stacy began to type onto one of her wrist pads, "One man's trash is another man's treasure," she said as she did so. "I'm just going to take note of where this is located."

"We'll never get around it," Peter said.

"It's okay to take our time," she said, sensing Peter's frustration. "No credits for this job."

"Speaking of," Peter said proudly, "I think I finally finished it."

"Your dead citizens account glove? That's great, kid!"

"I prefer to call it a credit glove. I don't like to think about where the credits come from."

"That's part of the point. When scrubbers leave their credits behind, it's usually because they care about the people left behind. They want you to think of them. I remember all eight of the people whose accounts were passed on to me."

"Eight?!"

"It was the reef collapse back in '35. My first crewmates. All but one of us got out of there initially, but I was the only one who made it through my injuries."

"I'm sorry. I heard you lost your first crewmates, but I didn't know it was in the reef collapse."

"Doesn't make a difference how a person is lost. Loss is loss. Pain is pain. And memory is a gift. I get to think of them when I use their credits. It may sound cold, but it's my truth."

"What sort of things do you buy?"

"Not anything really. Every birthday, solstice, new year, and scrubber anniversary, they give me a gift of credits into my account with a special note. Oh! And Rosh Hashanah and Hannukah, too."

"Really?"

"Levi was Jewish. It's not a lot at any one time, but I really love my life, so I don't need it just yet. You add what, seventeen years of credit gifts from eight people half a dozen times a year and I got myself a nice little chunk of change in there to retire on one day. It's all in my account. I'll deactivate each of them sometime in the last couple years of my work so that I don't have to maintain it anymore and just have one big account."

"You must be the richest scrubber in the GU!"

Laughing, "That's what Tatsu thinks."

"And the GU doesn't suspect anything?"

"Well, you have to be careful. It's not like my eight friends could live only by giving me gifts a few times a year, so I rotate between all of them and my own credit whenever we go into ports, which keeps my own credit spending low. I also spread around some love with all of the accounts, though. I buy supplies and food and any number of random things, and we stock up the '07 when the Global Union doesn't give us what we need. Like these suits. GU doesn't care enough about scrubbers to give us this kind of equipment."

"These aren't GU?"

"Hell no. Every dead citizen on the PS-1707 has bought one of these posthumously. My friend Howard is also particularly generous to the orphanages. And some of my DCAs provide real protein to some of the locals, extra rations to some of the families like Uru's.

He's hardly the only person who has found a way to have unpermitted kids. The GU won't supply for more than two children and, if they only gave one permit, they only supply the rations for one child. At the Lanai port, we knew a family that had quintuplets."

"Five children!"

"Had secretly. They didn't want to terminate any of them. Of course, the GU offered to put some of them into their homes, like Linda and Uru's kids, but the Global Union still hasn't gone so far as to be able to legally force parents to give their children over. They just assume that a family with five children won't find a way. Well, dead citizen accounts are the way. And I get to honor the lives of my crewmates by caring for others."

Stacy got quiet for a moment as she thought about the Lanai family, "I wonder if they made it out before the tsunami," she said and they were quiet for a bit before she moved, instead, from their present circumstances back to her past.

While they worked their way across the plain of garbage, Peter listened to Stacy's stories of Howard and the other lost crewmates. He heard about Olivia who was the brainiac in the bunch always figuring out more efficient manners of getting things done. Raina was strong, sassy, and sarcastic. Linét had a hard life but came out tough as nails despite her background. Kim was the business-minded one who taught the group how to maximize their credits. And Robert had been the steady foundation in the mix, always bringing calm to the high-energy group. Harrison and Kurt were new crewmembers and Stacy had just been starting to know them. Listening to her stories, for a little while, Peter was able to stop thinking about where they were and, when one is standing in the middle of refuse, that's not a bad thing.

"We're going to get a ton when we use the equipment later," Stacy said. Their packs were nearly full. "This is just the delicate samples, the charting of value zones. That sort of thing. It's not much different than our usual job, but it's trash instead of mussels."

"That makes it different," said Peter, laughing.

"Back to the '07," Tatsu called over comms. "Let's check in, drop our finds in the hold, and plan the areas for equipment usage."

Stacy pushed a few buttons on her wrist and directional tones began to guide them back to where they'd left the mining vessel.

"We must have gotten more turned around than I realized," she said. "I thought we'd come straight west."

"We've been out here for hours. Maybe we turned at some point," Peter said.

"I guess. Serves me right for chatting your ear off."

"I loved it."

"Well, looks like we need to go north," she said. Then, after a few steps. "So? Mercy's a nice-looking girl."

"Smart, too," Peter said. "She and your Olivia would have been fast friends."

"I'm sure that's what you saw when we first met her."

"Maybe not right off," He smiled sheepishly.

The time passed easily, albeit measured, as the partners made their way back to the PS-1707. Before they knew it, they started to see other pairs in the distance. They were all almost together again and it brought some relief to Peter. He was eager to get out of the rubbish abyss.

"Captain?" Khalil's voice projected from the comms.

"Go ahead, Khalil."

"Captain, the '07. She's gone, Sir."

"What do you mean gone?"

"I mean gone. Justin and I just got here, and we're supposed to keep going north, but north is nothing but ocean."

"Greasy scrubber stole your ship, Sir!" Marquise shouted.

"How is that possible? They would have needed your codes!" Amy shouted.

Their comms erupted with a collective panic stopped only by Captain Mageo shouting, "Calm down. It was me. Dammit. It was me. I had Peter key in the command code on Randall's station and I for-got to clear it. It was me," the captain said ashamedly. He felt so stupid. He may have just killed his entire crew because he'd forgot-ten to clear the codes when he'd shut down the engines.

"It's okay, Captain," Stacy said. "Don't lose your head. It could have been any one of us," she encouraged.

Whether or not Tatsu believed her, they couldn't undo the situation. He took a calming breath and rubbed the jagged lines of his facial scruff as he considered next steps.

After a beat, "Khalil, set yourself as home for our digital direction tones. We'll make our way to you. I can see some of you. We're probably half an hour from being together and we can collect our thoughts then."

Peter turned to Stacy, panic on his face and, for just a moment, he forgot the first beat of his next step. As if a trapdoor had dropped open beneath him, he plunged straight down beneath the water. Except, it wasn't just water. It was rubble and debris and it banged against his head and face and body like a flock of birds into a turbine. He felt the jerk of his rubber cord slowed by the weight of his partner, followed by a slow sink – but still a sink. He gulped water and fought the nearly involuntary impulse to gasp. He opened his eyes but, with the blanket of garbage above him, everything was black, and his vision was joining the darkness as well.

Peter began to pass out and the beat of his own nodding off reminded him of the rhythm they'd practiced: 'Breathe. Right-hand-man. Breathe. Right-hand-man. Breathe. Right-hand-man.'

For a moment, he only pantomimed as they had done on the surface. Then, he felt an abrupt tug on the rubber cord attaching him to Stacy as she pulled on him, and he slammed his hand against his left breast. It took only a second and a half. He regurgitated filth into his mask that got flushed out with the water and he took the most grateful breath of air he'd ever had in his life even while his face was coated in snot and vomit and unidentified film.

"I.... I got him, Captain," he heard Stacy saying with relief. "I got him," she coughed breathlessly through exerted effort.

Peter began to kick himself upward to help assist the tow from his partner. Finally, his face broke the surface and, lying flat, he crawled his way out of the deep, opposite of Stacy to keep their weight spread out, and onto the solid-ish surface. Then he rolled onto his back. He retracted his mask and just breathed for a little bit.

Finally, "Right-hand man!" he laughed to Stacy, pointing in her direction while staring upward at the clean sky above the crap below.

"Breathe," she raspily whispered back, with a gurgle.

Peter turned to face her. She was turning blue. He beat his right breast, launching his location drone into the air. Then, Peter began crawling toward Stacy, the four meters of their rope feeling like a kilometer.

"Hold on," he cried. "Hold on. I'm coming."

"Air. Broke," she gulped.

"Wait," he cried. "I'm getting there. Please. Please wait. I have air. Hold on."

It was agony being so close to his mentor and crewmate, having what she needed to live, knowing that, on either solid land or open water, he could be to her in a flash. When he finally was at Stacy's side, her eyes were nearly glossed over.

He pulled a connection hose from his own suit and attached to hers. Then, he pushed her mask button, so that it could force the air into her lungs like it was designed to do. But the button didn't depress. He hit it again and again, while tears welled up in his eyes. A piece of trash had wedged beneath the button and somehow wouldn't come loose. Peter began sobbing over Stacy. He attempted to push her mask release again, but she weakly caught his hand in her own.

"Glove," she barely managed.

"No. No," Peter cried.

Stacy's eyes began to close. From inside his suit, Peter fished out his credit glove, put it on, and held her hand in his own . . . until she stopped moving.

CHAPTER 32
YEAR 2908

Gubernatorial Grounds Zip Pad
Zoe Baja
Zoelands Concord

Inoke tried to understand what was going on.

He had opened as many doors as he could, both physically and figuratively. Tsunamic Defense Coordinator Doug Beamer was still roaming around the public side of the government building even though the warning, following the Zoe Chile earthquake, had passed. They would be sending assistance to their Zoe neighbor, but there was no cause for panic at Zoe Baja.

Deputy Governor Roberto Francisco wouldn't miss him if he took a whistler to the southern port. He hadn't been including him in any of the briefings since Governor Heirlinda had left on the Tatsu, anyway.

"Nina," Inoke said to the projection of his wife at home.

She was holding a chicken under one arm, wearing work clothes and a dirty hat, and had mud on her face. She never looked prettier to him.

"I'm so busy right now, love. What's going on?"

"I just wanted to say that I have to go to the southern port. I may be home late."

"What's going on?" she asked again, this time with knowing suspicion.

"Well, I'm not sure exactly. I can't find Harry. I need to go there in person. Something isn't right."

Nina stood still on the projection and her expression of exhaustion turned to one of concern.

"What aren't you telling me?"

"I wish I knew how to answer that. The truth is, I don't know what's wrong. But things have been . . . I don't know . . . suspicious ever since Miriam left."

"It's Francisco, isn't it? I don't trust that weasel. Hey, get out of here," she shooed away something out of the projection.

"Maybe it's nothing. I just wanted to say I'm going to be late, and I love you."

"Now I'm really worried."

"Don't be. I'm probably just paranoid. The governor will be back today, and everything will go back to normal."

"Okay. Be safe."

"I will be."

The projection disappeared and Inoke directed his zip chopper pilot to the southern port.

"We're just glad you let us prove ourselves to you after Ju...."

"Don't say her name!" Li Fang shouted at George. "You and Eric just do your job and then we'll see if you can prove yourselves."

"Yessir," said Erik. "We have to let their tsunamic defense coordinator know when the Tatsu crosses the two-kilometer mark."

"And then hightail it out of here," added George.

"I better not hear from you before the job is done."

"No Sir. Where will you be?" George asked.

Li Fang was stepping off of their small vessel onto his own but turned back and stepped right up to George to face off with him.

"Something I have to take care of before planning my sister's memorial," he said quietly.

The three men stood silent for a moment. Then, the head of the Wang Family Fleet boarded his speed boat, and his men made their way to the outermost seagates of Zoe Baja's tsunamic defense.

"Harry?" Inoke called running up and down the different piers and docks of Zoe Baja's southern port. Finally, he heard something around one of the buildings. He started to walk toward the sound when, around the corner, Potcake came walking. Usually the dog bounded toward Inoke, tail wagging, but this time he just slowly sauntered over to the chief of staff.

"Hey Potcake, where's Harry?" Inoke asked as he crouched down near the animal.

Vera came around the corner next and Inoke stood to greet her.

"He doesn't know. I haven't seen Harry in days. Found his boy wandering back and forth out here whimpering."

"Vera, are you kidding me? And you didn't think to let me know?"

"What do you mean? I left dozens of messages. I couldn't believe you hadn't come sooner."

"I didn't get any messages."

"I spoke directly with Francisco. He said he would personally see to it that an investigation was launched."

"What the hell is going on here?" Inoke shouted. "When did you last talk to him?"

"This morning."

"This morning?"

"Yes. I was up there to get the refugee, Mauga, to bring him down here. He's supposed to get passage on the Cityship Tatsu or something?"

"Hemi Mauga is down here? At the port?"

"Just the two of us. All other port activities cancelled. In fact, evacuated. He told me it was for Mauga's protection. Just the two of us are supposed to be here for the refugee transfer."

"You and Mauga here. Doug Beamer up there. I think I'm starting to put this together. Where is Mauga?"

"In the office."

"Take me to him."

Inoke, Potcake, and Vera ran to the office to find Mauga, dressed for formal travel and looking at peace, albeit his color wasn't great.

"Mr. Mauga," Inoke nodded. "We met when you arrived."

"I remember you."

Up close, Inoke noted that the refugee looked significantly worse than when they had met just days earlier. His eyes were bloodshot, and his skin had a jaundice appearance. The chief of staff had known others who suffered with Chloe but didn't remember them showing these symptoms.

"Listen. You don't have any reason to trust me, but I don't think what's happening here is what you think is happening here."

"What do you mean?" the man said, and his voice sounded raspy. Inoke wondered if Francisco had mistreated the GU citizen.

"I need you to come with me. Back to the capital," Chief of Staff Kalua insisted.

"I don't understand. I'm supposed to board the Tatsu. They're coming into port tonight."

"And if you come with me right now, that's exactly what can happen, but if you wait here, I think you're in danger."

"Inoke?" Vera asked, confused.

"Okay," said Mauga, looking bewildered.

Inoke and Hemi ran to the whistler while he called back to the shore worker, "Vera, get the fuck into the tower! Now!" Inoke yelled and his language shocked her. She never imagined the chief of staff cussing. "You do not want to be this close to the water. Get Potluck and go into the port observation tower until we return!"

"You're coming back?"

"We might have to. And if we do, we're all in trouble, so I hope not," the chief said. "Now get inside."

Back at the gubernatorial complex, Inoke Kalua and Hemi Mauga quietly slipped into a side door of the deputy governor's quarters. Inoke had great relationships with enough of the security personnel that a simple nod let them know he didn't want to be found out.

Coming around a corner, though, he found himself facing Doug Beamer. He tapped Mauga and signaled that he should keep his head down. Hemi pretended to look at something on the wall while Inoke addressed the tsunamic defense coordinator.

"What are you doing here?" Doug asked. "I thought you went home."

"I did. Forgot to leave my final report for the deputy governor."

"Why aren't you bringing it to the governor's office, then?"

"Well, it's his last day until Governor Heirlinda's return, so I though it would be most convenient if I left it on his desk here."

"No need to sneak around for that," Beamer said suspiciously.

"Didn't want anyone to know I was here again," Inoke whispered to Doug. "You know how it is when you're trying to get home. Don't want anyone piling on."

Seemingly satisfied, "Oh. Sure. Your secret's safe with me."

"Thanks, man," he patted the tsunamic defense coordinator's arm. "Shie shie. See you soon."

After Beamer moved around a corner, Mauga and Kalua slipped into the darkened deputy governor's office.

Shivering, "What are you looking for?" Hemi asked. The poor man must have been down at the port in the cold for hours in his travel clothes.

"I wish I knew. Just something to prove something, I guess," Inoke said as he swiped his way through the digifile on the desk and then began to open drawers; in one of the drawers, he manipulated a panel and a smile of satisfaction crossed his face as he put his hand on a second digifile. "And I think I just found it."

Inoke began scrolling through data, "Holy shit. We need to get out of here. And now."

Inoke returned the secret digifile to its drawer and left with the refugee.

CHAPTER 33
YEAR 2552

Pacific Nekros

It took forty-five minutes for the rest of the crew to reach Peter. They moved slowly across the island of trash. He lay there the entire time under the flashing drone above, holding Stacy's cold, lifeless hand. The tones being emitted from the location drone helped to numb his own thoughts and feelings.

Amy and the captain arrived first. The captain deactivated the drone. Little by little, the others arrived. Nobody could offer an embrace to their youngest crewmate or console him because they sat in a large, scattered circle, so as not to disturb the fragile surface of Pacific Nekros. With no physical consolation of their own to give, nobody said anything of Peter holding onto Stacy's hand.

As dusk wore on and silence wore thin, Justin was the first to speak.

"I loved Stacy, too. We all did. But we got some problems of our own we have to deal with now and laying here in the trash feeling like shit because of what happened won't do anything for solving them."

"Where do you think Wang went?" Cairo asked.

"Who the hell knows," Marquise shot. "He's always wanted to be in charge of his own ship. I doubt he even runs back to the GU. Maybe he goes rogue."

"You don't think he'll come back?" Samantha asked.

"No," Allen said. "If he didn't return when the location drone was up, he's not coming.

"Where does that leave us?" Davina asked.

"Up literal shit creek without a paddle," Patty said. "Or a flotation vest. Or a raft. Or a hope."

Tatsu tapped on his temple.

"Got anything, Captain?" asked Khalil.

"Nothing coming in. I was tied into the '07's system. If I were Wang, first thing I'd have done was jam me. Guess I'm offline until I have a new stream to connect with."

Tatsu looked at his people. He'd asked for their loyalty, and they had given it willingly. But he never really believed they'd pay with their lives. As far as he could see was garbage. If GU recon were to pass overhead, his team wouldn't even look like people, just more of the trash heap.

The days were long in the middle of the ocean with nothing to block the sun from its earliest and latest rays. Nonetheless, they didn't have a plan and night would come soon. He took inventory of the ration bars and waters amongst his crew. If they were cautious, they could last two more days. Two days to make it through the mess.

"And what about Stacy's ration belt?" asked Allen.

Peter, who still hadn't spoken, just shook his head no.

"Son," said Tatsu gently, "she didn't save you so that you could die out here. Get the belt. And her wetsack, too."

Peter ached more spiritually than he did physically as he pulled the wetsack, waters, and ration bars off of Stacy's suit. The act took longer than he'd wished. He had to move cautiously and didn't want to be disrespectful to her corpse. He continuously swallowed back the lump in his throat.

"She hadn't even touched them," Peter said, looking at her rations and he felt a new guilt because part of his job as her partner was to make sure they were drinking and eating, and he was certain he'd had some of his own water and a portion of one of his bars.

"Then she may have saved even more of us," Amy said. "Those rations buy us more time."

"We pay our respects tonight and make a plan in the morning," the captain directed.

Each crewmember spoke about Stacy. Peter, though he had been with the crew the shortest, had a glut of stories and had all of them smiling through their tears before he was done.

"It's a scrubber's honor to go while at sea," Tatsu said to Peter when the time came to let her go.

"Here?" Peter asked.

"We can't bring her with us," Amy said softly.

"Release the cord, Peter. It's the right thing." Khalil said.

The boy undid a latch that fastened one end of the rubber cord to his partner. With as much grace as he could manage in their precarious balance, he lowered Stacy into the water. The debris immediately floated back to fill in the water over the hole through which she'd dropped. Peter looked at his credit glove, tapped some keys on the back of it, removed it, and tucked it back into his suit.

"It's going to be dark soon," the captain said. "Quarter ration, two sips of water. Partners, take turns sleeping. Peter, you join Patty and Samantha, and you sleep first.

"I'm not tired."

"You sleep first," said the captain.

Not one of the eleven crew slept well. While they were in the open and the rubble, having lived on the ocean for ages, it didn't smell any different than the rest of the sea. The air still felt suffocating, though. Their suits were tight. The warmth was good in the night, but that didn't make up for the discomfort. As the second shift of sleepers arose, aching from stiffly held resting positions, they all faced the same questions and problems as they had before their eyes had closed the night before.

Tatsu forced them all to ingest some rations and water. They worked together to carefully stretch away the cramping they all felt, while still lying down. Then, they made their way to standing.

"We're going east," said the captain. "It's the most likely coast of this garbage patch to see another ship. That's the side most traversed by shipping vessels. It's not a big idea, but it's the only one I have right now unless anyone has something else to offer.

The crew was quiet.

"Okay, then. Stay in a net formation to disperse weight. Two beat steps. Right foot at the front of the group, right foot at the back of the group, left foot at the front of the group, left foot at the back of the group. You gotta piss, you piss in your suit and don't shift around while you're doing it. You need to stop, we all stop. We walk as a group. We rest as a group. We eat as a group. We drink as a group. Any questions?"

Lots of deep breaths, but no questions.

Together, as one unit, the corded crew began to slowly make its way eastward. As they started, Captain Mageo called out their steps like a cadence. Then, once he stopped, Peter could still hear the quiet mouthing of movements coming from Patty and Samantha.

They paused for a water and ration break, making their way to sitting cross legged on the rubble. Getting up again was difficult, so they opted to remain standing the next time they took a water break and to get low only when it was time to sleep and stretch.

As the second half of the day prolonged, Amy started singing. They all joined in for *When the Saints Go Marching In*, which they had danced to at Linda and Uru's wedding just a few days earlier. It felt like a lifetime ago, Peter thought. Then, he realized it had been at least one lifetime ago. Still, he sang, because it was better than not singing. And definitely better than thinking.

Sometime before dusk, they all fell into a numb silence. They moved forward, but almost robotically rather than with purpose. Right foot; feel the surface; adjust; step on the surface; pause for second team's right foot. Left foot; feel the surface; adjust; step on the surface, pause for second team's left foot. Repeat. They moved like zombies over the rubble, frustrated with their circumstances and powerless to change them.

It was hard to tell just how far they had come since they began their march at the start of the day. Everything looked the same as when they had set out because what does a giant floating pile of crap look like other than a giant floating pile of crap? They slept in shifts once more, not with any renewed hope, but at least knowing that they had all managed to stay together and nobody went under.

When Peter opened his eyes on their third day on Pacific Nekros, the captain was rubbing his one good eye repeatedly, squinting, and looking off in the distance under a hooded hand for shade. Tatsu had been awake when Peter closed his eyes for his sleeping shift and also awake when Peter opened his eyes after the restless hours. On the first night, he'd assumed it was because he was in a group of three that could spread the sleep out differently than the other partners, but now he questioned whether Tatsu had slept at all.

"You okay, Captain?" Peter asked. "When was the last time you closed your eyes?"

"I'm beginning to wonder," Tatsu said. "I think my sight is playing tricks on me."

"Get some sleep, Sir."

"I will. That's a good idea. Before I do, though, just assure me that I'm seeing things, will you? Look to your 2:00, to the shore. I see the water out there. But, before that, am I seeing...."

Peter could tell Tatsu didn't even want to say it out loud. He looked and did his own share of squinting and eye rubbing.

"I don't want to say what I think I see, either," Peter said with cautious optimism.

"I see it, too, Captain!" Justin said, yanking his cord to wake up his partner.

"It's really there?" Tatsu asked. "It's a ship, isn't it?"

With as gentle of tugs and words as possible so as not to upset their disbursement of weight, the crew each woke their sleeping partners. Enough eyes confirmed it. That day, they made their way toward the ship that was perched at the central eastern shore of Pacific Nekros.

The movements were as slow as they had been the day before, but—as they moved with purpose—the crew made great time and kept their spirits up even as the sun baked down on them. They didn't quite make their destination by dark as they had hoped, so they stretched out their rations a tiny bit more and toasted Stacy with sips from her waters before what would be their final night of sleeping in shifts.

The '07 crew began their fourth day knowing that they would reach whoever it was that had anchored near a garbage patch. It was all they had to keep themselves going because, after their morning rations, they were out. Only sheer will could carry them on at this point.

Every hour, one of the eleven released his or location drone, leaving a trail for anyone on that ship who might see them. As they closed in on the ship in the early afternoon, though, it became clear that this wasn't their savior pulled up on the shore. Rather, it was just another object from the past. But this trash was indeed a full-sized ship and Tatsu just happened to have with him the most dedicated crew a ship had ever been lucky to have.

One-by-one, the former mining vessel crewmembers helped one another board the beached behemoth of a vessel. To their sea-trained legs exhausted from almost four full days of traversing the trash vortex, they may as well have stepped onto paradise island. It was a massive water vehicle, far larger than the PS-1707 or even one of the recycler ships stationed over the Earth-Before-the-Melt cities. Tatsu had heard rumors of such sightings by other scrubbers, massive vessels that rolled and went under after the melt or during the space junk collapse. He'd never seen one in person.

They spread out and walked around the slightly angled deck of the ship. It wasn't going anywhere, and with something truly solid beneath their feet, walking on a slight angle caused by the manner of its beaching still felt like sturdy foundation. They were exhausted, but renewed in spirit, and so they began to do what they did best as a crew and work together to see how they could utilize their good fortune.

"Our objective has changed. We haven't given up on Uru and Linda, but we are no help to them until we help ourselves. Drop your wetsacks and your cords. You can strip your suits but know that there's a possibility we have to put them back on," he added, and he let the unpleasantness of that sit in the air. "Amy, Peter, and I will find the bridge and find out if this thing is seaworthy. Justin, you and Khalil see if you can find the engine room. Take Cairo and Marquise with you. Even if the engine runs, we need to see what it will take to actually get out of here."

Peter was in awe of Tatsu taking over. He'd only ever seen him in charge of the Mining Vessel but, on this strange sideways ship he didn't know at all, he was just as commanding.

"Do we need to dig ourselves out?" the captain continued, "If so, we gotta figure out how. Patty and Samantha, you're specifically on sustenance. I don't care if you walk into a room and it has a satellite connection, you walk out."

"You don't want communication?" Patty asked.

"Well, make a note," Tatsu laughed. "That wasn't really my point. I just mean that we need water and food, and we need it soon, okay?"

"Yes, Captain," she smiled and Tatsu remembered how nice it was to see his crew smiling. "Davina and Allen, explore. Anything else you can find that will help, grab it. Keep comms on, team. If you find something during your assignment that Davina and Allen need to know about, announce it."

Tatsu looked at each one of them, proud of who they were as much as he was of what they'd come through. He felt strong in spite of his hunger and thirst.

Clapping his hands together like a coach, "Alright. You have your assignments. Let's get off this garbage heap!" he said, and the huddle broke to the many assigned tasks.

Thousands of small round windows wrapped all around the ship that looked to be fifteen decks high. It had probably been white at one time, but now was mostly brown and green. Making their way to the bridge, Tatsu and his team of two passed recreational sports courts and a pool whose original swimming water was long gone and replaced with storm water combined with whatever mess had washed into the large basin. This thing was built for luxury. The bridge was surrounded by windows with glass long-since shattered or gone. Sand and stone and shells had washed into the space leaving most everything covered. There were some old-fashioned manual controls, but not so old fashioned as to work without the aid of power.

"If we could get it powered, this looks pretty standard, Sir," Amy said. "Apparently, not much has changed in the past – well – past however many years."

"250, give or take," said the captain.

"You think so?"

"I know so," he said pointing to a plaque on the wall. "Commissioned 2307."

"So, before the Global Union," Amy added.

"Seems like."

"It doesn't look very damaged," Peter said. "I mean other than being on Pacific Nekros.

"It's not," said Tatsu. "You both are right about that. But a ship is stronger than the bodies it carries. It could have withstood a storm that the people on it did not."

"What do you think happened to them?"

"Not sure. I mean it's possible people died here. But it could just as well be that they abandoned ship. Could be the ship itself wasn't even manned at the time it got caught in the vortex. Maybe a tsunami sent it loose."

"When the space junk collapse was going on, the whole world was in chaos. I mean, even more than it is now," Amy said. "People were boarding and abandoning ships all over the globe. So much was coming down at once that people never really knew when or where something would fall and whether it was man-made or an asteroid. They were wrong more than half the time about when they thought an object would burn up on impact."

"Meaning it would instead slam into the water flipping a vessel and all of its people over into the ocean," Tatsu finished.

"Captain, we got something!" Justin called over the comms.

"What is it?" Tatsu asked.

"Our way out," said Khalil.

It was going to be their last night on Pacific Nekros and nobody was going to miss this place. They all sat together around a fire they built on the bow of the deck of the massive ship. Thanks to the salvage efforts of the team, they were in new clothes found in storage. They were dated and even somewhat disintegrated, but they were better than the soiled dive suits. The crew ate birds that were cooked over the fire in wine boiled down to reduce the alcohol, although they didn't mind partaking of some of the 250-year-old treat at full octane. They drank the stalest water any of them had ever tasted. Old collected rain was pulled from the pool, filtered through a towel, and boiled. They didn't trust any of the perishable goods on the ship. Even dried and canned items of that age imparted concern at the very least. Their feast would not have been noteworthy at all, if it hadn't meant their actual survival.

Somewhat clean and with bellies a little less aching, they were able to focus on their wins. This ship was filled with items of use. They'd found plenty of quality supplies to bring back to Uru and Linda. They had batteries and fuel to carry it all. And, most importantly, was Justin's find . . . the small two-level ship with a hold, probably a lifeboat or dayboat for this old craft . . . in working condition . . . that could be lowered from the back of the huge vessel, mostly clear of the debris. While this city-sized ship they found probably could work, it couldn't do so in time to get Uru and Linda what they needed or, for that matter, get this crew their own sustenance. They would set out first thing in the morning and could be back to Nekros Baja in three to four days.

"We still have a problem," Tatsu said. "We'll need more fuel. We have enough to take us to the Columbian Province. I know a couple people there who can get us everything else we need, food and seeds mostly. Thing is, even my best connections aren't going to want a link to me. All my dead citizen accounts are gone with Wang. All of yours too. We just can't get supplies without revealing ourselves. We don't have mussels to trade this time. We have skills and abilities and can trade down the line, but we need help. Right. Now."

The crew was quiet. In the midst of the epic, they had unintentionally become fugitives from the Global Union. Their intentions would mean nothing to a GU court. They would lose their employ, their statuses, and the open water. They would be assigned to a GU penitentiary, with nothing but sustenance rations to see them through their days. When they picked Tatsu over Wang, Linda's and Uru's freedom over forced assignments, and even their earlier attempts to aid in recovery on Baja Province over quietly working their mining routes, they went against the status quo. And that just wasn't tolerated.

They hadn't even realized it while it was happening. It wasn't as if they woke up one day a year ago and thought, *'You know what? I think this is the year I go rogue from the Global Union.'* But that's exactly what happened. They went from a to b to c and on and on until here they sat at z . . . men and women without a home unless they figured out how to make one for themselves.

"I have credits," Peter said.

"You're burned, too," Amy said. "No matter how young you are."

"Not my credits," Peter said. "Stacy's. And hers are padded with the DCAs of—"

"The Reef Collapse victims," Tatsu said. "That was our worst accident ever."

"I know," Peter said, "she told me. Before she . . . before she asked me to use the glove. And the glove worked. I mean, they can try to find her, but I don't think they ever will. From what I understand, there's enough on this scan to at least get Linda and Uru started and maybe even us, too."

Tatsu nodded proudly to Peter.

"You all don't have to come," he said to the rest of them. "I can leave you in New Hispaniola. You can go to the authorities and say I forced you on this adventure over the last year. No hard feelings."

"What? and let you have all the fun?" Khalil asked.

"Okay, then. I guess we're on our own from here on out."

"No," Amy said. "We got each other."

CHAPTER 34
YEAR 2908

Pacific Sea Route
Cityship Tatsu IV
Cityship Regatta

"I can't wait to get off this ship," said Dr. Bradley.

"I'd love to tell you you're getting a little break after this, but I think we'll be doubling down on our efforts very soon," Miriam said.

"Governor?" Ensign Bintou-Keita asked, approaching the two on the deck with a digifile.

"Yes, Ensign?"

"You have a call from Zoe Baja, ma'am. A Nina Kalua?"

"Why would your head poulterer be calling you out here? Chicken emergency?" Jacob joked.

"I'm not sure." Miriam tapped a few buttons on the digifiles and, instead of Nina's image, she saw Inoke Kalua pop up in the air.

"Governor, where are you?" he said in a panic.

"Almost home, Inoke. One and a half, two kilometers out. I'm surprised you can't see us from the southern port."

"I'm on my way back there now, Miriam. Nobody else is at the southern port. Not even Harry. He's gone. You need to turn back. Now. Get outside the two-kilometer range."

"I thought the tsunami warning was cancelled."

"It's not the warning. It's Francisco. I saw a speech he's planning to give, ma'am."

"Always wanting to play the disaster hero, that one."

"No, Miriam! That's not it! The speech says you and Dr. Bradley are dead! Says you went down with the entire cityship and it's because the Global Union sent an infiltrator named Hemi Mauga to activate tsunamic defense. The speech claims that you died inside the two-kilometer range."

"But we're...." Miriam stood shocked for a moment before the reality dawned on her. "That monster. I never liked him, but I didn't think he was capable of...."

"Exactly, Governor. Turn around! Now!"

The berthing and mooring crews were just arriving, getting ready for the hours of work that they'd have to do to bring the Tatsu into Zoe Baja.

"Wait here!" Miriam said to Jacob as she ran toward the bridge with Ensign Bintou-Keita beside her.

"Mik! Mik!" she screamed as she entered breathlessly. "They're going to launch tsunamic defense and Harry is gone. Get us turned around! Quick!"

"Holy shite!" Kate called over comms from the aft bridge. The channel between the two ops centers must have been open.

Mik started calling a series of frantic commands out to his crew on the bridge as well as those who heard him over comms. Alarms started flashing and blaring. Before any noticeable movement of the Tatsu could occur, though, a deep rumbling sound started to echo throughout the ship. Miriam's eyes grew huge as she looked at the captain.

In seconds, the deck of the ship leaned deeply down, and a deafening metal-on-metal screeching noise overwhelmed all of the other sounds, including those of screams erupting throughout the cityship. The Tatsu was pushed forward violently in the water as water rushed up over the bow of the ship. Then, just as abruptly, she slammed down onto the surface of the ocean.

Equipment and people crashed to the deck with damaging impact. They had no time to catch their breath before shouts of "Help!" cut through the chaos. Mik ran off the bridge to find Dr. Bradley hanging over the edge. He had followed Miriam and Aida, but just hadn't made it into the partial safety of the bridge. In fast and enormous strides, the captain made his way to the scientist and grabbed him just before the doctor's grasp released.

"Murphy!" Mik screamed into his comms. "Open sideship bay number twenty -six!"

Two decks below where the doctor clung to the captain, the bay door concealing one of the workships began to open outward.

"I'm letting you go!" Mik called to Jacob.

Before he could object, the captain dropped the doctor, who landed on the platform beneath them. Then, for a moment, there was quiet.

Miriam, soaked and beaten, stepped off the bridge and saw Mik's face. The two exchanged a glance that was all at once fear and sorrow.

"Kate," the captain said over comms. "Get on the main bridge. You think you can get the Tatsu to ninety?"

"Mik?"

"A small ship might be able to make it to the manual release."

"Nobody can survive that."

"But nobody at all will survive if I don't."

Horror crossed Miriam's face and she ran to the edge of the ship where the captain stood. She grabbed his hand in her own.

"I'll take the ship," Mik said to Kate, but his eyes were locked on Miriam. "You get every fecking tool we've got onto turning the Tatsu. Got it?"

Kate was quiet.

"Got it?" he asked again, more forcefully as Miriam stared, unable to make words come out past the lump of panic that had formed behind her sternum.

"For you, yes," Kate said solemnly.

"You've got twenty minutes; eighteen now," he said. "I know you'll take care of her, little sister."

"Don't go." Miriam managed.

"You know I have to," he said.

"Mik," she cried as he kissed her.

She wanted to hold the kiss, memorize his lips, keep him here. There wasn't enough time.

"Callum," he said as he pulled away. "Say my name once for me."

"Callum," she said.

"Now, I can go," he said as he stepped over the rail and jumped to the platform below.

Mik checked on the scientiest and carried him into the bay, then hopped into the boat stored there, pulled a lever, and punched several buttons to manually activate the lifters that would lower the ship down to the surface of the water. As he was lowered, Kate had already activated the bay doors around the rest of the Tatsu and ship after ship was revealed at the ready. There were emergency calls echoing on comms ordering sideship operators to their vessels.

The waves were chaotic and the water between them appeared to be boiling like a violent cauldron. Mik hit the water and sped over the turbulence full throttle toward the manual release of the tsunamic defense sea gates at the southern port of Zoe Baja.

One-by-one, the other ships all around the Tatsu were lowered to the water – tugs, workships, and dayships all coming together for the effort of turning the gargantuan vessel. There was no line between citizen and civilian. They were all just Tatsian. Miriam watched for a moment before wandering, in a daze, to the bridge. Everybody else's world was moving frantically while hers seem to be standing still.

For a moment, Miriam caught Kate's eye. She hated Kate in that moment. It was irrational, but the anger crept into her being, nonetheless. She wanted Kate to have said "no," when Mik asked her to take over. Of course, she couldn't have done so. It was her captain ... and her big brother ... and she had a job to do. The short glance they shared could not have possibly conveyed all of those thoughts and feelings. It couldn't even have expressed the one emotion Miriam couldn't stop which was at the heart of them all. She was consumed by a selfishness to hold onto Mik—to Callum—even at the expense of everything and everyone else. She realized it too late. Dammit. She loved him.

Kate was amazing. She directed tugboats and commanded Devon to man their drones. She ordered workships and dayships to move quickly to one side of the cityship, bringing the full force of the flotilla's motors and strength to push the massive vessel to a ninety-degree angle between the two sets of sea gates. All six tugs were commanded to the other side with the work teams pulling like their lives depended on it . . . after all, they did.

"CLEAR THE DECK!" Murphy yelled into comms.

Crew efficiency Miriam would never have desired to see was set in motion. From a window looking out of the bridge onto the ship's deck, she saw Tatsian crewmembers and civilians rushing people to ladders and stairs that would take them away from the exposed deck of the Tatsu and to the levels that had elevators to move them even closer to safety. It was amazing how quickly they hustled. One young man, no older than Sefina, helped a large family, to evacuate the dangerous location.

"Devon, get me visuals on the stern. We gotta get our arse off that southern gate!"

"Yes, ExO!" they called.

"Second aft tug, more power!"

"Oui, ma'am!"

Meanwhile, Kate was moving her hands over her own set of controls in a manic manor, like a pianist bringing a complicated concerto to crescendo. The pace was nonstop. Each second that passed was filled with a combination of sideship monitoring, camera watching, and the engine and rudder movements of the Tatsu.

"Engine room, I need more!" ExO Murphy screamed.

Miriam never imagined being able to actually feel the shifting of a ship the size of the Tatsu, but she found she had to hold onto a bar to keep her balance.

"Out of the way!" Kate shouted as she moved to some controls behind the governor who stepped quickly to the side.

Miriam wasn't sure how much time passed since the nightmare began, but she quickly came to understand it had been twenty minutes – it was time for the next seagate to push up through the ocean in front of them. The low rumbling roar began once more.

"FECK! HERE IT COMES!" Kate screamed over comms. "BRACE! BRACE! BRACE!" she yelled.

With the push of a button, the command was loudly magnified on every deck of the great cityship: BRACE – BRACE – BRACE!

For a while, everybody held their breath, as well as the closest immovable piece of the Tatsu. This time the ship tipped deeply to a single side and more unsecured equipment flew about. Water rushed up over the side of the ship and washed away the young sailor Miriam had watched saving a family of Tatsians. The ocean was sovereign. Taking the boy was as simple as a wiper clearing a bug off of a zip chopper pilot's window. Then, the Tatsu slammed back down to the surface. Miriam flew into the air and bounced back down heavily. The entire ship echoed with chaotic cries.

The Tatsu then rolled deeply back in the opposite direction and equipment flew once more around the bridge. A heavy tool struck a sailor next to Miriam and the woman released her grip and fell to the ground bleeding. Nobody could help her as they each held onto their own parts of the ship for stability. The crewwoman was tossed around the bridge until she landed near to Kate who grabbed her with one arm while securing both of them by gripping the handle of an exit door.

Finally, accompanied by deafening metal creaks, the Tatsu leveled out and moved into a swaying and far less violent roll. It was a rolling that would have made Miriam ill just days ago.

The calls of the injured continued to pass through the ship. Kate stood and rested the wounded crewperson against a console.

"Roll call!" the Tatsu's de facto leader said into comms. The command assigned a dozen crewmembers to check in with the many sideships who had launched to help turn the Tatsu. The tugs led the effort, but—as Mik had ordered—they put every possible ship on the task, so there were plenty of others who had joined the task of turning the Tatsu to ninety.

Kate forced calm into her voice as she checked with all of her assigned ships. As each responded, a little more tension released in the executive officer.

"Kellogg family?" Kate asked.

"Kellogg family dayship, safe," the sound off was answered.

Next, she called, "Dixon family," into comms.

"Dixon family dayship, safe," a man's voice responded.

"First forward tug?" she continued down her list.

"First forward tug, safe."

"Workship Pan?" Kate asked.

No response.

"Workship Pan, respond," Kate said again.

Again, no response.

Workship Pan was one of six sideships lost in the effort to turn the flagship. It went down serving the citizens of the Tatsu just like its owner had said she would do. Miriam realized she'd never gotten that woman's name. The kind baker of the squash cakes whose cheek Mik had kissed. No, not Mik. Callum. Callum McMahon.

Kate set repair and medical units into motion. Then, she caught sight of Miriam's face, still ashen. The governor hadn't moved since the ship stopped rolling. The room went quiet.

Speaking into comms, but looking at Miriam, "Mik?"

"Can't hear! Repeat!" the captain's voice rang back.

"Mik," she shouted as clearly as she could. "We did it. We're at ninety," she said. "You don't have to do this."

"Kate, you know better," he screamed back, his voice strained. "You're okay for now, but if that water is pumped back out toward you, when each new gate adds to the sonic waves, you're not going to survive that. The Tatsians won't. I'm almost to the manual release. I've got this. You tell Miriam I'm just a drop in the sea now. Just like her."

"She heard you."

"Bitter waters," Miriam said under her breath as the comms cut out.

CHAPTER 35
YEAR 2553

Columbian Province
Southern Territory of New Hispaniola Land Nation
Global Union

The captain was growing concerned.

Tatsu Mageo and his crew had several close calls in the GU ports since leaving Pacific Nekros. Working to avoid any visual captures made it difficult to navigate the trade necessary to stocking their new vessel with supplies for Linda and Uru. The work was tiring, stressful, and—for the moment—unrewarding. Finally, they were ready to return to Baja, but one last stop was necessary as they did not have enough fuel to continue, just as was predicted.

"You're sure we can't make it?" Amy asked Captain Mageo.

They had just finished getting additional supplies at the port of the Columbian Province. When the crew had returned to the borrowed vessel, they found the captain unsure of whether they could leave once more.

"It's close," Tatsu shook his head in contemplation. "Not worth trying, though. We come up short and this could all have been for nothing. We'd be dead out in the middle of nowhere and my family would follow soon after. We're less likely to be seen here than in the

Northern Territory of New Hispaniola. I don't see as we have a choice," the captain said.

Tatsu gathered his crew on the deck of their claimed ship for a huddle. "I can't be the one to go," he admitted to all of them. "I'm the one we know is most likely to have his face across GU feeds right now. A couple of you even saw it when you were in the community buying resources. The authorities have me on going rogue with a GU vessel, a vessel I no longer even have. And since nobody goes alone, it has to be two of you who will go and—"

"I'm going." Peter said before the captain even finished speaking. "Me. I'm going."

Tatsu looked as though he wanted to stop the young man but thought better of it.

"And me," Amy said.

Tatsu sighed. The two people left on this ship to whom he was closest, and they were going to be the ones headed to the ugliest place he could imagine. "Okay. It's decided then. Make your way to the Columbian Vice Lounge on the southeast side of the city. Keep your heads downs. We need refueling right here in the port and I figure we've got less than three hours before the camera sweeps make it back to us in this slip. That means that if you're not back in three hours—"

"Leave," Amy said. "If we're not back, leave."

The captain nodded.

"I got it," Peter said, hardened. "Then let's get going."

He stepped onto the pier and started walking. Tatsu gave a glance to Amy who nodded her unspoken promise to watch over Peter, and then she followed the young man into the port city.

The port was bustling – GU commercial activities knew no sleep. One set of ships unloaded while another set loaded in a constant cycle across four daily shifts, each as busy as the one before and after. Food, power, and resources were conveyed through docks like this all over the world. From ships to pods, to markets, to districts, to quarters, and back all over again. What didn't come back for reshipping and usage came back for recycling and compost to be turned into the next food, power, and resources that would re-peat the cycle all over again.

Tens of thousands of citizens moved through each of the ports like this one at provinces throughout the world. It was all of the stuff of living, but none of the actual life. Because of that, the very hu-man-filled spaces felt more like machines. Walking through the chaos while not working as one of those machine parts felt strangely unfamiliar. These had been fellow scrubbers and dock workers, but they looked to Amy more like drones from her new per-spective.

Peter seemed like he saw none of it. He kept his head down and moved his feet quickly. He was on a mission.

After the port, the two crewmembers made their way through the city on pedestrian walkways. The route was slower than the public pod system, but less monitored. It took nearly an hour to get to the east side of the city. That left an hour to make the deal, and an hour to get back – if everything went well.

When they arrived at the vice lounge, Peter stopped for a mo-ment in front of the colorfully lit building. Until today, he'd never been to one of the vice lounges. The elder crew typically managed the runs without him. He'd heard stories about the activities there and—in his mind—the facilities had become a sort of adult play-ground where people went for a drink, a high, or to place a bet on the latest springball or soccer tournament. Peter and Amy slipped to the side of the building to watch the entrance for a few minutes and make sure it was safe to enter. It was there that the young man realized very quickly the reality of vice lounges was much darker than that of a playground.

In the alley next to the vice lounge, a group of several emaci-ated and filthy citizens huddled over a man's body. Peter initially thought the man might need help or, possibly worse, that they had just missed a murder. His instinct forced him to take a step toward the gathering, but Amy grabbed his arm.

"You don't want to look at that," she said.

"What if he needs our help?" Peter asked.

Shaking her head, "He's already gone."

Peter looked back as one of the starved people cut into the thigh of the corpse, pulled away a chunk of meat, and began to eat the raw human flesh. Peter turned quickly away from the sight as he swallowed hard against the puke that fought to come up.

"They didn't kill him. They're unpermitted citizens. No rations. The lounges deal in morgue sales."

"This is legal? Does the GU know?" he managed.

"Only the unclaimed dead are sold. The alternative protein movement a decade ago was sold as a humanitarian effort to stop blaming unpermitted citizens for their parents' mistakes," Amy explained. "One of Uru's three children would have been an unpermitted adult. An unpermitted birth can never become a full citizen."

"I thought they could apply."

"Never happens," she said flatly. "Never."

Peter shook his head in disbelief, anger replacing his nausea.

"The Global Union said they wanted to ensure that they used every available resource to care for its citizens, even those who never should have been born. That was the way it was sold, anyway. Nobody asked what the available resource was or from where the alternative protein sources came," Amy finished.

The two didn't look back and instead made their way into the building. Nothing inside could be worse than what was outside. The foyer of the lounge was filled with people in drugged stupors – patches were all over their bodies and they wore glossed over expressions on their faces. Then, the entire place became even more surreal when Amy and Peter reached a counter and were greeted by a man in a very vee fashion ensemble as though they had just entered a luxury entertainment complex.

"What would be your pleasure today?" he asked. "A first love for the young boy, perhaps? We have male, female, or machine. You can choose to watch or participate."

The well-tailored man may as well have been asking if they wanted pepper on their salads. He treated his menu as if it had the same innocence. Peter and Amy could have selected to participate in beatings—given or received—with human-like bots, tried an assortment of drug patches or beverages, or even old-fashioned addictions consumed through injection or inhalation. Betting was not done only on the latest sporting events or games of chance, but also on the survivor numbers in the earthquake zones, the death times of those left in medical wards, and the number of un-permitted children who would be forcefully aborted in various provinces.

Amy told the vice lounge maître d' that they wished to see a flatscreen movie, the code they were given for illegal trades. The man directed them to walk down a long hall to a double door on their right.

As they walked, they passed two naked women outside of the masochism room. The two were cutting on and licking one another. They were both covered in blood. Peter's boldness waned. He didn't want any part of this world. He wanted to be back on the ship.

"How did we become this?" Peter said. "How do places like this even exist?"

"The GU believes that if the worst of things are permitted in enclosed environments like these, it will keep them off the streets and out of the provinces."

"Is that true?"

"What do you think? You ever seen a drug patch outside of a vice lounge?" Amy asked.

Peter shot Amy a look. Of course he'd seen drugs in the world. They didn't talk about Wang's followers and how they always had small square rashes and black grime lines on their bodies, but it wasn't a secret, either.

"You know I have," he said.

"Well, if the patches get out in the world, what could prevent the rest of this from getting out there, too?"

The question was rhetorical . . . and Peter felt ill again.

They stopped before a door that had pictures of young children – very young. The images depicted sweet toddlers fully nude and in positions that belied their innocence. Peter felt rage build up inside of him.

"They're not real children in there," Amy said. "Images, 3-D representations, interactive mixed reality. It's sick. But it isn't human."

"No," Peter said. "It's monstruous."

The door opened and Amy and Peter slipped behind it in surprise as Wang and Erin stepped out of the room with a tall fair-skinned man. Wang zipped his pants, reached into his pocket, and handed a patch to Erin who was shaking in her withdrawal.

"You join next time, you get two patches," Wang said.

The opened door blocked Amy and Peter from Wang's view, but they held their breath and listened, hoping they could remain concealed.

"I was told that the Norwegian could reprogram a ship's hull. That's you, right?" Wang directed his question to the tall man.

"What are we talking about?" he asked Wang.

"It's official GU," Erin said. "Scrubber." Her patch was already on and serenity crossed her face.

"Toxic?" the man asked. "Was it a refuse miner?"

"No. Resources," said Wang.

Peter leaned more tightly against the wall and peered through the open crack of the door to see the conversation.

Shaking his head, "I don't know," the Norwegian said. "How did you come by this ship."

"That's not part of the deal," Wang said. "We pay you not to ask. You can have all of the equipment, top notch GU sea mining tools. It's more than fair for a paint job and metallurgic alterations so that the hull doesn't read like the '07 anymore."

"And what about the original crew? The original captain?" the tall man questioned.

"They won't be back," Wang smiled. "I fixed it so their pet boy would have a little accident."

Peter stiffened and Amy put a hand on him for calm. She felt his heartbeat quicken.

"How's that?" asked the Norwegian.

"Jammed his dive suit so that if he went under, not only would the suit not flush, but it would also force the water right into his oxygen supply. It wasn't a dive suit anymore. It was a drown suit."

"Are you sure he'll go under?" Erin asked.

"It's Peter. Have you ever worked a scrub with him? He'd have been a dead citizen eventually, I just put him out of his misery," Wang said. "I'm only pissed I didn't get to claim his credits." Then, turning to the Norwegian, "So, we have a deal?" Wang finished.

"I'll need three days," the man responded with a nod.

"You get two," Wang said, and he walked back down the hall away from the door behind which Amy and Peter stood.

The two moved quickly away in the other direction and made their way into the room for the flatscreen movie, which was truthfully the room for black market trades.

Peter fell against the door crying. "He killed Stacy," he sobbed. "That son of a bitch killed Stacy."

"And nearly you!" Amy consoled. "He sabotaged your suit."

Shaking his head in shame, "We switched. Stacy wore my suit."

Comfortingly, "You couldn't have known."

"But Wang knew. Wang knew that I would go under. And I did. And Stacy only went under to save me. I killed her just as much as he did. I don't belong out here."

"No. You didn't kill her. Wang did. And, if we don't finish this deal right now, we could join her. You with me?" Amy asked sternly.

Peter began to calm down and he looked at Amy as she continued, "We need your mind, Peter. That's just as important as being able to work the scrubs. Without you, we wouldn't have gotten this far. Do you understand?"

Peter took a shuddered breath, nodded, and stood up.

The actual fuel trade portion of their mission proved the easiest part of all. A woman with pink spiked hair asked what type of fuel they needed, how much, how soon, and where. They filled her in, paid with Peter's DCA glove, and left via a door that would avoid taking them past the cannibals.

By the time Amy and Peter returned to Tatsu's new ship, breathless from the high-paced trek from the east side of the city, the refueling had already been completed. They wasted no time shoving off. They were even more grateful to leave the garbage heap that was the Columbian Province port city than they were the one floating out on the Pacific.

CHAPTER 36
YEAR 2908

Small Scout Ship
Less Than Two Kilometers Off The Zoe Baja Southern Port
Wang Family Fleet

"Is that them?" George asked Erik.

Li Fang's men were staring through night-vision enhanced binoculars into the distance.

"You idiot! That's just a scrubber. You're looking for a cityship. Not like you can miss it. The thing is massive."

"I'm just ready to get the hell out of here is all," George said.

"As soon as we see the ship," he said. "Wait. Wait. Sorry, man. You're right."

"And I'm the idiot."

"I didn't recognize its size from the angle. That's it. You're right. Call up the deputy governor."

George pulled out a digifile and punched a few keys. Doug Beamer's projection appeared.

"Where's Francisco?" Erik asked.

"I'm the one who needs the message. You can say to me what you were planning to say to him."

"Fine. The cityship is coming in. They're just inside the two-kilometer mark."

"Thank you, gentlemen," the tsunamic defense coordinator said. "I'd get moving if I were you."

The boat sped quickly outward to sea racing a clock they would not beat.

Callum McMahon, in his role as the Tatsu's Captain Mik Ridgelin, dodged chop that rose as high as squalls in a ship meant far more for speed than stability. The water that came up over the front of the sideship slapped his face as sharply as if it had been stones being thrown at him from out of the deep. Each new splash smacked and cut and poured salt into his wounds.

As the captain made his way toward the massive nets that were part of Zoe Baja's tsunamic defense at the southern port, he spotted another vessel in the distance heading out to sea. Maybe they would make it before the next sea gates, maybe they wouldn't. He hoped it wasn't some poor fishermen with families waiting at home. Family was something he would never live to have. And the families of his own ship were what he needed to protect. The metal mesh nets were nearly in sight. He could see the lights of Zoe Baja's southern port in the distance.

"Mik?" he thought he heard from his ship's console.

His boat flew into the air over a peaked wave and slammed back onto the surface. He managed to slap his hand onto a button on the console, but he still barely heard the voice on the other side.

"Can't hear! Repeat!" he screamed into the air as he sharply turned the small ship between two violent whitecaps.

"Mik, we did it," his sister's voice cut through the chaos. "We're at ninety! You don't have to do this."

They made it. Kate did it. He was so damned proud, and he couldn't even tell her. His resolve was only strengthened. Not only would Miriam and his people be safe if he accomplished his task, but they would be in capable hands after he was gone.

"Kate, you know better," he yelled back, his voice strained. "You're okay for now, but if that water is pumped back out toward you, when each new gate adds to the sonic waves, you're not going to survive that. The Tatsians won't. I'm almost to the manual release. I've got this. You tell Miriam I'm just a drop in the sea now. Just like her."

"She heard you," Kate finished and, with another bounce on the waves, the comms dropped out.

Callum got the small ship right up to the nets at the port. There was no Harry on the other side. This was his task. He motored down the vessel and spotted the manual release. It was on the Zoeland side of the net. He would have to go under the net, through the gap where it connected to a stabilizing pole, climb to the lever, key in the code, open the encasement around the lever that would deactivate tsunamic defense, and pull the handle downward.

Sure. Simple.

The sideship continued to bang up against the nets and McMahon was tossed around the deck as it did so. He knew he was going to have to go into the water, but he had hoped he could choose the most opportune place from which to jump. It seemed the turbulence would end up making the decision for him.

Another gate must have closed as a rush of water capsized the sideship and Callum with it. He gulped the sickening seawater and gagged it back out in between gasps for air. The ship pinned him against the nets before he could get a deep breath, but the next wave pulled it back out. He kicked up out of the water and swallowed as much air as his body could hold before he went back into the drink.

It was nearly impossible to see. There were underwater port lights, but the tsunamic defense had churned up so much of the ocean floor that it was like working in a dust storm. He had to get above water again to get his bearings. As he did so, the boat was pushed back into the nets and the hull shattered near his head as easily as if it were sugar glass. A piece of splintered fiberglass struck him across his right bicep and nearly tore off his arm. He screamed out in agony.

Callum could feel himself losing consciousness as he continued to be tossed around and against the net, along with the razorlike ship debris. A leaf of water spinach floated by, and he thought of Jomo's gardens. He blinked heavily, marked his location between the net's stabilizing poles, and went under the water again.

Ten meters beneath the surface, the metal mesh net had an opening between its fasteners to the pole. Callum slipped through to the other side, his breath running short, and he began to kick upward. His pant leg caught on a piece of debris stuck through the net. He stopped within inches of the surface. He tried to kick free, but the water continued to control his movements and he was immovable. His lungs ached for inhalation and his head grew dizzy. He had no choice but to return beneath the surface, this time with no air left to guide him. His vision was blurred as he managed to yank his leg loose, violently causing a gash in his calf, and he kicked to the surface.

He gulped a massive breath of salty air.

A meter off the water, on one of the stabilizing poles, was the encased lever. He would have to climb to it. Callum grabbed a handful of net with his left hand and yanked his body upward. He grabbed the net with his right arm and, as he attempted to pull up his body weight, he wailed against the pain. A little more leverage supplied by his one good arm, and he was there.

Another wave slammed against the net from the seaside, and it threw McMahon back down to the surface. He landed on the broken, sharp bits of ships that once called the port home. He felt nails and splinters dig deep into the back of his already bloodied body. If a camera drone were to fly over him at that moment, one would assume the picture to be a corpse floating in the Zoe Baja port. His strength and breath were failing him. Pain coursed through every vein. His blurry-visioned eyes bulged with the salt of the water whipping they had taken, and his right arm was bent at an unnatural angle. The bone poked out of the drenched skin and the muscle of his bicep flapped in the water like a fish gill.

He knew this was a suicide mission. He just didn't know how hard and slow death would come. Using the debris in the water, he rolled himself over, dragged himself to the net one more time and, with only his left arm and sheer will to carry him, Callum pulled himself to the lever, typed in the code, and opened the closed case.

The lever was normally lowered by an automated tool, not the strength of one man. But one man was all Callum had. He threw himself at the lever, grabbed it with his left hand and pulled with the full weight of his body, shaking himself to gain momentum against the rigid release. Little by little, the lever began to shift downward. Callum hung like an animal on a meat hook. He'd lost more blood than he thought could be in a body. His eyes became slits, gazing in the distance. He thought he saw the Tatsu and, a bit closer, another ship, perhaps one of the sideships.

With a beastly cry that claimed the very last of his strength, He pulled his entire body up with his left arm and yanked it back down with all of his might. The lever snapped down and dropped the captain of the Cityship Tatsu and heir to the McMahon Family Fleet to the water with a backbreaking crack. A plank on the surface punctured his body and went straight into his lungs, stealing any breath he might have had left. The massive mesh nets came crashing down and landed in a mess on top of Callum pushing him under the water with the rest of the wreckage.

The waters grew calm . . . and so did Callum McMahon's body.

CHAPTER 37
YEAR 2553

Nekros Baja

Julian ran toward Linda and Uru's tent.

The family's nanny goat chased after the oldest boy as though this was a game.

"Are they back?" Linda asked their second oldest who had been on lookout duty for the '07 to return.

"No. It's somebody else," said the boy.

"GU?" asked Uru coming out of one of the two tents left by his brother's crew.

"I don't think so. Strange looking boat. Not very big."

After all they'd been through, very little in the world caused fear for Uru or Linda. Tatsu had been gone longer than they'd expected, but—with the continuing quakes and aftershocks taking place lately—they had assumed his brother had to travel a different route or occasionally dock for safety. Still, their supplies were running low. They could stretch an egg and goat's milk only so far after their rations were gone and the fish weren't biting in the waters that were so stirred up from the tremors. There was more hope that this arriving ship would be a friendly one than there was fear that it was an enemy. With curiosity beating out concern, the two walked toward the port's one and only remaining pier, the same place from which—

ten days earlier—they'd watched Tatsu and his crew of nineteen depart on the Mining Vessel PS-1707.

In the short time it took them to reach the water, Amy, Justin, Khalil, and their captain were already exiting happily with full arms, others just behind them.

"It is you!" Julian said as he ran up to the captain and hugged him, nearly knocking a crate out of his arms.

"Welcome back!" Linda said.

"I think you have a story to tell!" Uru said as he grabbed the crate from his brother while looking at the new vessel.

"You don't know the half of it. Looks like we're in this new world together!" he said before turning back to Julian. "Hey, big guy, go get all your little cousins. We have this boat packed to the gills for you guys!"

Mercy joined the welcoming party and Peter made directly for her. He took her into his arms, squeezed hard, and didn't let go. Uru looked at Tatsu recognizing that the boy appeared emotional about more than reuniting with his oldest daughter. He didn't look like he was greeting her with a young man's urges, but rather a need to be held. They were watching a much more adult embrace. Uru squeezed Linda's hand and she began to scan the group of Tatsu's crewmembers.

"Where is Stacy?" she asked.

Tatsu shook his head and opened his mouth to speak, but the words wouldn't come.

Amy put her hand gently on the captain, "She didn't make it," she told Linda and Uru.

Linda looked back at Mercy and Peter. He still hadn't let her go and his body shook as he cried onto her.

Julian was already returning with Dee and the other capable children. The many hands of the family and crew made quick work of unpacking batteries and compact solar panels, nutrient bars and fresh food, seeds and seedlings and garden boxes, two chickens that immediately began chasing Olive around the grounds that weren't yet surrounded in the new fencing that was brought, fully loaded individual education pads for each child, canvas tents, and even a kitchen unit. The family and crew worked all day and into the early evening hours rebuilding what they had lost. There was much left to do, but much done, as well. When they all sat exhausted around a fire that night, Tatsu approached the group holding one last small wooden box.

"I never gave you two a wedding gift," he said while sitting down. "Actually, it's from all of us."

"What is it?" Linda asked.

"I think the idea is you open it to find out," Khalil said.

The whole crew looked at the newlyweds like excited children in anticipation of a surprise. Linda and Uru glanced at one another and smiled, then opened the box together. It was an amplification pad, a pad loaded with music and built-in projection for the sound.

"The originals are gone, but we each loaded up our favorite recordings and, of course, all of Elsie Laurita's music, too," Tatsu smiled.

Linda cried. For the first time in her entire life, they were tears of joy.

"You all have given us so much," she sniffled. "I can never repay you."

"You already have," Peter said.

He was leaning up against a crate beside the fire while Mercy rested on his chest. He held her, but, emotionally, she was holding him.

"I mean that sincerely. We kind of have the world, now."

"Not to mention, we all get better beds now that we've unloaded all this shit," Khalil said, trying to make light of the emotional moment.

"I did wonder how you guys managed to fit all of this stuff on that ship!" Uru exclaimed.

"I slept on the food crates," Marquise said.

"Way softer than the kitchen unit," Cairo added.

"Speak for yourself," Justin said. "I was on the fencing!"

"Yeah, the captain had it easy in a canvas hammock on deck," Amy added.

"Easy! You all left me out there in the storm!" he chided, and they laughed heartily together until they were crying.

"Remember that time Stacy and Amy raced on the deck during that storm off of—, where was that, the western port of the Australian Province?" Patty asked, still laughing.

"Yeah! They were doing laps, all the while the deck was getting more and more slippery...." Samantha continued.

"And I was screaming through the rain for them to get their asses inside," joined the captain.

"But Stacy said, 'No. I'm winning!'"

"Which cracked everybody up because she wasn't. Amy was kicking her ass, literally had lapped her like three times and already had finished...." Patty said.

"But I kept falling," Amy went on. "And I had landed on my backside for like the fifth time after what we called the finish line, while Stacy was still doing this ridiculous wide-legged run really slow around the deck. And I was like, 'How the hell do you think you're winning?' and she said...."

"Because you're on your ass and I'm standing in the storm." Peter finished.

Everybody became still for a long time.

"That's all of us," Linda said.

She didn't speak often in the mixed company of crew and family. When she did, everyone listened.

"That's every one of us. Me. Uru," she said grabbing her husband's hand. "These children. You and your crew, Tatsu. All of us. The world just keeps throwing storms at us. Some real ones and some man-made ones. And we're still standing. We're still winning."

"*Stand in the Storm,*" Tatsu whispered under his breath.

"To Stacy," Justin said raising a glass of some of the 250-year-old wine that found its way into the hold of their small ship.

"To Stacy!" the others joined.

After just a few days together, Nekros Baja was as much a home as it could be with the start-up materials and resources that Tatsu and his crew had provided. They had a new pen for their animals, new plants in the ground and in garden boxes, and a tent city of their own with places for sleeping, eating and preparing food, learning, and recreation.

"It's not going to be enough for you," Tatsu said to his brother one morning. "It's a start. You'll survive. You're safe and provided for. But you can't grow. Not yet."

"You've done enough, little brother."

"I can do more," he said. "I know people all over the Pacific. People who barter and trade, who don't need credit. Stacy's accounts will eventually run dry, but I know people who might be willing to join you here."

"That's crazy."

"It's not. The idea of choosing a life. That's not unique to your wife. To you. Some of those people, others who want a different way of life, they have resources. I could bring them here. I don't have a life with the Global Union anymore after this. You know that. None of my people do."

"What does that mean for you?"

"I think I want to finally go live the life that I want to live, unapologetically and without excuse. This world—our world—can be a dark place, full of clutter waiting to engulf everything that makes us . . . us. It's the trash that pulls and holds us down, clouds our minds and spirits, keeps us from achieving our highest good . . . our greatest purpose. That garbage of the world lives in every nerve that tingles when we face something we fear; its stench-filled breath lives in the words we repeat to ourselves, telling us *you are not enough;*' its filth lives in our minds when we accept the lie that we cannot lead our own lives; and its claws are piercing our hearts when we feel hopeless and helpless. But the enemy of that rubble is in rebuilding on top of it like you've done with your family. It is in reconnecting with our own humanity like we've all been forced to do over this last year, making and doing for ourselves. And we have to continue doing that. We have to persevere. We can't stop now. We have to push forward for every inch we gain, just like my crew did. We were wearing our own piss while we crossed an island of trash, one two-beat step at a time and we came out clean on the other side. I'm not stopping now or what the hell was all of that for?" Tatsu finished with conviction. "We're in this together."

"What are you going to do, then?"

"I'm going back for the ship," he said as if making the decision in that very moment.

"The cityship?" Uru asked.

Tatsu squinted sideways at his brother.

"Well, your people have been talking about it nonstop."

"Is that what they're calling it? Well, it could hold a whole city, I guess."

"The Cityship Tatsu!" Uru mocked.

"Hey! I like the sound of that," Tatsu accepted.

"It was a joke, Little Brother!"

"Not anymore," the captain smiled.

"Are you going to be okay?" Uru asked sincerely.

Tatsu looked at his crew and saw, not just their faces, but their lives, and all that they had been through together. He felt their loyalty and their love. He watched their camaraderie as they laughed together, and their work ethic as they helped his brother's family build a new world of their own.

"We'll stand in the storm," the captain said. "What about you?"

"Ask Linda. She's the one who runs this place. I'm just basking in her sunshine."

Goodbyes felt different this time. Maybe because they weren't goodbyes at all.

"I'll be back, you know," Peter assured Mercy as he tucked her hair behind her ear."

"Oh, I know you will," she said teasingly. "And not just because we're one of the only places on the planet you can go, either."

"That'll change," he said. "This is the beginning of a movement."

And Peter was right. Right alongside the century of quakes and the second melting, past the revolutions and the forming of the fleet families, the independence of Nekros Baja and the Cityship Tatsu would light the way for the future.

Dr. Michele Richards would be the first new settler to Nekros Baja to start a medical clinic after defecting from the Global Union, but she wouldn't be the last. Tradesmen and farmers and professionals and scientists would bring life to the full-life land once declared dead. Even Elsie Laurita would one day apply for nekros status and come to Baja. She opened a little coffee shop and lived out her days singing to nobody but her plants and family and community. She smuggled out several of her dresses and gifted them to Linda, the unofficial matriarch of their independent land.

Ten of Linda's and Uru's children remained on the land all the days of their lives. Mercy began the first school and took in new students every year. Peter, Marquise, and Cairo eventually gave up their sea legs to live on land, too. They opened the first formal commercial port of the once-Global-Union nation. And when Peter and Mercy had a baby, with no permit at all, she became the very first child who was born as a Nekros Baja citizen.

In time, even the Global Union itself had to recognize Nekros Baja and become an international partner to them. And the Cityship Tatsu, which started its mission by running routes between Nekros Baja and other nekroslands of the world, would grow into a trade partner and world ally, shipping to and from ports all over the Pacific. More than three hundred citizens—including two of Linda and Uru's children, Julian and Sofia—eventually called the ship home.

They built an entire society of their own on the water.

As Tatsu and his crew stepped onto their two-story boat to head back toward the Pacific Nekros, they became the last people on Earth to sail to a new world.

CHAPTER 38
YEAR 2908

Southern Port
Zoe Baja
Zoelands Concord

Miriam never imagined the feeling of tragedy on her own shores.

In fact, she truly believed she already knew how it would feel. A hundred times in the two years she had served as governor there had been an extreme storm or a violent act on somebody else's land and she thought she'd felt sadness over it – even loss. She shared words of sympathy with the leaders of those governments and proudly claimed oaths of solidarity with the communities of other nations' victims. She meant the words she'd shared every time. But, as a Tatsu workship taxied her, Kate, and Dr. Bradley into Zoe Baja's Southern Port, she realized she'd never truly understood the experience of mass tragedy.

The workship moved slowly through ship fragments that were scattered in a line on the water marking where the tsunamic defense nets had once been raised. Miriam scanned the wreckage and swallowed back tears when a piece with the Tatsu logo drifted by. This had been the sideship Mik had taken . . . Callum had taken to his deathbed.

When they initially began their travel into the port, part of her hoped to see him clinging to the side of his boat, waiting for them to come pick him up. Maybe, she'd thought, he was fine. He was hurt, but not gone. When she saw what remained of the ship with which he'd navigated, that hope was lost. Now, she feared that, if she did see him, it would be in a way she didn't wish to remember him, bloodied and bloated, floating dead in what had been her safe harbor.

Miriam felt a hand on her shoulder, and she flinched, "He's in a better place," said Jacob.

She wasn't sure whether she believed that, but she appreciated Dr. Bradley for saying it. Why did it have to be here, she wondered? Why did her home have to have this awful stain?

Inoke, Vera, and the refugee waited on the pier of the otherwise abandoned port. Vera was still in her work clothes. Inoke was frazzled and dressed so plainly that Miriam could scarcely recognize her friend. They all looked visibly shaken, but Miriam could not find it in herself to be the picture of strength for them. She was as broken as the vessels that had once dotted the many slips around the southern port.

The workship moved at a snail's pace, pushing away the remnants of Zoean livelihoods to clear a path to land. The rainbow confetti of her fallen city was like a blanket over the waters. Finally, they reached Miriam's awaiting friend and he helped her down off the water taxi. Kate and Dr. Bradley followed.

"I didn't know where to be," Inoke said. "I've been back and forth between here and the capital. If I'd known—"

"It's not your fault, Inoke," Miriam said. "There was no time."

Vera couldn't look at Miriam at all. She'd lost somebody, too. Harry had been her mentor. Miriam touched her shoulder. She couldn't find the words to offer comfort to the worker, so the gesture would have to do.

"Mr. Mauga. I'm a bit confused as to why you're here," Miriam managed.

The refugee looked ill, shaken, and exhausted.

"Deputy Governor Francisco told him to be here at the southern port to await the Tatsu," Inoke said. "I think he was meant to take the fall for all of this," the chief of staff inferred.

Mr. Mauga twitched convulsively, "Funny," he said while shaking his head.

"What is it?" Kate asked.

His words and movements both jerky, "You know that deputy governor is some piece of work. I just was just here to shake the hands of a few dock workers," Hemi laughed. "Dock workers touch everything, right?"

Vera's eyes grew big.

"I don't understand what you're saying," Inoke probed. "What did he do to you?"

Laughing, "It's not what he did to me; it's what he did to all of you!" said the man. "Here he thought he was using me, but his sick little game is exactly what gave me access to all of you. Your deputy governor, your chief of staff, your dock workers," he smiled sickeningly at Vera. "Captain Ridgelin and ExO Murphy. Even you, Governor," he looked at Miriam.

Vera's chest rose and fell with equal parts guilt and pain.

"What do you mean?" Miriam asked.

"That's not what Chloe looks like," Kate said.

"He's a biological weapon," Dr. Bradley added.

The man began to seize and retch. He dove at the governor, but Kate stepped in between them, getting covered in his unexpected projectile vomit in the process. Hemi maniacally grasped at her. Inoke swung a fist into the man's mouth, bloodying his knuckles and causing the man to become unsteady on his feet.

Vera looked back and forth between the governor and Mr. Mauga as tears freely fell down her face. "I'm sorry," she cried. "I'm so sorry," she said as she charged the still dizzy Hemi and plowed him into the water, going down with him beneath the debris.

Inoke and Dr. Bradley each dropped to the pier and grabbed at the water after Vera. It was frightening how quickly she disappeared beneath the cloudy, cluttered water. Kate and Miriam joined the efforts, pushing away the ship fragments on the surface and grabbing for anyone, hoping it was their fellow Zoean and not the infiltrator.

Finally, "I've got her!" Inoke called. "I've got her hand."

He began to pull Vera up by her glove, but the glove slipped off and she began to slip away from him once more. Kate grasped the girl's arm before she went back beneath the debris and, together, she and Inoke pulled Vera onto the pier. She was gone.

"Governor," Inoke said, holding the dock worker's hand.

Miriam shifted her gaze at the same time that Kate said, "She's Global Union."

"Of course," Inoke said. "Hemi was not left alone down here. He was with Vera. Francisco was going to erase both of them."

Miriam barely even reacted. With all that had happened, she was beyond even shock and, if she weren't, she couldn't have begun to guess how she should react to these revelations.

Dazedly, "Are you okay?" the governor said to Kate. "And you?" she said to Jacob. "I'm okay," she added to Inoke. "What about you?"

The group of three looked at the governor, momentarily sharing her detached reaction.

Kate was the first to return to the importance of their work, "No time to tell," she said. "Let's get you to the capital."

The group of four stumbled wet, injured, and damaged, but still alive, onto a whistler and they set off for the capital.

CHAPTER 39
YEAR 2608

Nekros Baja

Linda sat solemnly looking out the window of her home. She was facing the southward waters and sipping her warm prickly-pear cactus tea. The sun was sprinkling glitter across the light ripples of the Pacific. Amy and Tatsu were in the room in quiet conversation that, for Linda, faded to wordless white noise. The rest of the family and friends had already returned to their lives and quiet was all that waited on the horizon. The sights, sounds, and people didn't hold Linda as her mind still lingered where it had been three days earlier.

Her husband wasn't sad, even though his breaths were short and time even shorter. She and Uru were surrounded by all twelve of their children. Just outside the room where he lay, filling the corridors of the medical center as no others could fit around him, were their children's partners, seventeen grandchildren, twenty-eight great grandchildren, and six great-great-grandchildren.

Surrounding the building were hundreds more keeping vigil and honoring Uru with their respects while he could still appreciate them.

Linda grasped tightly to the hand of her husband of fifty-five years while she looked down into his eyes. Her gray locks fell into a face that was filled with the wrinkles of a lifetime of laughter, joy, and hard work.

Uru's younger brother was at his other side along with his lifelong partner Amy and their three children. Tatsu wore a patch over his one bad eye that he hadn't had updated in over a decade. He allowed its software to stop working completely and accepted the technology blindness. Only his in-person present human connections entered his sights through his one good eye rather than the feeds and data that had filled his mind for most of his life.

"I stayed to die," Uru said to his wife. "Remember?"

"I remember," Linda said.

"I just didn't know it would take so long."

"I guess we both had to live a little first," she smiled. Then, bittersweetly, "Oh, my dear Tunes, what am I going to do without you?"

"Be Gloriously Human. Just like you always have been. Long before you met me. You're the mother of all of this. We, all of us, me too, we are all your heirs."

"This place has not been nekros, lo'u loto," she said as her tear fell onto Uru's cheek.

"No," he whispered more laboriously now. "It has been full of life," Uru said with closed eyes.

"Zoe Life," Linda smiled to him.

"Zoe Baja," Uru's last words were released with his last breath.

"…. anything else, Linda?" Amy finished.

"What?" Linda said coming out of the fog back into the moment and taking a sip of her tea. It had grown bitter and tepid.

"Where were you?" Tatsu asked.

"I was thinking about Uru. What he said before he died."

Amy put a hand on Linda's and looked at her lifelong friend with compassion, but Linda still wasn't really in the room. Her eyes were focused on something deeper inside of herself.

"He was right, you know," Linda said. "We haven't had a dead life."

"Of course not," Amy consoled.

"I don't want Mercy and Peter's children or their children's children, or generations of children from now to think that we were just dead in our lives," Linda went on. "We haven't been decaying since the Great Nekros Quake, we've been thriving. We've been advancing. We've become a people with traditions and music and literature and food and community. We're a whole culture. A whole society. We grow our own plants—"

Tatsu laughed out loud, spitting the water he'd sipped on the table as he did so. Linda never had overcome her brown thumb.

"Okay, fair enough," Linda smiled while wiping up the water. "Maybe not me, but some people do! And we raise our own animals. And not just us, either. But all of those who followed us. Nekros Chile and the Mediterranean Nekros. Amuria, East Africa, the Caribbean. I doubt they see themselves as dead."

"Who does?" Amy asked

Linda didn't answer but just gave a sideways glance and sigh to Amy. She rolled her eyes slightly in accepting agreement. The Global Union, after all these years, still didn't recognize who they had become. Occasionally, they were allowed to be partnered servants, but they were not equals.

"Forget them, Linda," Tatsu gestured with his hand brushing them away. "You're right. Uru was proud and deserved to be. So do you. You have a beautiful legacy."

"No," Linda said. "I mean, yes. He did deserve to be proud, of course."

"And you, too," Amy corrected.

"Yes. Yes. You two are kind, but that's not what I'm saying," Linda shook her head. "Yes, we have a legacy, but not because of what we finished together."

Linda stood up and turned her back to Tatsu and Amy. She walked to the window and looked, not out to sea this time, but to her home's surroundings. The shore was dotted with active trade ports. A school and park could be seen to the east and, to the west, natural power production facilities filled with real humans, colleagues working side-by-side and not in a lonely vacuum. There were small shops and homes and pedestrians – so many people – going about their lives with their loved ones. If she looked out her north window, she'd see the ethical poultry farms and edible plant gardens through which she and Uru passed for years en route to the cultural center where they would enjoy a cup of real coffee at Elsie Laurita's café. She looked down at her tea with dissatisfaction before turning back to her guests.

Putting her tea down on the table, "It's because of what we started that we should be proud," Linda said. She placed both hands on the table, took a firm stance, and looked wide-eyed at Tatsu with a fierce light in her eyes. He hadn't seen that fire since the day she'd first pulled Mercy behind her when he came ashore with his PS-1707 crew of scrubbers.

"We're not done, Tatsu," Linda said emphatically.

"Oh no," he shook his head. "I'm an old man now. You and Amy are lo'u loto, both of you," he emphasized, putting his hands upon his heart. "But you are old women, too."

"Excuse me," Amy smiled. "I got some life left in me."

"A quiet life. Haven't we earned that?" he said pleadingly to his partner as he stroked the back of her arm affectionately. "Life in our quarters on the Cityship Tatsu out on the open sea." Shaking his head, he stood up from the table, "I don't know if I have the energy for another revolution."

Linda moved to the chair Tatsu had vacated and took his hand. She looked up into his eyes like a child. "The revolution is done, my brother! We won but we continue to let ourselves be labeled as dead."

Dropping her hand, Tatsu walked away, keeping his back to Linda as she appealed to his courage.

"Did we really come this far to only come this far?" she begged Tatsu.

"Your adventures nearly killed me," he turned back to her.

"Her adventures," Amy said as she got up and wrapped her arms around him, "saved us from decades of lifeless monotony. Gave us a chance to have children with no permits at all."

Linda saw where she was making progress and stood again, pushing herself between Uru's brother and his partner. "Amy, you didn't just stand in the storm. You ran in it. Don't you want to do it again?"

"I fell on my ass," she said, not wanting to fully abandon Tatsu.

"And you got back up."

"I don't know if my hips could take it these days," she half-heartedly chuckled.

Tatsu turned Linda around. "This is not when you should do this. You're just hurting and looking for meaning. And that's okay. Everybody does that after they lose somebody. But mourn. Recover. Take some time."

"Time is the one thing we don't have, my brother and sister," she said with a hand on each of them. If there's one thing you've said that's right, it's that you're an old man and we are old women."

Linda stepped away, back to the window. She folded her hands on top of her head in frustration. She realized she didn't really have her own mind wrapped around what she was trying to say. Explaining it to Tatsu and Amy was frustrating and, in submission to Tatsu's truth, mourning over Uru wasn't helping her to find her words. After a moment of silence during which she felt their eyes on her, Linda took a deep breath, dropped her hands, and turned back to them.

"We may be old, but we are not dead yet and I'm not ready to let the world pretend I've been dead for the last fifty-five years," she said as emotion crept into her voice. "Where is it written that we have to slow down and stop driving toward a purpose just because we get old? Right when we finally figure out how this stupid world works? Isn't that when we should push harder than ever before?"

Frustrated, Tatsu jumped in, "What exactly is it that we should be pushing toward?"

"We demand to be more!" Linda shouted passionately. "We demand to be brought back to life. There are too many of us and we're too strong for them to deny us."

"You want us to go back to the Global Union?" Amy asked.

"No," Linda shook her head walking back to them. "Not a resurrection, that's not what I mean. More of a, a—" Linda moved around the room at a pace, gesturing with her hands while trying to think. She grabbed her teacup from the table and made her way to the kitchen space while Amy and Tatsu followed her with their eyes.

Tatsu crossed his arms, waiting while Linda dumped and rinsed out her cup, all the while lost in her own mind.

"Reincarnation!" she said at last, turning off the faucet and looking back at Tatsu and Amy. "We need to be reborn as something different. Something alive. Not a nekros people. Not a nekrosland, but a . . . a Land of Zoe," she said, forming the words faster than she could land on the thoughts behind them. "It's like Uru and you always said. Not Nekros Baja, but—" Linda paused, looking for the right way to phrase her thoughts. "Zoe Baja. It's that simple. Full life lands. All of them are Zoelands. Zoe Chile, Zoe Amuria, East African Zoeland."

"So, you want to rename Nekros Baja?" Amy asked.

"It's a start," Linda said as the idea began to truly form for her. She excitedly marched over to Amy and Tatsu, and then back and forth in front of them. "And not just the Zoelands. But, what about the cityships?"

"What about them?" Uru asked.

"Well, there are what? Eight of them, now?"

"So far," her brother responded, a touch of pride slipping into his voice that caused both Linda and Amy to smile.

"And," Amy added, "they're building a seastead in the middle of the Greater Lake."

"A floating city," said Tatsu.

"That's something, too. All of it. A major something if you ask me," Linda said, smiling fully now. "That's just as important as all of the independent Nekr—" Linda caught herself. "Uh. ZOE-lands. How many tens of thousands are living on those ships? And those ships travel between GU ports and transport their citizens. Some of your ships have even trained the scrubber crews that the GU uses. You trade with them, too. But on paper, cityship citizens are no different than outlaws. Their criminal reports don't read any better than those of your long-dead former crewmate, Wang."

A flash of fury crossed Amy's face. In unison, she and Tatsu each turned to their sides and made spitting noises.

"Ha!" Linda called out. "You still have fight. Both of you! You still have fire in your eyes!"

"Well," Tatsu half-grinned for the first time, "eye, anyway."

Linda laughed.

"You're right though," she said, lovingly poking her finger into his chest. "His watery grave deserves our spit!" she said. "And Erin who took over," Linda said to Amy. "She deserves it, too." Linda stepped away from both of them, back at her pacing. "And yet the . . . what do they call their little pirate groups?" she asked

"Fleet families," the two said blandly in unison.

"Well, their fleet families are not really looked at any differently than the people living on your cityships. They're all equally outside of the law. Equally unofficial. One of your Tatsians is no more likely to get assistance from the Global Union than a member of Wang's Fleet Family. You remember when Justin died a few years ago?"

Amy looked at Tatsu as he nodded with sad resolve.

"The GU had already declared him nekros. That broad-brush term is basically a do not resuscitate order they paint on the now millions across Earth who don't associate with the Global Union."

Linda shook her head. "Millions between the ships and the abandoned lands like Baja!" she emphasized. "They treat us like we are 'less than,' but we're not. We should be equals. We should all be working together in a world economy. The Global Union and the Zoelands and the cityships."

"And the fleet families?" Tatsu asked, shock in his tone.

"No. Of course not," Linda said. "There has to be a rule of—if not laws—at least human decency and respect for life . . . and for quality of life, too. I don't think you'll get that out of the raging pirate groups out there. They're no better than the mobs of the twentieth and twenty-first centuries. The closest they get to civilization are the vice lounges and those places just put legitimate prices on illegitimate practices."

"So, what exactly do you propose?" Amy put a calming hand on Tatsu as his mind was still on the fleet families.

"We have to deny the label of death," Linda finished resolutely. "As long as we keep letting ourselves be called nekros, we're accepting that word for ourselves. There's power in a name. We need to change our label and embrace a new identity – a gloriously human identity."

"Well, we can start with an alliance, right?" Tatsu said. "I mean, Baja and our cityship have always been partners. What if we make it official? We could draw up a treaty or document. And then we can use that to get others to join us."

Now nodding along as the three worked it out together, "We could unify the cityships as a legitimate on-water society next," Amy added.

"Exactly!" continued Linda. "And I could work to bring together all of the societies that the GU calls nekroslands. I could get them to adopt the new Zoe name and unify all of the Zoelands. The cracked lands that the Global Union thought we would fall into and disappear."

"You make it sound so simple," Tatsu said.

"Compared to what we've been through, isn't it?" Linda said.

Amy nodded. "I'm ready."

Both women looked at Tatsu who had crossed his arms again across his chest. He didn't have the physical strength he did in his youth, but his presence was still a commanding one. They needed his force. They needed the loyalty he brought out in those around him. It would take time and endurance to see through a global effort like this one. He stared holes through Linda and Amy with his one good eye. Without communicating it, the two women each simultaneously put a hand on one of his giant forearms.

"Oh hell!" he shook his head. "I guess I don't have any other plans before dying. I may as well try to get myself killed."

Forcing a smile through her unexpected tears, Linda clasped each of their hands. "For Uru," she nodded sharply.

"For Zoe Baja," Tatsu said as he grabbed Amy's other hand.

The three stood in a circle together at the beginning of the journey that would result in the Zoelands Concord and the Cityship Regatta.

CHAPTER 40
YEAR 2908

Governor's Residence
Zoe Baja
Zoelands Concord

The deputy governor stood before a room of reporters.

The carved bronze memorial of the unofficial founding of Zoe Baja hung ornately over the gubernatorial address backdrop. The memorial depicted Founding Mother, Linda, with stone-set eyes on the Cityship Regatta founders, Tatsu Mageo and his partner Amy Elm. The bottom of the mounted sculpture bore the Zoelands motto spoken first by Uru: *Be Gloriously Human.*

"People of Zoe Baja," began the Deputy Governor. "I come to you today with sad news. "While Tsunamic Defense Coordinator Doug Beamer and I both believed there was no need to activate this system as a response to the Zoe Chile earthquake, it appears the Global Union, in an effort to stop our own alliance negotiations, felt otherwise. They sent an infiltrator to our very own shores, Hemi Mauga."

Francisco barely contained a smug smile upon receiving the shocked reaction he expected. He pursed his lips and tried to pretend that the expression was one of pain.

"Though he and our own head longshore worker, as well as our longshore apprentice, were killed in this violent attack," the deputy governor went on, "Mr. Mauga managed to activate the system at an even greater loss to our own people."

Roberto affected a pause and the need to compose himself. "It is clear to me that partnership with the Global Union will never be possible after today and I believe you'll feel the same when I share with you the devastating losses that have taken place as a result of that infiltrator's efforts."

"It appears that this evening," the man continued with a false crack in his voice, "before we were able to inform those within the two-kilometer range of Zoe Baja, the Cityship Tatsu, while returning to us with Governor Miriam Heirlinda, crossed the threshold. Our oldest and dearest ally was caught in the very tsunamic defense that was meant to protect our land."

A collective gasp was heard amongst the news drone operators in the room. One camera-mounted drone closed tightly in on the face of Francisco, trying to capture his devastation. The deputy governor was quite skilled at putting on an emotional façade for the cameras. He even conjured up a tear to wipe away as he continued.

"It is with great personal sadness that I tell you of the death of, not just our governor, but the Cityship Tatsu, as well," he finished with labored breath.

It wasn't by accident that he raised his deformed right arm in front of his face, feigning a fist in front of his mouth. The visual was of a broken man covering his devastation, his disfigurement on full display in front of a grief-stricken expression.

"I believe that the only way to go forward from here—" Francisco began again as a lighting drone blinded him to the room.

A large door opened at the back of the address room, but Roberto could not see beyond the cameras until the lighting drone turned from him to find Governor Heirlinda, Chief-of-Staff Kalua, Dr. Jacob Bradley, and ExO Murphy at the back of the room.

"I'll take it from here, Francisco," Miriam said as she marched to the podium with as much poise as she could muster. "Do you mind standing with my security team, Roberto?" she said coldly.

With one glance from the governor, her security team made their decision and immediately flanked Deputy Governor Francisco. The message was clear.

"Feel free to join him, Beamer," the governor shot at the Tsunamic Defense coordinator and the deputy governor's cohort was put under guard, as well.

Miriam was filthy to the point of barely recognizable. Her hair was glued with moisture against her face and forehead and her clothing was tattered and soaked. Kate's uniform was covered in the bile left by Hemi. In defiance of her appearance, Murphy stook with the governor's security team. Inoke, who had a bloodied hand and disheveled clothing, took up position behind his governor. Dr. Bradley, out of his element, made himself small at the back of the room.

Miriam was still for a moment in front of the cameras, not saying anything at all. The drones closed in on her stone-faced expression.

"The former deputy governor was about to tell you that I was not informed that tsunamic defense would be activated. He was to tell you that the Tatsu, the flagship of the Cityship Regatta and home to more than a hundred and fifteen thousand innocent men, women, and children," Miriam punched the word "innocent" with grit, "was within the two-kilometer range of Zoe Baja's southern port. Thankfully, due to the incredible skills of Executive Officer Kate Murphy and the Tatsian crew and civilians, we survived."

There was no cheer or jubilance expressed amongst those in the room. Miriam was in a stunned pause and all who were present could feel that there was something more to add.

"I want to share my gratitude to the Deputy Governor for recognizing the malintent of Mr. Mauga." Miriam looked for the first time at Roberto as she went on. "He was right to suspect this man who was found to have been smuggling a biological weapon to Zoe Baja."

Francisco's eyes grew large. He was no longer able to put on a show for the cameras.

"He didn't make it," Miriam finished while turning back to the room. She swallowed back the lump in her throat to continue. "Also lost this terrible evening was Ca—" she stopped herself from saying the name that had so quickly planted itself in her heart and mind. "Captain Mik Ridgelin of the Cityship Tatsu IV. He was...."

Who was he? What possible words or descriptions could finish that sentence? An ally to Zoe Baja of course. A great leader? Nobody questioned it. Her future? She would never know.

"He was my friend," she said at last, choosing a word that couldn't begin to convey the whole truth.

Those in the room stood bewildered. Were it not for the lights, the governor would have seen the tears start to flow for many. Unseen around the world, the sentiment of sudden sorrow was shared by Zoeans, GU citizens, and cityship residents alike. . . as well as on the ships of at least one fleet family about which Miriam knew. She paused long enough to push her pain down beneath the shock, deep enough to turn it to numbness.

"The former deputy governor will be charged in his death, as well as with conspiracy to interfere with government relations." Miriam managed a fierceness in her voice as murmurs filled the room.

She was still processing the moments that didn't feel real to her. Her land was drowning. Her alliance to save it hung in the balance. Her longshore worker was lost. The prototype that could save them all was at the bottom of the ocean. The largest and most violent fleet family in the world saw her as an enemy. The Global Union, through sacrifice of one of its own citizens, had unleashed a virus on her people.

And, with all of that going on, she could only see one thing: Callum McMahon manually releasing a workship and speeding away from her life forever. His departure was the fault line centered at her core, shaking her soul, and ripping her apart. Miriam realized she'd been standing silently for a very long moment, unseeingly staring into nothing. Inoke made the smallest of possible throat-clearing noises accompanied by a touch to Miriam's back, unnoticed by the cameras. She blinked back to life.

"I will prepare a more thorough statement soon but will not be taking any questions at this time," Governor Heirlinda finished as she stepped away from the podium.

Miriam walked out of the room through a door on the same side as the podium so that she would not have to cross through the crowd again. Inoke followed and, while the large doors were still closing, Kate stood in front of them. Nobody even attempted to ask if they could go by her in an effort to get more information from the governor. Dr. Bradley joined her, feeling stronger after all he had been through.

"What do you need?" Inoke asked as he moved with the governor toward the private side of the residence.

Miriam marched stiffly with her head high until a whoosh sound told her that the heavy doors to the gubernatorial address room had closed. Immediately, her body slumped against the wall and her face fell.

"I've got you," Inoke said, helping the governor like a parent. "I'm not going anywhere," he said, pulling her close.

Miriam allowed herself to lean against Inoke while he partially carried her and partially led her to her room. He punched in a code for her private quarters to open and, when they did so, he sat her on the bed.

For a moment, he sat next to her while she blindly and mutely stared. Eventually, he put a hand on hers. Miriam looked down and, seeing his bloody knuckles, seemed to realize for the first time that the losses she felt were not just her own. She would have to be strong. She turned to look at her friend.

"I just need some time," she said. "Turn off the water regulators please."

"Of course," he nodded.

Miriam stood up and made her way into her shower, removing her clothing as she did so. Inoke pulled out his digifile and punched in a few keystrokes while he heard the governor's shower start. He picked up her clothing and put it into a laundry chute that pulled the attire away to be returned once sanitized, or maybe just burned and forgotten. Steam started to pour from the water closet. Kalua keyed a few more strokes on his digifile and a distressed image of Nina appeared in the air above it.

"My love!" Nina exhaled in exasperation. "I saw you on the feeds. It's the only way I knew you were okay."

"I need you to come to the governor's residence," Inoke said. "Miriam needs you."

"It's bad, isn't it?"

"It's not good," he responded in concern. "I'm not leaving until you get here. She's worse than when Susan died."

Nina shook her head and unfallen tears welled up in her eyes. "Worse than losing her mom? Got it. I'll be there on the next whistler."

"I'll send one for you. It will be hard for anyone who is not government to get a hold of a zip chopper right now."

Inoke sent the whistler for Nina and began to pace the room that was growing ever steamier. The governor's shower was well past the length for suggested water usage, but he suspected she'd be in there a while longer.

"I'm getting you coffee," Miriam's chief called to the governor through the steam. "I'll be right back," he said.

Miriam wanted to answer but she couldn't seem to find the strength to part her lips to make words. The hot streams rained down on her and she allowed her hair to flatten against her face and skin. Slowly, she got down on her knees in the middle of the shower stall and then she curled up over the drain. The water continued to fall all around her, beating her skin to a reddish purple with its heat. She cried into the floor of the shower, allowing her tears to drain away along with the filth on her body. Eventually, the tears transitioned to heaving and Miriam threw up. She didn't have the energy to keep the vomit away from her skin or hair. Rather she just let it flow around her.

Miriam wasn't sure how long she remained in the fetal position, but the streams turned to a trickle and then turned off. She wasn't cold. Her quarters were a steam room by this time and her body began to dry in the heated air around her. She heard steps enter the room and, as her stall opened, a large cotton robe was put over her body.

"Let's get you to bed," sounded Nina's sweet, soothing voice.

Nina lifted Miriam to her feet, wrapped the robe tightly around her, and tied a belt at the waist. She led Miriam to her bed, next to which laid a full cup of coffee on a small table. Miriam lay on the bed on top of the covers. Nina rubbed oil into her hair and began to pick through it, pulling out bits of puke and making her way as gently as possible through the knots that resulted from the loathsome last day. She hummed while she manipulated Miriam's reddish coils and waited for her friend to fall asleep.

Sleep came.

Nina tightly held Miriam in her arms until morning.

Over the next several days, Inoke and Nina hid the governor's depressive episode from the public. Her father visited more than once. As Chief-of-Staff Kalua, Inoke fielded the countless questions that arose and, finally—after three days—Miriam was ready to go back to work and face a world without Mik Ridgelin, without Callum McMahon, in it.

"So, your brother Inoke once told me you weren't picky about what ship you ended up on, but here you are on the flagship of the entire Cityship Regatta. What's that all about, Sefi?"

Governor Heirlinda entered the bow garden of the ship to find its newest crewmember standing at the front of the Cityship Tatsu IV with Captain Kate Murphy who Miriam didn't address at all. The sun was setting and making the ocean take on the appearance of an endless pool of liquid fire.

"Governor," Sefina said, standing up a little straighter. Her skin had a lilac tinge to it, her chosen color of dye for ultraviolet protection.

"Cut that out or I'll start calling you Ensign Kalua."

"That would sound odd coming from you," the young woman admitted.

"Exactly. We go way too far back for you to be so formal with me," Miriam smiled, though the expression didn't extend to her eyes and it seemed to have lost some of its warmth.

"Kate," the governor said in greeting while attempting a smile that didn't even come close to its intent.

Miriam knew logically that there was nothing that the captain's ExO—his sister—could have done to stop him. There was no other choice that would have saved the Tatsu and no convincing that she could have provided to change Callum's mind about his suicide mission. No matter how deeply she knew the facts though, seeing Kate caused her heart to tighten. She wanted to change the story somehow and needed somebody to blame for the fact that she couldn't do so. She found it difficult to even cross the rest of the distance to the rail where Captain Murphy stood with Sefina.

"Taking measurements to finally get rid of this useless park?" Miriam quipped in a weak attempt at humor that came across far more as the passive aggression she felt.

Without a reaction, Kate stood up and kissed her girlfriend on the forehead. "I'll visit you later in your quarters, Sefi," she said affectionately.

Kate paused by Miriam's side as she walked by. "My brother's garden stays," she said turning her head toward the governor. "The code is unchanged, and you will always be welcome on the Tatsu."

The women looked at one another for a moment before Miriam nodded, ashamed of but unable to overcome her own grief. She swallowed hard and watched as Murphy walked through the gate.

"I'm pretty sure Kate pulled some strings," Sefina said, pulling Miriam from her fog. "I mean, she's the captain now, right? I'm not really good enough to be here. To be on the Tatsu of all places. I don't have what it takes. Even to just shadow on the aft bridge."

"That's not what I hear," Miriam said making her way to the rail with Sefina. "But we're always our own worst critics, aren't we?"

"Kate says so, too."

"She's going to be one hell of a captain, that woman. Willing to make the hard choices and do what needs to be done," she shakily said. "I've seen it."

Miriam's voice cracked as she looked around the Tatsu's bow garden bittersweetly. She steeled herself not to think of the last time she was in this place. She invited apathy in place of the pain.

Sefina and Miriam silently leaned over the rail at the edge of the Tatsu while it rested in Zoe Baja's southern port. The water splashed against the sides of the ship and there was a slight rocking back and forth as the evening tide swept beneath it. Miriam wasn't even fazed by the movement. She stared out into the golden-light-reflecting waters of the Pacific.

"Mik's ceremony was really nice." Sefina said awkwardly.

"Yeah. It was. His crew really loved him."

"Everybody did."

"True words, Sefina."

"I wish he could have had a water burial," the younger woman said, and then she cringed at her own words. "Does that sound morbid?"

"It doesn't sound joyful," Miriam said.

"Disculpas. You're right. I'm just out of training and the people who work to be on these ships? The waters mean everything to them. It's an honor to have an at-sea burial. I just meant that it was a shame they couldn't find—" Sefina stopped knowing how unadroitly her words were coming out.

"There would have been nothing left to find after—" Miriam shook an image from her head. "It was a violent way to go."

"I'm sorry. I shouldn't have said anything."

"It's okay. You meant well."

Sefina fell silent for a moment. "It was nice that they honored Harry, too," she managed.

"Damn. Yeah. I'm gonna miss him. It was nice for Nina and your brother to take in Potcake," Then, after a pause, she added, "It's not a good month to be Zoean. Not a good month to be human."

"I don't know about that, Miriam. You're here. And you weren't supposed to be. I think that's a win."

Miriam looked heavy with the burden of leadership in a way far deeper than she ever had before. She was weighed down by the human cost of her personal crusade, one that she wasn't even sure would work – a crusade for resources and energy and human equality regardless of Zoe or GU or cityship status. And, even if they did achieve those things, what would it really mean for the future of humankind? What was next for them? She selfishly thought about Callum and her dying land and about what it was she was even trying to save.

"Did you see the stone trucks unloaded from the ships today? They're filling in our soil, Sefina. We'll be sending away our botanist and Nina after that. We won't need a poulterer without any poultry, and we won't have our chickens or their eggs when we have no land to keep them on nor food to feed them. We're an industrial Zoe now. We farm water and minerals and power."

"Power production takes us back to our roots, just like Linda, right? Your great-great-great-great-great grandmother?" Sefina smiled, trying unsuccessfully to coax the same from Miriam. "The world needs those things," she added.

"I suppose you're right. But, sometimes, I guess I just want a little something from the world, too."

"You should be so proud, Miriam. I know my brother is. You're hurting right now, but this whole Human Unification Movement you're building? It's going to change everything. It will put meaning to all that has happened."

Miriam said nothing.

"Do you think it's true what they say?" Sefina looked intently at her tired friend. "That we're at the start of another melting? Another century of quakes?"

Miriam looked down at the water as ripples formed on the surface from seemingly nowhere.

"I do, Sefina. Except, we don't have a century this time."

"What does that mean?"

"That we should *Be Gloriously Human* while we still can."

Be Gloriously Human | Stand in the Storm

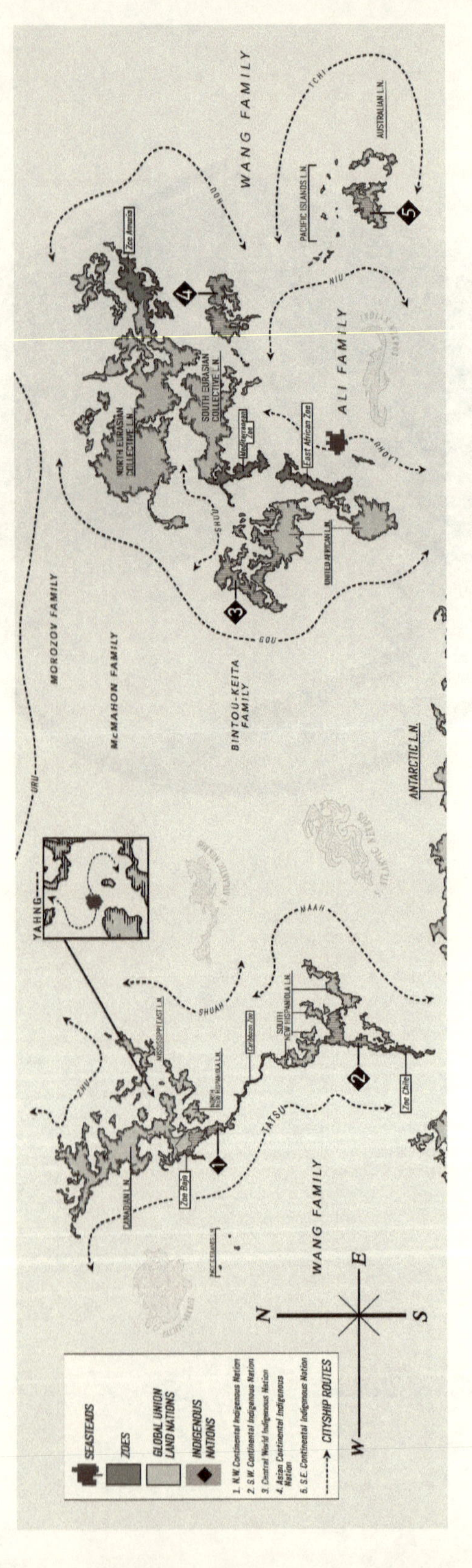

WANG FAMILY
MOROZOV FAMILY
McMAHON FAMILY
BINTOU-KEITA FAMILY
ALI FAMILY
WANG FAMILY
NORTH EURASIAN COLLECTIVE L.N.
SOUTH EURASIAN COLLECTIVE L.N.
Mediterranean Zoe
East African Zoe
UNITED AFRICAN L.N.
Zoe Atwood
PACIFIC ISLANDS L.N.
AUSTRALIAN L.N.
CANADIAN L.N.
Zoe Baja
MISSISSIPPI LAKES L.N.
NORTH W. ISLE HISPANIOLA
Caribbean Zoe
SOUTH S.W. HISPANIOLA L.N.
Zoe Chile
ANTARCTIC L.N.
YAHNG
ZHU
TATSU
SHUAH
MAAH
URU
SHU'U
GOU
HOU
NIU
TCHI
LAOU
N
E
S
W
SEASTEADS
ZOES
GLOBAL UNION LAND NATIONS
INDIGENOUS NATIONS
1. N.W. Continental Indigenous Nation
2. S.W. Continental Indigenous Nation
3. Central World Indigenous Nation
4. Asian Continental Indigenous Nation
5. S.E. Continental Indigenous Nation
CITYSHIP ROUTES

Miriam's World

EARTH AFTER THE MELT — YEAR 2908

Acknowledgements

It took a whole team to make this book come together and I sincerely pray I don't leave anyone out, as I appreciate and love each one of you. I hope I've done my part to tell you as much in person because these lines can't begin to convey the sincere and genuine depth of my gratitude. As my book moves beyond the creation of the content that goes into the acknowledgements, I'm sure there will be even more to whom I need to say, "Thank You." Please accept my gratitude here for those works that come during that pins-and-needles time between my letting go of these words and the world getting to read them. First and foremost, to my editors Stacy and Amy, you are both badass powerhouse women. I love you wholly and deeply respect your work. To my incredible designers and artists, Sara, Cas, and Mike, I thank you for adding your admirable talents to (and wrapped around) these pages. To my niche experts in no particular order, I hope I've done your knowledge justice in this book for both the real and pseudo-science of the *Fault Lines*, as well as to the culture of the world that I've built; thank you to Allison, Olivia, Bradley, Christopher, Laura, and Nick. To my reading team of Jeff, Jordan, Delia, Jim, Laura, and Daniel, as well as to proofers Laura and Jordan, you helped add to the intricacy of the *Fault Lines* world, as well as to the characters within it and I'm grateful. To creative consultants Joe, Kimberly, Jeff, and Doug, as well as to original C3 women Sarah, Liz, and Ashley, thank you for helping keep my head in this book when my heart wanted to run away with it. To Logan, Claire, Julie, Tonyia, Kimberly, Adam, Laura, Ramona, and Joe who all participated in the development of the book trailer, I can't wait until we can one day watch a screenplay version of this together, too! I'm proud to know and work with you all. To Rachel, Renee, Jeff, Stacy, Mike, O'dell, and Nick – my grassroots team – as well as to Kimberly who sprinkles the seeds on that grass, I appreciate you telling the world about the fault lines that are forming and encouraging others to join the journey. To my many followers who have joined that movement for the first time, welcome and thank you! Thank you to my chief encourager Jeff who helped keep my hand on the GO button with constant perfectly timed reminders that this project is so worthwhile and deserves space. Thank you to Mr. B who first introduced me to Lucy's Lantern. To my past (far-too-many-to-name) clients, students, ethical publishers, and collaborators from a long writing career, each past project helped feed into the development of this work and I appreciate you. To my incredible lifelong support team of family and friends including (but surely not limited to), Mom and Dad (Linét and Bob), Linda and Gerry, Kim R, Stacy L, Bradley, Shaina, Kimberly L, Laura, Adam, Sharon, Emily, Stacy B, Jeff, my RG family, my KW family, and my Rep family – I don't do this alone. I began with my editors and finally end on that note of not being alone. To my husband who has been on this writing roller coaster with me longer than anyone, your name is already here in a few places, but I thank you for getting on the ride one more time, and for your investment into the crazy adventure of marriage to an author.

About the Author

While Jeri Shepherd is new to the world of fiction, the author behind the *Fault Lines Series* has been in the writing industry for decades . . . under the name Reji Laberje.

As Reji Laberje, Jeri has 12 #1 Bestsellers in her 60+ books and plays, as well as another 17 #1 Bestsellers amongst those books for which she was a contributing editor; ultimately, her pen was on 29 #1 Bestsellers before taking on the new name and the genre of speculative fiction.

Before Jeri was "born," the author had combined print book sales of half a million copies across all of her works. She led more than 85 book projects in multiple roles including: author, co-writer, editor, designer, publisher, consultant, coach, and marketer. Her unique book marketing approaches helped lead more than 80 different authors to #1 Bestselling titles on lists with Amazon, Barnes & Noble, USA Today, and others. In addition, she consulted with numerous independent authors and publishing companies who went on to create successful books or imprints of their own. Hundreds of stories have been told, published, and sold through her professional gifts and services.

Jeri Shepherd can't remember a time when writing was not in her life, but she does remember when the writing became more of a career than an artform. She's excited to be back in the genre that will help readers create movies in their minds. She desires to share the art of making relatable characters, in diverse worlds, on dynamic journeys, that will excite and connect people.

The author is a veteran of the U.S. Air Force, where she served as an Arabic Linguist and earned her degree in international communications. She lives outside of Milwaukee enjoying children, grandchildren, and pets in a Wisconsin-based life. She spends time in the outdoors, service, the arts, music making and listening, travel, camping, hobbies, sports, and enduring family time and relationships.

For the author's full biography including past books, gifted and honored celebrity clients, and her many awards, please visit **JERISHEPHERDBOOKS.COM**.

Author photos by Paramveer Dhariwal